(Photograph by: Jeni Kendell)

Judy Atkinson is of Jiman and Bundjalung descent as well as having Celtic–German heritage. She has worked within the area of violence/trauma for the last fifteen years. As Professor of Indigenous Australian Studies at Southern Cross University she hopes to build bridges between Indigenous healing practice within western trauma recovery processes.

TRAUMA TRAILS, RECREATING SONG LINES:
The transgenerational effects of trauma in Indigenous Australia

Judy Atkinson

"When I put down all the different things in my own
personal story, things that had happened to me, the people
who had died, I didn't feel bad, just stronger that I had
survived all this. And lighter because it was really like
those blankets had been lifted. Also, I could understand
why. I made decisions to take care of myself."

SPINIFEX

Spinifex Press Pty Ltd
PO Box 5270, North Geelong, Victoria 3215
PO Box 105, Mission Beach, Queensland 4852
women@spinifexpress.com.au
www.spinifexpress.com.au

First published 2002
Reprinted 2009, 2011, 2013, 2015(twice), 2017
Copyright © Judy Atkinson
The moral right of the author has been asserted
Copyright on layout, Spinifex Press, 2002

Edited by Janet Mackenzie
Cover design by Deb Snibson
Typeset by Palmer Higgs Pty Ltd
Index by Max McMaster
Made and printed in Australia by McPherson's Printing Group

National Library of Australia cataloguing-in-publication data:

Atkinson, Judy.
Trauma Trails, Recreating Song Lines, the transgenerational effects of
trauma in indigenous Australia.

ISBN 978 1 8767 5622 2.

1. Spiritual healing – Australia. 2. Wounds and injuries – Treatment –
Australia. 3. Wounds and injuries – Psychological aspects. 4. Violence –
Psychological aspects. 5. Aborigines, Australian. I. Title.

155.93

Australia Council
for the Arts

This publication is assisted by the Australia Council, the
Australian Government's arts funding and advisory body.

Contents

This book could not have occurred without the support of my family. It is therefore dedicated to my family, across generations, to the mothers and grandmothers, the fathers and grandfathers who have guided me across my (hi)story. They have provided me with a rich and diverse cultural heritage and have contributed substantially to *who I am*. In particular I recognise Mike my husband, my children Andrew (who was accidentally killed during the time of the study—see epilogue), Carlie, Tim and Kate, and grandchildren Jessica, Sarah and Rebecca, who remind me that *I am responsible* for what I leave as a legacy to our future generations.

Acknowledgements

In 1992 I received a National Health and Medical Research Council Grant (Public Health) to investigate the various ways the First Nations people of Canada were addressing the dual problems of alcohol and other drug misuse, as well as violence within families and communities. The conceptual and foundational development of what is contained in this book was made possible by the grant I received from the National Health and Medical Research Council and the new concepts and understandings I gained in Canada during 1992. NHMRC and the people of Canada, who taught me well, must first be recognised.

A list of people deserve special thanks: Kayleen Hazlehurst, Robert Schweitzer, Jeni Kendell, Paul Tait, Shar Edmonds, John Cadden, Fran Collins and the Butterfly, Paddie Cowburn, Chris and Brigette Edwards-Haines, the Muir family, Priscilla Iles, Thalep Ahmat, Stacy Chamberlain, Hazel and Darryl Kaur, Cliff (Mosey) Mason, Dallas Fewquandie, Frank Kemp, Bronwyn Fredericks, Margaret Hornagold, Heather Toby.

More particularly I am indebted to the many participants of the We Al-li workshops and the Indigenous Therapies Program who individually and collectively have taught me more than they will ever know. I thank them for their gifts of courage and clarity, and the sharing of their wisdom. From our experiences, deep and sustaining friendships have been formed.

Definitions

Aboriginal and Torres Strait Islander peoples and communities: Aboriginal peoples and Torres Strait Islander peoples are separate cultural groups. In this book the word *Aboriginal* is used generally to refer to Aboriginal people as the primary group on which most of the writing centres. The word refers to those of Aboriginal descent who are recognised as such by the community in which they live, and who identify as Aboriginal. The plural terms *peoples* and *communities* acknowledge the diversity of Aboriginal peoples and communities within Australia, all of whom have different histories, political dynamics, social situations, cultural characteristics, economic resources and administrative capacities. *Indigenous people* and *Indigenous Australians* are also used as inclusive terms for the traditional or First Peoples of Australia.

Community: The word describes a group that is living, sometimes in close proximity, with similar interests, interdependent and interacting with each other for mutual support, in a "network of relationships". There may be a number of "communities"—that is, groups—of people with interconnecting interests and cultural/spiritual affiliations living within close proximity. Not all people living within close settlement feel part of "community", however. People may consider themselves part of a community which is separated by large geographic distances. Community therefore can also be a network of people and groups separated by space but interlinked by common concerns and consciousness. Hence, "the Aboriginal Community", which is in fact a "community of diverse communities" spread across Australia, and in some cases in other locations around the world. At a deeper level Rollo May has given a definition which reflects my intent in the use of the word.

> A group in which free conversation can take place. Community is where I can share my innermost thoughts, bring out the depths of my own feelings, and know they will be understood. ... Communication makes community and is the possibility of human beings living together for their mutual psychological, physical and spiritual nourishment (1976: 246–7).

Culture: The set of beliefs, values and rules for living that is distinctive to a particular human group. Culture is passed down the generations in the complex of relationships, knowledges, languages, social organisations and life experiences that bind diverse individuals and groups together. Culture is a living process. It changes over time to reflect the changed environments and social interactions of people living together.

Dadirri: A word from the language of the Ngangikurungkurr people of the Daly River area of the Northern Territory. *Ngangi* means word or sound. *Kuri* means water and *kurr* means deep. Deep water sound or sounds of the deep, also explains the word *dadirri*—inner deep listening and quiet still awareness. *Dadirri* can only be experienced over a period of time in the practice or activity: "When I experience *dadirri* I am made whole again" (Ungunmerr 1988).

Dysfunctional: *dys* is from the Greek, meaning painful or difficult. The word *dysfunctional* denotes people, as individuals or in groups, who are functioning with difficulty and in pain.

Family: The words *family* and *families* here denote the traditional concept of family, as blood relationships or extended kin networks. Many Aboriginal people, however, have been removed from their families of blood, and have been forced to make, through various means, other relationships in "families" where people care for and support each other. This construction of "family" is also honoured and recognised. At the same time it is understood that the word derives from the Latin *familia*, meaning all the slaves, women and children owned by the patriarch.

Healing: (from the Old English word *haelen*, meaning "a return to wholeness"). Chapter Five describes healing as an educational process of learning about the self at deep levels, about the transgenerational life experiences which have made me *who I am*, the life circumstances that have resulted, and my ability, through that knowledge, to make choices to help change those things that need changing.

Intergenerational: The prefix *inter-* is from the Latin, meaning *between* or *among*, *together*, or *mutually together*. Intergenerational trauma is passed down directly from one generation to the next.

Spirituality: An experience of numinosity or of the sacred. Religion, in contrast, is a system of belief. A person can be religious and never have had an experience of the divine, but live the rules and dogma of the religion to which they are attached. On the other hand, a person can be both religious and spiritual after having had an experience of the sacred. At the core of every great religion is an experience of numinosity.

Story: Used here in the terminology of Aboriginal people— "story place", "my story"—to denote a personal history, a narrative description of life events.

Transgenerational: The prefix *trans-* is from the Latin, meaning *across* or *crossing*, *through*, *beyond*, *on the other side*.

Transgenerational trauma is transmitted across a number of generations.

Trauma: Theorists and clinicians often distinguish between the terms *trauma* and *crisis*. These terms are used interchangeably here to denote circumstances that seriously challenge people's capacity to cope with ordinary living. Trauma is an event or process which overwhelms the individual, family or community, and the ability to cope in mind, body, soul, spirit.

Violence: The *Collins English Dictionary* defines violence as "powerful, untamed and devastating force; the instance or exercise of physical force, effecting or intended to effect injuries and destruction; unjust, unwarranted or unlawful force, as tends to overawe or intimidate, inflict harm upon, damage or violate" (Sinclair *et al.* 2000: 1335). To violate is "to break, disregard or to infringe on; to rape or otherwise sexually assault; to treat irreverently or disrespectfully; to outrage". In this book the term "violence" is defined as: "Unjust force, actions or words used, without informed consent, to intimidate or harm; actions that are irreverent or disrespectful of another or others, and that are used, consciously or unconsciously, to obtain power over another or others, causing pain to the whole person (body/mind/soul/spirit)."

Prologue
Great-grandmother's Gift

During a time of great pain and crisis in my life, my great-grannie came to me and gave me a gift. She sent me a dream.

Dream: 7 September 1993

In this dream, a daytime dream, I was walking—walking with a big mob of people to the place where my granddaughters would grow. And as we walked I could hear sounds of laughing, singing, sadness, crying. Big mobs of people together walking to some place—into the future.

I asked "Where are we going?" and the answer came "To a place." I asked "How will we know that place?" and the answer came "We'll know"!

We came to a place, the place? This place!

I asked "What do we do now?" and the answer came "We come here, and we sit with each other. We tell our stories. We grieve together. And we dance and we sing together. If we do this, as we listen to each other's stories, in our grieving, in our singing, in our dancing, we give power to each other for the healing to begin."

So in my dream we sat together, big mobs of people sitting on the ground.

In my dream, I was calling to my old friends to "come, come and sit and talk with me", calling all the names of those people I have known and loved over the years, "Come, come and sit with me and tell me what you have been doing, where you are going. Let me hear your stories as we travel together."

Then I saw my great-grannie and grannie, sitting with many other old, old women whom I did not know. They beckoned to me to come to them. So I went through the throng of people to where they were sitting.

We began to talk. I was so happy to see them but I could feel a great sadness around them and in them.

I went into their sadness and suddenly—suddenly, we were in another time and another place, and we were running, running in terror through the bush, running in terror from the thundering horses and the guns of the white men.

Tremendous fear—tremendous terror. I now know what it feels like to be a hunted animal with no place to hide.

… Exhaustion … We couldn't run any more.

Crawling under scrub, scrub that had been our home, our heart place, our nurturing companion over many lifetimes, to hide and rest.

After a while as we lay in our terror I heard a voice … my voice. "The children! The children. … Where are the children?"

In the terror of our flight we had lost our children.

And so … we women began to look for our children. The children, our lifeblood, our spiritline, representing our future generations.

Such intense sorrow, such a depth of pain, as one by one we found our children, … broken … ravished … wounded … the children the children … searching searching … We found our children, battered … bloodied … crushed … violated.

Gathering them to us, gathering them to us. And so … we women began our grieving for our children, with our children.

And the pain … the pain came like a raging fire consuming us; the pain came as swords thrust deep into our bodies splitting us asunder; and the pain came … and left us as sounds drawn from the very depth, the very core of our being, rising up through our throats as a wailing, as a song, as a prayer to the earth and the wind and the sky and the sea and we wailed in our grief until we were drained, emptied of all that had been—and all that had been done.

And the mountains and the rivers and the rocks and the trees stood in silent witness to our grief and our need.

And so it rained. The rain came in cloudbursts like waves in a storm bathing us clean. The rain came as blankets of mist covering our tears, the rain came cleansing us and cleansing the trampled defiled earth around us.

After the rain came the stillness, the silence, except for our breathing mingling with the breath of the earth. Listening to the silence in the stillness brought seeds of awareness and then a Deep Knowing—Spirit to Spirit. We are women.

With that knowledge came new life and movement and we women joined together and we rose up and danced a women's dance of birth and re-birth, of life healing, of re-generation, of re-creation.

My great-grannie gave me a gift—she taught me. We are Women. We are not victims. Nor are we merely survivors. We are Women. We have creation powers.

We are the Creators of the Future.

When I woke from this dream I lay there for many hours feeling the exhaustion, remembering the feeling of the bush tearing at me in my running, the great fear in my chest, the sounds of the horses running, and the stock whips and the men's shouts, and the women crying. My heart was beating so fast I felt I had actually been running and I felt half mad with the fear of what I had been through. For some time I really didn't know what was real and what was a dream. At one stage, for a brief instant, I felt myself swaying in the staggering exhausted run of a mother elephant with a calf at her flank, running from the guns of hunters. At another time I felt for an instant the pounding heart of a whale churning through the ocean with a calf at her side, fleeing from the harpoons.

I kept slipping from human to animal as if we were one in the terror of our flight. This was the first time I began to understand the terror of a massacre.

It was also around this time I began to think more clearly of the concept and impact of transgenerational transmission of trauma in the lives of Aboriginal peoples. I also, however, received a clear message in this dream about healing, for this was the first time I began to think about the power of people sitting together to tell their stories, and the use of dance and ceremony in healing.

I continue to have a strong sense of the "old women" of this dream, including my great-grandmother, being with me in many things I do today.

Chapter One

Dadirri:
Listening to one another

Value-free research is not possible and does not occur. Research may be most perniciously biased by the attitudes of the researcher when these attitudes are hidden from the reader or even from the researcher's own perception. Value-free research is not possible, but value-explicit research is more honest research in which scientists express and clarify their own value system.

Simpson 1993

This book is the result of a research project. Before beginning the study, I thought I knew something about violence.

I had previously worked for the Aboriginal Co-ordinating Council in far north Queensland. Established under the community services legislation of 1984, the council comprised the elected representatives of the fourteen Aboriginal Reserve Community Councils in Queensland. Beginning in the early 1980s, the council met monthly to plan and co-ordinate the movement from government-controlled Aboriginal reserves established under the *Aboriginal Protection and Prevention of the Sale of Opium Act 1897*, amended to the *Aborigines Protection Act*, to Aboriginal-controlled local government functions on what was to be called Deed of Grant in Trust (DOGIT) lands. The process was called self-management.

We sat in long meetings with an agenda controlled largely by government demands, with never enough time to give full consideration to the critical decisions being made. After the meetings, Elder men and women took me aside to talk of their concerns about local community problems. They named issues I never heard discussed as items of importance in government meetings where allocations of grant monies were decided. I heard of rape of small children; of women laughed at when seeking help at the police station after having been assaulted by their partner. I heard of abuse in police watch houses by law enforcement officers; evidence of escalating suicides and multiple suicide attempts; an increase in offending behaviours in young people, of homicides, of one young man after another being taken away from his community to serve a prison sentence after beating his girlfriend or wife to death.

I began to collect newspaper clippings and pin them above my desk to remind me of other needs, other concerns besides the agendas of government which were forcing us to "skip rope" to their demands.

> A man who bashed his wife to death late last year was today sentenced to six years jail. The court was told this man told police he had won a carton of beer at the community canteen the night of the killing and, while drunk, bashed his wife in a domestic dispute. The man told police he woke up the next day in bed with the woman, his arms around her, and found her dead. Witnesses told police the man had punched and kicked the woman during the attack.[1]

The Elders placed such problems in the context of increasing alcohol misuse, resulting from the government- and council-run canteens that had been established over the previous decade as alcohol outlets and economic development initiatives. As the Elders asked for help to make sense of this senselessness, I felt in them the essence of their own felt powerlessness. "Nobody listens to us", they claimed.

This seemed to be confirmed when, on their behalf, I approached the then Minister for Community Services and Northern Development for help. That week twelve children from one small Cape York community of 450 people were in

---

1 Extracted from the *Cairns Post*, 1987. In one year I counted seven such court reports. In each case both parties had been drinking before the assault took place.

Cairns Base Hospital[2] suffering the ravages of sexually transmitted diseases, one little girl of seven with four different diseases of the anus and vagina. I asked the Minister if he could direct his departmental staff to provide resources and help us find ways of addressing issues of family and community violence. He dismissed me by saying, "Oh, don't talk about things like that. People will think self-management isn't working."

Later that same week the Aboriginal Liaison Officer at the hospital organised a meeting with senior departmental and hospital staff about the future of the children in the hospital. The doctor felt they should not be returned to their homes and communities, but that they should be placed in foster care. In the emotion of the meeting the senior bureaucrat told us, "A lot more of your people are going to die until you people become responsible."

That same year, 1987, the Department of Community Services provided substantial funding, under a court-stipulated consultancy, for anthropologists, social welfare and other "experts" to determine whether it was traditional behaviour for Aboriginal men and youth to sexually use five-, six- and eight-year-old children.[3] Obviously, after consultation with Elders from the communities concerned, the report determined that such behaviour was not traditional cultural practice. My outrage at the time was that such questions were asked of and answered by "expert outside others". The voices of our senior people, our Elders, were repeatedly negated or considered as secondary expertise to the "expert outside other".

Around this time, when I tried to talk about such issues with police and senior government people, I would receive troubling responses: "It's cultural. What can we do about it?" Police were making regular charges for drunk-and-disorderly, while ignoring the more serious interpersonal

---

2 For a further understanding of this critical situation, refer Christine Choo (1990: 38–9, 84–9).

3 Confidential document, copy of which is in my possession.

violence that appeared to be escalating within our communities in far north Queensland.

In fact, while I was working in Brisbane in 1988, undertaking a review of policing functions within the Deed of Grant in Trust communities, a senior Queensland Aboriginal Affairs bureaucrat questioned why I was doing what I was doing and told me I was wasting my time. He informed me "the solution is clear ... just stop them from breeding".

I felt I knew what the political and bureaucratic face of violence looked, sounded and felt like. I came to believe that in response to this violence the despair and rage being experienced within our communities was being re-enacted by our people on ourselves in diverse and damaging ways.

At the same time, I saw links between colonial impacts and contemporary community circumstances in which interpersonal violence was escalating (Atkinson 1989, 1990a). I felt "insufficient research has been conducted for anyone to speak or write with authority on the issue of contemporary violence within Aboriginal Australia" (Atkinson 1989: 15). I was struggling myself to understand the context and extent of the violence within our communities.

In 1989 I was contracted by the Commonwealth government to work for a time on the National Domestic Violence Awareness and Education Program. This resulted, among other things, in the booklet and video *Beyond Violence: Finding the Dream*. Towards the end of that study, I was one of a group of Aboriginal women who were invited to Canberra to talk to senior staff of the Aboriginal and Torres Strait Islander Commission (ATSIC) about our concerns in regard to the violence in our communities. Twenty-three grey-suited white men looked at us from around the ATSIC boardroom table. During that meeting we asked if we could talk to the federal Minister for Aboriginal Affairs.

We were given ten minutes to meet with him. Two minutes into the meeting he interrupted what we were saying to demand of us: "I know the problems. You tell me the solutions."

This was an important and profound lesson for me. The decision to begin the "search for solutions" came out of that meeting. The difficulty was to find the time to stand back enough from the crisis of day-to-day survival to find "solutions" that were achievable and that could be implemented. A postgraduate study would, I hoped, provide me with the time, discipline and supervision to conduct research that would be meaningful and provide practical outcomes relevant to Aboriginal community concerns and needs. This book has resulted, in part, from that study, which I began in 1993.

A research purpose, topic and focus

The specific purpose of the study was to gain a contextual understanding of, firstly, the phenomena of violence and consequent experience of trauma; and secondly, the cultural and individual processes of recovery (or healing) from violence-related trauma, in the lives of a group of Aboriginal people living within an urban/rural coastal region of central Queensland.

The research questions were:

- What is the experience of violence?
- How does violence relate to child development, family and community fragmentation, alcohol and drug misuse, race and gender injustice, criminal behaviour and poverty?
- How do experiences of violence contribute to experiences and behaviours that influence situations of inter- and transgenerational trauma?
- What personal and social experiences assist change in such behaviours?
- What is healing and how do people heal?
- What cultural tools promote change or healing and how can Indigenous values and practices be supported to promote individual, family and community well-being?

The study took place in Central Queensland over several years, 1993–98. The region has a violent history that is well documented. The coastal area where the study took place is located at the periphery of a semi-circle, the centre of which is the site of a series of massacres that occurred from the mid-nineteenth century into the beginning of the twentieth century. There were large-scale dislocations of Aboriginal nations from their homelands both before and after that time. Consequently Aboriginal people subjected to these massacres and displacements moved and were moved across the country away from the milieu of the destruction, thus creating trauma trails running across country from the locations of the pain and disorder they experienced. Government reserves such as Woorabinda[4] were created as places of forced removal to contain people who were traumatised outcasts in their own country. Within this region there are also two orphanages where children who had been removed from their families or who had been orphaned were placed. A prison presently run by Queensland Corrections is located several kilometres outside the major town in the region.

The largest town in the region is Rockhampton, with a population of approximately 59,730 in 1996. Approximately 2870 of this population identified themselves as Aboriginal or Torres Strait Islander (Australian Bureau of Statistics 1996). Woorabinda is 150 kilometres from Rockhampton with a population of approximately 1500 people in 1996.

Indigenous people in central Queensland have regularly voiced concern about the many problems facing their communities. These problems include high unemployment; high rates of alcoholism and other drug misuse, including petrol-sniffing by young people; high levels of poor health; high rates of psychological distress articulated in depression and diagnosed mental illness; early deaths through ill-health and injury; a lack of personal safety resulting from personal and interpersonal violence (domestic violence, sexual assault

---

4 Established in 1927. The generation who survived the massacres was moved from the old Taroom reserve, which had given them some form of safety from the depredation of white settlers and the mounted police.

and different forms of street violence); high incarceration rates; and overall a general lack of personal, family and community well-being. Within this region Indigenous peoples generally have, for example, higher rates of heart disease and diabetes in comparison with Indigenous peoples in other regions and with the non-Indigenous population (Fredericks 1996).

In considering the question "what is the experience of violence?", I felt it important to establish a working definition of violence.

What is violence?

Violence is an activity: *brutality, cruelty, sadism, bloodshed, atrocity, carnage*. But violence is also defined by feeling words: *resentment, hostility, hate, enmity, lack of empathy*. Violence is generally considered to be the exercise of control over another person or group through destructive, demoralising, unjust, unwarranted and unlawful physical and/or psychological force (Sinclair *et al.* 2000: 1335). Violence is therefore both an activity and an experience.

The word *experience* is used to acknowledge that a person (including a child) who is violated in an act of violence experiences violence; that a person who commits an act of violence experiences violence, and that a person who sees or hears violence experiences violence. "Experience" is used as both a verb and a noun. The verb means: *to go through, to live through, be subjected to, to suffer, to endure, to undergo*. The noun means: *occurrence, incident, encounter, event, happening, feeling*; and *knowledge, skill, practice, understanding, wisdom, learning, education, scholarship*. Crolty (1996) says experience means: *feelings, perceptions, meanings, attitudes, functions, roles, and personal reactions to events*.

In spite of the fact that colonisers have disregarded the rights of Indigenous peoples, and have used force to dominate, intimidate, subdue, violate, injure, destroy and kill, they do not consider their actions, either morally or under their law, to be violence. On the other hand, they have defined many of the functions of Indigenous disputing processes as violence, while at the same time categorising much contemporary Aboriginal interpersonal violence, which Aboriginal people themselves have spoken of as unacceptable behaviour transgressing the cultural mores of our societies, as customary practice. In some cases Aboriginal people themselves, particularly male perpetrators (Payne 1992: 37), have also begun to describe actions of violence, specifically sexual violence on young women, as based in, and legitimised by, customary practice. It is reasonable to assume that a person or group who experiences violence has the most knowledge about experiences of violence.

Justification for the research

Violence in all its forms is a prevalent feature in many Aboriginal lives. The federal Minister for Aboriginal Affairs told his state counterparts in 1990 that violence among Aboriginal and Torres Strait Islander peoples had risen to levels that not only impair life, but threaten the very existence of Indigenous peoples (Australian Aboriginal Affairs Council Briefing Document 1990). The Queensland Domestic Violence Task Force estimated that "domestic" violence occurs in 90 per cent of Aboriginal families living in the Queensland Deed of Grant in Trust areas[5] (1988: 256). In one such community with a total female population of 133 over the age of fifteen years (and 107 over the age of twenty), 193 cases involving women with injuries due to violence were treated at the local medical centre over the twelve months ending 30 June 1990 (Aboriginal Co-ordinating Council 1990: 27). The Royal Commission into Aboriginal Deaths in Custody research paper No. 11 shows that 53 per cent of the men who died in prison or police cells were in custody for violent crime—9 per cent for homicide, 12 per cent for assault and 32 per cent for sexual offences. In Queensland over the period 1993 to 1998, 76 people were

---

5 Deed of Grant in Trust areas was the name given to previously designated Aboriginal Reserve lands under the *Community Services (Aborigines) Act 1984*.

killed in domestic homicides; 26 of the victims (34.2 per cent) were Aboriginal or Torres Strait Islander women and children, and 36 of the offenders (47.3 per cent) were Aboriginal or Torres Strait Islander (Aboriginal and Torres Strait Islander Women's Task Force on Violence Report 1999: 91).

Knowing and naming the statistics does not change painful situations. In fact, much research work has been centred on putting statistics together, while Aboriginal pain has continued, often defined as an "alcohol problem", a "suicide problem", a "juvenile offending problem", a "violence problem", and so on.

Research which has been imposed on Aboriginal peoples to define so-called Aboriginal problems has generally evolved from cultural and social engineering theories, which continue to influence current policy, research, government debates and social perceptions (Rigney 1997: 5). Linda Tuhiwai Smith, a Maori academic, writing from her own Indigenous perspective, suggests research "is probably one of the dirtiest words in the indigenous world's vocabulary. ... The ways in which scientific research is implicated in the worst excesses of colonialism remains a powerful remembered history for many of the world's colonised peoples" (1999: 1). Therefore it was vital to find a culturally safe way to research sensitive issues such as intra-cultural violence.

A culturally safe research approach

The research was influenced by a number of philosophical and ethical considerations. The National Health and Medical Research Council's *Guidelines on Ethical Matters in Aboriginal and Torres Strait Islander Research* was a guiding document. Aboriginal peoples with whom I was working gave the greatest ethical direction, however, as I listened to them and responded to their perspectives. Senior Aboriginal people from Rockhampton welcomed me "home" in the early stages of the study. This was my dad's birth and growing-up country, so for the next five years it was a "homecoming".

My design of an ethical and safe process for the study reflected my knowledge of the deep pain this country and its Indigenous peoples held from their colonial history.

The issues of greatest concern to me were the need to understand and to be responsive to the implications of hierarchical structures, and the potential for the intentional or unintentional misuse of power in the relationship between the researcher and the researched; the obligations of relating within an Aboriginal community environment, which necessitates reciprocity; and the ethical obligations and responsibilities of the researcher to ensure the participants' safety and confidentiality. This last was particularly important in research that was exploring the issues of violence and its related trauma.

"Power" over the acquisition and use of information is a critical factor in any research, but more particularly when working with people who have been victimised though oppression or violence (Gibbs and Memon 1999: 1–2). The absence of a demonstrated independent consciousness in oppressed peoples may be taken to mean that the oppressed have willingly collaborated in their own victimisation. Furthermore, Freire (1972) has said that the knowledge and wisdom of oppressed groups provides the most credible solutions to issues affecting their lives. These are not just ethical issues. They are vital research considerations. To deny the "independent consciousness", or appropriate the "knowledge and wisdom" of the researched would betray the ethical relationships formed with them and would compromise the research both in its integrity and fidelity, and, therefore, its value as a *documented body of knowledge*.

Insensitive and unethical research is characterised by the belief that the researcher can and will (as a result of the research) know more than the researched about their own experiences or their own lives. Yet it is not possible for an observer to fully know the experience of another. More particularly, a researcher can never fully know what oppression is more than the person who endures the oppression. As Schweitzer argues:

> the individual's experiential world is private and experienced by him or her alone. It is not observable and cannot be quantified and observed by another in the same way as a chemical reaction might, for instance, be observed (1997: 6–7).

A shared dialogue is also the core component in the chosen methodological approach: *dadirri*—listening to one another. I chose to base the research on the culturally informed philosophy and behaviours that are part of *dadirri* as a practice. This choice resulted from the struggle to find an appropriate research method which would reflect integrity to cultural safety in the research process.

It could be inferred that my use of *dadirri* is a form of cultural appropriation. On the contrary, I approached both the author of the paper "*Dadirri*: Listening to One Another" (Ungunmerr 1993a), and the Aboriginal people of Central Queensland, who helped inform the early design of the research approach, before the choice was made. *Dadirri*, as both an Indigenous philosophy informing investigative processes, and ethical cultural behaviour (in research), ensured cultural safety in the research design.

Dadirri is an Aboriginal concept which refers to a deep contemplative process of "listening to one another" in reciprocal relationships (Ungunmerr 1993a). While the word *dadirri* belongs to the language of the Ngangikurungkurr people of the Daly River area of the Northern Territory, the activity or practice of *dadirri* has its equivalent in many other Indigenous groups in Australia. The Gamilaraay have the words *winangar* (listening) and *gurri* (deep), so *winangargurri* has a similar meaning to *dadirri* (Judy Knox, of Tamworth Gamilaraay, 1998). Aboriginal peoples of Central Queensland talk of *yimbanyiara* (listening to elders), which has similar meanings and behavioural responsibilities to *dadirri* (Milton Lawton, Rockhampton, 1998). The principles and functions of *dadirri* have been explicated in English in

Ungunmerr's paper, presented in Tasmania in 1988 and published in 1993. These principles and functions were used as the philosophic foundations from which the research methods were developed, and they became the most essential functional component of the research methodology.

A narrative approach was used to help understand the context of Aboriginal lives, in relationship to non-Aboriginal lives, in the present. The research approach built on the following assumptions from Western research methodologies, which in turn informed the practice of *dadirri* as a research method:

- Consciousness-raising: The value given to community processes in raising consciousness within the researcher and the researched.
- Participatory Action: The valuable contribution people make in their activities of relating, defining and narrating together, their own life-being. All parts are recognised as essential to the whole.
- Phenomenology: The understanding of the relationship between the inner world of an individual and the outer world of social relationships.

Dadirri: Listening to one another

Dadirri has been called "the Aboriginal gift". Miriam Rose Ungunmerr (1993a) says it is a "special quality, a unique gift of the Aboriginal people. It is inner deep listening and quiet, still awareness—something like what you call contemplation".

The principles and functions of *dadirri* are: a knowledge and consideration of *community* and the diversity and unique nature that each individual brings to *community*; ways of relating and acting within community; a non-intrusive observation, or quietly aware watching; a deep listening and hearing with more than the ears; a reflective non-judgemental consideration of what is being seen and heard; and, having learnt from the listening, a purposeful plan to act, with actions informed by learning, wisdom, and the informed responsibility that comes with knowledge.

Stockton cautions the difficulty that would be encountered in any attempt to analyse *dadirri* by intruding into the "circle of meaning" (1995: 104) that it holds by breaking it into its separate parts. In fact *dadirri* is not a research methodology in the traditional Western scientific tradition, but a *way of life*. It gathers information in quiet observation and deep listening, builds knowledge through awareness and contemplation or reflection, which informs action. Nonetheless, I will make an attempt to break down *dadirri's* principles and functions into their inter-related parts.

Dadirri is informed by the concept of community. "Aboriginal people have a very strong sense of community. All people matter. All of us belong" (Ungunmerr 1993a: 35). At the same time *dadirri* acknowledges the diversity within community, in the complex and complete stories of each individual, all interpenetrating into the whole. There is inter-subjectivity within this sense of community, with a view that all parts are connected and informed by each other (Stockton 1995: 105). For example, it is not possible to know Aboriginal people's, or women's, full experience of violence without also knowing non-Aboriginal people's, or men's, full experience of violence and how these separate experiences inform and shape human behaviours in the whole. Similarly, it is not possible to know what healing is unless it is experienced and understood in the inter-relationships of diverse cultural protocols and practices. This understanding was brought to the methodological approach to the research, and is demonstrated in the inclusive nature of the study processes as they were chosen and formed by Aboriginal people themselves.

The principles of reciprocity ("in *dadirri*—we call on it and it calls on us": Ungunmerr 1993a: 36) are informed by the responsibilities that come with knowing and living *dadirri*. This principle shaped the dialectic between the researcher and the researched. "I will listen to you, share with you, as you listen to, share with me. Our shared experiences are different, but in the inner deep listening to, and quiet, still awareness of each other, we learn and grow together. In this we create community and our shared knowledge(s) and wisdom are expanded from our communication with each other."

A big part of *dadirri* is listening.

Through the years we have listened to the stories. In our Aboriginal way, we learn to listen from our earliest days. We could not live good and useful lives unless we listened. This was the normal way for us to learn—not by asking questions. We learnt by watching and listening, waiting and then acting. Our people have passed on this way of listening for over 40,000 years (Ungunmerr 1993a: 35).

Listening invites responsibility to get the story—the information—right. However, listening over extended periods of time also brings the knowledge that the story changes over time when healing occurs as people experienced being listened to in *dadirri*. This introduces tension into the research processes and explication.

The result of *dadirri's* profound, non-judgemental watching and listening is insight and recognition of the responsibility to act with fidelity in relationship to what has been heard, observed and learnt. *Dadirri* listens and knows, witnesses, feels, empathises in the pain under the anger, and, if the anger is accompanied by action, seeks to understand the thoughts and feelings behind the action. *Dadirri* then seeks to find the source of that pain in knowledge-building for a deepening understanding of the more complete story of the person. *Dadirri* is the stillness and contemplation, in the confusion of chaos as actions of violence are witnessed. *Dadirri* can also be, however, the chaos of feelings and actions as pain-anger-grief is articulated in processes of relating to the group which is in stillness and listening. In both cases, the observers understand that the actions have meaning, and that the body is saying something that the tongue cannot—and this shared knowledge becomes the growing awareness of the community. In "the circle of meaning" (Stockton 1995), all people have a story—"all people matter—all persons belong" (Ungunmerr 1993a: 36).

Dadirri at its deepest level is the search for understanding and meaning. It is listening and learning at its most profound level—more than just listening by the ear, but listening from the heart.

An example of *dadirri* can be observed in the documentary *Cry from the Heart* (Gaia Films), where the protagonist Chris Edwards is expressing the deep grief of his growing understanding: "every person that came into my life—I destroyed their life". At that moment each participant in the group is listening in stillness, at a deep level of knowing the truth as it is for him at that time, witnessing the pain and the courage, reflecting (perhaps unconsciously) the profound learning being witnessed and being experienced.

Dadirri reflects the mind-heart connection in the words " 'I'm thinking and feeling here', underlying the depth of critical thinking and intensity of feeling" (Aboriginal and Torres Strait Islander Women's Task Force on Violence Report, 1999: xvi), crucial to thinking, feeling, choosing to act in right relationship, in understanding of violence, trauma and healing. *Dadirri* therefore is a process of listening, reflecting, observing the feelings and actions, reflecting and learning, and in the cyclic process, re-listening at deeper and deeper levels of understanding and knowledge-building.

Dadirri means listening to and observing the self as well as, and in relationship with, others. This brings further responsibilities to the researcher—to know the self.

The researcher brings to any research her or his own subjective self. No research is value-free, for even in the choice of subject a value statement is made. In fact research must have value and *be of value*. In this, researchers must be able to know and acknowledge their own value judgements, and understand the beliefs, influences, assumptions and intrusions, the decisions and choices that come from their past and are active in the present in the day-to-day activities of relating in the research, and that therefore influence the research.

To summarise, the perspective of *dadirri* as a methodological approach was guided by the following assumptions:

- When conducting research within Aboriginal communities there is a need to honour the integrity and fidelity of community in both its dynamic diversity and its interconnected unity. It is important here to understand that within this essence of community there is often great conflict which has meaning in itself.
- It is important to work within the principles of reciprocity in ways of relating and behaving, and in sharing information, when conducting research within Aboriginal communities.
- Research using the protocols that are based within *dadirri* requires that the researcher be aware of any assumptions or bias.
- Aboriginal worldviews explain that learning comes from listening and witnessing, without judgement or prejudice, and in knowing and being responsible for the self, in relationship to others in this listening/learning process.
- Aboriginal worldviews consider that the activity of learning introduces a responsibility to act with integrity and fidelity to what has been learnt.

The question must then be asked: how can these principles and functions be applied as a research method? In other words, how is *dadirri* put into practice?

The research method was governed by a number of assumptions and principles, with actions based on these. The first assumption was that the success of the project would depend primarily on whether Aboriginal peoples themselves approved the research proposal with an invitation to conduct the research in the field. The principle was that the research would occur, and be located in a place, by invitation.

The second assumption was that the research could not proceed unless the researcher abided by the principles of reciprocity. The principle of reciprocity involves the researcher locating her or himself within community in time and place and in relationship to those who came into the research as participants. Again the essence of *dadirri* was reflected in these actions: "Through the years we listened to the stories … As we grow older, we ourselves become the storytellers" (Ungunmerr 1993a: 37), which is the power and processes of right relationship. A further principle of reciprocity was that, as the researcher received information from the participants, the researcher would be obligated to return resource materials to the participants through a participant organisation, for their future use. These materials include the knowledges derived that arise from the research activities.

The third assumption was that people would have to feel safe and be safe for the research to be successful, since in this instance what was being investigated was the experience of violence and of healing. A principle, therefore, was to establish a number of procedures to ensure the safety of each participant. To begin with, confidentiality is critical. Secondly, it is important to create a safe (ceremonial) environment, which in this research was the workshops. Thirdly, people must be allowed to actively influence the means by which the data are collected and to choose their own interview sites. In the current research it was found that people felt safer when we sat together under trees on the river bank or on the beach, in the safety of groups in which people had been relating for some time, before they were ready to share stories.

The fourth assumption was that, as the listening/learning function was adhered to in the collection of stories, there would be a change process as people began to access parts of themselves—their inner stories and outer lives—parts of who they are that they had previously denied or been fearful of acknowledging. *Dadirri* gives value to the human story, no matter how painful or shameful, naming the human story as sacred. "The stories and songs sink quietly into our minds and we hold them deep inside. In the ceremonies we celebrate the awareness of our lives as sacred" (Ungunmerr

1993a: 37). The researcher has the obligation to locate her or his own activities within those that affirm the courage and hope of people, and not in pathologising their pain. The principle was to provide support for participants, and to allow them to find new meanings in their experiences, to allow them to restructure their stories. In the current study, this involved documenting the trauma and recording the healing from trauma, using words of courage and hope.

> I never feel alone in the ceremonies. As a people we still survive. Survival is something that has become part of us from centuries of struggle and endurance. Culture keeps on growing. With education and interaction with other people we will grow strong again (Ungunmerr 1993a: 36).

The fifth assumption was that in the explication of data there would be the responsibility to act with fidelity. Making sense of the stories, from a *dadirri* perspective, involves allowing people to own their own data (or the intellectual property rights to their stories). The principle of *dadirri*—in watching and listening; waiting and then acting—also required me to reflect back to the group what was being said to check if the information was being explicated and presented with fidelity.

Finally *dadirri*, in common with many research methodologies, holds that the researcher considers ethical responsibilities to be of vital importance.

Putting *dadirri* into practice was very much the process of learning to stay within the flow of a community in which the river of need and of sharing would sometimes flow slow and deep, and at other times be fast and turbulent. At all times the role of the researcher was to listen to and stay with where people themselves needed to go, to take the direction they took as their experiences were defined and re-defined, as they found for themselves their own stories and their own healing paths.

Before the work started, however, I had to conceptualise the journey that links past with present.

Chapter Two

Song Lines and Trauma Trails

They live in a Tranquility which is not disturbed by the Inequality of condition. ...

Captain James Cook, Journal

At the Aboriginal Community Futures Conference held at James Cook University in Townsville in 1990, Isaac Hobson talked about the "first wave". He was describing the impacts of colonisation, from the latter half of the nineteenth century to the present, on the Aboriginal peoples where he lived. Isaac lives at Lockhart River, an Aboriginal community on the east coast of Cape York Peninsula. He said he was concerned that another wave was forming in the massive state-driven economic development proposals for the regions around Lockhart River. He asked that the neo-colonisers understand that his people had not yet recovered from the destructive forces of the first wave and requested that his people be included in any talking about, and implementation of, new economic developments in the Cape York region. At that time there were a number of proposals for large-scale developments on countries near Lockhart River, with little or no consultation with the Lockhart Aboriginal community: a space station, a 3000-bed exclusive resort, mining development.

Charles Figley, in his introduction to *Trauma and its Wake* (1986), describes the traumatic effect of extraordinarily stressful experiences as being like the waves created by a stone cast into a pond.

Waves radiate across the surface of the pond from the point of contact, and under certain conditions there is some discernible impact along the shore of the pond. Trauma—the point of penetration—and its wake—the psychosocial repercussions—are normal reactions to extraordinary circumstances (1986: xvii).

Hobson (1990) and Figley (1986) use similar symbolic language to bring attention to conditions of human distress resulting from human trauma experiences.

The persistent theme of the book is that experiences of violence are traumatic, and that trauma, if unhealed, may compound, becoming cumulative in its impacts on individuals, families and indeed whole communities and societies. The layered trauma that results from colonisation is likely to be expressed in dysfunctional, and sometimes violent, behaviour at both individual and large-scale levels of human interaction, and these are re-traumatising.

The first segment of this chapter is an exploration of Aboriginal worldviews or experiences of *being in the world*, before and continuing from colonisation. In this I discuss Aboriginal cultural and spiritual beliefs and practices that are vital to people in healthy relationships. I then consider the question, "What does violence do to human societies?" I detail the physical, structural and psycho-social violence of colonisation, followed by an examination of the research on trauma, reviewing the literature and sources in the context of the generational impacts of colonisation.

It must be stated here that research is only presently emerging that specifically explores the issue of trauma within Aboriginal and Torres Strait Islander contextual frameworks. A vital consideration, if we as Aboriginal peoples are to be able to deal with the violence within our families and communities today, is to begin the process of understanding the social, cultural and spiritual construction of violence as trauma as violence, and consider appropriate recovery from within Aboriginal ways of knowing, being and acting, in the world.

Cultures in collision

The land that was called *terra nullius* (land of no peoples) by the British colonisers after 1788, was in fact a living, breathing landscape inhabited by between 300,000 and 1 million people (Elkin 1954: 10–11; Butlin 1982: 120). An outsider, sailing near this continent which was later claimed to be *terra nullius* in order to legitimise its invasion and dispossession, wrote in 1770 of the Aboriginal peoples he saw:

> They live in a Tranquility which is not disturbed by the Inequality of condition. The Earth and Sea of their own accord furnishes them with all things necessary for Life ... they live in a Warm and Fine Climate, and enjoy every wholesome Air, so that they have very little need of Clothing ... in short, they seem'd to set no Value upon anything we gave them; nor would they ever part with anything of their own ... This, in my opinion Argues that they think themselves provided with all the necessarys of Life (James Cook, *Journal*, 1893 edn).

This land was not a paradise and our people did not (and do not) live in association with each other without conflict (no human groups do that). But in comparison to England, with its class distinctions and constructed poverty for the lower classes, an outside observer, comparing the two social situations as they were at the time, could well have agreed with Cook.

To Aboriginal peoples who knew no other place, the country was not so much a paradise, but more simply a homeland, and their associations with each other were the activities of normal human relationships.

Aboriginal peoples lived in small extended family units linked into larger language groups with distinct territorial boundaries. Both the family groups and the language groups were woven together by complex kinship systems, affiliations and rules for social interaction that bound distinct groups together.

Cultural diversity is illustrated by the 500 languages or dialects spoken (Berndt and Berndt 1988: 28), and the social and economic adaptation to the complex and distinct ecologies of the continent. Common organisational structures allowed people to interact with each other in relationships that gave depth and meaning to day-to-day life. The people were all hunters-and-gatherers who generally moved in semi-nomadic patterns according to seasonal harvesting and ceremonial responsibility. While people remained within their own territorial boundaries for day-to-day living, ceremonies were conducted across these boundaries to link groups in such a way that trade-routes and song-lines developed across the vast continent. Material artefacts such as flint tools and ceremonial shells, as well as the sacred songs and narratives—stories used in ceremony—were the commodities of sacred and secular business that drew people together (Clunies-Ross and Wild 1982; Ellis 1985). Such songs are narratives "of crucial forms of knowledge about the Dreaming" (Horton 1994: 1005–6), and about relationships between people and relationships with country.

Stanner has summarised the cultural and spiritual beliefs and practices of the people of this land, both in day-to-day living and sacred ceremonial practice, as "uniting hearts and establishing order" (1979: 143), in relationship both to the natural environment and to the other life forms, including humans, of the land.

Relationships with the natural world, and in particular the distressed feelings that accompany a natural disaster such a flood or drought, were ritualised and ceremonised so that healing, or a restoration of good relationships, could occur in the land with other living species, and between the land and the people. Order was maintained in relationships with the natural world by the rituals and ceremonies conducted to ensure increase and the healing of country, which were essential for survival. In turn it was known that, if people met their ceremonial obligations to the land, the land would nurture them. Similar principles applied to human relationships. Order was maintained in relationships between people by the activities of ceremony in management of conflict. If people met their social obligations in relationship to others, they in turn would be nurtured in processes of reciprocity (Berndt and Berndt 1988: 359–62; 121–2).

In fact, a strong sense of self, of belonging, of identity, was derived from experiences of validation of self in relationship—"from celebration, accomplishment, intimacy, ritual, occupation, avocation, affection, friendship, sexuality, management and resolution of conflict" (Clarke and Fewquandie 1998: 4).

Conflict is a normal aspect of all human associations. In Aboriginal relationships, when conflict occurred, ceremonial processes were used to bring the contending parties together, to find ways in which people could live with each other under lore. Lore here is used to mean Aboriginal traditional knowledge, wisdom, learning, erudition, information, and science (discussed further below).

In 1788 colonisation brought disorder and disharmony and a new law. Law here is used to mean Western systems of legislature, enactment, principle, enforcement, courts and incarceration.

Before looking at the impacts of colonisation, it is important to consider in more depth Aboriginal worldviews or ways of being in the world. Although trauma is essentially a universal human experience, the shock that accompanies colonising encounters may have profound effects on different groups, according to particular cultural elements and processes and the unique dimensions of the impacts. It is not possible to understand the lives of people today unless we also consider their experiences across generations.

Aboriginal worldviews

Land is a story place. Land holds the stories of human survival across many generations. Land shapes people, just as people shape their countries.

This land now called Australia was no wilderness. For

those people who have lived and loved here since the creation times, the land is more than a physical place. It is a moral sphere, the seat of life and emotions, and a place of the heart: "Come with me to the point and we'll look at the country. We'll look across at the rocks. Look, rain is coming! It falls on my sweetheart" (Song from the Oenpelli Region, quoted by Stanner 1983).

The people of this land, within the boundaries of their own countries, were intimately familiar with each rock and cave, watercourse and waterhole, mountain peak and sea headland, all humanised in the processes of the Dreamings. The social world of the people "was expanded to include this natural world which was humanised, formed by the Ancestral Beings of the long distant past" (Berndt and Berndt 1988: 28). Not only did the people have a spiritually intimate relationship with the land, they also had a detailed knowledge of the seasons and all other life forms, for they felt they shared the "same life essence with all natural species and elements" (Berndt and Berndt 1988: 136). An Aboriginal woman, Mary Graham, talks of "Being Aboriginal" as being made by our ancestors who also made the land in which we live, in a process that was, and continues to be, evolutionary, growing, developing, maturing, ripening. "Some Aboriginal people say we became human in this country, the spirit ancestors, the creator beings, spirit beings, made humans, made everything, made the land itself, and then made the people to look after the land" (Graham 1995: 61–76).

Anthropologist Deborah Bird Rose, in outlining aspects of an Aboriginal worldview, provides a conceptual essence of the land and its people connecting across lifespans, interacting, relating, moving, growing, nourishing and being nourished, transforming and being transformed, in this evolutionary process.

The Australian continent is criss-crossed with the tracks of the Dreamings: walking, slithering, crawling, flying, chasing, hunting, weeping, dying, giving birth. Performing rituals, distributing the plants, making the landforms and water, establishing things in their own places, making the relationships between one place and another. Leaving parts or essences of themselves, looking back in sorrow; and still travelling, changing languages, changing songs, changing skin. … Where they travelled, where they stopped, where they lived the events of their lives, all these places are sources and sites of Law. These tracks and sites, and the Dreamings associated with them, make up the sacred geography of Australia; they are visible in paintings and engravings; they are sung in songs, depicted in body paintings and engravings; they form the basis of a major dimension of the land tenure system for most Aboriginal people. To know the country is to know the story of how it came into being, and that story also carries the knowledge of how the human owners of that country came into being. Except in cases of succession, the relationship between the people and their country is understood to have existed from time immemorial— to be part of the land itself (Rose 1996: 35–6).

The land grew the people and people grew their country. Human spiritual and cultural processes within this landscape and with other life forms were, and continue to be, dynamic, proceeding, expanding, changing, growing, flowing, being mediated according to the movements and interactions that are natural to human, and non-human, associations. Rose names, in essence, "being human" as transforming processes, continuous movements of activity and energy, as people are involved together in the business of making sense of their actuality as they make relationships with both the corporeal and the non-corporeal world (1996: 36).

In this, there is recognition of those who have gone before and their contribution to the whole of who we are, of the connections and communications between people down the generations, between people and country, and between the corporeal and non-corporeal world. These are the inter-relationships, interdependencies, interconnections and continuities that form the whole. These inter-relationships must be considered in any developing understanding of the traumatic impacts of colonisation where irrevocable intrusion has occurred, and continues to occur, into the soul and fabric of the relationships that people had with each other and their country.

Relationships and land

It is important to understand people's relationship with land in considering trauma, for country can hold healing or traumatic memory and energy, by the human activity or ceremony that has made a place unique, sacred or profane.

For Aboriginal people, being human is relationship-centred. Being human is defined by the value given to *where we have come from, who we are,* and *where we are going* in relationship to country and kin. What we do to the country that is ours by birthright, to other humans and non-humans, to all with whom we are in relationship, is the essence of our humanity.

In this sense the land is central to Aboriginal identity and it provides a *logos* or guide for human interaction and sense of wellness or *well-being*. If the country is sick, people are sick. If the country is well, people are well. Stanner, writing from an Anglo-Australian perspective, describes the links between the people and their heartland, home or place of living:

No English words are good enough to give a sense of the links between an Aboriginal group and its homeland. Our word "home", warm and suggestive though it be, does not match the Aboriginal word that may mean "camp", "hearth", "country", "everlasting home", "totem place", "life source", "spirit centre", and much else all in one. Our word "land" is too spare and meagre. We can now scarcely use it except with economic overtones unless we happen to be poets. The Aboriginal would speak of "earth" and use the word in a richly symbolic way to mean his "shoulder" or his "side". I have seen an Aboriginal embrace the earth he walked on. To put our words "home" and "land" together in "homeland" is a little better but not much. A different tradition leaves us tongueless and earless towards this other world of meaning and significance. When we took what we call "land" we took what to them meant hearth, home, the source and focus of life, and everlastingness of spirit (Stanner 1979: 230).

Stanner writes through the historical, patriarchal "he". Women also have equally strong bonds to the homeland or heartplace, through their ceremonial responsibilities, including the significance of conception or birth sites. Miriam-Rose Ungunmerr, an Aboriginal woman, confirms:

> You might like to hear how I feel about the bush. I never get tired of going back. My relations have told me about the origin of these places. This history of my ancestors has real meaning for me. I learnt about trading trails, a track that neighbouring tribes used to follow, the place of our ceremonial grounds. All these places mean a lot to me. They are part of me. All the bush is part of my life. I was born under a tree. My mother showed me the place. She showed me where I used to play, and where I would hunt for wild honey. The feeling I have for this place is very special. This place where I was born, it's me (1993: 36).

In fact conception and birth sites set in place much of the journeying across country that the physical body undertakes, and the inter-relationships with people, which are re-enacted at death, in mortuary rituals, determining the continuing journeying of the spirit into other realms and realities (Morphy 1984).

> Land has recuperative aspects that are essential to Aboriginal well-being. Our land also has an important role to play in healing. The land is a powerful healer, as is the sea. When your ancestors have walked these places for millennia, they hold an energy of timelessness that invokes serenity and the feeling that one is not alone, but in the presence of these ancestors, who are able to communicate via the senses and convey the feelings and thoughts that are most conductive to healing. When we are able to sit on our land in contemplation and hear, feel or see the spirits of our old people, then we have been to a place within ourselves of great depth and connectedness. It is this place that we need to go to in order to truly heal ourselves; and once we have learnt how to do that, then we can move forward (Clarke and Fewquandie 1998: 3).

Relationships with land are mutually life-giving. Within the homeland or heartplace, the people have been, and still are, part of the creation or evolutionary process. In their responsibility for country and kin in social and spiritual interaction they are its continuing stewards as well. The Dreamings are not something that happened in the long distant past. Dreamings are the processes of human action in co-creation with the great Creators and the ancestral beings, which continue in the present, the continuing birth, life, death, rebirth, renewal that is human activity across millennia.

Ceremony and ritual as articulation of relationship

Ceremony was (and is) central to Aboriginal life. Ceremonies were used to re-establish the sense of creative power after being made to feel powerless, and to help heal the distress that accompanies natural disasters and as a consequence of human conflict. Ceremony in "looking after country" had its own essential responsibilities for the continuation of the ongoing life cycles. An Elder of the Ghungulu people of Central Queensland says, "There are three devils, Fire, Water, Wind. If we don't do our jobs [ceremony], they will come to destroy us. If we are doing the right thing, they'll work for us, do the right thing by us" (Ghungulu Elder Lindsey Black). These three elements are both predators and cleansers of the natural world.

Ceremonies are also a time when feelings can be articulated in creative action. Ceremony is the process and responsibility of mediating with the living entities that are part of the physical world, the land and other non-human and human life forms (Rose 1987: 264–7; Edwards 1987: 12–25). Ceremony is a time of communicating with the ancestral beings and the creation powers as well as other people. In using the sacred names, songs, dances and art in ritual, in telling the past and present life stories in ceremonies, people are preparing themselves for another stage of a journey they managed and started before birth: a journey that continues after death, a journey that is continuing (Edwards 1988: 65–76; Morphy 1984).

A central concept of Aboriginal life is the notion of spiritual continuity of the present—and the future—with the ancestral past (Stanner 1979: 24–7, 1987: 225–36). The ancestral past is used to refer both to that period of time called "Time Before Morning", or "The Dreamings", and the ancestral beings who were active in that past (Berndt and Berndt 1988: 227–300). These are the creators of the known world. By giving form and meaning to the creation powers, in the allocation of rights to human groups, to land, to sacred objects, songs, dances and art forms, the ancestral beings have created a continuing and interconnecting relationship between past, present and future (Berndt and Berndt 1988). They—*we*—in ceremony and in actuality are one. Song, dance, art and ritual, used in ceremony, remind the ancestral beings to continue to release their powers, to ensure the ongoing reproduction of life cycles (Edwards 1988). Within the action of the ceremonies, the human mediators are reminded of their responsibilities, of the need to mend and preserve relationships between people and country and people and people, to care for country and to care for kin (Rose 1988: 264).

In ceremony we become storytellers and teachers. "We pass on to the young ones all they must know. The stories and songs sink quietly into our minds and we hold them deep inside. In the ceremonies we celebrate the awareness of our lives as sacred" (Ungunmerr 1993a: 34). In so doing the rules and knowledges for living across generations are confirmed and affirmed.

Stanner implies that people do not just have a spiritual link with the past and the future (1963: 255). We have control by what we do in the present; in ceremony we become co-creators, as well as stewards of the ongoing processes of creation.

Ritual and ceremony also provide structure to the

essentialities of social life; the core reality of the ancestral past with its connection to the present (and future); relationship with land; group interactions, and kinship responsibilities (Berndt and Berndt 1988: 227–300). Ritual not only confirms and reaffirms responsibility to kin, it is a potent tool for affirming, articulating knowledge and power over life—and death (Rose 1987: 264). Men's sacred trust in ritual, particularly male initiation, is well known. What is less well understood is women's ceremonial responsibility that is central, for example, to birthing and mourning rituals that are affirmations and confirmations of life cycles (Bell 1983).

While birth is an affirmation of the continuity of relationships, death in any group is a potential threat to social harmony. The emotions of love and attachment to the dead person are replaced by feelings of sorrow, anger, fear, despair and hopelessness. Janice Reid asserts that ceremonies conducted at the death of an individual are an "affirmation of the relations and beliefs of the living" (1979: 342).

At the ceremonies that commemorate the death of an individual, a number of things happen. The person's life journey is re-enacted. People who at various times had responsibility for aspects of that journey have to be there to reaffirm their knowledge of responsibility, and to ensure a safe future journey of the spirit of the person who has died. If those who were present at birth, first initiation and so on have died through old age, their place is taken by their ritual representatives in the next generation: grandmother—granddaughter; grandfather—grandson. They come together to celebrate and reaffirm the individual aspects of that particular person, the unique life journey (Morphy 1984).

Reid (1979) describes such ceremonies as doing two important things. Firstly, ceremonies dispel feelings of despair and hopelessness as they provide testament to people of the power they hold over life and death. In this, ceremonies reaffirm the future of the ancestral past in the lives of the living. And secondly, by allowing people to work through their feelings of anger and sorrow, in utilising those interconnecting webs of relationships between groups and among kin, such ceremonies unify the community. In the process, the vital essence of the sacred in both the individual and communal identity is reaffirmed and the future as inclusive is confirmed.

The wilful denigration and destruction of Aboriginal ceremonial responsibilities and processes by the colonisers has therefore had profound transgenerational effects on the people of this land. Aboriginal people have been prevented from engaging in ceremonial processes for healing from trauma. The distressed feelings that accompany loss, death and devastation remain as destructive forces within the land and the people.

Relationships between people

Trauma disrupts and restructures relationships between people. In particular this has been so for Aboriginal men and women and for the various Aboriginal groups across Australia. Stanner writes of the Aboriginal

> creative drive to make sense and order out of things. ... there has been an unusually rich development of what the anthropologist calls "social structure", the network of enduring relations recognised between people. This very intricate system is an intellectual and social achievement of a high order (1979: 33).

Aboriginal men and women among themselves have always been diverse individuals involved in a tensely creative process of mediating and negotiating their relationships and responsibility to each other. Aboriginal relationships, in particular gender relationships, were (and are) dynamic. While some have described Aboriginal society as patriarchal (McGrath 1995), others such as Meggitt (1966) use the word "egalitarian", which suggests that all members of the social group are seen as having equal status. Sackett writes of the Aboriginal people he observed:

One aspect of the traditional belief system is the notion that there should be no bosses. Ultimately, it is thought, all humans are equal in that they are all less than the Dreamtime-beings whose edicts they have to follow. Humans cannot make or change the law—it is established and laid down for all time in the creative epoch—so there is supposedly no need for leaders (1978: 42).

Nonetheless, a more precise term would be "egalitarian hegemony". "Egalitarian hegemony" is described as a significant masculine stature balanced by woman's sovereignty and authority in the social, economic, and spiritual domains. Egalitarian political systems generally incorporate some distinctions based on gender and age, in so far as men in general have authority over women, and older people have authority over younger people (Edwards 1988: 58). Hamilton feels Aboriginal men's power over women was based on the threat of physical force (1981: 74). Cowlishaw (1990) concurs, suggesting it is this threat that teaches women caution. Burbank (1994), in writing of "fighting women", sees Aboriginal women as aggressors in asserting their rights, not victims of men's authority and dominance. Bell (1983) writes of Aboriginal women as autonomous in their own right in all domains, economic, social, political, spiritual, ceremonial. Aboriginal women have said they feel the essence of Aboriginal relationships is the management of conflict, the continual mediation and negotiation that occur between men and women, within both the personal sphere and the political domain (Watson 1987).

Aboriginal women have the right to mediate between the corporeal and non-corporeal world through their own ceremonial processes. They themselves are co-creators working with the ancestral beings to ensure life processes continue. Women had and continue to have power and autonomy, as well as full responsibility in these regards. Although Aboriginal societies were gendered, Aboriginal women believe they are not victims of men's power, but assertively affirm their place, their role in the whole of community. According to Catherine Berndt, this provides both independence and also an essential interdependence between gender groups (1989: 6).

While diverse opinions debate the role and status of men and women in societies before colonisation, one thing remains clear. Gender and age relationships have been fractured and dismantled in colonisation and have changed considerably as a result of colonising impacts. The relationships between Aboriginal women and men are continuing to be de-constructed and re-structured.

A flowing of good (social) relationships is essential for the well-being of both individuals and groups (Bell 1983: 149). Social relations are mediated by those possessions upon which we place the greatest value. If the possession we most value is a car, for instance, our social interactions will be centred on cars, as is the case with many young people today. If it is a business, then business activities, and good social relationships around the business, will take precedence. If it is the right to drink alcohol with our mates, then our predominant social interaction will be the activity of drinking with other men or women.

In Aboriginal Australia BC (Before Cook), "the most cherished possession of men were women, children and their sacred heritage. For women it was men, children, their domestic circle plus their sacred heritage" (Berndt and Berndt 1988: 225). Men's corporate power was based within the sacred and "looking out for the mob", while women's communal power came both from familial circles and the sacred. This would suggest that rich social interaction would have occurred among women in their domestic circles and in sacred ceremonial responsibilities. Rich social interaction would also occur among men in their responsibilities in the sacred, and relationships with each other. Communal activities across age and gender groups and extended kin networks ensured that the richness of social and ceremonial interactions acted as a uniting force for social cohesion.

Adults had gender-specific responsibility to nurture, protect and teach children. Adult responsibilities centred on teaching children proper behaviour through example, while allowing the child autonomy to grow and learn naturally. Adults who did not fulfil their responsibilities to teach children, to pass on knowledge for life, were censored and chastised themselves (Burbank 1994: 77). Stanner observed:

> Aboriginal culture leaves a child virtually untrammelled for five or six years. In infancy it lies in a smooth, well-rounded coolamon which is airy and unconstraining, and rocks if the child moves to any great extent. A cry brings immediate fondling. A child may still cry at three as a sign that it wants something—water, attention, carrying. Its dependence on and command of both parents is maximal, their indulgence extreme (1979: 99).

Any adult who allowed a child to be severely hurt would themselves be punished for their negligence. To actually harm a child would attract severe punishment. While children were reproached, severe physical punishment of a child was unheard of (Roth 1984: 1905, 7). In fact, physical or emotional punishment of a child in the way of Western child-rearing practices of the time, was incomprehensible (Hamilton 1981; Stanner 1979: 99). Roth, a medical doctor and ethnographer, said he found no instance of what would now be called child abuse by white society, during all the time of his work with the tribal groups of Queensland early in the twentieth century (1984: 1905, 7). At this time, many of these groups had already been severely traumatised, yet the transgenerational effects of the trauma had not, at that time, overwhelmed the child-rearing practices and the cultural attitudes and behaviours towards children.

Aboriginal society has been described as gerontocratic, that is, the authority of Elders was paramount (Berndt and Berndt 1988: 210). Elders were, and are, respected. They were believed to have grown into knowledge and wisdom by their involvement in life and the incremental ritual stages of ceremony. Aboriginal clans allocated certain responsibilities to Elders, who were usually, though not always, the older people in the group. An Elder of the Quandamooka people (Moreton Bay) has described their role:

> In Traditional times leaders were not born into a position, there were no hereditary titles. Elders chose through a process of initiation the person responsible for taking on a particular responsibility. No one person knows all, which prevented the development of the cult of the individual. Decisions were made by a group or body responsible to that country, not one individual person. ... Basic protocols are standard good manners, they are universal and may differ according to language but not in practice. The first point is self-respect which is a prerequisite to respect for others. It is also important to be polite and courteous, to be unselfish in what you do and have and to be helpful. If we identify as Aboriginal we should accept responsibility to live by community protocols (Uncle Bob Anderson 1999).

Not all older people are equally respected. People are given their title of Elder much as people earn the title of doctor, professor or statesman in Western society, by their pursuit of knowledge and its application in wise action, and the communal judgement of the contribution they make to the community as a whole.

Much is written and spoken about the Aboriginal community, or more definitively, Aboriginal communities. Indigenous worldviews recognise being part of a whole that is called *community* (Duran and Duran 1995). Communities are made up of diverse groups of people who function separately and collectively, generally for the common good of the whole group. There will always be conflict in the relationships in such communities (Langton 1988; Dodson 1995), but *community* is made when human groups choose to work through and resolve conflict. In this sense *community* can be defined as:

> A group in which free conversation can take place. Community is where I can share my innermost thoughts, bring out the depths of my own feelings, and know they will be understood. ... Communication makes community and is the possibility of

human beings living together for their mutual psychological, physical and spiritual nourishment (May 1976: 246–7).

The essence of "Being Aboriginal" was the dynamic processes of engaging in communal activities of communicating, expressing and managing conflict, which would often be challenging, and invariably entertaining.

Relationships, at the individual level and between groups, were renegotiated, redefined and healed on an ongoing basis, in ceremonial pursuits and day-to-day activities. This is in keeping with an ethic that allows diversity and honours community, and which places great emphasis on, and effort in, the maintenance of relationships. Men and women came together in ceremony both in separate gender groups and as community, through dance, art, music, theatre, crafts and storytelling, used and acted out in day-to-day secular and sacred ritual. Thus relationships and interconnections were established, maintained, strengthened and healed. In the speaking, singing, painting, dancing, enacting of stories, people in the present are following the patterns of speech, designs, symbols, rhythms and steps that the ancestors have created in the continuity of ceremonial processes (Clarke and Fewquandie 1998: 3) used to "unite hearts and maintain order" (Stanner 1979: 143).

Stanner, having written on Aboriginal cultural and spiritual beliefs and practices, observed that the process, the business, the religion, the profession of being Aboriginal, is "probably one of the least material-minded, and most life-minded, of which we have knowledge". The invading Europeans saw excessive leisure, social entertaining and great ceremonial gatherings. In fact, these were activities of relationship, of making connections, of creating, maintaining and healing relationships, in which the primary virtues were "generosity and fair dealing", working to "unite hearts and establish order" (Stanner 1963: 234–6). Such activities were and are hard work, because they reflect the conflict that comes as we mediate and negotiate relationships in a sometimes harsh environment.

In examining the transgenerational consequences of colonisation, the disruption to family and community relationships must be considered. It is vital to understand the manner in which children were taught proper behaviour and the roles of men, women, and more particularly Elders, in this generational responsibility. It is also vital to understand how the responsibility to nurture, protect and teach children has been fractured and dismantled under colonisation and how much of the learning of children today comes from witnessing acts of violence in institutional situations, in families and communities, and in Western media. The fractured relationships between men and women as partners are also important in understanding the dysfunction in Aboriginal families and communities today.

Lore and law

Aboriginal societies before Cook were not perfect harmonious groups of people living in paradise. Neither the ancestral beings, nor humans as co-creators, are perfect, and the land now called Australia has an environment that is often harsh and unpredictable, a land of great contrasts that evoke deep feeling. Land forms people.

All societies have conflict. All humans have ego, bad behaviour, hostility, resentment, fear at the death of a loved one or at the unknown, the tensions between generations and gender groups, passions in sexual encounters, and attempts to control others. Then and today, there was and is continuing tension between the rights of the individual and responsibility to the group, the role and place of women and the role and place of men within the whole as community. There will always be tension in the relationships between old and young, conflict in the interactions between groups.

The absolute essence of Aboriginal relationships, however, was the vibrancy of mediating the conflicts natural to all human associations. The effort that went into maintaining good relationships, abetting balance, was hard work: it was necessary to continually mediate the conflict between the right to individual autonomy and the responsibility to the well-being of the group, of community.

Lore was the functional foundation of these interactions. Lore is defined here as the body of traditional knowledge based on the wisdom that comes from experience, and transmitted in practical teachings across generations. The word *law* on the other hand, is used to refer to the functions of legislature, enactment, policing, courts, and prisons in the imposed application of colonial domination.

Women and men, equally, had full responsibility before the lore. Women were lore keepers; they were more likely to call people to account for wrong behaviour. Men were lore enforcers. There were two aspects of lore: interpersonal standards of behaviour between individuals, in families and within groups; and forms of interactions between the corporeal and the non-corporeal world.

In any society, lore and law should be a set of rules or principles that enhance the lives of a people. Aboriginal lore ensured all people lived within a set of known precepts that provided clear standards for interconnecting relationships within both the human and non-human world.

The land is the land. But it was the lore that held people together. The lore is what is educated here [head] and here [heart]. Each family was responsible for the family education of the children as they grew up, the mothers, the fathers, the grandmothers and the grandfathers, the aunties and the uncles. The lore is always there. The breakdown was when the families were broken down when the white men brought their law (Alice Kelly, taped interview by author, 1990).

Aboriginal lore differed very little from one group to another. Sacred lore does not change. Secular lore was a dynamic process of group interaction, for disputing, mediating, arbitrating, conciliating, and articulating the rights of individuals over responsibilities to group. As stated before, there was (and is) an energetic tension within Aboriginal society, between women and men and young and old. In this process individuals are enabled to express their feelings and assert their rights. At the same time they would be reminded of their responsibilities. Other members of the group had the responsibility to listen and respond appropriately to articulations of distress. Confrontation in these interactions was often forceful and physical. "To not show 'proper feeling' in one's interactions with others is to question the relationship, and to violate not just an expectancy, but to threaten a severing of connectedness, which is critical to a sense of self and well-being" (Reser 1990: 31). In relationships, both in families and in community, how one is feeling is of paramount importance. Thomas Moore (1992) has written of the soul as the place of deepest feeling, giving value to feelings as the place and process that connects us to the spiritual essence of *who we are*. According to Joseph, spirituality is "The drive, need, power or capacity ... the underlying dimension of consciousness which strives for meaning, union with the universe, and all things; it extends to the experience of the transcendent or a power beyond us" (1987: 13).

In this, it is the deepest feelings, worked through in the processes of clearing conflict, which allows relationships at their most profound, spiritual and creative level to occur. Aboriginal people were spiritual people at its deepest level of meaning as they strove to make explicit and create order out of the conflicting and often chaotic relationships that govern the corporeal and non-corporeal world.

Transgression of lore, and the personal and group conflict that came from transgression, was managed in many ways.

The Tjunparni is a statement of authority and an expression of dissatisfaction with a promise of subsequent retribution to remedy wrongs if they occur in the future. The institutionalised "growl" is an important way by which some men and women attempt to establish and maintain their authority within their own camps by demonstrating their moral strength and opinions (Mow 1992: 1).

Women's "ring place or business place" (like those of men) were areas where offenders were brought to trial and disputes resolved by ritual means (Bell 1983: 124).

Clan meetings and community moots were methods of dealing with disputes which attempted to reach outcomes that were acceptable to all and implementable by the group (Williams 1987: 49–65). Ritualised aggression was also used, particularly, as stated before, in ceremonial processes to manage or resolve large group conflicts, but also at the interpersonal level between individual disputants.

Such ceremonies were not just functions of lore but also functions of health or *well-being* in the healing of relationships within the cultural aspect of who the person is, and the collective experience of being in the world.

The closest word for health within the Aboriginal languages is *well-being*. The word *punyu*, from the language of the Ngaringman from the Northern Territory, sometimes translated as *well-being*, explains the concept and functions. *Punyu* encompasses *person* and *country* and is associated with being:

- Strong
- Happy
- Knowledgeable
- Socially responsible (to "take a care")
- Beautiful
- Clean
- Safe—both in the sense of being within the lore and in the sense of being cared for (Rose 2000: 65).

In Ngaringman cosmology the known universe constitutes a living system the goal of which is to reproduce itself as a living system. Each part of the cosmos, country, Rainbow Snake, animals, people, etc is alive, conscious, and is basically either punyu or not punyu. That which is punyu is not just alive but also contributing to life (Mobbs 1991: 289).

Rose explains that "When people and country are punyu the flow of energy keeps both strong, healthy, and fruitful." *Punyu* and being well connect People, Place, Lore into a whole. Being well would therefore be an "achieved quality, developed through relationships of mutual care" (2000: 65).

This is the whole-of-life view and it also includes the cyclical concept of life-death-life (National Aboriginal Health Strategy Working Party 1989: x). How does this translate to an urban situation? Mobbs suggests that " 'being well' means having harmonious social relationships with kin, with others who are not kin, and even with strangers" (1991: 289).

The word *safe*, both in the sense of being within the lore and in the sense of being cared for, is vital in well-being for Aboriginal individuals and groups. The experience of safety determines all the other factors of well-being. We know ourselves as strong, happy, knowledgeable, socially respons-ible people when we are in a safe environment, cared for and caring for others. Lore is clear rules and boundaries. Lore provides a structure for proper behaviour, and creates a sense of safety. When we know lore we know how to behave towards others. We also know how we can expect others to behave towards us. With the impacts of colonisation the world became unsafe. People neither knew how to behave towards others, nor could they understand why the others, were behaving towards them in the ways they did.

In traumatised populations, lore collapses. Environments and the relationships within them become chaotic and unstructured. They collapse into lorelessness. In this sense, according to Aboriginal worldviews or ways of being in the world, health/well-being and lore or law cannot be separated.

Aggression (or assertion) as instrumentality

Aboriginal people accept aggression as a normal human trait (Langton 1988). Conflicts were valued and owned. Reser points out that "what might be viewed as highly emotive and aggressive behaviour from a non-Aboriginal perspect-ive, is often simply an expression of genuine concern, distress and real feeling" (1990: 7), as individual and group relationships are mediated with meaning and responsibility. Burbank (1994), writing about aggression and authority in gender relations in Aboriginal Australia, makes the point that what is known so far about conflict through aggressive behaviour has largely been formed by what Western observers have written about behaviour between Aboriginal men and women. Less attention has been given to what Aboriginal peoples have said or written about their own relations and behaviours and the cultural meaning they ascribe to such behaviours.

Langton (1983, 1988), an Aboriginal woman, explored the expression of feeling in the role of swearing and fighting in the management of conflict. In these studies she quotes Stanner (1979), as she draws together the threads of past conflictual interaction to make more meaning of those in the present.

> I was an eye-witness of many fights in which more than a hundred men came to an appointed field. There would be a warming-up period given over to threat-signals and other ritualised gestures of hostility but once the true fighting started it might go on fiercely for hours. Their lives certainly had a full share of conflict ... but in some ways they were more skilful than we are in limiting the free play of man's combative propensity. ... The impression I received in watching their large-scale fights was that an invisible flag of prudence waved over the battlefield. There was a tacit agreement to call a truce or an end when a few men on each side had been grievously wounded or at the worst killed. Each life in a small group was a great treasure. ... The conquest of land was a great rarity. And the war of extermination, with one group bent remorselessly on the complete destruction of the other, as far as I have discovered, was so rare as to be all but unknown. There were few or no "total" enemies. It was much more commonly the case that groups which fell out contained a proportion of people who were closely tied by kinship, marriage, friendship, trade, or some other precious bond. ... The ties that bound overrode the conflicts that divided (Stanner 1979: 229).

A further example of aggression as instrumentality is provided by Roth (1984: 1902, 15) in his description of the *prun*,[1]

---

1 Or *Brun* as it is presently pronounced by Gimuy people near Cardwell.

a structured ceremonial process of conflict management from North Queensland. In this ceremony feelings of anger were articulated and discord was settled in creative activities in which all community members had specified roles and responsibilities.

The *prun* ground was a large, cleared, circular space which was shifted every two or three months. *Prun* was held every seven to fourteen days. The hosts, on whose land the *prun* ground happened to be, were always the first to arrive. A few days prior to the scheduled event, a messenger was sent to various camps reminding them of the date. As groups came to the *prun* ground they camped on the edge of the circle, and came forward into the circle only when they were fully prepared. Those who were decorated were the *Ulmba*, the ones picked "to uphold the honour of their particular mob". Well-recognised laws ensured that fighting would not occur outside the circle. One group would ceremonially enter the circle and another would follow. They would then "fight" for ten minutes, with much shouting and spear-throwing. They would retire and another two groups would perform. Sometimes one group would come to the aid of a group they had previously been *prun*-ing with, if they felt their previous adversaries were disadvantaged in the present conflict. Spectators were also participants. *Prun*-ing would continue until dark, then friendly relations would be resumed and corroborees would be performed late into the night. In the morning at sunrise, they would have another final bout of *prun*-ing, then all would return to their respective homes. "Evidently the prun both helps to settle old scores, and at the same time promotes social intercourse and amusement" (Roth 1984: 1902, Bulletin 4).

Such ceremonies sound similar to the contemporary workshops on large group conflict management that I have attended over recent years. They also resemble stress-releasing sporting activities such as the Olympic Games which function to "unite hearts and establish order".

The Warlpiri fire ceremony is another example of

ceremony in the maintenance of relationships and management of large group conflict. The ceremony is both a statement of Aboriginal ownership of land, and a process used to "settle up old quarrels and to make the men friendly disposed towards one another" (Spencer and Gillen 1904: 392, quoted in Langton 1993: 76). The ritual brings people together along song-lines that stretch from Central Australia to Port Keats on the northern coast.

> Like other religious traditions, its celebration is founded on the exploits of ancestral beings, of Jardiwarnpa (the snake) and Kankirri (the Emu). ... Yuendumu is on the path of the great journeys which these Beings made. Along their tracks are places sacred to the Warlpiri and other Aboriginal people. The journeys of Jardiwarnpa and the Yankirri, and the places they visited, are celebrated in the songs and dances of this particular fire ceremony named after the Snake. This is one of the bodies of knowledge conferring ownership of land and governing Warlpiri society. The places visited and the activities performed by the ancestral being are recreated and represented in dances, body designs and sand paintings. ... The ceremony does not concern any fire totem, but rather the name refers to the spectacular use of fire. Of all the public ceremonies or public sequences of Warlpiri ceremony, this is the most visually spectacular. Fire, a powerful and polysemic symbol in the Warlpiri iconography, has the special significance of ritual cleansing as, for instance, in the practice of seasonal burning of tracts of land (Langton 1993: 75–7).

In the Warlpiri fire ceremony grievances are settled by means of ritual process in which individuals of one moiety shake sparks onto their featherdown body decoration and allow it to briefly ignite, relying on the men of the opposite moiety, who may wish to punish them, to beat out the flames or embers on their shoulders and backs. If a man wants to severely punish another, he will delay beating out the embers for as long as he can within the restraints of the ritual (Peterson 1970: 200–15).

These descriptions show how Aboriginal societies have worked to manage conflict within the context of large groups, but individuals also used aggression as an instrument of assertion and articulation of distress in day-to-day interactions. In fact, it could be theorised that, within the structures of the ceremonial processes of conflict management and in the day-to-day emotional expressions of distress or anger, Aboriginal peoples had a deep knowledge of the negative psychological and physiological effects of strong feelings suppressed and held in the body, with resulting ill-health.

Hunter writes that some observers called much of what has been described above "ritualised, structured violence, interpreted by whites as savagery" (1993: 175–6), but it was not violence. Those who participated in these activities did so out of a cultural context of informed consent. This was *assertive aggression* used ritually to aid the process of managing the conflict in human relationships, to assert autonomy and to promote physical and psychological well-being within individuals and in group relationships.

Violence occurs when there has been no informed consent. The *Collins English Dictionary* defines violence as: "powerful, untamed and devastating force, the instance or exercise of physical force effecting or intended to effect injuries and destruction; unjust unwarranted or unlawful force intended to intimidate, inflict harm, damage or violate". To violate means: "to break, disregard, or to infringe on; to rape or otherwise sexually assault; to treat irreverently or disrespectfully" (Sinclair *et al.* 2000: 1335). Violence can only occur when there has been no informed consent. Violence certainly occurred within Aboriginal societies. However, many of the activities named as violence by the colonial observers would be better defined as assertive aggression. Assertive refers to the firm, self-assured affirmation of the right to be heard, to express dissent; aggression refers to actions which express opposition, antipathy, resentment, or anger.

Assertive aggression was structured to provide individuals and groups with mechanisms to assert autonomy, for expression of self-restrained anger or distress. Such processes also provided the opportunity for kin to help mediate and ensure boundaries were maintained, and that the aggression did not become violence (Roth 1984: 1903; Myers 1987; Williams 1987; Langton 1988; Burbank 1994; Dodson 1995).

As with all human groups, violence did occur. If boundaries were transgressed and violence occurred, there was always the communal pressured agreement to "clean, or square up". Processes of lore also dealt with offenders who were not willing to abide by the rules of the group. Ritualised aggression was controlled, approval was given for expression of feelings, and the process was recognised and appreciated by all participants.

Who Aboriginal peoples were and what they did prior to the invasion, however, is of secondary importance to knowing and understanding what has happened since 1788, and how what has happened has changed Aboriginal relationships and life experience. "Savagery" and "violence" came with the colonisers, who acted out (without consent) their own aggression on those whose lands they were trespassing on. This "savagery" is the key to understanding the situation of violence in Aboriginal families and communities today. Large-scale epidemics, massacres, removals of whole populations to detainment camps called reserves, removals of children, splitting apart of family groups, physical and cultural genocide—these formed layers of traumatic impacts down the generations. The cultural and spiritual ceremonial practices of repairing and healing human distress were in many cases outlawed and destroyed under the conditions and enforcements of colonisation.

The questions must be, what were the effects on the people as their lands were stolen and desecrated, relationships destroyed, children taken and violated, lore and ceremonies devalued and dishonoured? What long-term impacts have these separate yet inter-related tragedies had on the survivors? Answers to these questions will provide answers to present distressful circumstances.

What does violence do to human societies?

Increasingly since the early 1980s, theories of traumatic stress reaction and post-traumatic stress disorder have been applied to many recent human disasters, catastrophes, tragedies and criminal violence experienced by individuals and groups. Hiroshima, World Wars I and II, the Vietnam War, environmental catastrophes such as the Buffalo Creek disaster in the Appalachian Mountains of West Virginia, criminal violence including homicidal attack and rape, domestic violence and child physical and sexual abuse are some examples of such traumatic experiences. Such theories are now being extended to encompass the experiences of Indigenous peoples of the impacts of colonisation (Danieli 1998; Duran *et al.*, 1998; Gagné 1998; Raphael, Swan and Martinek 1998).

Figley defines traumatic stress reaction as the natural human consequence in response to a disaster or tragedy: "A set of conscious and unconscious actions and behaviours associated with dealing with the stresses of catastrophe and the period immediately afterwards" (1985a: xix). The *Diagnostic and Statistical Manual of Mental Disorders* defines post-traumatic stress disorder as the trauma which occurs when:

> The person experienced, witnessed, or was confronted with an event or events that involved actual or threatened death or serious injury, or threat to the physical integrity of self or others—and the person's response involved intense fear, helplessness or horror (American Psychiatric Association 1994).

The *Diagnostic and Statistical Manual* does not highlight the chronic, ongoing stress of particular situations or where the stressors are cumulative over time. It is therefore inadequate as a diagnostic tool when considering colonial conditions and cumulative traumatic stress situations. It does, however, provide a starting point.

Victims of violence, and those who work to provide

meaningful responses to their needs, should not view the
traumatic symptoms as signs of personal weakness or mental
illness. This assumption is important to bear in mind even in
the use of the *Diagnostic and Statistical Manual*'s definition of
traumatic stress reaction. The feelings and behaviours that
come from traumatisation are the natural and predictable
reactions of normal people (Figley 1985a, 1986; Ochberg
1988: 74; Silver 1986: 213) to abnormal experiences (Simpson
1993), defined here as a disaster, catastrophe or atrocity in
which great violence is experienced.

A disaster, catastrophe or atrocity is a violent event, either
natural or man-made, which causes great distress or
destruction, a core wounding to the body/mind/soul/spirit
of human beings. Words such as *ferocity, intensity, fierceness,
force* are associated with the violence of natural disasters.
Words such as *hostility, brutality, carnage* and *bloodshed* are
associated with a catastrophe or atrocity that has occurred
because of the actions of humans.

Erikson writes "every disaster is a unique private tragedy,
inflicting its own special wounds, its own peculiar species of
pain" (1976: 48). In the report of his study of the environmental flood disaster of Buffalo Creek, Erikson defines four
kinds of disasters or conditions of extreme stress. They are
those that are natural and those that are man-made; those
that are acute and those that are chronic. He shows how what
can appear to be an acute natural disaster may in fact have
arisen from chronic conditions imposed by men in their
attempts to exert power over and to exploit the natural
environment and/or human beings as a resource commod-
ity. He also shows that an acute disaster can elicit an
emergency state intervention, which establishes chronic
conditions that increase the resulting human injury by
actions which compound the traumatisation (1976: 47).
Erikson looks at the individual trauma or state of shock,
which is compounded by the collective trauma, or loss of
communality, that can result from large-scale experiences of
violence.

Collective or communal trauma refers to traumatic experiences which are experienced by large groups of people, who may therefore share some of the psychological, cultural, physical, spiritual, social and mental distress that results. Erikson lists the classic symptoms of traumatic loss, grief and bereavement as people are exposed to violent devastation and death. They "withdraw into themselves, feel numb, afraid, vulnerable and very alone" (1976: 154). He shows that the survivors of the flood, while feeling bereaved for the loss of loved ones and the loss of their known world, also felt victimised and dehumanised by the attitudes and actions of the mining company. They were further victimised by the actions of the officials who intervened into their tragedy and intruded into, and disrupted, the social fabric that connected people to each other, the web of relationships and responsibilities for each other which helped people heal together from disaster.

Collective trauma is compounded and made more complex as the bureaucratic response dismantles the natural support and caring that people have for each other in extended family and community networks during times of distress (Erikson 1976: 47). This, in part, is an apt description of how government interventions into Aboriginal lives subsequent to invasion have dismantled the social support systems and collective healing ceremonies that were integral to Aboriginal well-being, and have therefore compounded the traumatisation.

Although collective trauma does not have the same acute impact normally associated with trauma, it has distinct— and, in many cases, longer-lasting—repercussions. It seeps slowly and insidiously into the fabric and soul of relations and beliefs of people as community. The shock of loss of self and community comes gradually. People, feeling bereaved, grieve for their loss of cultural surrounds, as well as for family and friends. Feeling victimised, the same people may also carry a deep rage at what has happened to them, but may be unable to express their anger at those they perceive to have violated their world and caused the death of their loved ones. They are not sure what to do, for often "both their inner compass and their outer maps for what is considered 'proper' behaviour" (Erikson 1976: 200) are lost.

Furthermore, Erikson showed that, when the physical space of home or place is violated, the boundaries of a group's moral space might also collapse. Feelings of distress and helplessness may then be expressed through violence (1976: 182). Herman describes psychological trauma as an "affliction of powerlessness" (1992: 33). May says, "when we make people powerless, we promote their violence" (1976: 23). Anger and aggression are natural human responses to traumatic loss. Violent behaviour against others and self are often therefore a product of trauma. This is often complicated by the increase in alcohol and drugs used as coping mechanisms during times of traumatisation (Erikson 1976: 171). Misuse of alcohol and other drugs is now a well-documented response to the stresses of warfare, to natural disasters, and to human atrocity. After the bombing in Oklahoma City, for example, it was shown that alcohol and other drug misuse, suicides, homicides and violence against women and children increased substantially for a period of about eighteen months within the city.

Similar to the events at Buffalo Creek is the destruction of an Ojibwa community in Canada documented by Shkilnk (1985). Within the context of colonisation, two further things happened that interacted to almost destroy the community. In 1963, without adequate consultation, the government relocated the people after an international papermaking company dumped thousands of pounds of methyl mercury into the network of lakes and rivers surrounding the Grassy Narrows Reserve. These now-poisoned waters had represented both the life support and spiritual identity of the people. Within a short period following relocation, sexual assault, child neglect and abuse, extreme alcohol abuse, petrol-sniffing and death through violence became epidemic within the community. Men beat women and abused children, women discarded dependent infants and abused children, and older children beat and raped younger children. Hierarchies of power abuse and misdirected pain and anger were expressed in community violence. Old people could remember the "time before"; in their shame at the "time present", they felt powerless to effectively intervene. In fact, they were often victims of violence themselves. Abuse became transgenerational.

> There is no easy way to communicate the cumulative effect of a succession of violent deaths in a small community, only half of whose residents are over the age of fifteen. Grassy Narrows is a place where everybody is related by blood or marriage. Death therefore affects not only one's immediate kin, but a much wider circle of relations. A not uncommon reaction in those who have been touched by violent death is to repress grief, guilt or anger until these powerful emotions can be released by the disinhibiting effects of alcohol. The feelings of aggression and rage normally suppressed in face-to-face encounters find expression during drinking parties which are the contexts for beating, rape or other acts of violence that may lead to death. The drinking parties become part of the vicious circle in which the mourners often become those who are mourned (Shkilnk 1985: 11).

Shkilnk uses the following words to describe the individual and collective trauma: anxiety, rage, and depression; subjective feelings of loss, a sense of helplessness in the face of conditions over which they felt they had no control; disorientation; apathy; a retreat into dependency; a general loss of ego functions; and a numbness of spirit.

> I could never escape the feeling that I had been parachuted into a void—a drab and lifeless place in which the vital spark of life had gone out. It wasn't just the poverty of the place, the isolation, or even the lack of a decent bed that depressed me. I had seen worse material deprivation when I was working in squatter settlements around Santiago, Chile. And I had been in worse physical surroundings while working in war-devastated Ismailia on the project for the reconstruction of the Suez Canal. What struck me about Grassy Narrows was the numbness in the

human spirit. There was an indifference, a listlessness, a total passivity that I could neither understand nor seem to do anything about. I had never seen such hopelessness anywhere in the Third World (1985: 4).

With the destruction of "place" with its central meaning to the body/mind/soul/spirit of the people, social order was also destroyed and chaos became the norm. Homicide and suicide prevailed, with the contributing factors of domestic violence, rape and child abuse, facilitated by drug and alcohol abuse, in layers of pain and distress.

Shkilnk's story of Grassy Narrows builds a picture of people in extreme anguish. This is the often-unrecognised place of pain that covers multiple layers of trauma, the behaviours that are then criminalised and pathologised by the Western world that further compounds so much of this distress. Grassy Narrows was both a group of colonised peoples, and a community suffering under the impact of environmental disaster. The compounding factor, however, was the intrusion into the community by a bureaucracy that determined what should be done about the community, without proper consultation or consideration of its whole-of-community needs and cultural ethos. Again the parallels can be drawn to Australia in relationship to Aboriginal peoples.

This is made all the more pertinent by the observations of Nordstrom (1993a; Nordstrom and Robben 1995) in her work with the people of Mozambique. She realised that accounts of the horrendous physical violence of the civil war in Mozambique were not the focus of people's concerns. Their concern was for a deeper, "more enduring type of violence; the destruction of home and humanity, of hope and future, of valued traditions and community integrity. Psychological, emotional and cultural violence rank equally with, and in many cases outrank, physical violence" (Nordstrom and Robben 1995: 29). When the trauma of the original experience is unrecognised by both abusers and abused, the pain "sticks like a rash on the soul and continues on and on ... into the communities, into the families to ruin us" (Nordstrom and Robben, 1995: 23). The effect of violence becomes inter-nalised and is expressed in further self- and other destructive behaviours.

All societies experience natural disasters. Individual and group conflict occurs in all human relationships. The long-term consequences of violence in its diverse forms are only just starting to be recognised, understood and documented. Simpson argues for the development of a "greater under-standing of community trauma and communal responses to trauma", which must include a greater comprehension of the "nature and effects of continuing and recursive violence and the interplay between multiple traumata". Most importantly, he calls for recognition of "the political context of trauma and its effects and the fact that structural violence, such as that inherent in oppressive systems, has potentially severe and continuing posttraumatic effects" (Simpson 1993: 601).

The disastrous consequences of war and colonisation

Nature's capacities for violence are small compared to the destruction human beings enact on each other. The *Diagnostic and Statistical Manual of Mental Disorders* notes that trauma is greater, more severe, longer-lasting and different when the stressor is of human origins, as opposed to a natural disaster (Figley 1986: 20). Nature may leave people feeling bereaved, but human acts of violence create feelings of victimisation (Lifton and Olsen 1976; Ochberg 1988). When such victimis-ation occurs, the person or group no longer feels secure in the world and further experiences of victimisation become more likely. Trauma such as this becomes harder to remedy, for people "feel their humanity has been desecrated" (Figley 1986: 20). While individual ordeals may differ, the felt experience of the group may be collective public violation and trauma (Deloria and Lytle 1984; Danieli 1998; Napolean 1991; Rintoul 1993; Rowley 1971).

Large-scale man-made disasters, for Aboriginal societies worldwide, occurred as European countries practised colonialism from the late fifteenth to the early twentieth centuries. These activities have reshaped the social and cultural face of the globe with disastrous outcomes that were unforeseeable at the time (Giddens 1989: 52).

Worldwide European colonialism was a "brutal age; an age in which swarms of savage invading males slew, raped, plundered and enslaved ... or decimated with exotic diseases, after which they replaced them in some instances by hardier and more complacent slaves" (Price 1963: 51–2). Colonialism has been a major trigger in this evolutionary process. The ideology that drove such activities was the belief that some individuals or groups have rights to power over others and that they can establish and maintain this power by force (Giddens 1989; Baker 1983).

Colonisers came from patriarchal societies in which the strata of class and hereditary male privilege determined whether the coloniser would be commandant of a colonising force or foot soldier, merchant trader or clerk, slave-ship owner or blackbirding seaman, military convict overseer or convict. Generally, because of economics and socialisation, women were "camp followers". Their contribution to, and impacts within, the colonising processes are still continuing to be evaluated and felt (Huggins 1994; Moreton-Robinson 2000).

Studies of the impact of colonisation on Indigenous groups in the United States, Canada, Australia, New Zealand and South Africa shows three distinct periods in the relations between coloniser and colonised (Price 1963, 1972; Baker 1983). These periods are invasion and frontier violence; the intercession of well-meaning but often ethnocentric and paternalistic philanthropic and religious groups; and the reassessment of government responsibility to Indigenous needs around the 1930s to 1960s. Under principles of disaster theory, this last period has proven to be as damaging as the first two, as state interventions have increasingly intruded into Indigenous lives, creating dependencies and dysfunctions that have re-traumatised Indigenous peoples.

Within these three periods, principles of systemic power and control of others prevailed, facilitated by three main types of power abuse or violence: overt physical violence, covert structural violence, and psycho-social domination (Baker 1983). These forms of violence are often used inter-actively, both at the personal level and in political groups. Across generations, Indigenous families and communities have been severely affected.

Physical violence: invasion, disease, death and destruction

Physical violence—as in military invasion, wife assault, rape —is the quickest, most effective way to establish power over others (Schechter 1982). Thereafter, the threat of violence is all that is needed. Such violence terrifies and intimidates victims and witnesses, so they feel they have no other choice than to comply. In Australia, Memmott describes the initial impact of colonial violence as involving "dispossession of land, population decimation, murder, massacres, maltreat-ment, fatal diseases, opium and alcohol addiction, slave labour exploitation, *all resulting in chronic anxiety*" (1990: 2, my emphasis). The story from an Aboriginal point of view is more personal:

> We were hunted from our ground, shot, poisoned, and had our daughters, sisters and wives taken from us ... They stole our ground where we used to get food, and when we got hungry and took a bit of flour or killed a bullock to eat, they shot us or poisoned us. All they give us now for our land is a blanket once a year (Dalaipi quoted in Petrie 1904: 182–3).

The arrival of the prison hulks at Sydney Cove in 1788 set in motion a series of disasters, one precipitating another, to propagate trauma on trauma on trauma. Aboriginal peoples did not abandon their ways. They resisted. But some of the man-made disasters perpetrated by those who came to the country in 1788 and thereafter were outside the compre-hension, the previous experience, of Aboriginal peoples. In many instances, resistance was not sufficient for survival.

Disastrous epidemics came with the diseases incubated in the back streets of London and transported like sewage over the water on the stinking prison hulks. Aboriginal peoples had no immunity to European diseases such as the common cold, influenza, tuberculosis, measles, chickenpox and smallpox.

In 1789, smallpox (or chickenpox) swept like a bushfire through the tiny settlement at Sydney Cove and its sur- rounds, killing half the Gamaraigal, and sweeping down to what was later called the Port Phillip region (Victoria). These diseases were virulent. Whole families died. Children were left orphaned. Babies suckled on the breasts of dead mothers. One writer recalls: "After a week or so, they were unable to bury the dead, and day by day kept moving onwards, leaving their dead on the ground" (quoted in Broome 1982: 58). Such devastation would have had a shocking effect on the survivors. They could no longer conduct the essential ceremonies for the dead, for the living were also dying. They believed the diseases came from evil spirits from which they no longer had protection. Their world was suddenly fragmented and shattered. It became a world that no longer made sense. For people who had lived in a known world of meaningful relationships and relating at deep levels of com- munity, this disaster would have been incomprehensible. There are no written records of the suffering, the heartbreak, the despair, the confusions of that time, but if we try to imagine what it would have been like for us, we come closer to understanding that this would have been a "fatal psychic wounding".

Another level of trauma of that time is that people existed at starvation levels. They were unable to forage for food because of illness or because they were denied access to their traditional hunting grounds, continually on the run in their attempts to escape white persecution. They were "mere lumps of misery; their legs and arms shrunk like anatomical preparations, their eyes fixed in a state of insensibility, and looking altogether as if they were waiting to give up the ghost" (quoted in Harris 1990: 149).

Frontier violence continued at different levels across the continent into the early twentieth century. At the end of the nineteenth century, Archibald Meston provides some insight into the trauma of people seeking shelter from the violence in the Cooktown region when he wrote to the Home Secretary: "They come in here like hunted wild beasts, having lived for years in a state of absolute terrorism. Their manifest joy at assurances of safety and protection is pathetic beyond expression" (1896, quoted in Reid 1985).

During this time sexual exploitation, physical violence and institutional racism were endemic. The missionary Daniel Matthews records an inquest into the death of an Aboriginal woman who had been camped with her husband near Barmah Forest on the Murray River. A mob of drunken saw-mill workers attacked them. The husband was knocked unconscious. She was raped, kicked and burned with a hot iron, and later died of the injuries she sustained. Her three white assailants were let off because the Coroner decided her death had been from natural causes (Cato 1976: 44). Other evidence documents the imprisonment of women in rabbit-proof runs so they could be used sexually by station hands; of children as young as five being "brutally ravished"; of groups of young girls of seven and eight years of age kept in concubinage by one station hand, to be discarded when the venereal disease they caught from him became evident (Evans *et al.* 1975: 107, 106; Harris 1990: 237).

The abduction of Aboriginal woman and children for both economic misuse and sexual abuse was common. At Lake Macquarie by 1837, the missionary Threlkeld, writing of his distress at being unable to stop the kidnapping of young women by drunken white men, reported all that remained of the original land-owners of the region were twenty-eight men, two boys, two women and no girls (Harris 1990: 244). Harris points out a whole language evolved in Australia around the sexual violations of Aboriginal women: *"gin"*

busts, "gin" sprees, "gin" jockeys, "gin" shepherds,[2] and so on.
Such terminology places sexual violence against women in
the context of sport and contextualises Aboriginal women as
animals to be used for sporting pleasure. Just as many
"respectable" white men boasted of Sunday afternoon
"buck"-hunting parties,[3] this same society viewed sexual
violations of Indigenous women as familiar male sporting
events. White women maintained their silence in their denial
of the reality of this violence.

Aboriginal women and girls were sometimes able to make
choices (Bell 1983; McGrath 1987), but most often they were
driven by the need for food or protection from marauding
white males, or violence had been the first persuader. "Sex as
instrumentality" (Merlin 1988) was a means whereby both
Aboriginal women and men initiated friendly dialogue with
other groups, and established diplomatic relations with
strangers. The invading males, who carried cultural baggage
with stereotypes about women's sexuality and acted
accordingly, misunderstood this. Harris observes:

> the point must be made that Aboriginal people were not
> naturally a promiscuous or immoral people. Despite the fact that
> missionaries spoke out unceasingly against sexual immorality, it
> was they who, of all people, came to realise that in their
> traditional state Aborigines were a moral people. That is, they
> had an exceptionally strict code of sexual behaviour and stern
> punishment for those who broke the code (1990: 236).

The myths that all Aboriginal women went willingly to the
white intruders, or that the sexual trade of Aboriginal
women by Aboriginal men was normative on the frontier,
must also be put aside. Sexual violence, as well as physical
violence, was rampant on the frontier. What also must be
named is that the experiences of colonisation were different
for Aboriginal women in comparison to Aboriginal men.

---

2 "Gin" is a slang and derogatory term for Aboriginal woman.
3 "Buck" is a slang and derogatory term for Aboriginal men, and for "negro"
   slaves in the USA.

This created tension and disharmony in relationships between Aboriginal men and women that continues into the present. Such issues must be taken into consideration in the exploration of violence in its cyclical form. Aboriginal male status and authority was placed under threat, and attempts were made to subordinate Aboriginal women to the economic and sexual needs of the white male invaders and immigrants.

Physical violence had been widespread on the frontier. This violence pushed people from their traditional lands, their spiritual heartplace. It prevented them from conducting their essential ceremonies that ensured the continuing life cycles. It denied them access to their natural bush foods, their economic resource.

> They hardly had any food in the camp ... I asked them why they did not go into the bush and kill possums, and dig yams. They replied, "Whitefellow along a yarraman [horse] too much break him spear, burn yambo [humpies], cut him old man with whip; white man too much kill him kangaroo" (quoted in Evans *et al.* 1975: 88).

Dispossession of land was complete in the southeast. After the violence of first contact, traumatised and looking for a place to "lay their heads in safety" (Lamond quoted in Loos 1982), Aboriginal people sought protection on the fringe of white settlements and on stations, where the land autocracy began to profitably use their labour. Many such landowners obtained the services of Aboriginal people by paying for their labour with opium and alcohol. "It was common practice to entice men and women with bribes of tobacco, adulterated liquor or opium dregs" (Kidd 1997: 34). Apart from their addictive potential, these substances became the means by which people could medicate their own pain. In too many cases, the original owners were a traumatised people, disoriented and reduced to begging for food, living in fixed, unsanitary camps, in forced submission to new laws and new ways. Disease and starvation were common plights.

"Many orphans [were] already addicted to alcohol and opium, a consequence of, and incitement for, juvenile prostitution" (Kidd 1997: 40).

The traumatic experiences of introduced diseases, physical violence, rapes, starvations, torture and death are not those of individuals alone. Rather, these traumas were both individual and collective. Furthermore, any one of these disasters as a traumatic event could be passed through the adult and child survivors to their children and grandchildren. The multiple layers compounded the trauma. Today the trauma remains in the hearts, minds and souls of Aboriginal families whose ancestors survived these times. Listen to Alice Kelly and hear the pain explicit in her words.

> The violence, where our people were massacred and slaughtered. They rounded them up like kangaroos, my people. Women and children too. They drove them on foot from horse back, with whips cracking over their heads. They shot them and the sands covered them over. Still there today. I weep as I walk through the massacre sites today. Barbarians. Saxon barbarians. They showed us no mercy (Taped interview by author, 1990).

It is easy to recognise and name the human experiences of acute trauma on (both sides of) the frontier, "the events that involved actual or threatened death, the threat to the physical integrity of self or others" (American Psychiatric Association 1994). The fear, helplessness or horror that people feel under these circumstances is also understandable. It is more difficult however, to quantify or qualify. We cannot fully understand the impacts of the chronic conditions (Erikson 1976, 1994), the covertly violent structural conditions of the state (Baker 1983), which were set in place by government and mission agencies, in their response to the normal human reactions to original trauma. This, in Erikson's words, is the "seeping and insidious injury into the fabric and soul of relations and beliefs of people as community" (1976: 47), as colonisers set standards of behaviour and established systems of control through legislation and removals, which permeate Australian consciousness and structural conditions today.

Structural violence: enforced dependency, legislation, reserves and removals

Colonial governments, at different levels, voiced disapproval of the violence of the frontier; but, in the way of government, they either turned a blind eye or, when forced to respond, established commissions of inquiry. From the time Queensland was established as a state in 1856, a number of inquiries into frontier violence and policing activities have been held. In each instance, the inquiries censured the brutality of police activities; but analysis of the government response to the tabled reports shows that police powers over Indigenous lives increased. In fact, in every instance when there have been proposals for reform because of police brutality, police powers and Aboriginal incarceration rates appear to have increased (Reid 1985: 23–56).

The response to the concerns expressed by Archibald Meston in 1896 demonstrates this. Meston, a private citizen, wrote an essay titled *Queensland Aboriginals: Proposed System for their Improvement and Preservation*. He suggested a series of large reserves be established throughout Queensland as special places where people could live in "accordance with their own laws and customary practices" (Meston 1896, quoted in Reid 1985: 182–94). The Home Secretary, Sir Horace Tozer, requested Meston make a fuller report, and this report makes "appalling reading" (Kidd 1997: 43) because it detailed physical trauma in Aboriginal lives of shocking dimensions. Forced to act, Tozer appointed William Parry-Okeden, the Police Commissioner, to implement a response to Meston's proposal. Parry-Okeden became responsible for the *Aboriginal Protection and Prevention of the Sale of Opium Act 1897 (Qld)* (Reid 1985), and Meston was appointed the Southern Protector for Aborigines under the Act. Through to 1939, a series of amendments to this Act resulted in a total control instrument, with power vested in the Director of Native Affairs, and state police acting as his enforcers. Meston's original proposal to establish special places where people could live in accordance with their own laws and customary practices became, over time, a total system of government legislation and bureaucratic (police) controls over Aboriginal lives. The special places became substandard refugee camps for people dislocated from their own countries. The controls written into each new layer of amended legislation, as the Act was reviewed over the years, gave full power to the Protector, or Director of Native Affairs, and the police who were his protectors in each regional area.

The established reserves became strictly monitored, closed to public access, and any Aboriginal person could be transferred at the direction of the minister or his designated Aboriginal protectors, often under brutal circumstances.

Two women and two men were forced at gunpoint, chained together for 240 miles [380 kilometres] and force marched across the peninsula to Laura for transportation to Palm Island. A previous group were beaten by the police, flogged on route several times, including one woman who was six months pregnant, and sexually assaulted (Kidd 1997: 121).

Once at the reserves, such people found that the Superintendent's regime of control included "head shaving, flogging, chained work gangs and confinement in small iron sheds or watchhouses". The Myora mission was closed after the matron beat a young girl to death (Kidd 1997: 121). These are descriptions of prison conditions. Kidd claims Protector Bleakey understood "that his network of police protectors were often indifferent or inept in controlling prostitution or stamping out sexual abuse" (1997: 104), yet often his public service police protectors were the sexual violators. The fact that they were given the name and function of "protector" by the state is itself another form of abuse. Police themselves have a long and documented history of sexual violence against Aboriginal women, often in the course of their duties, which continues into the present (Human Rights and Equal Opportunity Commission 1991: 88).

The Protector was the legal guardian of every Aboriginal child in the state under the age of twenty-one and could authorise marriage and adoption at the flick of a pen; could determine that a husband was to be sent to one place, his wife to another and the children to a dormitory at another location (Kidd 1997: 140). The protection legislation was supposed to create safety for people who had been traumatised. Instead it enforced dependency while denying essential services. It gave power to people who used their power abusively. It tore families apart. It destroyed any sense of self-worth and value in culture, as it outlawed ceremonial processes and use of language. Feelings of frustration, fear, anxiety, anger, rage, hatred, depression, as well as the essential need to suppress these feelings, became part of the day-to-day lived experience. Although alcohol was outlawed, the use of it was promoted in binge drinking, in secret. The consequential brawling release of emotions produced further traumatisation. Such drinking, as a form of self-medication, enabled life to continue under the trauma-inducing conditions of a total control system. But it promoted violence at its most base level—within the families and groups incarcerated. By 1959, the Director of Native Affairs, O'Leary, could proudly state of this total control system: "We know the name, family history and living conditions of every Aboriginal in the State" (quoted in Kidd 1997: 189).

What the Director of Native Affairs did not do, with his acquired knowledge and government power, was to improve these living conditions. Rather, state policies increased the dependency of Aboriginal peoples. The government programs were inadequate, as they were not designed to meet the needs of traumatised groups.

Having been dispossessed, those invaded were dependent on the invaders. This dependency was then reinforced by institutional controls (Rowley 1970, 1971; Baker 1983: 30–41) which increased the dependent conditions of the oppressed. The institutions and systems of the colonisers were imposed on people already traumatised by physical violence. Again I emphasise that research shows that, all too often, when the state intervenes in the recovery process of trauma victims, it re-traumatises the people concerned (Erikson 1976: 175–201). Government interventions into Aboriginal lives have been multiple, protracted and many-layered, and at various levels have acted as traumatising agents, compounding the agony of already traumatised individuals and groups.

Even when Indigenous people wanted to use the systems of the state, they were denied or restricted access to the power and resources within these newly imposed systems that were now controlling every facet of their lives (Baker 1983: 33). The Royal Commission into Aboriginal Deaths in Custody highlighted the reality of this total control, documenting the individual lives of those who were psychologically crushed in government files, sometimes fatally, those who were murdered, those who committed suicide in police or prison cells.

No matter what their age at death they all had files—in many cases hundreds of pages of observations and moral and social judgements on them and their families; considerations of applications for basic rights, determinations about where they could live, where they could travel, who they could associate with, what possessions they could purchase, whether they could work and what, if any, wages they could receive or retain. Welfare officers, police, court officials and countless other white bureaucrats, mostly unknown and rarely seen by the persons concerned, judged and determined their lives. The officials saw all, recorded all, judged all and yet knew nothing about the people whose lives they controlled. ...

Aboriginal people were removed at the whim of others, crowded into settlements and missions and in impoverished camps on cattle stations. Always there were non-Aboriginal people giving orders, making decisions in which the opinions of the Aboriginal people were not sought nor, if volunteered, heeded. Aboriginal families could be separated, children removed if judged too light skinned, placed in homes or boarded out as servants of non-Aboriginals (1991: vol. 2, 502–503).

This is a description of a total control system encompassing both structural and institutional violence. It is a system that made people powerless and dependent.

As we make people powerless, we promote their violence ... Deeds of violence in our society are performed largely by those trying to establish their self-esteem, to defend their self-image, and to demonstrate that they too are significant ... Violence occurs when a person cannot live out their need for power in normal ways (May 1976: 23).

Psycho-social dominance: cultural and spiritual genocide

Baker calls psycho-social domination, in its various components, cultural genocide, cultural imperialism, thought control or brainwashing (1983: 35). Aboriginal people would call this the greatest violence, the violence that brings the loss of spirit, the destruction of self, of the soul.

Cultural and spiritual genocide occurs when oppressors believe that the oppressed are non-persons (Harré 1993: 106), with no culture or identity as human beings, or with a culture or identity that is inferior. They deny the oppressed the right to a separate identity as a group or as individuals within the group. Such beliefs allowed the oppressors to feel justified in their attempts to destroy customary social and cultural processes that worked to "unite hearts and establish order", providing a strong sense of an individual and group self and a sense of life purpose to Aboriginal people. By defining Aboriginal people as non-persons and continuing to do so across the colonising histories, the oppressors justified their behaviours, and in turn, the oppressed came to believe this about themselves. It was this belief that enabled authorities to remove Aboriginal children from their families, among many dehumanising and oppressive acts.

The stories of the child removals have been extensively

documented in *Bringing Them Home*, the report of the National Inquiry into the Separation of Aboriginal and Torres Strait Islander Children from Their Families (1997). This report says the inquiry was "not raking over the past" for its own sake, but that "the past is very much with us today, in the continuing devastation of the lives of Indigenous Australians" (p. 3). The report details "multiple and profoundly disabling" layers of abuse in the lives of all those affected, causing "a cycle of damage from which it is difficult to escape unaided" (p. 177):

- separation from primary carer
- effects of institutionalisation
- physical brutality and abuse
- repeated sexual violations
- psychological and emotional maltreatment
- loss of cultural and spiritual knowledge and identity (pp. 177–228).

The results are a group of profoundly hurt people living with multiple layers of traumatic distress, chronic anxiety, physical ill-health, mental distress, fears, depressions, substance abuse, and high imprisonment rates. For many, alcohol and other drugs have became the treatment of choice, because there is no other treatment available. "If they hadn't used alcohol they probably would have committed suicide. … Having flashbacks of traumatic events can cause such psychic pain that the person might start to drink heavily or use other psycho-active substances" (p. 199). For others, acting out the alienation and violence they had experienced meant a cycle of offending and re-entering other institutions of containment, juvenile detention centres and prisons.

Anger is a normal human response to a violation of the self. For some, however, the anger becomes disabling. They cannot express it safely to others or themselves because the places in which they live are unsafe.

One of the effects that Eric identifies in himself is that, because of the violence in his past, when he himself becomes angry or confused, he feels the anger, the rage and the violence welling up within him. ... Eric's symptomatology is obviously severe and chronic. It is clear that he deals with many deep emotional wounds that do not clearly fit [a post-traumatic stress disorder] diagnostic classification. His deep sense of loss and abandonment, his sense of alienation, and his gross sense of betrayal and mistrust are normal responses to a tragic life cycle (p. 180).

Identity becomes fractured and fragmented. The sense of self appears to be become lost.

Most of us girls were thinking white in the head but were feeling black inside. We weren't black or white. We were a lonely lost and sad displaced group of people. We were brainwashed to think like a white person ... [but] were not accepted because they[4] were Aboriginal. When they went and mixed with Aborigines, some found they could not identify, because they had too much white ways in them. They were neither black or white. They were simply a lost generation (p. 152).

Rowe (1987) has described the greatest human fear as the experience that our identity, our self, is being annihilated. This is the basis to understanding Pat Swan's statement about cultural genocide (1988: 12–13). Cultural genocide not only works to destroy the cultures of oppressed peoples, it also eradicates the sense of self, of self-worth, and of well-being in individuals and groups so that they are unable to function from either their own cultural relatedness, or from the culture of the oppressors. They feel in a world between, devalued, and devaluing who they are.

Cultural and spiritual genocide attacks the very heart, the locale of *who we are*, more so than physical violence. Order and continuity were central components in Aboriginal cultural and spiritual ways of Being in the World, mediated by ceremony and ritual on an ongoing regenerative basis. Bessel Van de Kolk says the essence of psychological trauma is "the loss of faith that there is order and continuity in life.

---

4 Note here that the narrator changes from the first person (personal) to the third person (impersonal).

Trauma occurs when one loses the sense of having a safe place to retreat within or outside oneself to deal with frightening emotions and experiences" (1987: 2–3). This is what Duran *et al.* refer to as the "soul" (1998: 341–54). Moore (1992) has defined the soul as the place of deepest feelings; these feelings may connect people to each other and the country which has formed them in sustaining relationships, or in a core wounding, which separates people from each other and the country from which they come, in destructive relationships. These corrosive impacts dismantle the spiritual fabric of persons. Trauma, then, is spiritual at its deepest level (Van de Kolk 1987). Cultural genocide—or psycho-social dominance—at its most destructive, must be understood from this aspect.

In cultural genocide, people come to believe that they themselves are of no value, that their cultural practices and traditions are inferior and hence so are they, that they are non-persons with no value. Consequently they may "build their own prison and become simultaneously prisoner and warden" (Baker 1983: 40), and even executioner.

Hassan (1990), in studies of suicidal behaviour among American Indian and Aboriginal Australians, affirms:

> One of the grim lessons social scientists have learned from the history of colonisation is that to destroy a society we do not need to kill all its members. The destruction can be achieved through the devaluation of society's social and cultural institutions through which social life is sustained and reproduced. This devaluation of social institutions produces anomie, hopelessness, despair and depression which condemn its members to a gradual and slow social death (quoted in Ratford *et al.* 1990)

The violence of colonisation has long-term compounding impacts. As previously stated, Aboriginal experiences of violence have been integral to the colonising processes in this country.

An important consideration in understanding colonisation as violence is the manner in which "the anthropology of violence" is constructed from a single disciplinary approach, and from within the limitations of Western research methodologies and theories without being informed by a deeper listening to and understanding of the colonial experiences in all their ongoing complexity and multiplicity of factors.

The anthropology of violence

Violence can be best understood when it is examined over a range of cultural settings and in complex and varied social situations (Riches 1986: vii).

Within Anglo-Celtic colonising cultures, violence was labelled as the behaviour of the *Other*, that is the colonised. At no time did the colonisers consider their own colonising functions as illegitimate, unacceptable, or in fact, as violent. At the same time Indigenous peoples observed and experienced behaviours they considered to be unacceptable, illegal, and in many instances, incomprehensible. Riches argues that people will view another's acts of physical force as barbarism but consider their own actions as heroic. He makes the point: "violence is a word used by those who witness, or who are victims of certain acts, rather than those who perform them" (1986: 2, 3).

In Knight's description of "Fighting in an Aboriginal Supercamp", included in a book titled *The Anthropology of Violence*, he placed cultural context on constructs of disorder. He wrote, "fighting appears to be the main social activity" (1986: 138), He goes on to say:

> traditionally some types of fighting were hedged in with rules and rituals which undoubtedly helped to prevent them from becoming too serious. In a ritualised fight e.g. a "square up", opponents performed their totemic dances as they approached each other. First they threw light spears from a distance. It was the rule that as long as a fighter is holding his weapon he may be struck, and this is so even if he is lying half-stunned on the ground. It was also a rule that if a man dropped his club, or it was struck out of his hands, then he could not be hit (1986: 146).

Knight agreed that it is "quite likely that the incidence of fighting has increased because of European influence", and "to give the Kaiadilt their due it seems that they were most likely the recipients rather than the perpetrators of violence when contact occurred with outsiders" (1986: 142, 143). However, he is selective in his research. He focuses on the fighting of men in an "Aboriginal Supercamp". While he details that fighting in the "Supercamp" has more likely increased because of European influence, he does not elaborate on the statement "older people publicly expressed concern about the high incidence of violence" (1986: 141, 142). What did they define as violence? During the mid-1980s many of the older women from this community expressed deep concern about the increase in various sorts of violence that they were observing, including sexual violence. At the same time they were speaking out about other forms of cultural imperialism that were occurring within their community, namely government actions and outside cultural influences.

The construction of self or identity, and the social nature of that construction, has many ingredients: it is also necessary to critique the functions and dysfunctions that contribute to these personal and political constructions of the individual and collective self. Knight's paper highlights the point made previously: that research provides a static database, while the researched continue to form and shape their world, sometimes functionally and sometimes dysfunctionally. Knight conducted his fieldwork in 1966–68. He writes that no deaths occurred while he was in the field, but that ten years later a number of deaths had occurred connected to fighting and alcohol (1986: 140). By the time he wrote the paper referred to here, in 1986, a $6 million tavern had been built within the community; and a white male state government worker was importing pornography (from Canberra) into the community, which he used as an enticement to young men if they would procure young girls for him. By the time the research was conducted by the Aboriginal and Torres Strait Islander

Women's Task Force on Violence in 1999, the community was attempting to cope with the deaths of twenty-four young men in one year, most of which were suicides (1999: 19), as well as high levels of domestic violence, and high rates of sexual assault.

More particularly, to provide context to the suicides and the physical and sexual male–female violence within the community, it is fair to say the context and functions of the violence, in particular sexual violence, had changed completely.

> A three-year-old child was sexually assaulted by three (young) males and about ten days later another male returned and after sexually assaulting her, assaulted her again using a mangrove root. ... Two of them were juveniles and one of the offenders saw me recently and explained he had been sexually assaulted as a four-year-old child. It is further evidence that children who are victimised become offenders in the longer term (Task Force on Violence 1999: 15–16).

It is evidence also, that violence is learned behaviour (Riches 1986: 16–18). Social and cultural factors, together with ecological settings, influence the type and frequency of violence in any social situation (Riches 1986: 23).

As Marx (1976) and Riches (1986: 25) argue, violence fulfils both instrumental and expressive functions, and can only be understood in terms of its relationship to power. Although Riches claims that trying to understand "violence as disorder" is futile (1986: 5), I argue that the forms of violence now being documented within Aboriginal Australian situations are a clear and impassioned articulation of disorder: the powerless are being impacted upon, victimised, and reconstructed in the form and shape of the colonisers, while allowing them little or no voice, and restricted access to the services that could address the (dys)function that has been created by the use of power over them.

In order to understand the grief and anger that occurs in violence, we need to distinguish between victimisation and loss. Colonisation has been profoundly violent on Aboriginal peoples. Two specific elements are the multiple victimising experiences, with resulting feelings of victimisation, which continue and are sometimes disabling in people; and the multiple losses that have not been adequately acknowledged or grieved.

Victimisation, loss and grief

Survivors of violence and the resulting trauma may have a number of emotional experiences. Although related, these need to be understood in their separate components, while never losing sight of where they fit into the whole. Before discussing trauma and trauma behaviours, we will look at the differences between victimisation and bereavement through loss, particularly in relationship to the layered losses in colonisation and victimisation.

A person who loses something significant feels grief or deep sadness. The person is bereaved and must be able to grieve the loss—of significant others; of the diminution of themselves in the severed relationships; of hopes and dreams; of a sense of security and sometimes community (Ochberg 1988: 12), the destruction of their world as it was.

In victimisation on the other hand, there have been deliberate individual acts of violence, or violence that is imposed or sanctioned by structures or institutions. To deny that some people have been, and continue to feel, victimised, negates the extent of their suffering and denies the right of people to be heard, and to understand the layers of their oppression (Stark and Flitcraft 1988a; Kirz 1988). It denies the right of a group of people or individuals within the group to look at what behaviours are harming or destructive to them and by them.

According to Ochberg, victimisation is different to bereavement; it has deeper destructive impacts on the psyche of people, just as man-made disasters—in which a victim has been deliberately, unjustly harmed or coerced by other human beings—leave deeper scars than natural disasters.

The bereaved feels loss. The victim feels like a loser. The bereaved feels sad. The victim feels humiliated. The bereaved may feel as though part of him/herself has been ripped away. The victim feels diminished, pushed down in a hierarchy of dominance, exploited and invaded (Ochberg 1988: 11).

The differences that Ochberg points out are important because terms such as *diminished, pushed down, exploited* and *invaded* describe the "reason for the act of victimisation as much as the feelings of the victim" (1988: 11). Victimisation also has other dimensions from bereavement. Traumatised survivors of violence often feel diminished and defiled. Adult and child victims of sexual violence may feel self-loathing, shame and self-blame (Butler 1978; Hartman and Burgess 1988; Herman 1988; Ochberg 1988). They can feel hatred towards themselves, and/or they may feel hatred towards the abuser, which may be expressed in outbursts of anger or rage at other objects or people or in self-harm. Some, however, may feel a paradoxical gratitude called the Stockholm Syndrome (Graham *et al.* 1988; Romero 1985) towards their abusers.

Oppressed minorities, women and children who are generally less powerful than those who hold power, those who assault or oppress, are more likely to feel victimised as well as bereaved. The impacts and outcomes of these separate forms of victimisation are translated through the socio-cultural constructions of race, gender or age (Yllo and Bograd 1988; Walker 1979; Martin 1976; Butler 1978; Taylor and Hammond 1987; Hampton 1987).

After victimisation, people are likely to enter a downward socio-economic spiral because of "psychological, social and vocational impairment" from the abuse (Ochberg 1988: 11–13). They are more likely to be victimised again, or to victimise others. Many victims, for example women who have been beaten and children who have been abused, are also likely to be re-victimised by the medical, legal, welfare and political responses to their trauma (Hart 1988; Hartman and Burgess 1988; Kirz 1988; Rosewater 1988; Scutt 1982; Stark and Flitcraft 1988a, 1988b).

Ochberg points out that, after victimisation, the single most important factor for recovery is a supportive family: "Over 90 per cent of people seeking residential treatment for traumatic stress came from non-supportive families" (1988: 23). It seems that a healthy family is the best prescription for recovery from trauma. This, more than any other factor, underlies the tragedy and criminality of the wilful destruction of Aboriginal family systems by the governments of Australia. It emphasises the need to focus on rebuilding Aboriginal families for a whole-of-community, whole-of-government approach to violence and trauma in Aboriginal lives.

Violence experienced as traumatisation

Survivors of violence also describe other feelings besides grief and victimisation. Survivors often have deep feelings of depression (Figley 1985a, 1986; Ochberg 1988; Van de Kolk 1987; Wilson 1986, 1988a). They cannot find meaning in either their past experiences or present circumstances (Hartman and Burgess 1988; Mollica 1988; Wilson 1986, 1988a). They often have no clear sense of themselves as worthwhile people (Herman 1988). They feel they can no longer trust the world they know (Erikson 1976; Graham *et al*. 1988). They feel isolated from others (Erikson 1976), powerless, helpless and hopeless in the face of forces they feel are outside their control. They come to believe that they are unable to change their life circumstances (Wilson 1988). They feel they cannot describe their feelings and experiences to others. They also find that no one wants to hear—or cannot understand—when they do try to articulate their feelings or talk about their experiences (Danieli 1988b; Wilson 1988a).

Trauma permanently changes one's personal construction of reality. Particularly after trauma is inflicted by another human being, people may begin to appear less benevolent, events less random, and living more encumbered ... trauma is qualitatively different from stress, though one might consider both to be anchor points on a nonlinear continuum of negative experiences.

Negative stressors leave an individual feeling "put out", inconvenienced and distressed. These experiences are eventually relieved with the resolution of the stressor. In contrast, traumas represent destruction of basic organising principles by which we come to know self, others and the environment; traumas wound deeply in a way that challenges the meaning of life. Healing from the wounds of such an experience requires a restitution of order and meaning in one's life. The wounds of trauma wear many masks: anxiety, panic, depression, multiple personalities, paranoia, anger, and sleep problems; tendencies towards suicidality, irritability, mood swings and odd rituals; difficulty trusting people and difficult relationships; and general despair, aimlessness and hopelessness (Root 1992: 229, quoted in Cameron 1998: 6–7).

Trauma expressed as violence

One aspect of traumatisation that is rarely discussed in depth is the feelings of deep anger or rage. Anger usually masks a hurt (Wong and McKeen 1998: 164) and is a normal human response to any loss, boundary violation, or unmet need. At the time of violence the primary feelings are fear or terror. Anger expresses the person's affirmation of their "right to life". If they do not feel anger they are in a state of apathy and passivity (Wong and McKeen 1998: 164). When an individual or group violates the personal boundary or space of another, it is essential to renegotiate rights to a safe living environment so that balance can be restored. When environments are supportive and safe, the intense feelings of anger can be worked through with safety and with responsibility to all people within the group. For Aboriginal people and for children growing up in environments where there are multiple violations, the anger that is experienced as a natural and essential consequence has no safe outlet. It is stored in the body for expression under duress. This invariably occurs in unstructured and explosive violence, aided by alcohol (Task Force Report on Violence 1999; Hunter 1990a, b, c). It also results in hypertension-related diseases within the respiratory and circulatory systems of the human body. The early death from disease of important people in families creates added layers of loss and trauma. Again, anger is a normal human response to the death of loved ones.

When there are layered multiple losses and boundary violations by authority figures who have made themselves powerful over particular groups, the source of anger, which can become a deep rage, is sometimes unrecognised, and often denied. This anger may be displaced onto others or turned inwards (Williams *et al.* 1992; Wilson 1988b). Often the suppressed rage suddenly erupts, triggered by some seemingly unrelated event. The explosion can be extremely dangerous because the rage is always physically intense and without boundaries. The triggering event may be a sudden unbidden memory, an intrusive image of a stressful experience, a word or even a smell. Heightened, out-of-control feelings, vulnerability, extreme anxiety or fear can rise suddenly from the triggering event. Emotional flooding occurs; the person is overcome with intense sadness, depression and remorse, "loss of the sense of self in a confusion of various negative impressions" (Ochberg 1988: 10). Violent behaviour is often both a symptom of trauma and a symptom of recovery from trauma (Figley 1985a; 1986). In this regard trauma expressed as violence contributes to criminal behaviour. Wilson in his work with Vietnam veterans says, "the unconscious reliving of a traumatic experience may precipitate criminal behaviour" (1986: 305–7); however, variables of environment, disposition and demography also apply.

In colonised societies there have been multiple layers of both acute and overt acts of violence, and chronic and covert conditions of control have been established. These separately are traumatic and oppressive. Collectively, and compounding over generations. the pain may become internalised into abusive and self-abusive behaviours, often within families and discrete communities. The rage is not only turned inwards, but cascades down the generations, growing more complex over time. The bureaucratic interventions of the state—the processes of law, social welfare, and health care—

have not addressed the core issue of human traumatisation. These interventions have, in many cases, compounded the trauma by creating and increasing dependency on the state which, while intensifying feelings of victimisation, also enforces beliefs of being powerless to change destructive circumstances.

Transgenerational aspects of trauma

Trauma may be transmitted across generations in a number of ways. Sociological and psychological conditions are established by the systems and structures that triggered the original trauma in previous generations; these become entrenched in societies and become cultural norms. The transgenerational psychic impacts and imprints on individuals, families and communities through parenting and communal conditions must also be considered.

> The psychological impact of the experiences of dispossession, denigration and degradation are beyond description. They strike at the very core of our sense of being and identity. ... Throughout Aboriginal society in this country are seen what can only be described by anyone's measure as dysfunctional families and communities, whose relationships with each other are very often marked by anger, depression and despair, dissension and divisiveness. The effects are generational. ... I recognised all the things that had happened to me through my grandparents, and their parents; their brothers and sisters whom I had known as a child; through my mother and her siblings; through my cousins and my siblings. I recognised the things that happened to the thousands of other Aboriginal families like our family, and I marvelled that we weren't all stark, raving mad (O'Shane 1995: 151–3).

Berlin (1986) says that when violent behaviours in American Indian communities are studied systematically, in their various forms and context, transgenerational patterns reflect poverty, low self-esteem and self-image, epidemic alcoholism and other drug misuse, and a family history of violent behaviour. Nordstrum writes that "families in Africa cite an oral history of disorder that links the cultures of violence apparent in their countries today with those operating in the times of the slavers" (1993b: 2). Duran *et al.* have expounded on the "soul wound", also called historical trauma, historical legacy, American Indian holocaust, and intergenerational post-traumatic stress disorder (1998: 341). Brave Heart-Jordan (1995) traces the family and community history back to show different levels of traumatisation from original profound trauma, such as the Battle of Wounded Knee, being repeated into the third, fourth, fifth and later generations. Connie Hunt, an American Indian psychologist, outlined what she called four layers of trauma—historical, kin-group, extended-family and individual—in a presentation at the "Healing Our Spirit" conference in Sydney in 1992 (author's notes 1992):

- Historical trauma is the socio-political genocidal impacts of colonisation.
- Kin-group or communal trauma includes the diseases and massacres of first contact, removals to reserves and removals of children to residential schools, experienced by whole communities.
- Extended-family trauma includes the articulations of distress of the other unhealed layers of trauma in homicides, domestic violence, rape, child physical and sexual abuse and neglect, and alcohol and drug abuse.
- Individual trauma includes suicides and suicide attempts, mental illness, and individual victimising experiences from the above.

Gagné demonstrates that trauma dramatically changes the system of human relationships, which consequently directly affects future generations. She names four tiers:

- colonialism
- political and socio-economic dependency
- the cultural genocide of residential schools and the alcoholism and substance abuse which has direct relationship to the residential school experience, and to interference by federal governments with introduced

social programs such as housing projects and welfare
- cultural bereavement, family violence, accidental deaths, child abuse and sexual abuse (1998: 357–69).

Raphael, Swan and Martinek show how psychological reverberations of traumatic events can affect people in both extended family parenting patterns and communal disorder: family breakdown, impaired parenting and relating skills, violence or antisocial behaviours (1998: 331). The effects of original trauma compound down the generations, until healing action breaks the cycle (Duran *et al.* 1998; Brave Heart-Jordan 1995; Gagné 1998).

The multiple violations of the historical experiences of American Indian nations and Aboriginal Australians, inter-linked with the institutional destruction of American Indian and Aboriginal families, have resulted in violent behaviours across generations (Berlin 1986; Deloria and Lytle 1984; Unger 1977; Duran *et al.* 1998; Brave Heart-Jordan 1995; Gagné 1998; Raphael, Swan and Martinek 1998). These create chronic endemic crisis. Government interventions may increase the trauma. And thus, trauma behaviours become the norm. They have

lost their shock value because the community is in continuous mourning. … the community becomes so desensitised to violent acts that they are unable to perceive the patterns of violence across families and generations, or the *inherent strengths* in the community itself that can be mobilised to counter such behaviour (DeBruyn *et al.* 1988: 64, my emphasis).

Studies in Queensland in Aboriginal communities (Wilson 1982; Aboriginal Co-ordinating Council 1990) show longitudinal or historical trauma, expressed as violence on self and others, across generations. This begins with the displacement onto the reserves, as a result of frontier violence and land dispossession, leading to situations described by the Aboriginal and Torres Strait Islander Women's Task Force Report on Violence: "Violence and death is such a common occurrence in [such] communities that every family, directly or indirectly, suffers the consequences of murder or serious assault" (Wilson 1982).

Individual men as perpetrators also carry behaviours and attitudes across generations which reflect the social construction of masculinity as power and control. The Queensland Domestic Violence Task Force listed a range of studies which showed that men who saw their fathers use violence against their mothers or siblings, and/or who were abused themselves, were between 65 and 90 per cent more likely to use violence in their adult relationships than those who did not witness violence as a child (1988: 82). Witnessing spouse abuse as a child is an even greater predictor of abusing an intimate as an adult than being abused as a child. Later we will see that some of the most significant traumatic memories of Aboriginal adults are the childhood experiences of seeing close male relatives abused by authority figures, and/or watching their mothers and grandmothers being beaten by male family members. As the adults reconstructed these events, they always identified a relationship between the childhood experiences and their subsequent behaviour.

Observation is the primary mechanism for child learning for most types of aggression (Bandura 1973), where behaviour may be learnt in the family of origin. In the broader environment of immediate social contact, and through symbolic modelling of the broader society which communicates social norms and behaviours, other complex factors are also present. Childhood experiences, passed on between and across generations, and adult peer group attitudes and behaviours, support and reinforce such behaviours. Hunter (1993) has also defined the loss of male role models through separations and the criminal justice system, and the interruption of models for progression into mature manhood. It is not inconsequential that the two communities in Queensland with the highest rates of sexual violence were also the two communities who had a high rate of consumption of pornography in the mid-1980s. In both communities canteens for the sale of alcohol had been imposed, and church functions had interfered with previous parenting patterns. In both cases, outsiders introduced the pornography to barter for access to girl children for sexual purposes. The "observational learning" of watching pornography provides a distorted and destructive construct of manhood for these young Aboriginal men and women. The attitudes and behaviours of many young Aboriginal males come not only from observational learning, or lack of positive parenting, but from experiences of trauma in their own sexual victimisation.

Well over half of the perpetrators of child sexual assault have been sexually abused as young boys without healing intervention to break the cycle (Butler 1978: Martens *et al.* 1988). At the same time, studies show that sexually abused girls are at greater risk of entering marriages or associations with an abusive partner (Herman 1988). "About four in five of these incidents first happened to these persons when they were children or youths." Female victims were more than twice as likely (23.8 per cent) compared to male victims (11.1 per cent) to have sought assistance (Badgeley 1984: vol. 1, 175). Herman shows that over half the women she surveyed with an intra-family sexual abuse history reported witnessing their father beating their mother and/or siblings (1988: 178). Women who have been abused as children, or who have seen their mothers beaten, are more likely to enter relationships believing such behaviour is the norm. Consequently they are more likely to be re-victimised or to abuse their children in the same or a similar manner (Queensland Domestic Violence Task Force 1988).

Observation, fieldwork and statistics in Indigenous populations support the theory of the relationship between the colonising catastrophe and the intra-cultural and transgenerational transmissions of traumatic behaviours. Today violent assault, suicide and homicide are endemic in many colonised Indigenous communities worldwide. A study by the Ontario Native Women's Association (1989) found that

89 per cent of Aboriginal Canadian women surveyed had been either sexually or physically assaulted. The Queensland Domestic Violence Task Force claims that Aboriginal Australian people consistently estimate that domestic violence affects 90 per cent of families living in Queensland Deed of Grant in Trust or former reserve areas (1988: 256). Aboriginal families today experience the trauma of the varied and multiple impacts of colonisation as being internalised and re-experienced in the lives of the children of survivors in new and even more traumatic ways.

Aboriginal experiences may be compared with Epstein's statement about the transgenerational transmission of the trauma of the Nazi concentration camps (1979: 338). Vogal (1994) and Danieli (1982, 1988c, 1998) provide additional context to the transgenerational transmission of trauma through the experiences of Holocaust survivors and their families. Both discuss gender as a factor to be taken into consideration.

Danieli presents concepts of transmission of trauma "within and *beyond* current notions of post-traumatic stress disorder". She shows trauma can continue into the third and succeeding generations when the trauma is unrecognised or untreated. Trauma victims adapt their behaviours and beliefs to compensate for their traumatisation, compounding their traumatisation. She believes this applies not only to Jewish survivors of the Nazi concentration camps, but to other victim/survivor populations throughout the world. Many such families become closed systems, teaching mistrust of the outside world, carrying massive rage and grief. Because society could or would not recognise and allow opportunities for expression of this rage and grief, and having no place to express it but within the family, they continue the victimisation on self and close others. Danieli believes male survivors are at a disadvantage in achieving psychological recovery and re-establishing their place within the family and community because of social norms about male expression of distress. There is greater social acceptance of female expression of distressed emotions (1985: 295–311).

Solomon's 1997 study of Israeli society during the Gulf War showed that the most traumatised group were those who had been previously traumatised (that is, those elderly people who had survived the Holocaust). Furthermore, there was a clear difference between the way men and women reacted to the stress that came with the war. Finally, family violence increased dramatically during the time of the war. The points made in the Israeli study, added to the knowledge that in colonised populations oppressed males may take on the attitudes and behaviours of their oppressors, gives us a greater understanding of what has happened, and is happening, within Aboriginal society today.

Vogal writes in the context of survivor women who have not been able to articulate their experiences because they can neither find the words to describe what had happened to them, nor tell their feelings around their experiences (1994: 35–47). In the social and emotional circumstances of the home environment, their children found much of what their parents were, and how they behaved, incomprehensible, yet took the trauma on as their own. She quotes Herman (1992: 52), observing, "A secure sense of connection with caring people is the foundation of personality development", and suggests that if the connection is shattered the developing self becomes confused. Children are therefore likely to take on the emotional and communicative constrictions of the parents. Vogal says:

Psychic trauma can be named transgenerational when it is the client's parents or other adult care-givers who have experienced the traumatic events, in response to which this person now suffers inexplicable symptoms of fear, anxiety, depression, flashbacks of things never experienced, nightmares and obsessions with phenomena out of their range of experience (1994: 37).

Grof (1976, 1984, 1988, 1990, 1991) takes this a step further. He believes that we have a genetic imprint or cellular memory, perhaps in some way related to Jung's collective unconscious (1964). He states, however, that "we know nothing about the human psyche", underlining how much we still have to learn in our consideration of traumatic imprints on human beings across generations. Grof links human experiences across the biographical into the trans-personal. His work is relevant in understanding traumatis-ation in Aboriginal peoples because of the close relationship between the corporeal and non-corporeal world in Aborig-inal ways of being in the world. In acknowledging the essence of *spirit* in the continuity of birth, death and rebirth in human activity, Grof has coined the term "spiritual emergency" to describe the condition that occurs as human trauma experiences across generations emerge in individuals and in social groups in the present, often at times of crisis, with the potential to create further traumatisation.

Trauma trails: fractured identities, families, communities

Within Central Queensland, trauma trails run across country and generations from original locations of violence as people moved away from the places of pain. These trauma trails carried fragmented, fractured people and families. They are a record of the distress that occurred when relationships between people and their land and between people and people were wilfully destroyed.

The Hornet Bank massacre potently illustrates many points already made, demonstrating the trauma lines that now run across the Central Queensland region. The massacre did not arise out of a single issue. It is used here to show the contextual ingredients of the frontier continuing into the present, changed into contemporary situations. Hornet Bank also points to issues of female and male Aboriginal sexuality at point of contact with the intruding white males.

In October 1857, the Fraser family of Hornet Bank station were attacked and killed by the Jiman (sometimes spelt *eoman, yeeman, e:mon*) of the Upper Dawson River in central mid-west Queensland. When Christopher Hodgson travelled through this country in 1845, looking for signs of the Leichhardt expedition, the Jiman were friendly, and appeared "so confident of our kindness that I could not help fancying they had been for some time with him [Leichhardt]" (Reid 1982: 16). This was before squatters moved into the country, seeking land for cattle and sheep. Reid shows that what happened at Hornet Bank was an inevitable result of the way in which white settlers, supported by governments and their agents, occupied Aboriginal territories. The attack by the Jiman was in response to, and in retaliation for, the indignities they had suffered in the ten years of white intrusion into the Dawson. This included stolen lands, deprivation of food supplies, the killing of hunters, the poisoning of waterholes, and—the final trigger for the Jiman attack—the sexual violations of young Jiman women by the Fraser men and others.

By mid-1857 the abuse of Jiman women had reached a crisis. The Native Police, instructed and assisted by their white supervisors, had been taking Jiman by force. Station shepherds had brutally violated Aboriginal girls and women, as had the Fraser men. Mrs Fraser had asked a visiting police constable to rebuke her sons for forcibly taking the young women. The Fraser men were "famous for the young gins" (Reid 1982: 55). In fact some days previous to the attack, two Jiman girls had been abducted, whipped and raped by a station employee (Reynolds 1981: 66).

The Jiman attacked the homestead on the night of 26 October 1857. Eleven white inhabitants of the station were killed, including Martha Fraser, the matriarch of the family, and her daughters. Although the older three women were raped, the two younger girls (nine and three years old) were not (Elder 1988: 138–9). The most telling behaviour by the Jiman in their killing of the whites was the rape of the Fraser women: "this was extremely rare behaviour for Aboriginal men at the time" (Elder 1988: 138–9). Gordon Reid says he had been told it was the Jiman women who told their men to commit the rapes, as punishment for what had happened to them.[5] The Jiman women would have seen this as fitting punishment for the violations they had suffered, similar to the forms of punishment that Aboriginal women would enact on men who raped. Under Aboriginal lore all members of a tribal group were held equally responsible for violating lore (Reid 1982: 5). The Jiman enacted their punishment according to their lore. Even so, their actions confirmed the observation of Roth that "unnatural offences, including criminal [sexual] assaults on children, are unknown" (1984: 1905, 7) at that time.

There was immediate retaliation. Over the next few years around the Dawson, over 300 Jiman were hunted down and slaughtered in a genocide that almost obliterated them. Those surviving few fled their lands, moving closer into more settled areas for protection. The Taroom Aboriginal Reserve became the home of a number of Jiman until the reserve was closed and the people were relocated to what is now called Woorabinda in 1927.

There are several reasons for relating the Hornet Bank story. It shows how the powerful define what violence is, who is violent, and who are the victims. In Australian history, the behaviour of the Jiman has been described, then and now, as savagery and treachery; the behaviour of the whites, both before and after the Jiman killings, is described as the right of white males and the strong, avenging arm of white "justice". Labelling Aboriginal women as promiscuous or sexual predators places responsibility for their violations on them, and removes it from their violators.

The narrative also illustrates that what happens to colonisers in the violence of invasion is easy to access in written historical records; the stories of the colonised, however, remain locked in the psyches or souls of the survivors, sometimes passed down in fragmented memories and feelings of terror and rage, of profound loss and grief. The oral histories which could have validated the intense pain and grief are too

---

5 He was told this during research fieldwork for his master's degree. Gordon talked to many people including members of my family for oral histories, corroborating his findings with official documents.

often untold because of the pain; or if told, are not believed. As people moved away from the original battle fields of Hornet Bank, they carried with them these stories. To various degrees, the traumas of their experiences have continued on into the families and communities which formed, and hold them as prisoners of the past. As the descendants of Jiman work together on Native Title claims, they are finding that their kin across the generations have also been victims of the institutional violence of the orphanages in this region, of the local prison, and increasingly, of suicide and murder.

Summary

Aboriginal worldviews and colonising impacts have been themes of this chapter. The collective and diverse Aboriginal world was one of relating, where social organisation, structured and informed by relationships with country, was the foundation of all thinking, feeling and behaving. Colonisation brought violence in forms inconceivable to a people who had lived removed from the incursions of colonisers that had been occurring in European countries for centuries. The invasion which is called colonisation or settlement occurred without informed consent. It involved actions designed to diminish the power of, and subordinate, the colonised, which re-formed and reshaped the constructions of individual and communal selves. Such activities created complex and compounding experiences of individual and communal traumatisation for Aboriginal peoples across generations.

People felt victimised, which is different to bereavement. In victimisation people begin to feel like losers, humiliated, diminished, pushed down, defiled, exploited, self-blaming, self-loathing, and invaded, which also explains in part the reasons for actions of the victimisers. Although the most important factor for recovery is a supportive family, interventions by government and others, sometimes well-meaning but more often virulent, actively worked to destroy the social systems which could have ameliorated such distress.

Man-made disasters have increased as men[6] have demanded the right to have power over and exploit the natural environment and other human beings. Such demands came generally from patriarchal societies with class hierarchies that spawned colonialism—racism, sexism and ageism. All are dependent on ideologies of superiority and inferiority of race, culture, gender and age. When physical, structural or psychological violence is used to achieve the objective of domination, the outcomes may not only produce acute trauma, but may set in place chronic conditions of ongoing victimisation and traumatisation at different levels, compounding the traumatisation across generations. The symptoms of post-colonial trauma include illness, dependency and dysfunction. These symptoms should not be seen as mental illness, but rather the normal human responses of traumatic violations that remain unhealed.

Such activities, acting as both cause and effect, include increasing destruction of natural environments as humans become more removed from their capacity to have a healing relationship with their country. Again, government interventions often work to increase the traumatisation. Violence becomes both cause and effect in an ongoing spiral. While feminist analysis, for example, says the violence in wife assault must be seen as the problem and not a symptom of a deeper malady, to understand and respond to the problem of violence in Indigenous families, it is imperative to look beyond the obvious physical violations. Situations, events and relations have meaning for people; they are largely determined by psychological needs, and these all occur within political, economic and social situations controlled by the dominant society.

Chapter Three now takes us into the stories of people living in the present in our attempt to listen to and understand the transgenerational products of colonising impacts.

---

6 I use "men" deliberately to emphasise the historical patriarchal He.

Chapter Three

We Al-li:
A program of healing

"I will tell you something about stories."
"They aren't just entertainment."
"Don't be fooled."
"They are all we have,
all we have to fight off illness and death."
"You don't have anything if you don't have stories."

"Their evil is mighty,
but it can't stand up to our stories."
"So they try to destroy the stories."
"Let the stories be confused or forgotten."
"They would like that."
"They would be happy,
because we would be defenceless then."

In *Ceremony* by Leslie Silko

We Al-li: fire and water, anger and grief

We Al-li was the name given to the program that evolved from the participatory action focus of my research project. A series of workshops was developed and delivered to promote the exploration of personal and collective stories in a safe environment. The program was built around a number of considerations. Firstly, it was informed by the work of Alice Miller (1983), who has listed what she believes are the five interactive ingredients into the construction of a truly violent person:

- being profoundly hurt and abused as a child
- being prevented from experiencing or expressing the pain of that hurt

- having no other single human being in whom the person can confide their true feelings
- having a lack of education or knowledge which do not allow the person to intellectualise the abuse
- having no children on whom the person can repeat the cycle of abuse in socially approved floggings or other forms of extreme punishment which help, in part, release the pent-up feelings resulting from the abuse.

Secondly, it was considered that a culturally safe environment had to be established, so that the stories of violence could be told in self–other relationships, during which each person could experience and express the pain of past abuse, and have others in the group witness the truth of those experiences. At the same time the purpose and structure of the workshops was to allow the group to work together to "intellectualise", or "make sense" of the abuse.

Finally, all the work we did would be based on the integrity of Indigenous cultural and spiritual practices. The name We Al-li was part of that cultural integrity.

In the Woppaburra language, *we* means fire. For us, fire was also symbolic of the great anger or rage we felt in people, often expressed on self or others or in ill-health.

Fire is an awesome force in the natural world and a powerful spiritual symbol. It has the potential to create and to destroy. It can nourish and comfort or it can threaten and harm. It can give life and it can blind. Fire transforms solid forms into pure energy. In its most powerful form—the sun—fire is a cosmic principle without which life would cease to exist. Aboriginal people used fire to cleanse the earth, to make way for new spring growth. Looking after country was a sacred responsibility, as was looking after people. Fire was used in ceremonies to ensure procreation and regeneration of all life forms. Fire provides warmth where people can sit to share, resolve conflict and restore harmony. *We* signified the spirit of cleansing that is essential to healing and re-creation, regeneration. It also symbolises the spiritual and cultural strength of the Aboriginal life forms that have been kept alive since the beginning of time, and in particular over the last two centuries.

In the Woppaburra language, *al-li* means water. Water was also symbolic of the deep grieving that needs to be done to restore health within our communities. Water is the source of all life. Without water we die. Our bodies comprise 70 per cent water. In spiritual literature water is often used as a metaphor to describe mystical states of conscious. The parallels drawn often derive from the pure fluid pristine qualities of water in its natural state and its lack of boundaries (all can be healed).

Once a place has been fired (cleansed), the rains come, green shoots give evidence of new life. One explanation of life says we are water. The water leaves the earth and returns again in the form of rain. Rain enters the ground, cleansing, creating new growth, sustaining all life forms. Some water runs into small streams which move across the landscape, creating waterways and pathways, interconnections. A small stream becomes a bigger stream, and finally a river, which eventually runs into the sea. The cycle of life continues. *Al-li* signifies the essential life-giving force of water. It acknowledges the healing that takes place in and with water. And for this region it acknowledges the waters that are a source of food and nourishment to us and our lands. This country is crisscrossed by water tracks which show the journeying of Moonda Nghadda, the Rainbow Serpent, and of the creators. Aboriginal peoples celebrate their journeying as they conduct rain-making ceremonies. After the sacred rituals of song and dance, people join together in great fun-filled water fights, and all conflict is swept away in the laughter and fun that comes with the cleansing from water.

In the design of the We Al-li workshops a number of activities were developed to help people find their stories that had been suppressed or denied:

With that first workshop "Lifting the Blankets", all the hurts came up. We saw them in the blankets and we wrote them on the wall. Some, you wouldn't even of thought of naming yourself. I think sometimes we just look at ourselves, this is what happened to me. But now I could see the whole picture. The men there, and the other women, all of us, we all shared our experiences. I was sexually abused as a child and I thought that was a separate issue but now I could see that other people had also had that happen. And all the other things. I could see that it was part of the bigger picture (Atkinson, Fredericks and Iles, 1996: 6).

The workshops were designed to help people connect their stories into a whole, to aid understanding and provide insight. People compiled genograms (diagrams of inter-generational stories) and were shocked at what they saw. Their story was an individual story but it was also part of a collective story.

Aboriginal people were connected to other Aboriginal peoples, non-Aboriginal to other non-Aboriginal people and Aboriginal to non-Aboriginal peoples. People from the same communities, Aboriginal and non-Aboriginal, were joined through genera-tions of hurt that had never been acknowledged. All the stories were linked by history and by experiences of pain (Fredericks 1996: 3).

Stories of pain and stories of healing

I was sitting with Hazel Kaur, Mosey Mason, and a young man, early in the morning before the We Al-li workshop started for the day. In the style of the workshop we were talking and reflecting together about the feelings that had come up for us from the previous day's work, which had been emotionally turbulent. We went on to talk generally about Halo House, the organisation with which we were running the We Al-li workshops that week.

Hazel and Mosey are both counsellors with Gumbi Gumbi, the Alcohol and Drug Awareness Program in the Central Queensland region. At that time, the young man was a client at Halo House, the residential centre from which the Gumbi Gumbi program was being run. As I listened to the talk about the happenings at Halo House, I commented that I could see a therapeutic community emerging. The young man asked what "therapeutic community" meant. I explained: *therapeutic*, medicinal, restorative, curative, healing from ill-health, dis-ease or pain. I went on to describe *community* from my perspective. "Similar to what we do here—sitting together—talking together—a place where people are safe to share their deepest thoughts, to bring out all of their hurt, to reveal their pain and know they will be accepted, supported and understood" (paraphrasing May 1976). I went on to explain that I believed we were building community as we come together in the activities of We Al-li and at Halo House, talking with each other, listening and sharing our pain and joy, and providing each other with psychological, physical and spiritual nourishment.

Halo House was a place where people came: some to spend a time in residence; some to attend the regular Alcoholics Anonymous and Aboriginal alcohol abstinence support programs; some for a cup of tea, a yarn and maybe a cry or a laugh; and some to offer services such as massage, meditation, reiki, and reflexology to complement the alcohol and drug counselling programs available at the house. I finished by saying that I could see that Halo House was more than a place to get off the grog: it was becoming a place where people could come for healing, which, we were beginning to understand, was much more than stopping drinking, or naming violence as a problem in our lives. With tears in his eyes, the young man leaned over and gripped Hazel's hand.

"Then", he said, "I can call Gumbi Gumbi my healing place."

This statement opened for me, in a profound way, a deeper understanding of the depth of pain, and the yearning for healing in the lives of those with whom I had been working.

The following dialogue takes the reader into a group of which this young man is part. Imagine that this group has sat in long discussion, been involved in heated processes of meaning-giving conversation, sharing themselves in group dialogue, exploring their own life experiences and listening to those of others in the group. They have been involved in this cycle of action-reflection-action for many months, which has taken them into deeper and deeper layers of under-standings about themselves. They are now sitting together within a We Al-li workshop in deep reflective discussion, or *dadirri*, to explore and share what they have learnt and their expanding self-knowledges. The challenge for the reader is to sit with me in *dadirri*, to read from a deep listening place, without judgement or analysis. I ask an occasional question, but allow the activity of *dadirri* to occur naturally. Listening to this dialogue is *dadirri* in action.

"What do you remember most about your childhood?"

Lorna: *I remember what I seen as a child. My dad, a great big man, on the mission. I remember being with him and holding his hands. He was talking to this white man and this white man told my Dad not to look him in the eyes and Dad had to drop his head. I couldn't understand it, not for a long time in the years growing up. This big man, with the biggest hands I could ever remember, and here was this white man telling him, "Don't look at me like that. You look down at the ground when I speak to you."*

I remember the smell of carbolic soap—it was black stuff and you had to clean your house with it and wash yourself. I hated that smell. I remember the little tins—oh dear, I don't think I have ever talked to anyone about this—the little tins that they brought to the house, just little tins with lids and we had to give a sample of our poo, for worms and stuff like that. I used to hate that. But we did it because we all had to do it. Even thinking about it now, feeling it, we were just bloody guinea pigs for them.

I remember our home. We really had a lovely home—we had flowers and a vegie garden and my brothers helped my dad. Mum was a good mum, clean and caring, but I remember her face. I remember Mum's face when these white people would come into her house to see how clean the house was. I think that was something that was in every home [on the reserve]. They would go through and check us all.

My biggest memory of my childhood was that I wasn't good enough, I could never be as good as the white man that was in charge, that was the overall feeling of my childhood. I was not a good person. I just felt, even back then, that I could never be good enough for anything or anyone.

Ben: *I was fearful in my childhood, always afraid, afraid of a lot of things. I felt very insecure, so afraid, so alone like no one would ever see me or hear me or help me.*

Jackie: *The greatest feeling that I remember was the feeling of always trying to please people, so I could to be told that I was good and that I wasn't stupid and that I could do things, but I was never given that feeling and I always felt that I was never good enough and that I was a bad person.*

Len: *I would have liked to have had a childhood, a proper childhood. I love my parents dearly and I can't blame them for what happened, but I would like to be a child again, to have another chance.*

Mary: *I never used to have memories of myself as a child, well before I was about eight or nine, I didn't have memories except of a feeling of being frightened—no—terrified—yeah, terrified is a better word. I was frightened of everything. Something happened around eight or nine that I do remember, all of it, every bit of it, like it's in slow motion, almost frozen. It's as clear today as if it just happened yesterday. But I don't have memories of normal things before then. My feelings of that time are of being no good, of being really bad, of being a dirty black gin. Something happened around eight and I do remember that really well. It's like my life started and finished then.*

Lorna: *That feeling, of not being good enough, that's the feeling I took into my drinking times. Now when I think back to those times I believe the feeling came from being black and never having enough of anything. We managed in the family. But I remember my mum* *forever worrying about things. Where we were going to get the next tin of milk, the next packet of Weeties, and it was just there all the time. And just not being as good as the white people. I was born [on a reserve], and I guess, well, not that I guess, I know that was part of the feeling of the place, of not being good enough, of never being as good as the white people who were there. I didn't know at the time, but I do know now, that's where a lot of the stuff, of the feelings that I had then, and the feelings I had through my drinking career came from. Something happened to me there too at the age of about three or four. Those feelings, I'm just feeling them now, going back into those feelings, of not being good enough also came from my sexual abuse as a three-year-old child.*

Jackie: *The feelings I had of being a bad person came from something that happened when I was around three too. I was playing in the front garden of my house with another friend and a man came along on a bicycle and leaned over the fence and offered my friend a sweet and he took it. Then this man offered me one too and I went to take it, and he grabbed hold of me and took me over the fence and put me on the cross-bar of his bicycle and—our house was the last house in the street, it backed onto the fields and the football pitch—and he took me down there into this bush area behind and he sexually assaulted me and when he finished he shook me and told me that what I had done was very very bad, and if I ever told anyone I would be punished for it. So I think the feelings go back to there. Even now, I know it's not logical, and I think to myself I am not a bad person, but the feelings are still there.*

Ben: *I was sexually abused when I was only ... I can't remember the exact years of it, but between ages of three and six. I've carried those feelings with me for the most part of my life. I've sort of ... it wasn't explained to me when I was young that this was a bad thing. I was led to believe that this sort of thing happened all the time and when I found out it didn't, I felt so angry, so hurt that somebody else could do this to me, so shamed of myself for taking part, I just felt really deeply hurt about it.*

Lorna: *I carried a lot of guilt about that sexual abuse. I'm forty-nine years of age and it has only been in the last three or four years that I have started to really look at and talk about my abuse. Those days back then you couldn't go to anyone and say those things have taken place because you would be flogged and told you were a naughty girl. It was your fault. You had no right being around those men who would do that. I carried that for many many years, that guilt. And my drinking stemmed from that very feeling, that I wasn't good enough and nobody would want me anyway. I will always remember that. These are the things I can remember when I was a kid [on the reserve].*

Mary: *I been trying to work this out in my head, right. I got raped. It wasn't sexual abuse, or molestation, it was rape. When you're raped it's ... like force, and this was force—[yet]—I felt I allowed this thing to happen, I didn't run and get away. I felt really bad that I didn't stop it. I've been angry at myself ever since. Something happens now and I slide back to that time.*

Len: *A lot of my childhood was ... has been practically blanked out. A man lived with us once and ...* [begins crying] *I get funny when I watch movies like the one the other night [a documentary on sexual assault in the boys' homes] and I get angry, really angry. I rang the TV station and abused them for putting it on. I felt bad in myself for days afterwards. I get funny, like last night, at the church social the children came and I feel, very, I get frightened ... when a child hugs me, I feel I shouldn't hug the child. You know what I mean. At the last ... I went to the toilets and two kids went into the toilets and I thought to myself, I'm not going in there, but I had to because I had to go to the toilet. I felt frightened, afraid that somebody would call me ... a child molester, you know. But I am not.* "Do you have a belief that you might repeat on others what somebody else has done to you?" *Yeah, yeah* [crying more deeply]. *I'd love to get married and have kids but ...* [sobbing]—*Oh, I would never put a child through what I've been through.*

Don: *I'm one that was sexually abused when I was a child too. My drinking, my drugging came because I was not allowed to cry when I was a kid—I was not allowed to shed a tear. The things that was wrong with me, was nobody would listen to me—nobody would sit down and talk to me about my problems—about the violence—the blood on the floor—the blood on the walls—the blood on my grandparents.*

Ben: *The strongest memories of my childhood were the times I got beaten. Sometimes I probably deserved it—but I felt sometimes that I got more punished than what I deserved. I was too young to have any memories of one time I got beaten, but when I was one and a half I was in hospital for two weeks because of it, and that stirred up, ... when I heard about that ... I only just found out ... it stirred up a lot inside of me just to find out this had happened to me at such an early age. I feel that I'm only understanding the pain of it now. I've seen my mother being bashed and I was always afraid for her. I felt for her when she got bashed. It was only when she was drinking that this sort of thing would happen. I remember one time when I was getting older, I tried to help her. I seen Mum getting bashed and I tried to help her and I ended up getting bashed up myself because I had run up and hit this fellow to try to stop him and he just backhanded me. He had kinghit mum and broke her nose and jaw, and when I tried to stop him, he just backhanded me, and Mum and me, we ended up on the floor together holding onto each other—blood everywhere and somebody was holding him back.*

Len: *I saw a lot of violence, in a lot of ways, got beaten a fair bit, and seeing other people beaten. My father used to take us down to the pub and we would wait outside but we could hear and see what was inside. Mum used to work and he used to bring us drinks outside, but we knew what was going on inside. Where I come from, I suppose I saw violence in a lot of ways. All sorts of violence. I saw other people getting bashed, seeing blokes in fights, my father putting this man through a wall. I think I was frightened then, but I also skited about it, so kids would think, better not touch him, he's got a big father.*

Don: *Violence was just practically there every weekend and on pension nights and on pay nights. It was just there, it was a normal way of life, that's what it seemed anyway. That's the way the family passed that belief down to me. They probably didn't know it at the time, but now that I am older and I've got a little bit of understanding of what happened, that's what they passed down to me. My stepdad, he probably thought he was only mucking around and that, but he used to grab us like a crab bite, on the leg or the upper leg. You don't know what to do, cry or laugh or what to do, because he made you say these silly poems and that, things like that, and Mum would be saying "you're hurting the kids—you're hurting the kids", and everybody would be laughing, all the grown-ups who were drunk and everything and all us kids would run. It wasn't just me but all his nieces and nephews and my sisters, we all ended up with marks and skin ripped off our legs.*

Lorna: *I can't remember any violence in the home on the reserve, but I remember when we left, I remember violence outside, with my dad always drunk and us kids always running away, taking the littlies with us and sitting up on a hill while these two people were fighting all hours of the night till the early hours of the morning, sitting up on a hill or under a tree somewhere, all cuddled together, waiting, waiting for everything to settle down. I have no memory of violence by my dad on the reserve, of having to run and hide, but outside, when we got outside, when he got the exemption, that's what you call it eh, I remember it then. Dad was a strict man. He was the man of the house and that's the way he reared us kids up. And that was the way he was with Mum. I guess you could say he was a kid of his past. We had to jump. When he said move, we had to move. That was even at the reserve. But when we got outside, that's when he started to use his power in an abusive way. He'd get us all out of bed at three in the morning. We knew his whistle. He only had to give one whistle and we would all have to round up like cattle and he'd line us up, at three o'clock in the morning. We all had to sing his favourite songs, while he was drunk. Stuff like that. He started to use his power in an abusive way. And if we didn't sing we'd get flogged. Can you imagine that. Seven or eight kids* *standing in a line, half-asleep, trying to think of a song. I can see now there was a relationship between him having to stand in front of a white man and being told not to look in his face and now him having the power to line his kids up like this and have them do what he told them to.*

Len: *A leather belt or a coat-hanger or cane, that's what he used. Pretty scary. He was a big man and when I did something wrong if he didn't hit me over the head straight away, I would be in my room and I had to wait for him, and sometimes it would take hours for him to come in and I think that was the most scary. Always waiting. Never a chance to explain. But I cannot blame him. He didn't know any better. He apologised to me a few months ago. Good words. He said I didn't know what to do. I apologise for all the beatings I gave you, but I didn't know anything else. And it was true. He didn't know any other way.*

Don: *My father would come home drunk all the time — "Where's my boy? Where's my boy?" — looking for me and the boy would be under the blankets with a pillow over his head — you know, a six-year-old boy — or he would be under the bed hiding — from his uncles. You know — in my life, I thought, for me to be normal, for me to be like my uncles and fathers I had to go and steal — thieve — from just about everybody I knew. I had to go and drink at the age of eight years old — just to be a man — I had to go and drug on when I was twelve. I can remember from the age of eight, probably even younger, my name was Monkey John. I didn't like it but I accepted it and grew with it. You know when you don't like anything, like a song on the radio all the time, you get used to it and you accept. My mother and father they split up when I was at a young age and I was passed around like a football from family member to family member — relation to relation — and it didn't matter which family member I got to, they were either drinking or smoking yarndie [marijuana] or things like that, and I just followed suit because that's what I thought life was all about. Chaos — that was me, going this way and that way — don't know which direction half the time. I was like that — uncontrollable. And to block all that outta me I*

*just needed to escape and to escape I found a world of glue-sniffing
and taking drugs and drinking to get away from all of that so I
could be by myself in my own little world. When I was about eight,
before I turned into my teens and I was still only a child, I was
probably drunk the Tuesday night, the Friday and the Saturday
night. That was until I turned twelve.*

Mary: *Mum and Dad, I can't remember them hitting me. I think
they were trying to be the best parents they could be. If there was
anything, it was just that they couldn't show love to me. I can't
ever remember them giving me a hug or a kiss or showing any
affection—never saying I'd done a good job, that I was a good girl.
I don't think they knew how to show affection. But they was never
violent—they never hit me.*

"What was it like for you growing up as a young man or young woman?"

Don: *When I got in my teens it was probably just on the weekends,
we used to go to drive-in and it wasn't just alcohol it was glue-
sniffing, practically every day until I turned fifteen years old.
Stealing glue from the shops and going under the bridge and
sniffing it because I wasn't at school—I was wagging it [playing
truant]. I had a mate, a Murri fella, we was about fourteen or
fifteen, he never used to sniff. I didn't know why but I know why
now. He was there to look after me while I was having my trips on
glue, and drinking was part of it too. In my teens on the weekends
I used to sniff glue and drink at the same time just to get that high,
to take me out of the society world and the problems that were at
home all the time with Mum and her husband, my stepfather, my
sister's father. They always used to fight. It wasn't until my teens
that I got hit. Didn't get hit until my teens and that was from my
stepfather. He would get into Mum all the time. Only when they
were drinking. When they were sober and that, you couldn't get
nicer persons. When they had the alcohol in them, my stepfather he
would get stuck into her all the time. If I would rush in to do
anything, to try to stop it, he would say "You next" and I would
cop it. When I had a project with TAFE, if it didn't go too well, or*

the family wasn't going well, and you would be the only one cleaning up all the time if you were not drinking that day while the family was drinking, you would be cleaning up their mess, and you would think to yourself, "Why am I cleaning up their mess, what the bloody hell, can't they clean up their mess". That was hard when I was trying to do the TAFE course.

Ben: *I was about fourteen the first time I was bashed by the police. I was walking down the mall and there was a fight between two bikies. I was watching it, and the cops came. I went to leave and one of them grabbed me and asked if I had anything to do with the fight, and I said no but he backhanded me anyway, and I fell against a car and I heard people in the crowd cheer him on. I believe it was because I was black. Another time I was walking along the road with some friends when the police drove past and stopped. My friends ran off and left me and they—the police—grabbed me and gave me a flogging. I didn't know what I had done, they just gave me a flogging, and when I asked what I had done wrong they said I shouldn't be out on the streets looking for trouble. I started drinking when I was about sixteen. I'd been bashed twice by the police before I started drinking but I never started drinking before sixteen because I was always afraid what my mother would do to me if she found out I was drinking, you know. So I never drank until I got a bit older.*

Len: *When I was young I started doing things that were normal, well I thought it was normal at the time, from where I come from, pinching milk money and things like that and shoplifting, and it started growing and I was taken to juvenile aid and I got expelled from my last school. I suppose I was lucky because my father got me a job out west or I could have got into bigger things, but the police never forgot, never let up. It's my drinking that got me into the most problems. I was sent to this school in Brisbane, and one night there was a dance and a rock band was playing and there was a big fight outside. I was watching. A bloke said, pass me that knife, and he was just about to stab this kid on the ground and three blokes had to hold him back so he wouldn't stab this kid. You never got* caught outside by yourself. They say this [violence] is only happening now but this was going back twenty years and this was a "white" school. You couldn't walk outside the school grounds. You really had to watch yourself. I have experienced a lot of police violence—we used to call one station the black eye factory. If you got put in there you would come out with a black eye, a broken nose and cracked ribs. They would just go looking for you. I remember once five of us were living in this house. We weren't doing nothing, not hurting anybody and they broke our door down, went through the place. One of my mates only had one leg. They threw him around the house like a bit of rag. My friend Billy and me, we was coming out of the rubbish tip in his car and the CIB stopped us and they gave us a bit of a going over. I was living away from home then, on the streets of Acacia Ridge. Most people would put me up for a few days. There was always violence on the streets there. I been arrested maybe a dozen times, everything from disorderly behaviour, obscene language, assault, grievous bodily harm, to possession of drugs. Never got convicted, [laughs] can you believe that!

Ben: I've been afraid for most of my life. I was pretty much fearful all the time and when it came to fighting I tried to avoid getting into fights and that. If I remember correctly, it was when I had been drinking when I got into my first fight and I won my first fight and after that, realising how much, sort of, anger and strength I had inside me, it happened on a regular basis that I would get into a fight. It was only when I drank that I got into fights. I wouldn't have had the guts to get into a fight when I was sober, but when I was full of grog I was always getting into fights with other people. What they were about? Sometimes I can remember but most of the time I can't remember what they were about—sometimes I can't even remember the people I was fighting with. I wouldn't go out with the intention of fighting, but I would feel so stirred up inside and I would just be waiting for somebody to do something wrong and then I would just up this person and take all my anger out on this innocent person. I been arrested more times than you can count. Ohhh, it's almost too many. What got me to decide to stop drinking was I had a chance to see my file at the police station and *see how long it was. It was almost two pages long — more than fifty arrests for drunk and disorderly, resisting arrest, obscene language — I've been drinking for the last twelve years and that's what I got from it — a big fat police file.*

Lorna: *Even when I was a teenager, Dad, with his drinking, used to have a bull strap and that's what he used on all of us. In my own drinking years there was times when, one night I just about had my throat cut. I was drunk. It was a sexual thing. Other times I was left out bush. You'd go on a party and people were drunk themselves and they would take off and leave you still out there. The next day you would wake up. There was just lots of things like that that happened to me. There were many times I could have been raped, I've been pinned down and that kind of stuff. Someone must have been looking after me in my teenage years when I was drinking.*

Jackie: *The most significant thing for me in growing up that I remember was I was at school one day, I think I must have been about eleven. Mum had never bothered to tell us the facts of life and some other girls at school were talking, and I understood, they were talking about sex, and I suddenly realised what this man had done to me and the feelings of being dirty and untouchable were absolutely overwhelming. There was no one I could go to talk to about it and I really withdrew for a long time.*

Don: *By the time I was thirteen, before I even got to thirteen, I had to learn about sex. Before I was thirteen I had to use a stuffed-up dirty pillow to make love with. Little girl friends, at school, feeling their legs, in grade one. For me, sex was a dangerous thing. When I got drunk I could have raped anyone. But I have a higher power and I believe in the old ways of my ancestors. That higher power is Moonda Nghadda — the Rainbow Serpent. To many people, it would be just God and the Jesus on the cross. But without Moonda Nghadda and faith in my God and without the faith of We Al-li and Gumbi, and the fellowship of AA, I wouldn't be here. I wouldn't be talking about this now with youse.*

"Have you ever hurt yourself?"

Don: *Going back to my school days, something would happen that would hurt me and I'd punch the walls. As I got older, I was drinking and drugging more and more. When I was drugged up or drunk, I thought of suicide all the time. Back then I didn't have plans. When you are drunk you just don't plan, you just don't care. It's not your mind doing those things. I started walking out in front of cars, hoping I would get killed or something. Way back, even in my glue-sniffing days, I didn't want to live anymore. There was no lights on the streets in those days and what would happen, I was just drinking scotch straight and on top be yarndied up. You'd just feel it was the right time to go and run out in front of a car, smash yourself up against one or run into it. Sometimes the publican would come out and grab me, or call the police. It was just that I was tired of the pain, sick of it, the way that my life was. Why!! Crying out for attention! I could have been doing that—just wanted somebody—I just thought the way to get attention was to get somebody to realise that there is a person inside me, and I had to go and do these things—you know, cut my arm up and that— just because I needed somebody to talk to and, I don't know what, just to listen to me. I wouldn't do those things when I was sober. If you are talking about before I really felt I had lost control a lot of times, I was killing myself very slowly. My suicide attempts were anything from what I said, running out in front of cars, smashing myself up against trucks, punching windows out—glass windows, sometimes I would just stick a needle into me or cut myself just to feel the pain. Other people saw my suicide attempts but I didn't see them then. I look back on it now and think it was silly, but it wasn't at the time.* "So what's the change now?" *Now I am sober and straight. I can get those feelings out in another way now. The memories come back now but I wouldn't do it now.*

Lorna: *I have suicidal thoughts time and time again. I've tried it a couple of times, overdosed on tablets. I remember an incident at home when I just felt that nobody, nobody, not even my husband, thought I was good enough to stand up for and I felt I couldn't blame him [crying] so what I did, I got all my Serapax and took* them all and sat on a chair. I'm thinking about that now, and I can see myself sitting in that chair again in a state of "I've had enough. I can't take any more." It was crazy because there was some part of me that felt I just wanted to die—I can't take any more. And the other part of me was feeling, "I hope somebody finds me soon before anything happens." Now I think I was asking for help. It was true that I felt life wasn't worth living, but it would have been worth living if someone could see me and listen to me and be there for me in my hurt, just accepting me for who I was [crying].

Mary: I've tried to kill myself a number of times. The closest I came was in 1981. One night I couldn't sleep after another flogging. My body was dead tired and real sore, but somebody else had control of my mind. It was running around in circles, like a dog chasing its tail. It was trying to figure out what to do. I'd think "I'll leave him." Then I'd think—"Yeah! where are you going to get the money", what with the kids and all? We was living you know, way away from anybody I knew. All my family was in another state. My mind was going round and round, coming up with ideas how I was going to get away. I thought, "Well, I'll go without the kids. I can hitchhike out." Then I thought, "You'll never be able to live with yourself if you left the kids behind." He was pretty toey with them too at that time. Then I thought, "I'll talk to him tomorrow—he'll be better without the grog in him and he'll listen." You couldn't talk to him when the grog was in him, you see. Then I thought, "He's not going to listen, he's not going to change. He's getting worse." He's a good man, you know, but he needed the grog in those days and he was getting worse with the grog and his fist. That got me feeling sorry for myself—I couldn't leave—even thinking about how sent me into a spin—it was too hard with the kids and all. And I reckoned he wasn't going to change. I just couldn't see a way out. Looking back on it now, all I can remember was the biggest jumble—my mind running round and round in circles like a dog chasing its tail, but the rest of me was frozen. I couldn't do a thing. I couldn't see a way out. Then it was real clear in my mind. There was no way out. So I went and took every tablet I could find in the house. I woke up three days later in hospital. At the time I thought, "Hell. Who did that?" I wasn't happy at all that they stopped me from dying.

Ben: Before we split up I had a feeling everything was falling apart—there were a lot of arguments and nothing was ever sorted out. We would fight at least once or twice a week—there were times when it got physical. Once or twice a year it got physical. After we split up I walked the party line. I was going through a big depression. That's probably why I drank so much. I think I drank so I didn't have to wear the pain. I didn't drink so much in the relationship. But after we split up I started getting into more and more fights, more trouble with the police, humiliating myself in front of people. I was thinking suicide at least once a fortnight, I attempted it once and I failed, and just before I went into rehabilitation I was starting to feel very strong about it again, to feel hopeless and that I was no good. I was pretty close to doing it again. My father is the only person in my family I know that went through with it. Other family members have tried but been unsuccessful. Dad was the only one I know who was successful. He died in prison and that was the same year my ex and I split up. When I heard about my dad, I was angry at him for what he did, and angry and shamed at myself for feeling like that. He was never a father for me, but just before he went to jail that last time, he contacted me and I thought we might have been able to get together, get to know each other, and then that happened. I think that might have been why my ex and I started to have problems and then we split up. Not being the kind of father for my children like I wanted to be, and wanted my father to be for me, really hurts me. I want to be there for my children and now that we have split up I only get to see them once a fortnight.

Len: Over Christmas I had a really hard time and I was thinking of admitting myself [to hospital]. I used to have suicidal thoughts depending on the state I was in. They started in my late teens and they would be strong at the end of a relationship or if I didn't have a relationship but I wanted one. This last Christmas, I wasn't *drinking or drugging, but I was having a hard time and I shoulda got myself in a safe place over Christmas but I thought I had to get through it myself. It was very hard and I tried to suicide on Christmas Day. Kinda of hung myself—cut myself. I never had a real plan. I was really upset and angry. A few people around me had done the wrong thing, what I thought was the wrong thing anyway. I was sick of it, sick of people doing this to me, of being alone and I went and hung myself. Now I think how lucky I was. The rope broke. I had a scar around my neck for months and I broke a couple of ribs. A few other times I have cut myself, my arteries. I would get a razor blade and would get rushed into hospital, self-abuse with blades. I was nineteen the first time I cut myself with blades. I would never have a gun—I used to have a gun for about two months. I was sleeping with it but I gave it back to my mate because I didn't trust myself.*

Don: *We had a baby, I went to see the baby being born and we were living in a flat. I did all the right things. Her family was a Christian family, supposedly a Christian family, and I did all the right things I could do for her and the baby, and I suppose because I had being doing drugs and alcohol and stuff like that, the family came one day and took everything. It was the first time I cut my arm, cut myself up. I just grabbed the serrated knife and sliced my arm a couple of times, fourteen times actually. I did it out of pain to let her know that nothing can hurt me, to show her how much hurt I was going through.* "I didn't know you have a child. Where is the baby now?" *What happened, after we split up, I went and seen a solicitor to get me access through the courts to see baby and they had a warrant out so I had to go and turn myself in. I did that and then her solicitor got in touch with mine and they wanted me to go for a DNA test. I went for the test, after eighteen months, two years, of believing that the baby was mine, I find out she wasn't mine at all. That was another pain, another loss. I sung to that baby when my ex was carrying it in the womb and then I find out it wasn't mine.*

"Have you ever experienced any form of violence as an adult?"

Lorna: *There was physical violence between my husband and me. I've been dragged by the hair, thumped, flogged with the hose, choked, on many many occasions. I used to have marks around here [motioning to her neck]. remember once I had to go to work and I had a broken jaw and I was wired up—just a little gap that I had to suck soup through. It was all done to me when I was drunk because I became very very violent when I was drunk, only with my husband, only with my husband and son. Nobody else would have ever known that was what I was like.*

Mary: *I've been flogged up many times, bruises, split lips and that, but I'm telling you the worst violence is the mind games. Twisting what you say and do around. Sometimes I felt I could never do any-thing right, I'm telling you, no matter what I did, I did it wrong. If I tried to defend myself I just got into more hot water. And I would try harder and harder and harder. But you didn't have to tell me I was stupid and no good. I knew it anyway. In the end I was going crazy. I'd tell him what I was—stupid bitch—before he'd start on me. Mind games. I called it mind-fucking and I was doing it to myself in the end.*

Jackie: *I was in an abusive relationship for over twenty-three years. It was living in constant fear, never knowing whether he was going to explode, always being made to feel no good, and useless and worthless. It didn't matter how hard I tried to make him happy, or do things for him, I never felt like I was of any value. I was always being put down. The abuse was physical as well as all the other forms, sexual, psychological. He kept me totally isolated. I wasn't allowed to have any friends. If someone came I wasn't allowed to socialise or give them a cup of tea. I wasn't allowed to do anything I wanted. Every minute of the day—one of the hardest parts was he wouldn't go out to work for eight hours like other men, we worked together on a property, so it was twenty-four hours a day. When I stood up to him and tried to defend myself, the violence* got worse—that's when I got the most injuries. Once when I tried to defend myself he just picked me up and slammed me against the wall and I got broken bones out of that. If I didn't retaliate it might be one to two good punches and he would leave me alone so I learnt not to retaliate. But I lived on a knife's edge, waiting for the next bout of physical blows. The other abuse was even harder to heal than the physical abuse—the emotional, mental, psychological and spiritual violence which came with the verbal abuse, swearing, shouting, taunting, put-downs—"You're a stupid, useless bitch", "No good, ugly and worthless", "You can never do anything right", "If you were more feminine I would not be able to hit you", "It's you that makes me hit you, apologise for it"—that was even harder than the physical abuse to heal from. When the blows came, your wrist snapped, your ribs cracked, your teeth broke, the stock-whip cut your legs, and yet, you can't feel this physical pain because the pain, the devastation, the betrayal, the piece-by-piece dismantling of your very being, the destruction of the soul which is writhing in agony inside of you, the desolation of living totally isolated in this world of violence, that is unbearable. You would ask yourself, "What have I done?" "How bad I must be to receive this much punishment?" "How can I survive living like this, minute after minute, hour after hour, day after day, year after year?" The only way I knew of surviving was the same way I survived my early traumatic episode, to shut down and switch off. I created a block, a steel door in my mind, behind which I put what remains of me, my feelings, emotions, the things of importance to me. People ask me, "Why did you stay?", "Why didn't you leave?" My answer—the only one I have—is "How could I leave? I was not there." "What do you mean by that?" I guess I dealt with most of what was happening by withdrawing inside myself, putting all my feelings behind a door, just trying to keep it all under control. One thing I did was to have an imaginary world—that is how I lived. I made a world for myself that was livable and that's how I survived. It started in my childhood and it continues today. It was the way I got protection, otherwise I would have gone mad. It was an imaginary world and when things got really bad I would go back into it. In that world I had a mother figure who loved me and protected me, and I would do things that were heroic and so people—she—the mother—thought I was very good, that everything that happened was good in that world. I told a counsellor about it once and he said I shouldn't be doing that, I should be through that behaviour now, that I should be over it. But he never really knew what had happened to me, about the childhood thing, and at that time it was about five years since I had got out of my violent marriage and all the feelings of it were coming up for me. He didn't even know about the violence in the marriage, he didn't want to know. He never asked.

Len: *I had a girlfriend that hit me all the time, but hitting a woman, that's one thing I could never do. I always always always held that part in me that I could never hit a lady or a child. Yet one of my girlfriends used to hit me. I remember one night she hit me so many times it wasn't funny. That night I had a few in me too, but I just sat there and took it. She laid into me, but I knew if I hit her I'd have nothing left. I just couldn't do it, I'd crumble. I'm a violent man, but I've never used physical violence on a woman. I had a girlfriend that hit me all the time, but hitting a woman, that's one thing I could never do.*

"Have you ever behaved violently towards another person or thing?"

Jackie: *I've really always tried hard never to hurt—the other thing I've done I think—I was so hurt by the hurt I felt, that I have always been really careful not ever to hurt anyone else.*

Don: *With my last woman, I never hit her. Just verbal fights. But I had a relationship with another one—I was a no-good back in those days anyway, and before that, the first one, like I said, I seen my parents, my mother, getting slapped around and choked and physically mangulated and I seen my uncles bashing their women around all the time, and I just thought it was normal to bash a woman. I thought that was the way to live too, so when I got a girlfriend I just got her on the ground and I kicked her head in, and smashed it up against the wall, like she was a rag doll. I didn't* *know no better. It's not that I wanted to. You wouldn't do those things if you were sober. It was different when you was drunk. You got jealous if she looked at one man, she looked at the guy across the street and when you was drunk you remembered that. One time she said I did hit her and grab her by the throat and was throwing her around, but I don't remember that. I can't acknowledge it. It is not an excuse. I was drunk that night, and I just don't remember.*

Len: *I've destroyed lots of property [chuckles] a lot of property. Oh yeah. I remember one charge I went up on, I can still remember this night. I walked into the place and I kicked every piece of fibro wall on my way to my room, smashed the machine, kicked the walls in, the windows in, must have been a good noise. Oh it was. And there was blood everywhere and I kicked holes in my room and fell over on my bed and there was blood everywhere and they woke me up in the morning and asked me if I did it and I said no [laughs]. No! Wasn't pretty obvious, eh. Yeah. I've destroyed cars, myself in them, my body got scars, yeah, just smashing things a lot of my life.*

Ben: *I can't count the number of times I got into physical fights, heaps and heaps and heaps. I've kicked in, punched in a few doors. When I am inside I feel trapped and I'll just lash out at anything. Outside I don't feel that same feeling of being trapped and I don't damage things in the same way. I'd say about once a month I threaten to punch somebody's lights out, but I've never used a weapon on another person, and never threatened use of a weapon. I got me fists, hey.*

Len: *A lot of time when I was drinking, I've threatened violence, without a weapon, and with a weapon. First time when I was thirteen, I told the first man I would shoot him. I'd get into a blue every week. I stopped carrying a knife with me after my last attempt. I had a fight, I had this man up against a wall, a very good friend, a brother, and I was just completely off my face. I picked him up off the ground by the neck and I had my knife out of its pouch and I was ready to open his belly up and I'm glad my friends pulled me off him, and it didn't happen. That kinda slowed me down about* *using weapons against people. When I woke up the next morning in the hospital, I had to get out before the coppers came. That really shocked me that night cos he was a real good friend of mine that I'd known for a long time.*

Lorna: *With my children, I been violent with my children. I'd start to smack my children and I'd end up punching them. I just wanted to punch all the time. I think I told you about this finger, you know, how it got broke. I had my son in a corner of the room with a knife and I was going to cut his throat and he broke my finger to get away. I don't know what happened, something clicked in and I fell in a heap on the floor and I just cried and cried. Yeah, I was really aggressive. You know how big my hubbie is, he is a strong man, and I'd get ten feet tall and ten stone and I'd attack him. I'd be ripping his shirt off. I'd just dive at him with the anger in me. I remember a time when he had just finished a shift and was going to bed, you know the railway shifts, and I was hungover from the night before and I was having a reviver at the kitchen table, drinking a stubbie at the kitchen table and he didn't say anything to me. Just talked to our daughter, and I got her and put her down in the cot and I walked in with a knife behind my back and I thought when this man goes to sleep I'm going to get him back for everything he has ever done to me. Something must have clicked in him because he jumped off the bed, he somehow knew that I had a butcher's knife, and he wrestled with me and took it off me. I remember times when I would sit in the lounge and I would hear him snoring, he would be that tired from work, and I would think, I could go in there now and just stab him and stab him and stab him, cos, I just [crying], because people hurt me. I just wanted to get a bit of my own back. There were things like that. I just wanted to kill [crying more deeply]. My poor son. I used to just beat him around. He was someone when I couldn't get at my husband. I'd just punch and punch, but I was too frightened to touch the younger two because they were his [the husband's] children and I knew if I put a mark on them, somehow in my madness, I knew he would probably kill me. So it was my oldest son that got most of my anger, my son that I had before I got married to my husband, that took all my anger, yet through it all he* *remains just what he is today, my best friend and loving son, but I guess if we dug deep enough in him we would find all that pain and hurt that I gave him still there. I took a lot of my stuff, my pain, out on him.*

"Were the police ever involved in any of this?"

Mary: *The police came once. He tried to kill himself. Cut himself up pretty bad and smashed up the house. I got in the way, trying to stop him, and got hurt too. The kids called a doctor who was treating him for depression. A locum came instead—took one look at the damage and called the police. You should never say never, but I tell you it would have to be pretty big before I'd ever call them after what they did, how they came into our place. Five squad cars—if I'd have called them, I bet they wouldn't have come, but a doctor calls them and five squad cars full of cops. They ran into the house with their guns drawn. One of them jumped through a window onto our daughter who was in her room in bed. By this time we had got him settled and he was asleep. But now the police were there it all started again. They didn't help in any way. Just made things worse, so then and there I thought to myself, good lesson here, don't ring that mob. Sort it out yourself. And I always have, no matter how bad things have been, I sort it out myself.*

Lorna: *Have I ever been arrested, is that what you mean? No. Not yet! [laughs] I was a good actress you see. When I was drinking, I used to put on the hard-done-by wife act and they'd take me home and get up my hubbie, you know. I would be the good little wife that's hard done by and as soon as they drove away I'd start screaming and ranting like a mad woman at him. I know now it was terribly hard for him at the time. We've been through a lot, a hell of a lot, the pain that we both have been through.*

"Tell me more about the alcohol and drugs you used."

Ben: *I came into rehab because I had a feeling that drinking was a problem in my life. It played a major role in my life and I had to do something about it. I didn't drink every day but I went out to* *nightclubs and parties and when I did drink I drank pretty heavy, binge drinking. I used to also smoke cannabis, use amphetamines and cocaine.*

Don: *In the beginning glue-sniffing was a beautiful experience for me. I was able to leave those things that were painful to me behind. The glue took me into another world. I could blot everything out. Nothing of what was happening to me mattered any more. I started drinking when I was about eight and using glue when I was twelve. Things that were happening for me, the domestic fighting at home, and what was happening for me at school which wasn't a good place for me either, I felt like I was treated as stupid, I just couldn't face up to what was happening for me. So around twelve when I was introduced to glue I found I could get away from my reality for a couple of hours. Glue-sniffing was a way I could escape at that time and I sniffed glue from twelve until I was fifteen. For about two years, sniffing glue, I would go into a world of my own, a real beautiful world. Then the nightmares started, the real bad trips. I began seeing things that were not very nice. I didn't like the trips I was taking any more, on the glue, because they started becoming bad ones. Seeing right in front of you, cows getting their heads chopped off, and blood spurting everywhere. People saying, you are going to Mars now, and they get the dogs and the sirens all going off and the big explosions, and you really think you are going. Around sixteen I found yarndie. At sixteen I could get the dole and could go out and buy yarndie in the pubs. It was expensive but now I had the money from the dole, the glue was giving me bad trips and the yarndie was relaxing my body at the time, the yarndie gave me a better feeling, so I started to use yarndie which I used, with all the other drugs, until I was twenty-eight.*

With the yarndie, I thought it was giving me good ideas for my artwork. I would get stuck on my artwork and I'd have a couple of cones with my uncles and go water the plants and a great idea would come to me, and I thought it was from the yarndie. But eventually it would just put me to sleep. I started sleeping longer and longer, all day, so it became a bad medicine for me too. Eighteen years — I sniffed glue, smashed up Mogodons, Serapax, Valium and snorted them up through my nose—speed, mushrooms, all kinds of different hashes, yarndie, cannabis—ever since I was twelve years old. My family was proud of me. I was living in the normal way. I was like them. Today I'm a reformed alcoholic and a drug addict, but my problem is not alcohol or drugs no more—my problem is living today in a sober and straight life—an everyday life.

Len: I started drinking around eleven—twelve. I went to a party with my bigger sister, and everybody was drinking and I thought I would have a go. I made such an idiot of myself. The second time I just wiped myself out completely. Then it came that every time I got drunk I would wipe myself out. Since then I have never had a social drink. I just wipe myself out. I get these funny things when I am drinking. You start going into your feelings a bit more. I used to get cranky about why I had to have a drink to feel. But when I was drinking I could release my feelings. I could cry into my beer, or I could get angry. I could say what I wanted to say. These were good feelings but there was a price. At the end of the night I would be on the ground or in the lock-up or in hospital. Self-abuse to the body just got out of control. In the end I was drinking just about every day. My capability level of handling alcohol wasn't there any more. My build-up level, being able to handle it, I would still drink a lot, but if I had three or four beers at the pub I would be well on my way. I wouldn't stop drinking until—I would drink 100, 150 dollars of alcohol and I would fall over in a heap, just obliterate myself in one session. I was also using a lot of other stuff—coke, hash, dope, amphetamines, uppers and downers. Wouldn't touch heroin because I hate needles.

Prescription drugs were great—oh, I shouldn't say it was great, but any time in the middle of my drinking, I would say to the doctor, "Hey look, I've got a problem." But going to the doctor wasn't the answer because he would sit me down and talk to me for fifteen minutes and then he would prescribe me Valium, Serapax, anything I wanted, to control my mood swings. It was great because you knew you could sleep and you could be completely off your face, but you wouldn't be drunk. Overall though, in the short term, they didn't make me better. Bandaid approach to holding me *in that place where I was. Made things worse in the long run— when I did go out and drink, I would be drunk with the drugs. I couldn't cope without the drugs in me, but I was coping less and less with the drugs. Couldn't go out, couldn't do anything unless I had the drugs in me, wouldn't meet anyone without popping a Valium or Serapax. I had to make sure I had these drugs in me before I went out, to calm myself down, so people wouldn't see how high-strung I was and so I would be in a relaxed state of mind. Even if I was going out with ladies, before going out I would take a few pills just to calm me down because of the nervousness that was inside of me.*

Lorna: *There were times when I was just too sick to drink, but otherwise I drank every day. My son, my eldest son and my husband would come and pick me up from the river bank and I would go home and get cleaned up and go to bed and just have all this stuff in me, the guilt, the shame, and I used to lay in bed for days on end until I started to feel I was all right within myself. Yeah I drank heaps. I drank every day. That's all I knew from ten o'clock in the morning to ten o'clock at night. My life ran, I guess, on the times of the pub. There were other drugs too. You know, I've had joints, sessions with people, marijuana but mostly my drugs, apart from alcohol, was Serapax and Valium. I just popped them. It was nothing for me to take four or five Valiums. If I didn't have alcohol this was what I washed down. I got them from doctors. I went in and told them a story that I was in need and I was nervous, I was this and I was that, and I always got them. The prescription drugs —at the time they were the only thing when I didn't have alcohol, the only things that helped me get through the day. But I used them even when I had alcohol. My drinking stemmed from never feeling good enough and that nobody would want me. I did feel a part of a group on the riverbank and as good as the rest of those people down there. I wanted to be just like anybody else, and the drinking helped me because I didn't have to think about those feelings, that I wasn't good enough. When I had a drink in me, I felt that I was as good as the person I was sitting next to in the pub, or on the riverbank, anywhere I sat. I was as good as anyone.*

"What was/is being in a family like for you?"

Ben: *When I get questioned about family life, I don't feel that I ever had a family life. My idea about a family is two parents, brothers, sisters, aunties, uncles. Most of my life was me and my mother, and I wouldn't call that a family. I have never felt contentment, except when my first daughter was born and I thought I had a family, but I never felt I had a family life back then, and I don't feel I got one now.*

Mary: *My father, he wasn't a violent man—he just drank. He was a hard worker and there was always food on the table. He worked his guts out, but what he did was he drank and that was the closest he ever came to showing us love, when he had been drinking. When he had been drinking he would give us kids a bit of a cuddle, but real clumsy but it was a bit of a cuddle. I hated the smell of the grog on him so that's what I remember most about him, the grog on him and him falling over and Mum having to help him to bed and that, and people taking advantage of him, taking his money. But there was never violence to us kids. And I never saw them, my parents, have a fight like what happened to me after I got married.*

Don: *I got family problems. My family don't understand. A lot of my people [in this town], especially my family—my family— helped my emotions to be blocked up. When I went and stole, they laughed at me. When I got disciplined, they laughed. When I first got drunk, they wanted to know where I got the grog from so they could have some. When I went and stole the money, my family wanted a little bit of that money so they could go and buy drugs and they could go and buy alcohol. They never disciplined me in whichever way, and then I got so uncontrollable that one family couldn't hack me any more, and they would pass me on like a football, to the next family and they would pass me on, when this one has had enough of me, enough of my carrying-ons and my silly ways, my madness that was in my head, when they had finished with me, they would pass me on again until I was going around in the circle, around in the circle, and I just kept getting passed from* *family to family. Yeah—chaos—that was me, going this way and that way—didn't know which direction half the time. I became like that—uncontrollable. Basically four–five families but all the time —all at various times, sometimes from one to another and back to the other. It was like a big circle—just being moved around all the time. I stopped living with Mum probably because she was still drinking and she was never home, she was working as a barmaid at one of the pubs. And each family member I got passed on to, they either were drugging on, thieving themselves, or they were drinking—what kind of life is that for a kid, especially a black kid?*

Len: *The family rules in my family came from my dad. Yeah, my father was a very strong powered person. I can see where it comes from, my grandfather. We had a lot of rules in the house, very strict and powerful man in a lot of ways, and if the rules weren't kept, he got obsessed after a while. I get into that too, like chewing with your mouth open. Once I hit a man chewing an apple with his mouth open. Crazy, eh. But in our house, you couldn't leave the table until everything on your plate was gone, and I can remember eating brussels sprouts and tripe and force-feeding it down my throat until I vomited cos I couldn't leave the table until I had eaten it.*

Don: *With my father's side, there were practically no rules. Just get dressed for school. With my mother's side the law was really laid down. My mother's family sent me to a home when I was a young boy, a children's home, I don't know why, I still don't know why. They said it was for a holiday but it wasn't any holiday. I didn't like it there and I tried to run away.*

Ben: *I grew up with my mum and we were close sometimes, but it was hard because we moved a lot. Mum did a lot of geographicals. We never had a place of our own. We always lived with other people. I went to every school in [our town] and heaps in Brisbane. We would have had more than twenty moves when I was a child. As I was getting older I was very restricted, yet in another way there were no rules.*

Len: *I can sit and talk to my mum these days. She listens now. Before, she always wanted to listen but maybe it was me, eh. I always wanted to talk. My dad came down to see me a couple of weeks ago and I was really scared of him, being sober and straight. How were we going to get on? But I think the gap is starting to come together now. My mum and me, we can talk things through, but my dad, I find it very hard to talk to him one on one, cos we still blow up with each other. We can't be in the room more than ten minutes and it's just a total disaster sometimes. I love my father greatly but there are things that need to occur, are starting to occur, there has to be a healing. We can sit on the phone and chat like normal but before there wasn't a relationship, five–ten minutes and we would be at each other's throats.*

Don: *With Dad—I feel that Dad—he doesn't have a great understanding in what I experienced. He still believes what his brothers and sisters believe, that I had a nervous breakdown, that I was going crazy, that I lost my mind, that I was going womba. They've always believed I was womba from the time I was a little kid. When you get a three-year-old kid walking 500 yards from his mother's place to his grandparents' place just to have a yarn and a cup of tea before they go to work, at the age of three years old. They said I was womba because I did things like that. Because I played with myself—playing games, always by myself, talking to myself. When somebody would leave I would cry, the emotions of not seeing them again even if they were just going down to the shop, I was thinking "that person is leaving me now", the shock, and because I cried they thought I was mad, bad. And when something went wrong, even when I didn't do it, I had that guilt feeling, that I did it. I don't know why. And my father's mob, to this day, they glad I got off that alcohol, the drugs, but they won't look through the skin and find out why and how, because they are afraid of what they'll find.*

Jackie: *Being in my family, in some ways it was good, and it was bad. I wanted the love of my parents and I never felt that I got it because they didn't show any love towards me. I was never told that* *they loved me and I was never hugged. And I desperately needed that. I had always worked really really hard to please them and try and get that love. It was kinda just how it was I think back then— they were working hard—my mother worked as well. Although there was those feelings and the things that went along with it, but the other thing that came out of being in a family like that was that we had complete freedom. When we came home from school, there was no one home, and so my brother and I would just take off down the lands and the streams and just play and so I had a good free childhood with my brother. It was just the other part that was really missing that I really needed. As children we gave each other loving —we would all sit on the settee or laying on the bed and we would all be facing one way and we would all scratch each other's backs and we would time it, would scratch for five minutes or so and then the one in the middle would have to go to the far end so each one got a turn of being in the middle and would get two scratches in a row. I never really thought of it as nurturing and loving until you said that, but we liked the scratches and the touching. In the relationship I had, I strove to get love and to please again, and for a couple of days I would be told that I was loved and I would begin to think, maybe he does love me, maybe I am lovable. But it would [be] two days at the very most, and it was all taken away again with the physical abuse and being told I was stupid and useless and no good. So it was like I was being given this love and it being taken away all the time, so I would still keep trying hard, hoping that if I tried hard enough it would be given and not taken away. I have no family—in the true sense of the word—but I have made friends with people, I'm building a family. It's still hard, for although I consider some people family, because the blood tie is not there, you don't know whether it can survive the turmoil of relationships. I still feel the isolation of being alone.*

Lorna: *Back in the drinking days, I don't think you could say we had a relationship. Maybe you could say it was more or less because of the littlies, the babies, that we were together. There really wasn't much of a relationship because I had a lot of trouble in my marriage earlier, with having to live with my mother-in-law and my brother-*

in-law. I felt I never really ever had a husband to myself. I was sharing him with his mum and his brother. They were always with me, and that was a part of my drinking also, because I needed to have my own home, to have my own family around me. I realised a long time ago that this was the way it had to be, with my mother-in-law and brother-in-law, and I've accepted it. I had to or I'd die drinking. And that was my own choice. I made my own choice. I decided I would accept that, simply because I needed to be with my husband and my family. They were more important to me than the drinking and if it meant that I had to have other people in the house, then so be it. And that decision only came to me when I put down the drink. It's changed heaps with my children now I have put down the drink. When I was drinking I didn't have a relationship with them at all because my husband and my mother-in-law were with them most of the time because I was drinking down the river-bank. I never had much contact with my children at all in them days. There were times when I was a good mum and I was home for three weeks and I would bath them and play with them and look after them. I'd be there for a couple of weeks and then I would be off again and they would be left with the grandmother and father. We were like strangers. I would come home from a drinking spree—three or four weeks on the drink and I would come home and these babies would peep in the door to see this woman lying on the bed, you know, "Is that our mum?" I never liked the kids coming into the room when I was home, cos I felt they were just coming in to look at what I looked like so they could run up and tell their grand-mother. I used to hurt them and chase them and tell them I didn't want them around. After going through rehabilitation and not drinking, I came home and needed to build the bridges with my children. There were times when I didn't think they would ever forgive me. I guess there is still stuff in them that comes up for them at times, but all I want to be today is the best person I can be. I have a different relationship with them—I like to think it is different. It's a long way better than it ever was. I can say that today. So now I have a fairly good relationship with my two sons and daughter— my two daughters-in-law. Very close relationship today.

Don: *Mum is very good. She is very understanding because she has gone through the same things I've gone through, a spiritual awakening. When she was going through it, I thought she was mad [laughs] because she was, I thought she was crazy. She had all these sicknesses, she was scared to go outside, she was scared to be locked up, she didn't want to sleep in her own room, she didn't know where she was, and I didn't know where she was either, and I thought I had better get out of this place in case this woman does something to me. But she got through it and she is a lot happier in herself. And when I realised what I went through I went back to her and I said, "Mum, I had a spiritual awakening. I wasn't going off my head. I wasn't having a nervous breakdown. I was having a spiritual awakening and nobody told me. Why didn't anybody tell me?" I'm still asking. But some things you learn spiritually, in quiet communion. It's not like they come up to you and say "hello" and pass all this wisdom and knowledge on to you on a silver platter. It's not like that. It's when people say to you "Gee, that's a coincidence" and you know it was meant to be. Things like that. Coincidences are meant to happen. They are spiritual things.*

"Can you talk about feelings?"

Lorna: *I would wake up with the fear. I used to have heaps and heaps of dreams. Especially when I was drinking, the fear in me was full on. I'd be sleeping, sick from the booze, the shakes and stuff from my childhood, like my sexual abuse stuff would come up. I guess it's like a movie—it's all in front of you, happening all over again, and the fear of it takes over your whole body and you're hiding and running, yeah, running running forever. Oh, in my dreams I ran full of fear, always looking back behind. The days when I was getting over the drink, the feelings came back—the fear, Jeez, I haven't thought about these things for ages. I've never put them into words like this.*

Don: *Jealousy—they call it the green devil. The fear I would feel that she would leave and what would I be then. She would talk to somebody else, she would just look at somebody, walk past* *somebody, and inside me would be a big jumble of feelings that would twist and turn and I would hate her for thinking she could just walk out on me, and would be frightened she was going to go and I would get angry, why wasn't I good enough for her? Crazy thinking, heh. But I tell you, no matter how many times she told me she loved me and would never leave me, all I ever knew was that she was going to find somebody better than me and she would go. I drove her away with my jealousy.*

Len: *A lot of little things trigger me, scary things. Like times when I've gone fishing, fifty yards from the car, no light and I have to leave because I'm so scared. I just run. Frantic, a frantic run. I'm not scared from the … I'm sober and real scared—I don't know what it is … I just run and run, it's feelings but I don't know where it's coming from. Yet other times I can't feel anything. I never feel close to anybody like a friend or like my mum or dad. You see families that are close. Well, I've never felt that. I have friends. But it's just I can't seem to feel anything. It's like I'm dead. I've never been able to feel any deep feelings except scared. When I get into a relationship with a girl, I usually hang onto that like it's my last chance at life, and yet the word love, I don't know what that means. I've never had a relationship with a woman that has been successful. I don't know how to have a relationship. I suppose it's always been me that has scared them off, my drinking and such. My drinking and drugging played a lot of problems, and a lot of the time they were drinking and drugging too, so how could we have had a good relationship, eh?*

Ben: *When I see or hear anything that reminds me of my past, I feel very concerned, very angry about it, because it sickens me to know that it still happens today. I don't know what the rate was at my age, but it seems to be getting worse all the time. I feel for a lot of people out there who have been through the same thing as me. Now I am an adult I have never experienced sexual violence. I won't allow that sort of thing now, never. When there is physical violence around me or I hear loud noises I feel upset but I don't feel frightened. I can hold my own now.*

Lorna: *There are still things that set me off even in my sobriety. There was one morning recently I came in here and a young fella here was getting a cup of tea and I came in and said, "Good morning, everyone" and started to get my cup of tea, and he pointed to his watch and said, "You're supposed to be here at nine o'clock" and straight away I felt that thing in me like "Don't tell me what to bloody do." It took me back. I get really sensitive about things like that and something in me came up because I remember my dad spoke to me like that. And my husband. These feelings came up for me in a big flood. We talked about it later on and I admitted to this young man, he was only joking cos we don't run to a timetable here, and I admitted that I am very sensitive about things like that because it presses buttons for me. So there are things that can still trigger me even today.*

Jackie: *When I am talking to you like this I can't go into the feelings of it—I've never been allowed to feel the feelings of it—the feelings sometimes are overwhelming—the continual pain of how someone could hurt me like this, is with me all the time. When I do release it and start to cry, it is for a confusion of things and it gets mixed up in my mind and I can't analyse it or name it because it is all confused. I never told anyone about the early instance in my life or I never told anyone about how my husband treated me until you. My family, my mum or dad, my brothers or sisters—they, I never spoke to them about it they still don't know to this day. Then after I split up from my husband I started to talk to someone about it and it was good, but they were only there for a few hours and then they went away, I had just started to open up a bit and they left. It was like I had opened the door and it couldn't be closed again and everything that was inside of me was trying to come out. I just couldn't handle it, there was so much of it. I was really depressed and upset all the time and I just didn't really know what to do or how to handle it. Alcohol and drugs have never been a problem in my life. I never used them to handle my problems. I have never drank or smoked. When I got really depressed and started to open up and I went to the doctor and he put me on drugs for depression and I found these made me worse. I had never, never considered* suicide until I went on these drugs. It was kind of something that was always in my mind after that. I thought of suicide—it was always there in the back of my mind. There was a lot of pressures on me, financial, obligations to other people, and sometimes I just don't know if I can cope with it, or whether it is worth hanging around to cope with it. With feelings—I feel really high fear a lot, but now most of the times it would be okay. It takes things to trigger it. Most times fear would be triggered if I thought someone was angry at me. The fear comes and I would get really upset. It was fear I was feeling on Saturday when I almost blacked out when you were talking to me because I thought you were angry with me. The feeling of being anxious is really high but most times I can block it out, all the responsibilities, and then it would get on top of me and I would feel really anxious about things that were happening. Today I am contented a lot when I am out driving around the animals, I feel really contented and other times it would drop right down it would go back to being really anxious when I am with people. It swings a great deal from being contented and anxious, fearful. Big swings. When you asked the question about love—I was thinking that you can't trust humans to love. My ex would give love for a day or so and then take it away. But with animals, once you have earned their trust, they do love you no matter what you do, who you are. They just love. I cried a lot when I first started talking about it. The smallest thing would make me cry. But now I have more control over it. I cry when I feel hurt or when someone I love is hurting me. I have nightmares which are really frightening. I had one recently where this guy I know sent these people, two other men, after me, and they get into my house, it's a lonely place, and they torture and rape me, and I feel really churned up and anxious about it and I'm afraid, and I know it's not reality but I still feel uneasy that it could be more than a dream. "Was there anything in the guy that reminded you of something, that could have triggered that dream?" He's got a lot of anger in him and he is abusive and he frightens me because of that.

Ben: I was a very negative person. I lost faith in myself on a number of occasions. I felt very hopeless and I couldn't have cared *less about what was happening to me. I'm pretty much able to feel everything now but there was a time when I felt nothing. Now I cry a lot. Never stop now. My feelings are like a roller-coaster. I always worry. I worried a lot about everything. It's been more of an eating disorder for me. When I worry I don't eat. Sometimes I feel happy but most times I am miserable. I feel sad lots of the time. I feel angry all the time. Lots and lots of anger. I couldn't love. I couldn't. Not the way I was feeling. I didn't know how. I am always fearful. I feel lots of hate, all the time, really intense, sometimes for no reason. I never feel contentment, except when my first daughter was born and I thought I had a family. I was very, very depressed when I first met you. I did two workshops which helped me to make up my mind I had a drinking problem. I had to do something so I moved into the house [Halo House]—I was starting to get the shakes before I moved into the house, the trembles. I was suicidal and very depressed and I was really frightened of losing control, especially when I drank because I would just—I had all this anger inside me and I was getting into all these fights all the time, but I was also afraid all the time. That was the only time when I got into fights, when I was drinking. I was afraid of my actions when I'd been drinking. There was one time when I was really going to do a person some harm, and I asked somebody to come with me because I was afraid I would go too far.*

Len: *I used to have no interest in what was happening around me. When I was drinking, I couldn't give a damn. Sometimes I go back to it, you know, when it's a really hairy day, but I know I can't just give up now because things are starting to change but before it was just, couldn't give a damn, you know. I still feel sad and angry lots of time, and fear a lot of the time for reasons I don't understand. I suddenly get really anxious, and get a massive headache and the runs [diarrhoea]. Loud noises. I duck sometimes, feel a bit stupid, my heart runs and I get agitated and I have to get out. I get angry and I've got to get out. I still have to lock everything, the front door, the back door, the windows. It's not as bad as it used to be because I'm owning up to a lot of things inside me, but I can remember a stage where I would double-check windows, double-check them, and*

sometimes I would sleep with a shotgun. Don't know why I was so
scared, but I was scared. Something was coming. Now if there is a
fight I get out, get away as quick as I can, now that I am sober.
After I came out of rehab, I used to cry every day, but now it's
getting less. I cried for months and months and months, when I
first came out.

Lorna: *I've had feelings for a lot of my life that I am not part of
anything. I'm here but I'm not taking in anything that's around
me. I have whole days when the numbness sets in, like yesterday I
sat in the group and shared that I didn't feel anything for anyone
and talked about it, and then I have days when I feel everything
around me. For the last couple of days I've not been interested in
what's been going on around me at all, and I feel guilty because I'm
part of this house but I couldn't care less. But I know it will pass.
Before I stopped drinking I can never remember feeling happy or
contented or love for anything, but lots and lots of sadness, lots and
lots of anger and fear and hate—I hated everyone and was jealous
and suspicious, but after I stopped drinking, those feelings
changed. After I got sober I cried and cried, and I'm still a good
crier. Loud noises still frighten me. My heart goes ten to the dozen
and I feel shaky and I want to run. In the old days I would get
under the bed or just put heaps of blankets on me and lay as still as
I could, trying not even to breathe so that nobody, whoever it was
that was in the fights, would know that I was there. I would get in
a cupboard or under the bed. Today if I hear a loud noise I might get
a quick heart beat but now I'll go and investigate it today. For most
of my life I have been very, very depressed. I would be in the darkest
depressed state anyone could get in. It was like a great big black
hole and no one could help me. At the same time I would feel very
anxious. Couldn't eat. Didn't have much weight. I think I was
about five stone. I would sick it all up, and my heart would go ten
to the dozen. I used to run out on the street like a mad woman and
just scream abuse at these people in my home, my mother-in-law
and brother-in-law, my husband and my children. I always feared I
would lose all control, go right over the edge and kill someone, yet
there was something talking to me, in the back of my head saying,*

"You can do this, but you won't ever get away with it. They will lock you away. Just remember if you stab your husband, if you damage your son you will be punished. You will be jailed, locked away." There was that fear of not wanting to be locked away because I was locked away many many times for my drinking, in 3C [the mental health unit at the local hospital]. I didn't like that feeling. "Did they help you in there?" No. Most of the times I was given tablets. I was sedated. I remember on the veranda waiting for my husband one day and I didn't know it at the time, but he says he came through the door and he said, "Hello sweet, how are you going?" and he says I said to him, "Oh, hello. I don't trust too many men, but you look like a nice man so I'll talk to you. I'm just waiting for my husband and babies to come." I don't remember that but he says that is more or less what I said. He was very upset and went and spoke to the head doctor. I was just so pumped up with tablets. I didn't like that feeling either because I wasn't in control of anything. People would lead me from one room to the next, to the toilet. I didn't like that. There was nothing I could do about it because I was bombed out of my brain. It didn't help me. "Did they sit and talk to you about the kind of things we are talking about now?" Oh no. I was just given tablets and at one stage, I'm not too sure, but they wanted me to have—oh shit, I haven't thought about this for years—they wanted me to have shock treatment. Yeah, but my hubbie just refused. Just as well I had him there to say No. Thank God for my man.

Len: I used to be really scared of losing control. But today I have worked on a lot of my anger, and I don't get to that point of losing control like I used to. Today I know where to go and what to do if things start to get really bad. It's only been four–five months since I felt like that. I've been sober twelve months now, but that kind of feeling of losing it, is starting to dwindle away.

Don: When there are loud voices I just feel like taking off, running, just getting away from that place and not being able to hear it, but that's no good either. When I was a kid, I had a real fear of the window, scared of the window, sleep with my face away from the *window, with my back towards the window. I thought because I was having all these nightmares, it came from the window—the nightmares came from the window. They'd say the boogie man's at the window, he's going to get you tonight, and I thought all these nightmares were coming through the window.*

Ben: *I have real difficulty sleeping. Even now I can't get to sleep before twelve and I go to sleep and if I am feeling stressed, something bothering me, I can't get to sleep until 2 o'clock. I wouldn't be able to get to sleep until late, and I would wake up early. I always wake up early between 5 to 6 a.m. I find it hard to remember what I dream about because I am so worn out, fatigued, stressed out that I go into a deep, deep sleep.*

Len: *I still have trouble sleeping. I'm thirty-five years old and sometimes, last week, heh, I had to sleep with my light on again. My bedroom, most of the time I sleep facing the door and I wake up in the middle of the night and I am so scared that I rush out to turn the light on and I go out and sit and watch TV. I used to have a lot of trouble to get to sleep. Sometimes I wouldn't sleep for two days. But now I get to sleep around twelve … two o'clock in the morning and I wake up early, I don't have so much trouble. I've always had problems—I just can't get to sleep.*

Mary: *Do I ever have nightmares? [laughs] I used to—my whole life was a bloody nightmare. Like how can I explain—I could never make out what was real and what was a dream but even when I was a kid I had bad nightmares, always the same kind of dream, and it's only in the last few years that those kind of dreams have stopped. Sometimes I think that I'm crazy and one day they'll lock me up.*

Don: *I was wanting to get off the grog so I come down to Halo House to the AA meeting to talk to somebody. Auntie was there doing some paintings that particular day. She said, "Sit down and have a bit of a talk. They are not having an AA meeting—they are having a bit of a yarn—but sit down with them." So I sat down and listened to them. After, they gave me a lift home and asked me if I* wanted to come to the next AA meeting, but before that my grandfather, Wednesday morning, he took sick and we put him into hospital. He collapsed in the toilet and I carried him from the toilet into the bedroom. He felt as light as a feather. I could lift him with one arm. Then I had to carry him from the bedroom into the dining room, but I couldn't lift him, he was like a wardrobe, real heavy, too heavy for me. I had to get help. The little bit of CPR we gave him, Grandfather's got a hole in his throat [he had had throat cancer] and we knew if we blew through his mouth, it would just come out his throat. We couldn't get his heart going and the ambulance people pronounced him dead before they got him to the hospital. But a nurse came in and said, "Hey, this man's heart is still going here." And he was in hospital for a while in a coma and the spiritual awakening started happening to me then.

My body—during that time, my body was doing crazy things. I thought I was going off my head. The things that were happening to me were unbelievable. I tried to accept it but I thought I was going off my head. I was walking up the big hills, up to the hospital and I wasn't even tired. I wasn't puffing. My legs weren't tired. I was taking a shower, I got gumbi leaves and I was rubbing them on my body, but I felt I wasn't rubbing my own body, it wasn't my body. I was standing in front of the mirror and my legs started twisting, you know, like in shake a leg and it wasn't my mind telling them to twist. Something was happening and I didn't know what it was. Sometimes I felt like I was floating, not just part of my body but my whole body, was floating over the ground, yet I knew my feet were on the ground.

About that time, they said I was schizophrenic. I got sent to a doctor. He didn't want to listen to me. Life experience. That's what these doctors haven't got—these psychiatrists haven't got—life experiences. And they expect sick people to go to them and listen to them, talk with them, and psychiatrists sitting there, "Yes—yes— yes—true—well this is what you should do. Take this tablet in the morning and this tablet at night-time." I just wanted somebody to listen to me, to explain to me what was happening. My auntie and my cousin, they saw me one day when I was walking down the street and they knew I needed help, and I was talking to them and they said it was up to me. I could go to that doctor to the hospital, or I could move into Halo House. I made that choice. I moved into Halo House. That is what helped me the most, being in that safe place, that healing place.

I feel I've always been a spiritual person. I believe in spirits coming to you to give you guidance. Even when I was on the drugs and alcohol, I always had a great belief in my ancestors and the old ways. I believed personally it was his [Grandfather's] time to go. But he didn't go. He hung around. I feel when the uncles found out I was going to AA, they were yarning on like they usually do, and Grandfather must have heard about it and he probably thought, "Well now, one of the grandsons is getting off the poison." Grandfather's job on this earth had been done and it is time for him to move on. But he wouldn't go. He was in a coma, but it felt like he was trying to make the family strong before he did go.

I believe my spirit can contact his spirit or any other spirit that I want to contact. I used to go and talk to him in the hospital. My family, they thought I was silly. But a doctor told me "He can hear you" so I started taking dadirri up there and the relaxation meditations I learnt in Halo House. I started sending healing power to him so he could see the light and I asked my Creator, Moonda Nghadda, my God, my Rainbow Serpent to guide him towards the light because Nan was on the other side waiting for him. It took seven weeks before this happened, before he could see the light and go to it.

You know, it's still unbelievable but I've got to believe it because I've seen and experienced spirituality within my life. They say it's a spiritual awakening, and that's what I've got to believe it was because Grandfather was there to make us all strong for him. The real old people [the ancestors] and Grandfather and Nan,[1] they think it great what I am doing. Especially Grandfather. He's the one that has shown me how to dance spirituality, passing the spiritual wisdom and knowledge down in the meditations in the mornings to me. I wouldn't have been able to do it without his help and the help of youse all. All my life I've been dreaming—dreaming about being

1 All these people are dead, but they are still real to this person and he regularly communicates with them.

like my ancestors, not fifty years ago, or two hundred years ago. I don't want to be like them ancestors. I wanted to be like the thousands of fifty years ago when my ancestors used to heal themselves—go out bush—let all their energies out in the bush—and heal themselves. I want to be like them ancestors.

"Can you talk about healing, what does it mean?"

Don: *The reason why I came here was because I had to make a decision whether I would go into hospital and be pumped up with drugs and have the psychiatric doctors try to make me well again, or come down to Halo House. I knew people here. Some of the people here had been in the same kind of experiences I was going through. My cousin, and my aunty, tribal way, gave me a choice to either come here or stay up at the hospital. I made the choice. I knew I had to go into Halo House if I was going to get well. The best thing about Halo House is I feel safe here. I know it's a safe place for me. And there are people who don't live here but come here with my medicine. My medicine is people who will listen to me, like you and Uncle, when I want to talk about what is happening to me, with my spirituality. These people understand what I am going through. My medicine is listening to other people too. First time I was in the meeting like this, and I listened to the others talking, I thought they were talking about my life, their experiences were like my experiences. Their feelings were like my feelings. They were stealing my story—I wanted to know how did they know my story and what it felt like to be me?*

Here, I've learnt that it's good for me to cry and let out my anger in a way that doesn't hurt myself or other people—that it's good to be mad, silly, womba. I found out a lot about my spirituality. It has always been there but it just needed to come out. The dancing. I never thought I could dance until six weeks ago, when I was told I could. I didn't know no movements. I didn't know nothing about dancing, about shaking my leg—where to put my feet, I didn't know nothing until I did a healing workshop with We Al-li. I feel safe in the workshops. Before, when I was in the TAFE college and we used to go down to the Haven, we would smoke yarndie when we were there and doing college work. Nothing ever worked for me when I was in that state. I always thought the yarndie was giving me this power and ideas to put in my paintings but eventually it just got me down, just dried me up.

Mary: *After the first workshop I went home and that night I had this dream. I wrote it in the journal you said to keep. I am camping with a group of desert women and we are watching children play as we talk together. The children are beautiful fat babies who keep crawling all over the place. They keep crawling down into a river which is muddy and turbulent, flowing fast and full of rocks and tree limbs being tumbled in the current, and the babies keep falling in. I am frantically rescuing them while the women are just watching and letting it happen. I am angry at the women—"Come on", I am calling at them, "We have to stop these kids from drowning." A woman gets up to help me and she too falls in and is swept away. Another woman tries to help her and she too becomes a victim of this river. Finally, because I have pushed the women, they all get washed away and I am running around frightened and alone still trying to rescue the babies. A white man comes and watches—he is some kind of administrator and he is just watching and does not care that people are dying. I get on a piece of timber to try to help rescue the babies and the women and I get three little fat babies to safety but the women are gone and it is as if their life is of no consequence, a natural thing and life goes on without them. I feel all alone. I am terrified of the river, what it could do to me if I fall in, because it goes down a big opening in the ground and I am really frightened of this. I wake up crying and as I lay in bed thinking about it, I realise how exhausted I feel and ask myself why I am always trying to rescue people all the time, and begin to understand how angry I feel because they are not doing what I think they should be doing.*

Jackie: *After I split with my ex I went into a deep black hole for about four months—depression. I couldn't see any way out of it. Then I realised how nice it was to be free. I seemed okay for a while but a couple of years later I knew I was in trouble and that I would* have to start talking to someone but when someone came who I could trust and I started to talk they weren't there long enough but once I started to talk I couldn't shut the door. I had no control over all the stuff that was coming up. The feelings were just flooding and everything was just overwhelming me. I'd got really depressed and I'd been to a doctor who put me on anti-depressants but they made me worse. They seemed to make me suicidal. I had never thought of suicide before.

I went to a psychologist and talking to him was okay. He was a quiet, gentle type of person but he talked way above my head about things I couldn't grasp and couldn't understand, about spirit. I had no concept what he was talking about. It didn't seem to relate in any way to my problem or the things I needed to talk about. He wasn't really into the story of what was behind why I was feeling like I was. He said the story didn't matter. He was into, if you believed in spirit and your inner-self and not let your mind, which was just a computer, guide you down the wrong path. He said you should be following your innermost thoughts, and if you could just relax, spirit would heal. I was really trying to understand what he was trying to put across to me, and I did understand in one way, but I wasn't in a place where I could put into practice what he was trying to say even if I could understand it. You have to be in a certain stage through the pain before you can allow things to just work themselves out. It was just not possible. The other voices I had, of being no good, of being bad, I had no concept really, who I was. I'd been in a relationship for over twenty years. I didn't go into any of the stories, the detail of the abuse I had experienced. I told him it had been physically abusive, but he said the story didn't matter anyway. I just had no real concept. I was really mixed up and I didn't know really, who I was. I'd been controlled and manipulated for so long that I didn't know who I was or what the real me was. I couldn't separate what bits of me were really me, and what bits had been formed by pressures from outside. So I applied to get into the We Al-li program.

The first workshop was the best—that's when I started to understand about myself and how you had to look at your story, about how you became who you are. It was the safest workshop. It was where we bonded into a family and I felt a really good feeling at the end of the workshop that I had met this really good group of people and that we were all moving in the same direction. There were people who I could talk to, who would listen to me. And I knew that talking would help me find out the bits of me that were really me and the bits of me that were not really me.

Talking in the circle was the most important thing for me, also the painting—which I didn't think I would be able to do—but that was very important. It helped me express myself in a different way besides words. It made me see different sides to me that I didn't know about. It was something I could do that was uninhibited, whereas other things that were in the workshops I felt silly and I didn't want to do them.

Healing is a really confusing word. When I first thought of it I thought I would go along and all this pain was going to be healed and at the finish I would just walk away and I would be healed, but now I know healing means learning. Learning about yourself—learning about looking at things in a different way. Understanding how those things came to be. Owning your own things, but not taking on board other people's things. Being responsible for what you are responsible for, but not for other people's responsibilities. Learning how to deal with different situations—how to interact with people—how to lessen conflict—seeing your own things differently.

Ben: I had done two workshops at The Haven and I would have to say before I did the workshops I was very, very depressed. I done the two workshops and that's what helped me to make up my mind that I had a drinking problem. You know what I was like at the first workshop—suicidal—very depressed and it was the workshop that helped me feel I could do something for myself and so I moved into Halo House and kept coming to these workshops.

Mary: You know, I don't think most Murri people have any idea about healing. A lot of people I know think healing is just going to the doctor and getting fixed up—getting some pills or something like that. Or getting somebody else to do something for them. Faith *healers—religion—stuff like that. Saddest thing is they don't even realise that they've got all the coping mechanisms, and they've been healing themselves all these years. If this was pointed out to them, things would really start to happen. They would build on it, because they know things are wrong, but they just don't know what to do about it. What I've learnt is, healing is facing up to the fact that you've got choices, and there is no need to live all your life in this pain. You can always get out of it. Yeah, just knowing that fact is a healing thing itself, and it shifts you from that place you have been in all the time, and you never thought you could get out of. You just accepted it, you know, you can't change anything. One of the things I've learnt in the workshops—the pain isn't a bad thing, even though it might seem like a really bad thing. Going into the pain was some of the best learning experiences I've ever had. You go back into the most shittiest experience, and afterwards you realise that if it hadn't happened you wouldn't be who you are, you wouldn't have grown.*

Lorna: *Healing happened when I realised I had to look to myself. I had spent half my bloody life looking at my husband and trying to get him to change, his family and my family, and the only time the changes began to come was when I put down the drink and started to have a really good look at me. There were things in the rehab that I started to like about myself, things that I never did like, [grins] my ankles! I still have a little thing about that, but seriously, being black—being black. For a long time I never ever wanted to be a black woman. It was just too painful. Putting down the drink helped and then I was able to take a good look at myself and change happened. My attitude toward my marriage, my husband, me. I realise today that I am only in control of me. I am not in control of my husband or my children or other people. I can't control them and I am not responsible for them, only for myself.*

Len: *When I walked into the first We Al-li workshop I thought I'll go with the flow. To be truthful I was looking for a spiritual thing, like the church. Then once we got into it, it was far different than what I had expected. I was looking for something really spiritual* *and cultural, I thought so anyway, and I thought, in the work-shops, we would be talking about what was spiritual. What we talked about was ourselves. Ourselves!! Yeah! It really opened my eyes. It was a big turn-around for me when I began to understand that we are sacred beings. It was spiritual but not in a church way and it was cultural but it taught us about ourselves today. Yeah. That was good.*

Lorna: *The word healing—it means to me [that] I need to look at all my pain. Feel the pain and release it. Work with it, talk about it, and let it go, rather than holding on to it, locking it up inside myself. I need to have a safe place where I can talk about my pain, all the pain that I have had in my life, my drinking in my marriage, my childhood, to be able to sit and feel free enough to talk about it to get it out of me. I had it in me for so long, too long. I believe that's when the healing takes place, when I can feel well enough in myself to talk honestly about how I feel, what happened to me, what it was like for me. It is action healing. That is what I found for myself. It is action. I can sit around and talk about healing, but I had to do the work to make it happen, and it was, it is, hard work because it means for me, to go to the workshop like We Al-li where I can clean out that pain and I do it, the action is called for.*

Don: *It seems like a dream now. Mother Earth and everything about her seemed to be within me from when I can first remember. Aboriginality, culture, corroboree, paintings, music, singing, dance—not that I could do these things then. But I know now they were in me. In 1996 we knew Grandfather was getting old, we knew it was time for him to go. I used to come home from the nightclubs and Grandfather would be awake because he was an early riser, 4 or 5 o'clock in the morning. This was before he had his last collapse and went into the coma. Just before he died he said to me, "If you ever want to get yourself well again, get yourself better, you do whatever you need to do. Don't worry about anybody else. Do what you have to do for yourself to make yourself well." And that's what I'm doing now.*

Ben: *I really enjoy the workshops. Sometimes they get a bit hard because they stir a lot up inside me but I know it will benefit me to stay with it. At the time it is a bit stressful but I know the workshops are sort of like a lifeline. When I came to the workshops I had feelings—for the first time ever—feelings of security, of safety. After the first workshop I knew I had to come back because I needed more. They, the feelings, the easing of all the pain and anger and all that—it's really given me new life, more than anything else. It's sort of like a new beginning, being able to deal with all that stuff I've carried for so long. I love them—I really enjoy all the closeness, the sharing with the other people. That was my problem. All my life I sort of felt, nobody ever really cared about me but since I've been in the workshops, I've met other people that also have problems and they share the same pain, the same anger and we all care for each other. It makes me feel good because I know I am wanted. I feel a part of something. It's just given me new life.*

Jackie: *Today I think differently than I did two years ago. How I perceive myself is different today. I always had a certain fear of myself that I thought other people held as well, and so I was still in that frame of mindset where I had to please everybody. I was always apologising for things before they happened, and I never thought I was good or smart, or that I could stand my ground with anyone. I've looked at all those things and have a better understanding of them. I've been able to overcome a lot of my negative beliefs. I know I've got a long way to go, but I've shifted from a totally negative person to feeling some positive things about myself. The change in me is all tied up with self-concept. Now I don't see myself so negatively. I suppose it's about believing in yourself. Part of it also is when you name the story, when you start to accept the story that has made you, you can hear all the words that you tell yourself, the jumble of words that have been how you put yourself down and under those words you start to hear and know the other part of you that has always been there. As you find out who you really are, you start to believe in yourself, and that's healing.*

Len: *The best thing about the workshops was seeing other people that you thought "I got to watch myself with him—he's been there—done that", but being there with him and being allowed to see him doing it—his story coming out and seeing that you don't have to be a big man or tough. Sometimes I would look around and see people and it really amazed me what came out of people [who] I thought would just hang onto it. When I first got there, sussing a few people out, I thought, "Nothing will ever come out of this fellow", and what came out of people has opened my eyes a lot. I been in a lot of rehabs but this, how it came out, it flowed out, it wasn't forced out, it came out naturally and it was allowed to come out in a real sacred way. There's a difference between allowing something to come out and bringing it out. I've seen that a lot in rehabs and when you talk to psychiatrists. You have to think it out. But in the workshops, it just flowed out, it came from the heart, and it was a heart healing. It didn't come from the head.*

Summary

Within this group narrative, which demonstrates *dadirri* in action, is potent courage, clear insight and great wisdom. The words on the pages belong to those people whose stories provide a deeper understanding of acts of violence experienced as traumatisation, and how such experiences shape people and the relationships that are formed both on an individual level and at the group level. After I had put the chapter together, I copied it and sent it to each of those whose stories make up the complete narrative, for their comments. They rang me or wrote to me with further comments. It is appropriate that this chapter closes with impressions gained as one of the group made comment on what she read.

Jackie: *[I read of] a group of kids all sitting together and playing under a big tree. Happy kids. Good kids. Clean pure kids. One at a time we all get up and go away, some for a few minutes, some for hours. When we are all back together, we are all different. We have changed. The laughter has gone. Our innocence, the very protection of childhood has been stolen. We all feel afraid, not good* *enough, even dirty. Our confidence has gone, replaced by self-doubt and insecurity. ... [I also read of] people sitting together in a healing circle, maturing through their stories, realising change only comes if they make it come. I learnt it is only possible to change myself. No one else. Change is hard work and painful. My changes started with Lifting the Blankets [the first workshop within We Al-li and the Indigenous Therapies Program]. Sharing stories, feeling strong, because of the support of others. Bonding into a family. Coming to know I was lovable. Learning we are all unique and important. Healing is regaining power over myself and not letting anyone else control me. Gaining confidence—being responsible. Conquering my fears and speaking out for what I believe in. I still need reassurance. Self-confidence is still a major battle. Changing and healing is painful, hard work. I don't know if the process ever ends, or if it gets easier as time passes. I just have to keep working at it.*

As people involve themselves in the sharing of their life experiences, they also share with each other—and in this instance, the reader—a shared deep learning, a collective insight and wisdom. The participants in this *dadirri* or We Al-li circle have shared here not just how violence affects human groups, but, more importantly, they demonstrate the first principles of healing from trauma. These are the creation of safe places for sharing where the unspeakable can be given voice, where feelings can be felt, and where sense can be made out of what seemed previously senseless.

Chapter Four

The Way of the Human Being I: The trauma story

I can't feel. I can't talk about it—if I did I'd get mad. I'd go really mad and kill someone.

Atkinson 1998: 7

As people reflected on and discussed their lived experiences a number of major themes emerged, which we will examine in this chapter. It exposes the links between the child, adolescent, and adult experiences of violence to traumatisation, listing the feelings and behaviours that have resulted to show that cyclic situations of repeated and compounding traumatisation and re-victimisation may result. The experiences, thoughts and feelings are all interconnected and cannot be separated from each other. What is important is to make the links, to name and know that present behaviours may be based in unresolved past experiences.

Trauma experiences, thoughts, feelings and behaviours

The narratives in the previous chapter outline a range of experiences which have resulted in feelings and thoughts, and resultant harmful behaviours which are invariably re-traumatising.

Experiences include: institutional racism; structural violence; constructed poverty; police violence; witnessing domestic violence; being sexually assaulted; being beaten as a child; being psychologically abused; having no experience of loving family relationships; mother–daughter conflict (relationships full of pain at generational child rape);

father–son conflict; being removed from family; experiencing adults drinking and fighting; having family members suicide; broken relationships; living in chaos—being told one thing and experiencing another; constant moving from places of pain.

Thoughts and feelings include: being black which meant never feeling good enough; feeling anxious, nervous, sad, angry, hate, jealousy, suspicious, sick, seesaw of fear (taking over whole body); anger; the need to punch, stab, kill; flooding with feelings; flashbacks (like a movie all in front of you happening again and again); not being part of anything; numb; never feeling happy, contented, loved or love; feeling depressed, bad, stupid, dirty, shame, ugly, useless, worthless, of no value; totally isolated; desolation is unbearable; stranger with family but part of the drinking group; wanting to die; constant feelings and thoughts around suicide.

Resultant behaviours or re-traumatising experiences were: drinking; misusing prescription and other drugs; screaming and ranting "like a mad woman" and being locked away; being charged with drunk and disorderly; being afraid of fights yet getting involved in constant fights when drunk; running and hiding; violence against children where smacking would turn to punching; knife at son's throat; loud noises triggering excessive reactions; eating disorders; being unable to establish and maintain stable loving relationships; when in a relationship, clinging to it "like it was a last chance at life" or wanting to kill the other; multiple suicide attempts; cutting or mutilating the self; working with and trusting animals but never trusting humans; isolating the self from society.

Don illustrates the complexity of compounding trauma: *We had a baby—I went to see the baby born. I did all the right things I could—but I suppose because I was doing drugs, the family came one day and took everything. It was the first time I cut myself. I just grabbed the serrated knife and sliced my arm a couple of times—fourteen times actually.* **I did it out of the pain to let her know that nothing can hurt me ... to show her how much**

I was hurting. When he went to a solicitor to obtain access to "his child" through the courts, he found there was a warrant out for his arrest on unpaid fines, so he had to turn himself in and serve out the warrant. Then the woman's solicitor demanded a DNA test, and Don found, after eighteen months of believing he was a father and wanting to be a good father, that the baby was not his. Three years after the birth of the child, and a year and a half after Don had learnt the child was not his, the Commonwealth government was still sending monthly demands for him to pay maintenance; this sent Don into further mental and emotional distress at serious, life-threatening levels. This has continued to compound in his life and has influenced all other relationships, including the birth of another child in another relationship, where for some time he would not accept that the baby was his.

Observed in isolation, his behaviour made no sense. Linked to other layers of experiences and trauma, the behaviour has meaning.

Self as inadequate consequent to child harm/trauma

All the participants describe having experienced different forms of violence as a child. When Jackie said, *we are a group of kids all sitting together and playing under a big tree. Happy kids. Good kids—clean pure kids,* she names the experience of feeling whole and being happy as a child. The childhood experiences of violence and trauma changed those feelings of well-being: *[now] we all feel afraid, not good enough, even dirty. Our confidence has been replaced by self-doubt and insecurity.* Jackie gives a powerful word picture of children changed by distressful and damaging early experiences that can only be described as traumatic.

Consequently participants have feelings and thoughts of inadequacy and insecurity that continue to influence their adult behaviour and therefore sustain the traumatisation. Experiences of commission range from witnessing racist violence on a parent; experiencing racist violence on themselves; witnessing violence by a father on a mother; witnessing violence on other family members; being abducted; being sexually assaulted; being subjected to excessive forms of physical punishment or physical violence (for example, crabbites); being subjected to psychological abuse (for example, wakened to perform poems and songs late at night). The experiences of omission range from living in constructed poverty; having little experience of loving family relationships—no hugs or loving touch; having little or no family support in times of abuse and being blamed for the abuse.

The experiences left scars that have lasted and continue into adulthood. Each person in this group, in their own way, came to feel themself as inadequate—*the greatest feeling I remember was of always trying to please people so I could be told I was good and wasn't stupid*; contaminated—*the feeling of not being good enough came from being black and never having enough and being good enough*; marked for life—*I felt like my life started and finished at that time.*

All the participants describe feeling and, to various extents, being unsafe and insecure in the world. The overall sense of childhood was described by the women as never being/feeling good enough—*I could never be good enough*; of an innate badness—*I was a bad person*; of being unclean and unlovable—*dirty ... untouchable ... nobody would want me.* Childhood was experienced by the men as a *fearful, frightening, lonely, shameful, unsafe,* place.

Lorna describes the memories, feelings and learning she acquired as she observed the racism of the institutional environment of the reserve where she grew up. *I remember what I seen as a child* (her father being subjected to racist abuse*); I remember the smell* (of the experience of being labelled dirty—the carbolic soap); *I remember our home* (the conflict of having a lovely home and a mother who was clean and caring, yet intruders entering the home to subject her mother to racist and demeaning inspections); *I remember Mum's face* (the powerlessness, shame and anger). Her biggest memory, however, is violence on herself, a violence that was both overt and covert. *My biggest memory was I wasn't good enough—I could never be as good as the white man.* This memory, and the feelings that are a part of it, are linked to the sexual abuse she experienced at the hands of an authority figure and the witnessing of physical violence on her father.

Even as a small child, Lorna feels and knows the injustice of the situation but she feels, and is, because of her age, powerless to change it. She senses her mother's worrying for things—whether she has enough food to feed her children and the humiliation of having her home inspected by reserve authorities. Is Lorna describing a transference of traumatic feelings from parent to child, feelings of distress, humiliation, shame, of feeling inadequate and never being good enough? Is her father's suppressed anger or suppressed rage, later released on his own family after he has left the reserve with his exemption papers, transferred to her too? Certainly Lorna made that connection, and the connection allowed her to understand her father's behaviour through knowing his pain which was also part of her pain. Her feelings that she *could never be good enough for anything or anyone* are perhaps also the feelings her father and mother had from their own experiences of racist abuse on the reserve, the messages transferred from those in authority to both her parents. Is the suppressed rage of her childhood part of her own rage, expressed on her husband and child?

Trauma appears to prevent healthy adult functioning. For example, the words Ben repeats over and over again, giving emphasis to the results of the harm he experienced as a child, *fearful—afraid—insecure—so alone*, are linked to his adult feelings of *anger—hurt—shame*, and explain much of his complex adult compensating behaviour. In describing the memories of his child sexual abuse and the physical beatings he received, Ben says he has *carried the pain for the most part of my life.* Ben witnessed the violence of his mother getting beaten, and again demonstrates the transference of feelings from mother-to-child/child-to-mother that sometimes becomes confused and complex. *I was always afraid for her, afraid for myself.* Children often experience the violence they witness against their mother, or indeed another person, as a threat to their own life.

Ben can now see the link between his childhood experiences and the drinking and drug-taking behaviours with the offending patterns that resulted in multiple charges for drunk-and-disorderly and assault. Ben demonstrates that childhood trauma also may prevent the formation of enduring, nurturing relationships. His adult relationship with a woman breaks down when he hears about his father's suicide in prison.

His father had been unable to provide Ben with childhood parenting, in fact had never been a presence in Ben's life. Ben is angry at his father when his father suicides in jail, yet feels guilty that he feels this way. The suicide of his father triggers feelings of inadequacy in himself, and he begins to blame himself for not being the kind of father to his own children that he wanted his father to be for him. He has layered feelings of inadequacy, insecurity, fear, anger, and guilt which influence his adult functioning and which contribute to the breakdown in his own relationship with his wife and children.

Jackie demonstrates the clear child messages which may result from childhood sexual violence: her belief of an innate badness in herself makes her unlovable, and she believes if she works hard enough, and if she is good enough, she will please people and therefore be loved. She internalised the messages from her assailant that *she was the bad person* who made him do what he did. Until recently, even though common sense told her otherwise, she believed she caused the abuse because she was the *bad person*. Her parents, for whatever reason, were unable to provide her with the love and support she needed to recover from the child rape, thereby reinforcing her belief that she was unlovable.

Jackie says her most significant memory of growing into

her teenage years was at school one day, when she suddenly realised when the girls were talking about sex that this was what the man had done to her when she was abducted. The feelings of being *dirty* and *untouchable*, that she was to blame for what had happened to her, become *absolutely overwhelming*. These feelings governed much of her adult behaviour. It is important to understand that something as innocent as a group of young schoolgirls discussing sex in a normal situation has the capacity to trigger another layer of trauma in the life of an abused person. Jackie clearly illustrates how child trauma can place an individual at further risk of abuse. She enters an adult relationship in which she stays for an extended period (twenty-three years), where there is extreme domestic violence. Throughout the situation of domestic violence she continues to strive for the love and the affirmation of being loved and of being a good person to counter the beliefs that she was the bad person and unlovable. Once again, in this relationship she experiences feelings of being bad and unlovable, resulting in severe depression and suicidal feelings. Yet at the same time, she works long, hard hours and becomes successful in her chosen career.

While Don also names the childhood experiences of sexual violence, and of witnessing members of his family fighting, he also describes the chaos of families in crisis. His words— *the things that were wrong; nobody would listen to me, about my problems, about the violence; the blood on the floor, the blood on the walls, the blood on my grandparents*—highlight again the traumatising experience that the witnessing of violence is for a child and the normalisation of violence in some families and communities. Don names the forms of escape he used— the alcohol at eight, wagging school and glue-sniffing at twelve, and using other drugs by the age of fifteen. *When I was eight I was probably drunk the Tuesday night, the Friday night and the Saturday night. That was before I turned twelve.*

He also demonstrates the compounding traumatisation when children who have been violated do not have their needs met; when their pain is unrecognised and unheard;

when adults, for whatever reason, are unable to listen and respond to the pain in the child. He relates the experiences of being in an extended family that appears to be functioning in considerable pain and disorder. He talks of the *madness in my head*, relating this chaos in himself and his surrounds to the child in turmoil and the *feeling and being uncontrollable— feeling mad and bad, being sick of the pain*, all linked to his own drinking, drug-taking and suicidal thoughts and behaviours. His family call him *womba* (mad) and bad; society also has given him similar labels, calling him "criminal", "perpetrator", "schizophrenic", for various behaviours which have been a response to his childhood trauma experiences.

Though an adult of thirty-five, Len uses a number of childish words—*scary, it was the most scary, really frightened*—in much of his conversation. Often when relating the episodes of child trauma on tape and in workshops, he would alternate between crying and conflicting angry episodes. He says he *never had a childhood*, that a lot of his childhood has been *practically blanked out*. In fact he experienced high levels of physical, sexual and psychological violence in various situations which he does not describe in detail on the tapes. These experiences have had the effect of preventing him from having any enduring relationships in his adult life.

Len has a long history of so-called offending behaviours, starting from early adolescence where he does things he thinks are normal—stealing milk money—escalating to life-threatening acts of violence involving other men when he has been drinking. While Len has been violent towards other men, his violence against himself and multiple suicide attempts demonstrate the close link between self-harm and harming of others.

Participants reported numerous responses to the trauma, which included losing trust in the world around them; feeling unsafe; struggling to control situations that were uncontrollable; attempting to regain a sense of power out of their felt powerlessness.

While the destructive coping mechanisms have been

outlined above, the creative coping strategies illustrated by
each of the group must also be acknowledged. For example,
during the group sessions, each individual demonstrated a
variety of coping strategies. When the situation became
tense, Don would curl up in a foetal position. Len would get
angry and struggle to be in his anger without losing control
(he never did lose control and he taught the group much
about how trauma is held in the body). Mary would walk
around whenever things got tense or she felt threatened—
which she came to understand was a child's response to
critical situations. Lorna would cry and have a cigarette
break. Jackie brought her dog to the group and this dog
became a therapeutic companion not just for her, but for all
the participants in the group. Ben cried for his own pain in
the group, while at the same time comforting others in
distress, just as he had previously comforted his own mother
in her, or his, needs.

Childhood survival strategies had included Jackie and her
siblings giving each other "loving touch" by rubbing each
other on the back in a ritual manner each evening, the loving
touch they needed but were unable to receive from their
parents. Similarly, Lorna and her siblings gave each other
comfort up on the hill when there was violence between their
father and mother. Don talks about the young companion
who sat with him in his glue-sniffing, never sniffing himself,
but protecting Don from harm when the trips became
terrifying and the potential for self-harm was high. For Ben,
fighting on the streets was both a destructive and a creative
strategy, insofar as putting his anger out on others prevented
him turning it on himself, as he did later in life with his
suicide attempts.

Individual feelings of self-worth are invariably determined in childhood. Once the child's sense of self as safe in
the world and their sense of value or worth is damaged,
considerable repair work has to be done to allow the individual to feel safe again and to feel of value. The adult who
does not feel safe in the world cannot pass on to their child

feelings of safety and security. Many of the experiences described by Lorna, Ben, Jackie, Len, Mary and Don are commonplace for large numbers of children, including Aboriginal children (see, for example, Task Force on Violence 1999: 2–35). The participants demonstrate that the feelings of insecurity and inadequacy that result from child trauma influence adult behaviour; they also demonstrate that repair work can be done, but only if safe places are established so that the stories can be explored in depth, and healing education can be supported to occur.

Victim/perpetrator/survivor roles in family and community violence

I now examine the forms of family and community violence which emerged from the narratives in the context of victim/perpetrator/survivor conduct. The interconnections between childhood experiences and adult behaviours in relation to male violence against men and against women, and women's violence, will be considered in the light of people's experiences in the narratives. I will analyse the differences and similarities in the experience of violence of the men, compared with the women in the group. The narratives provide evidence of links between forms of violence in families and adult victim/perpetrator behaviours.

Ben demonstrates the link between forms of violence in families and fighting in the community as he describes his victimising experiences as a child and his young male attempts to protect women (his mother), which result in him being further victimised, and his move to fighting in the streets and becoming a perpetrator. *I've* **seen my mother bashed** *and I was always afraid for her. I tried to* **help** *her and I ended up getting bashed up myself because he had king-hit Mum and broke her jaw, and I had run up and tried to stop him. He just backhanded me and* **Mum and me we ended up on the floor together, blood** *everywhere.*

He talks about the fear which is transformed into anger, which gives him strength when he gets into street fights.

Fighting on the street became a regular occurrence for Ben. His police file is full of arrests for drunk-and-disorderly and assault, and he says he *can't count the number of times I got into physical fights.*

The suicide of Ben's father in prison triggered many unresolved issues. His coping behaviour was to drink more, which in turn created tension in his relationship, resulting in domestic fights and violence as well as increased fighting on the streets. After one suicide attempt and increasing suicidal thoughts, he demonstrated survivor behaviour by seeking help and entering rehabilitation.

Len and Don and Lorna also report episodes of street or community violence. Like Ben, they, too, demonstrate the link between childhood trauma and offending behaviour. Street violence is defined here as behaviour that occurs outside the family arena; often this behaviour may be on other Aboriginal people, including members of the family of the offender, but it is enacted in the public, non-Aboriginal domain. Such behaviour may be considered petty offending like that of Len and Don, or the behaviour of a *mad woman*, as Lorna describes herself.

Len and Don began petty offending at an early age, with Len pinching milk money and Don breaking into houses for food and later stealing glue from shops. Both were drinking by the time they started to offend, and their drinking also involved them in street or pub fights with other young men.

Len was born in the islands of Papua New Guinea and grew up believing he was black. He demonstrates social learning in a household where child punishment was Westernised and physical, and he observed male parental role models of drinking and pub fighting, balanced by male–female superordinate–subordinate roles. In these roles some women are protected, so he can say, *I would never hit a woman.* On the other hand, male children in this environment are taught to be aggressive, and this aggression results in male-on-male violence while drunk or under the influence of drugs.

Len talks about witnessing his father's violence on other men in fights in pubs and elsewhere—*I think I was frightened, but I also skited about my father—putting this man through a wall*—illustrating the conflicting seesaw of emotions that may be part of the same experience: the relationship, for example, between fear and excitement, or fear and arousal which can lead people in adult life to engage in risk-taking behaviour. He also points to the male-child learning that comes from witnessing violence, the confronting socialisation of boys into men. *Better not touch him—he's got a big father*, brings the message that to be a man a young boy has to be prepared to be tough and aggressive—to fight—*to be able to put a man through a wall*. Len's situation is interesting because, while he says he has seen his father in many violent situations and talks of the violence which he experienced from his father as a form of punishment, he never mentions any domestic violence by his father on his mother. He describes himself as *a violent man* with a record of extreme male-on-male violence—*I had my knife out of its pouch and was ready to open his belly up*—yet he says he could never hit a woman. *That's one thing I would never do. I always held that part in me that I could never hit a lady or a child.* This statement and his behaviours support the Aboriginal concept of primary learning by observation—unfortunately, in this instance, it is family and community environments that legitimise and help perpetuate different forms of violence.

Len describes social learning and the formation of personality in the early interaction between father and son. There is fear and the need to suppress anger in these interactions.

Len also describes the child moving into community—or juvenile—offending with the links between street-living for young people, the drug and grog culture, and violence on the streets. He begins to put his anger out on others at an early age, and this escalates into substantial forms of physical violence, which he recognises. *I stopped carrying a **knife** with me after my last attempt ... I was just completely off my face ...*

I had a knife out of its pouch and was **ready to open his belly up**
*... When I woke up the next morning in the hospital I had to get
out before the coppers came ... that really shocked me ... cos he was
a* **real good friend of mine.**

The rage in him is directed not only at people but also at
property. Again the pattern is that he is generally "blanked
out" at the time of his offence. ... *I've destroyed lots of property
...* **kicked every piece of fibro wall** *...* **smashed** *the machine—
the windows ... kicked holes in my room.*

While giving a picture of aggressive male energy wreaking
havoc wherever he goes, Len also articulates the movement
beyond victim/perpetrator and self-blame or blaming of
others, which is an essential part of reclaiming the self in a
change in attitudes and behaviours. He speaks of the truce
which is developing between himself and father (the rage at
his father has previously been directed outwards into society
on other men) and he demonstrates a deeper understanding
of why people act as they do. *I* **cannot blame** *him—he
apologised a few months ago ... It was true ...* **he didn't know
any other way.**

Don, an Aboriginal man, within the intensity of his words,
clearly shows the child trauma of witnessing violence. *My
problems—the* **blood** *on the walls, the* **blood** *on the floor, the*
blood on my grandparents. This may have been only one
incident (he was not asked to elaborate). It is, nonetheless, a
significant incident in his childhood that still holds traumatic
memory for him as an adult. Don makes the link between
childhood trauma and juvenile offending. **Stealing** *glue from
the shops ... sniffing ... to get away from my reality for a while ...
I was able to leave those things that were painful to me behind.*

Don also links school dropout situations with what was
happening in the home. *I wasn't at school. I was* **wagging it.** *...
School wasn't a good place for me either.* Further, he describes the
stress of having to try to cope with the responsibilities of a
TAFE course when his family are drinking, and he has to
clean up after them at the same time as keeping up with his
studies. He highlights the problems that victims of violence

—particularly children—have in trying to cope with learning responsibilities in formal educational settings. He understands and names the childhood behavioural modelling which can become adult criminal behaviours. *The family passed that belief down too—I seen* **my mother** *getting slapped around—***choked and physically mangulated** *and I seen my* **uncles bashing their women** *around all the time. I just thought it was* **normal to bash a woman.** Don is a gentle person when sober: *You wouldn't do those things if you were sober.*

People who experience trauma often describe a feeling of being outside themselves, watching what is happening but not feeling anything. This may be the child seeing *blood on the walls.* Similarly, people who have perpetrated violence on another—or, as in the case of Len, smashed objects—have described the experience as one of being outside themselves while acting in a frenzy over which they have no control. They may also claim to have no memory of committing an assault. Don has no reason to lie when he says, *One time she said I did* **hit her and grab her by the throat** *but I don't remember … it's not an excuse—***I don't remember.** He readily admits to others and describes himself as *a no-good back in those days* and implicates himself in his description of many of his own acts of violence, so it is important to ask what were the steps that occurred within him as he committed an extreme and potentially lethal act of violence, while at the same time having no memory of it. These questions must be answered if relevant programs are to be developed within prison environments and outside, to address so-called criminal acts of violence.

Many Aboriginal men who are convicted of a crime have no memory of committing the offence. This is not to say they did not do it, but that considerations of trauma should be included in sentencing summaries and in prescribed treatment programs. Treatment programs which address the person's perpetrator behaviour without also helping to move them out of the victimising experiences which may still be controlling much of their behaviour are a waste of time and money. In the course of the fieldwork one young man, serving a life sentence for double murder, while not denying he may have committed the offence, said that he had no memory of the event. He said his strongest and most painful memory was of seeing his mother's face as he looked back at her as "the vehicle" took him away. When questioned further it became clear that he was confusing two separate events: his removal from his mother as a child, and being taken to prison for a life sentence. In both cases he was driven away in a "police" vehicle. Both, in fact, were life sentences. In another case an Aboriginal woman, who had served a prison sentence for the stabbing death of her brother, talked about the time when her brother died. It was only after some confusion that it became obvious that, some years before she stabbed one brother, she had seen another brother stabbed and killed. She often conflated the two events when talking, which confused those who were working with her.

Lorna provides another clear link between the childhood experience of violence and adult behaviour, in victim/ perpetrator/victim roles. She begins by linking the construction of powerlessness and its resultant articulation in violent behaviours within the institutional situation of the reserve. This felt cycle of powerlessness/power-over is demonstrated or acted out by her father, once he has left the reserve compound, on his own family. Lorna names this cyclic process: *He started to use his power in an abusive way ... I can see now there was a relationship between him having to stand in front of a white man and being told not to look in his face and now him having the power to line his kids up like this and have them do what he told them to.*

Lorna herself repeats the cycle across the generations as she expresses her own felt powerlessness in the way she acts on herself, in her drinking and suicidal behaviours, and in violence on her own husband and children. Lorna names the intergenerational victim/perpetrator roles her father played in her own victimisation, and her own victim/perpetrator behaviours that can potentially continue the trauma across generations. In this instance she has worked to break the cycle; however, only she and her children will know if she has been successful in preventing the transfer of her pain, and her parents' pain, to her grandchildren.

She also articulates the interactive violence that may occur between husband and wife, out of a cultural response to the construction of traumatic distress. *There was physical violence between my husband and me ...* **I've been dragged** *by the hair,* **thumped, flogged with a hose, choked,** *[once] I had a broken jaw and I was wired up ...* **I became very violent when I was drunk,** *only with my husband.* Here she moves from describing her husband's violence on her to acknowledging her own violence. While she acknowledged, at various times, her husband's violence, she was always more particularly concerned, in the interviews and in all the work that was done in the workshops, to deal with her own power and ability to change her life. (It should be stated here that the relationship between Lorna and her husband is now a balanced and nurturing association free of violence.)

Lorna describes her violence on her son. *I been violent with my children ...* **I'd start to smack and I'd end up punching** *...* *I had my son in a corner of the room* **with a knife and I was going to cut his throat** *and he broke my finger to get away.* While Lorna names the victim/perpetrator behaviours— **somehow in my madness**—she also demonstrates survivor conduct as she breaks the cycle in naming the links between her father as the victimised, incarcerated man and her father as the abusing patriarch. The subordinated man uses what small portion of power he is allowed in a hierarchical, dominant society as he plays abusive patriarch within his own family. In this there is no blaming, but rather understanding and a commitment to work to change such cycles in her own family and community for the future.

She is able to see the links between her own "victim" experiences and her own "perpetrator" behaviours, which re-victimise and re-traumatise her. She was placed in a mental health unit where she received no help, where in fact she was *pumped up so full of tablets* she could not recognise her husband when he came to visit. Authorities in this institution wanted to give her electric shock treatment, yet they never did find out the story that had driven, and provides context to, her behaviour. For Lorna, it is knowledge of the links that enables her to make choices to own and change behaviour that will continue to harm her. The strength and courage she demonstrates are substantial.

Lorna names something that is vital for workers to understand if they intend to work with Aboriginal and Torres Strait Islander peoples. In this case, Lorna's husband knows from a deep place within that Lorna's behaviour has meaning, and that even behaviour some may call abusive—criminal—psychotic, is a call for help, a cry of pain. Although he felt frustrated at the behaviour that resulted when she was drinking, he did everything he could to help her, for he knew she wanted help and that she was not getting what she needed from the Western mental health and social welfare systems. Lorna and her husband used these systems because at that time there was nothing else available.

Jackie demonstrates clear links between the childhood situation of sexual violence consequent to her abduction and the messages she has internalised, and her victimisation in her adult life when she remains in an abusive relationship for many years. Jackie gives a classic description of "domestic violence". She talks about the constant fear, of never knowing when he was going to explode, as she describes the intense brutality that was part of her life for twenty-three years.

Jackie knows from her own experience that victimisation is much more than physical injuries. *The other abuse was even harder to heal than the physical abuse. The emotional, mental, psychological and spiritual violence ... You can't feel the physical pain because the devastation, the betrayal, the piece by piece* **dismantling of your very being**—*the desolation of* **living totally isolated** *in this world of violence is unbearable. [It is] the* **destruction of the soul**. As violence enters the body/mind/

soul/spirit it begins to reshape who the person thinks they are and what they understand themselves and their world to be. Their view of themselves changes. They feel damaged, contaminated by the humiliation, shame, pain and fear that comes with the experience. The pain is inescapable and indescribable. They believe they cannot explain how they feel to anyone and so they close down, withdraw, become numb and dumb—silenced by both their abusers and their own inability to describe the pain of their experiences. Jackie shows again the link between her childhood messages that she was bad and would be punished for her sexual assault, to the patterned thinking in her adult relationship. *What have I done?* **I must be bad** *to receive this much* **punishment.**

People find different ways to survive such abuse, and Jackie's worked for her. She shut down and created another world for herself. *The only way I knew how to survive was—to shut down.* **I created a block**—**a steel door** *in my mind behind which I put* **what remains of me**—**my feelings**—**emotions.** *People asked me "Why did you stay?", "Why didn't you leave?" My answer—"... How could I ...* **I was not there."** This other world made her real world more bearable. *I [had] an imaginary world ... that is how I lived. I* **made a world** *for myself* **that was livable.** *... It started in my childhood and it continues today ... otherwise I would have gone mad. ... I had a* **mother figure who loved me** *and* **protected me**, *and I would do things that were heroic so ...* **she ... thought I was very good.** This imaginary mother-person now provides the love and protection her mother was unable to provide for her when she was a child. The patterning is still there, however. She has to prove to this mother figure that she is good by committing heroic deeds and earning her love.

Jackie also demonstrates that some traditional forms of therapy—for instance, counsellor-and-client with hier-archical structures and with no analysis of race and gender oppression—are unhelpful to abused women and to Aboriginal peoples. *I* **told a counsellor** *about it once and* **he said I shouldn't** *be doing that.* [Of living in the imaginary world]: *I should be through that behaviour now ... But **he never really knew** what had happened to me, about the childhood ... my violent marriage and all the feelings of it were coming up for me.* He never asked, and was not interested when she tried to talk with him about the childhood violence and the domestic violence, and learning from his response to her needs, she blamed herself for not being able to move on from her victimisation during his therapy sessions. He also blamed her and labelled her as not wanting to help herself: "she doesn't want to heal" (personal conversation with author by therapist).

Jackie's survivor behaviour has enabled her to begin to rebuild her life. *I'm building a family; however, I still feel the isolation of being alone.* Her life revolves around animals whom she can trust, but her relationship with people is governed by a decision she made after her own experiences and perhaps by her need to be loved, which for her is safer than being bad and mad and angry.

While the narratives comprise a small group, their cases are typical of the majority in the extended workshops of We Al-li, which show that there are both differences and similarities for men and women in the experience of violence and the articulation of their distress.

All the men drank and used drugs; of the women, only Lorna drank. All the men engaged in male-on-male violence; only Lorna articulates her distress in (physical) violence on others. All the men have long histories of involvement with police, with multiple charges for drunk-and-disorderly. All the men, at different times, have experienced police brutality. Ben says he felt police behaviour towards him was because of his Aboriginality. Don has experienced selective police attention because of his Aboriginal appearance (my personal observation and his own feelings, resulting from experiences). Len, a white man, has also experienced the "black eye factory", and has been arrested often but never convicted. Len is non-violent towards women, while the two Aboriginal men have a history (to varying extents) of violence against women, which was part of their own childhood socialisation in families where there was considerable chaos and distressed acting-out.

Lorna, Mary and Jackie illustrate gender differences in response to trauma as well as race differences. Lorna, born on a reserve, articulates the feelings of her distress in aggressive action, both on her husband and child and on the streets; she drinks as part of her coping strategy. Her interaction with the law, however, is different to that of the men in that she does not fight the police but receives a form of protection from them.

Mary, a more urbanised Aboriginal woman with a Christian background, does not drink; she has used prescription drugs to cope, however. She does not appear to be physically violent, but acknowledges verbal and emotional abuse in her interaction with her husband and children. In her urban environment, when the police were called to what could have been considered a domestic dispute (in fact it was a suicide attempt by a distressed and drunk husband), police intervention increased the potential for disaster, and Mary vows she will never involve the police again.

Jackie was born in England; she is shy yet resilient (which could be an inherited cultural trait or it could be a personality development from early childhood, or a combination). She has never experienced racism and therefore does not fully understand the construction of racism in its transgenerational impact on Aboriginal people. Jackie's ex-husband, a white man, over a period of twenty-three years committed horrendous acts of violence on her, yet was never apprehended by the police. On the other hand, Ben and Don have numerous convictions for minor offences such as drunk-and-disorderly.

Alcohol and other drug misuse: a self-medicating response to trauma

This theme refers to the evidence in the narratives that traumatised people may use alcohol and other drugs as forms of self-medication to meet particular needs. Lorna refers to the use of alcohol as a means of coping with feelings when she talks of her years of drinking down on the river-bank: *the drinking helped because I didn't have to* **think about those feelings of never feeling good enough** *and that nobody would want me*. The re-creation of a sense of community is also a part of what she is referring to: *I wanted to be like everybody else and ...* **I did feel part of a group on the riverbank ...** *as good as the person I was sitting next*.

However there were also the negative consequences: *there were times I was* **too sick to drink** *and I would go home and get cleaned up and go to bed and just have this stuff in me—the* **guilt—the shame**. During these times, as the effect of the prescription and other drugs leaves the person's body, the underlying trauma begins to emerge. While drugs at one level may have a medicating effect, the long-term conse-quences may be devastating because they both mask the underlying trauma and compound its consequences. Alcohol and drug misuse may be a slow form of suicide.

High-risk behaviours, often associated with alcohol and other drugs, are relevant in traumatised groups. *One night I* **just about had my throat cut**—*I was drunk—it was a sexual thing. Other times I was left in the bush*. Here Lorna names a contradiction that has been part of her narrative. While she feels part of a group when she is drinking on the riverbank, the group is not *community*, for when alcohol is involved it is not a *safe place* for her.

Alcohol and violence are clearly linked. *It was* **only when she was drinking** *that this sort of thing would happen*. Violence against children also occurs more frequently when adults are drinking or using other drugs. Under such circumstances the child's pain is unrecognised, and may be intensified not only by what is happening around him or her, but also by not being seen or heard at times of crisis. *My father would come home drunk all the time and* **the boy would be under the blankets** [note how his language changes into the third person as he distances himself from his fear and pain] *with a* *pillow over his head—hiding. My drinking my drugging came because I was not allowed to cry as a kid—I was not allowed to shed a tear—**nobody would listen to me**—sit down and talk to me about my problems—the blood on the walls, the blood on the floor, the blood on my grandparents.*

What Don also names as he talks is the early age at which children who have experienced trauma may start to use drugs. *I was drinking from the age of eight—to **block all that outta me** I just needed to escape.* He names reasons why people start to use drugs. Drugs help people escape from reality and people may feel better for a while. ***Glue-sniffing was a beautiful experience**—it took me into another beautiful world … a world of glue-sniffing, taking drugs and drinking to get away … so I could be in **my own little world.*** While drugs may take a young person into another world, there is always a cost. *Then the nightmares started … real bad trips … I began seeing things— cows getting their heads chopped off—**blood spurting every- where**.* Does this blood have any relationship to the blood he saw when he was a very small child, on the walls—on his grandparents? *People saying "**you are going to Mars**"—dogs and sirens.* Again, do the sirens and dogs relate to the number of times he was apprehended by the police as a small child for breaking and entering, stealing money to buy food and drugs? Is the reference, *you're going to Mars*, reflective of the threats that were made to him that he would be taken away—and indeed was, when he was sent to a children's home? Or do they have transpersonal implications, memories across generations of massacres and removals?

During the time of the fieldwork a clear generation gap emerged regarding the kinds of drugs people used. On the whole, alcohol belongs to one generation, other drugs of various kinds to another. In the men we see the conglomerate of drugs young people are using today, as they grow increasingly able to access them on the open market (com- pared to what their parents used). *At sixteen I found yarndie. … I started sleeping longer … so it became a bad medicine too. … Eighteen years **I sniffed glue, smashed up Mogodons, Serapax,***

Valium snorted them up my nose, speed, mushrooms all kinds of hashes, yarndie, cannabis. The study illustrates that the world of young people is radically different from the world in which their parents and grandparents grew up, where alcohol was not only the drug of choice but more often the only drug available.

From a Western perspective and in the Aboriginal context of learning by observation, male children who witness drinking by adult males are more likely to begin to drink at an early age themselves. *My father used to take us down to the pub—we would wait outside **but we could hear and see what was inside**—he used to bring us drinks ... I started drinking around eleven—everybody was drinking and I made an **idiot of myself**.* The fact that he makes a fool of himself at his first drinking episode does not stop Len from continuing to drink. Indeed, right from the beginning of his drinking career it is clear he is going to have a major problem with alcohol and other drugs. *The second time I **wiped** myself out. After that every time I got drunk I would wipe myself out. ... When I am **drinking you start going into your feelings more.** I could **release my feelings ... cry into my beer or get angry**.* Once again there is always the cost: *At the end of the night I would be **on the ground or in the lockup or in hospital**. I was drinking every day of my life. I was also using a lot of other stuff—coke, hash, dope, amphetamines, uppers and downers.*

There are a number of questions that need further research in relationship to prescription drugs. *Prescription drugs were great. I would say to the doctor I've got a problem and he would prescribe me Valium, Serapax. In the **short term they didn't make me better. Made things worse in the long term**. I would be drunk with the drugs. I couldn't cope without the drugs in me but I was **coping less and less with the drugs**.*

All of the participants who contributed to the group narrative had used prescription drugs to alleviate their pain. There were gender differences, however. Women were less likely to be involved in other drug-taking and more likely to use prescription drugs. Neither Mary nor Jackie drank. Jackie used a variety of prescription drugs, including benzodiaze-pam tranquillisers, but found anti-depressants made her suicidal. Mary would not drink because she had seen her father drink, and she did not want to lose control as she had seen the effect of alcohol within her family, but she became addicted to benzodiazepam tranquillisers after she was put on them by a doctor. Lorna drank and used prescription drugs as well. *Mostly my drugs apart from alcohol was Serapax and Valium, it was nothing for me to take five Valiums. I got them from doctors ... went in and told them a story—they were the only things that helped me get through the day.* Such drugs may have their short-term value, but questions must be asked about the actual benefit to traumatised people in the long term. Research should be undertaken to establish the long-term benefits, or otherwise, of prescription drugs to Aboriginal people who are suffering traumatic stress.

None of the women used the mix of drugs, or the hard drugs, that the men did. This may have something to do with age—the women are all over forty, while the men are all under forty. It also could reflect learned behaviour—male children see their fathers and other men drink, and begin to drink themselves at an early age, then escalate into the use of other drugs as the trauma compounds. Female children saw their mothers coping with family crisis because of the drink but choosing not to drink because of family responsibilities.

There are also intergenerational considerations. Both Lorna and Mary saw their fathers drinking and their mothers coping with the consequences. Their children have been involved in the use of a variety of soft and hard drugs. *There were times when I was **too sick to drink but I drank every day**. My eldest son, and my husband would come and pick me up from the riverbank.* Note again the observational learning of the son, seeing his mother drinking. Indeed, the son later has his own drinking and drug-taking problems. Both Lorna and Mary have children who have repeated their mothers' suicidal and self-harming behaviours. Jackie's parents did not drink, and she does not have children. It is also worth noting that parents, by their pressure, can delay the drinking age. *I started drinking when I was about sixteen. I never started drinking before I was sixteen because I was always afraid what my mother would do to me if she found out I was drinking.*

The participants showed that the use of alcohol and other drugs, whether prescription or otherwise, may have both positive and negative consequences. Such use may allow people to cope with or express feelings: pent-up anger, rage or despair can be expressed without having to take responsibility for the consequences. Consumption of alcohol, in particular, within a group environment, allows a person to feel a sense of community, albeit a distorted and false community. Alcohol is associated with being drunk, with felt powerlessness, with aggression in articulation of feelings of anger and distress, and with actions of interpersonal violence; however, as an enabler, it also perpetrates and recycles the traumatic distress. While one generation has used alcohol, with the consequent violence as an outcome, the next generation(s) is using a more complex and lethal mixture of drugs to cope with their traumatic distress. These are real issues that must be considered in any therapeutic response to the trauma in Aboriginal lives today.

Suicidal and other self-harming behaviour

Suicidal and self-harming behaviour refer to the Western term that indicates the desire to kill, to destroy or to harm the self. The data indicate that suicide and other self-harming behaviour may be an outcome of the trauma of victimisation. People who have been victimised may consequently engage in acts of self-victimisation, which can take many forms. Self-harming behaviour can involve substance misuse and chronic suicide feelings: *as I got older I was **drinking and drugging** more and more—when I was drugged up or drunk I **thought of suicide** all the time, **you don't plan you don't care**—it's not your mind doing those things;* and self-mutilation: *a few times I have **cut myself—my arteries**—a **razor blade**. I would get rushed into hospital;* and risk-taking: *I started **walking out in*** *front of cars.* For some women, repeated involvement in abusive or dangerous relationships is a form of self-harm. All are linked to articulations of pain: *the first time I cut my arm I grabbed the knife and sliced my arm a couple of times, fourteen times actually. I did it out of the pain.*

To various extents, all are linked to low self-worth or self-esteem. Self-esteem is "the measure by which people regard themselves, the value that they place upon themselves, the respect that they have for themselves" (Wong and McKeen 1998: 50). Other words for low self-esteem could be self-loathing or self-hatred, a lack of self-acceptance or self-compassion as illustrated in Lorna's words. *I just felt **nobody,** not even my husband **thought I was good enough** so I got all the Serapax and took them.* These are feelings many people have about themselves after experiences of childhood abuse—they could never now be "good enough".

There is a variety of reasons why people attempt suicide or engage in self-harming behaviour. Two particular reasons stand out in the narratives. The first to be discussed is the obvious cry for help which accompanies many suicide attempts. *I **didn't want to live** any more I was **tired of the pain—sick of it**—the way my life was.* Don recognises what was at the base of his multiple attempts at suicide and self-harm when he asks and answers: *Why? **crying out for attention**—wanting somebody to realise **there is a person** inside me.* So does Lorna: *I've had enough—there was a **part of me** that wanted to **die** and the other part **asking for help**—life wasn't worth living but it **would have been** if someone could **see me and listen** to me ... to be there in my hurt and just **accept me for who I was.*** Lorna is externalising onto others her own feelings about herself, saying in effect, "If I don't like myself, how can anybody else like me?" Later she speaks of the beginning of her process of self-acceptance and self-love: *my ankles, I always had a thing about my ankles, but seriously—**being black being black.*** She names the place where her pain is located, and her first memories of oppression. Baker's work, which names psycho-social violence or cultural and spiritual genocide as the most insidious and destructive form of violence, is relevant here (see Chapter Two).

Suicidal feelings may begin early in life. Both Len and Don say their suicide attempts began in early adolescence. Mary's first suicide attempt was at the age of fourteen. During the time of the fieldwork, children as young as seven and eight attempted suicide, and in one case a nine-year-old boy suicided near a community in another state in which we were delivering the We Al-li workshops.

Suicide attempts increase at particular times—after family reunions, relationship break-ups, and particular holiday periods. *Over **Christmas** I was thinking of admitting myself, I was having suicidal thoughts.* Len said that it was usually at the finish of a relationship that he would harm himself or attempt suicide. The failure of a relationship was experienced as another failure in his life.

Men and women use different suicidal weapons. Generally, men are more likely to use a gun or a rope, while women are more likely to use tablets, as demonstrated by both Lorna and Mary, or to cut themselves. Len talks of his last suicide attempt: *Kinda **hung** myself. I never had a real plan … the rope broke. I had a scar around my neck for months and I broke a couple of ribs.* Len has previously pointed out that he stopped keeping a gun in his home because he was frightened he would use it—it is unclear whether he meant on someone else or himself. The link between suicide and self-harm is clear. One is an attempt to kill the ego, or undergo an ego death, while the other is to hurt the ego and demonstrate that the ego is hurting. When Don talks about cutting his arms with a knife, he uses contradictory language—*to let her know that **nothing can hurt** me … to show her **how much hurt** I was going through*—which has a certain logic even in its contradiction. It is the cry of somebody who is hurting so much they feel nothing else can hurt them.

Suicide often runs in families and communities. A successful suicide can trigger an attempt by another family member or someone else within the community who knew the person and is also feeling that life is not worth living. *My father is the only person in my family I know that went through with it. Other family members have tried but failed. My dad was the only one who was successful. He **died in prison**.* A suicide by one person can trigger unfinished business in another and set in motion a series of difficult situations, which can lead to another suicide or attempt. *I was **thinking of suicide** at least once a fortnight … had attempted it once and failed and just before going into **rehabilitation** … was starting to feel very strong about it again, to **feel hopeless**.* Ben refers to risk indicators that, taken in their whole, point to reasons for serious concern for his well-being at that time. There were other reasons for concern, and a healing response to any one of these concerns could have been helpful to him. *That was the year **my ex and I split up**. Everything was falling apart—I was going through a big **depression**.*

Suicidal actions can result from inwardly directed rage. *When I heard about my **dad, I was angry** at him for what he did and **I was angry and shamed at myself** for feeling that way.* However, it is generally not the bereavement as such that triggers the suicide attempt, but deeper unresolved issues. Ben was angry at his father because he says he never had the relationship he wanted with him—*he was never a father to me*. His father's death destroyed Ben's dreams that their father–son relationship could occur in the future. Consequently he started to drink, and tension increased between him and his wife until they split (this was within twelve months after his father's death); his drinking increased further; he was increasingly involved with street fighting and consequent trouble with the law; and a "big depression" set in, which is a critical risk factor. Ben's feeling of hopelessness was also compounded because he feels a failure in one important aspect of his life: he wants to be the kind of father for his own daughters that he wanted his own father to be for him, that is, *to be there*. In this, he feels he has failed. He now is allowed only limited access to his children.

The second type of suicide or suicide attempt is when the

person loses the will to live. This is not the same thing as "being suicidal". People in captivity (which each of the narrators has been to varying degrees) live constantly with the fantasy of suicide and homicide, between which there is a thin line. Mary and Jackie both talked, at different times (not in the transcripts), about fantasising that their husbands would be killed on the road, at work, or die of a heart attack—then they would be free. Neither allows herself to fantasise that she could kill him. Lorna, on the other hand, is able to name her desire to kill, not her actual abuser(s), but *her poor husband* who, she says, has taken a lot of her pain. The compulsion to kill is acted out on her child, who escapes by breaking her finger. The power to kill the abuser is generally limited, and so the rage is turned inward or on other members of the family.

Occasional suicide attempts are not inconsistent with a general determination to survive. Lorna gives a clear example: *It was crazy because there was some part of me that felt I just wanted to die, I can't take any more. And the other part of me was feeling,* **"I hope somebody finds me soon before anything happens."** While Lorna is effectively saying "acknowledge my humanness and the pain of my reality", she may also be the child hoping somebody will find out about what is happening to her as she dies inside, isolated in her disabling experiences.

Mary's suicide attempt comes from feelings of despair, helplessness and hopelessness. She cannot see a way out of a situation that has become intolerable. She describes the body tiredness that may accompany a suicide together with a cold clarity of intent. *My **body** was dead tired but **somebody else** had* **control of my mind** *[which was] running around in circles—I just couldn't see a way out ... my mind running around and round but the rest of me **frozen**. Then it was real clear—there was no way out so I went and took every tablet I could find.*

It is important to see the connecting factors that comprise suicide ideation and other self-harming behaviours, and the compounding triggers that may result in a successful suicide.

It is also important, however, to see that people can look back at that time of pain, and reflect on how the past and the present connect and allow them to grow; they can move on once they have made the connection and decided to change some of their circumstances. It is appropriate to give Don the last word: *Other people saw my suicide attempts and I didn't. I look back now and think it was silly but it wasn't at the time. Now I am sober and straight I can get those feelings out in another way.*

The search for identity: fragmentation and separation

Identity refers to the experience we have of ourselves as an "integrated self" and a self in relation to others. Each of the participants talks at different levels about the construction of identity. The data show considerable fragmentation and separation of the self from the Self, and how, as others have labelled them, they in turn label themselves.

Lorna expresses her distress at being treated like a guinea-pig on the reserve, and also at seeing her father lined up and inspected, being treated with disrespect and *hating it*, the white-on-black power misuse. She experiences the confusion of a similar situation with her father when he lines all the children up late at night, forcing them to sing songs for him. This is a conflicting sense of identity—families are supposed to be places of caring and sharing, particularly black families, yet her family is a place of pain and distress, as well as a place and experience of love and companionship.

Mary talks of the feelings of being a *dirty black gin*. This is an identity ascribed to her by another that she took on for a large part of her life. It is only recently she has begun to like the "black woman" that she is, and, significantly, it is the fact of having to face herself that gives her the direction of wanting to find out more about her family and Aboriginality. She also assumed or took on the powerlessness of the abused child/woman who is fragmented and separated from the whole and powerful child she was born to be. Later, when in crisis during domestic abuse, trying to work out how she can leave her abusing husband, she feels the only power she has left is to "kill herself". She describes thoughts running around and around in her head *like a dog chasing its tail*, fragments of a self that can see no other way out of her pain but to kill the Self. She took on the labels others placed on her, saying, *you didn't have to tell me I was stupid and no good. I already knew it. I was just **a stupid bitch.*** This is part of what she has assumed as her identity. The incompetence she feels in not having prevented the abuse she experienced as a child, the dislike of her blackness based on what others have ascribed to her, her self-defined stupidity—all these are the constructions others have placed on her.

Len thinks that people may call him a child molester because he believes that this is what he would be labelled if others knew what had happened to him as a child; that they would assume that he might do to others what has been done to him. (This, and a deep shame that they would be considered less than men, was a recurring theme and fear in all the men in the workshops who disclosed childhood sexual abuse.) Len also had to sit in a room waiting for the leather strap as a small boy. This constructs two conflicting aspects of identity: a scared little boy and a grown man full of rage. As a child he is both scared and unconsciously angry at his abuse, but he has to suppress the anger because it is unsafe for him to feel and express it. As an adult he transfers this anger into actionable rage and, with the enabling alcohol and other drugs, he is dangerously violent on other men. Yet he says he could *never hit a woman, that is something I could never do.* His adult identity is conflicting as he rages in the adult male body, but continues to have the child's feelings of being scared and fearful. Len has another conflict in identity that is not discussed in the interviews but is relevant to this discussion: for the first eight years of his life he thought he was black. Apart from his parents, all the other people in his early childhood were black, so at the age of eight, when his parents returned to Australia, he experienced a crisis in identity from which he is only now recovering. He couldn't speak English on his settlement in Australia and he experienced his cousins and children at school laughing at him for this. Members of his Australian family thought him an oddity because he behaved differently to other Anglo-Australian children, and they expected him to behave as they thought white Australian children should behave. Today he does not relate to white Australia, but finds his companionship with Indigenous peoples and is more comfortable in their company.

Ben was fourteen when the police bashed him as he stood as a bystander at a street brawl. Others cheered the police who bashed him, and he believes *it was **because I was black***, yet he also talks about *not being black enough*. In reality it is not possible to tell, at a glance, that Ben is black. Ben's conflicting identity also comes from being a male child wanting to protect his mother, but being scared and fearful; and then being the adult man fighting on the streets with all the anger of the child at his violations, and winning, yet still being punished by the police.

Through his words Don indicates the removal of himself from a painful situation when he talks about his father coming home *drunk all the time—where's my boy—looking for me and the boy would be under the blankets with a pillow over his head*—as though it was not Don but some other boy that was hiding from his father and uncles and the potential violence. He also talks of the *chaos—that was me going this way and that way don't know which direction half the time*, and the need to escape, which he did with the alcohol and drugs *just to get high—to take me out of the society world and the problems that were at home*. Don names the fracture in identity in his mother and stepfather which is triggered by alcohol: *When they were sober you couldn't get nicer persons ... when they had alcohol in them my stepfather he would get stuck into her all the time*. Don resents being called a name, a label given in his family—Monkey John—yet accepts it, *cos you get used to it*. As he is passed around *like a football from family member to family*, he is in *chaos—that was me—uncontrollable*. Don enters a crisis in identity when he thinks he is a father and later finds out through DNA tests that the baby is not his. Don's family labels him *womba* and the hospital labels him schizophrenic, but Don also has a spiritual belief, in Moonda Nghadda and in the ways of his ancestors, and these are what sustain him. He begins to re-label himself and grows from this.

Jackie takes into her identity the words given to her by the person who abducted and raped her. She is a *very very bad* person. As a consequence of the abduction and rape, her sexual identity is formed so that when she hears other young women talking about sexual matters, she feels *dirty and untouchable*. In her adult relationship she was kept isolated, not allowed to have friends, and was called—labelled—*stupid, useless bitch*. While she accepts these labels, and they become part of who she thinks she is, as a survival technique she creates a fantasy world where her identity is heroic and good so that she is loved. She has had constructed, and constructs for herself, a number of identities which are both painful and helpful.

Each person uses particular labels as they talk that describe the fragmented and distressed feelings of a traumatised identity: *the madness in my head—womba; the mind-fucking that I did to myself; mad woman; child molester; dirty and bad—I must be really bad to deserve this*. Such fragmentation is a product of trauma, of sexual abuse and domestic violence, among other traumatic experiences. The fractures and fragmentation of identity being described here are not unique to Aboriginal people; however, they have been complicated and made more virulent for Aboriginal people as a group because of the racism that produces and compounds traumatisation.

Jackie was in a crisis when she first began participating in the workshops. She talked of going to a psychologist for help but being unable to hear or understand what he was saying to her because *I was really mixed up—I didn't know who I was. I'd been controlled and manipulated for so long that I didn't know what the real me was. I couldn't separate what bits of me were really me and what bits had been formed by pressures from outside.*

One night when she was feeling really distressed, *damaged* and *broken—contaminated—unhealable*, as she said, I told her, "You are whole. Even though you feel broken, you are always whole, for the whole is present in all the parts of you, of who you are." The next morning she phoned me to share the work she had done for herself overnight with the following picture concept. She made sense of the confusion and hurt that she was feeling, and articulated a purposeful healing approach to her pain. *I have been thinking about what you said yesterday and this is how I describe myself and what happened to me. As a child I was like a jigsaw puzzle picture of the many parts that made up the whole picture of me. I was a complete picture of who I was even as a small child but I had not yet reached all my potential. I was still learning and growing. I used to talk about my innocence being taken away from me at three, but I've realised now that nothing was taken away from me. Things were added. The picture of who I was became a jigsaw that was all broken up. The picture became shattered. Bits of pieces all over the place. And over the years more parts have been added—when I was sexually abused at three and the man told me I was bad, dirty, I took those words into me and believed them about myself. When my parents couldn't love me, I took that into me and believed that I was unlovable. Later when I got married and my husband beat me all those years, I took his words into me that I was stupid and no good for nothing. They became my beliefs about myself. These beliefs were parts of his broken jigsaw puzzle that had been added over the years, not mine, but I still took them into me. So there was the real me that I was born to be as a child, but I became separated from me. There was the parts of me that I came to believe that other people gave me—all the negative things people said to me that I took into myself and let influence how I felt about myself. And because I wanted people to love me so badly, I constructed another person who was always trying to please everybody, always trying to win people's approval, always trying to do the right thing, always apologising. Now I have got to find the real me again, by sifting through the different parts of the jigsaw and discard those bits that don't fit, and find and give value to those bits of the picture that do fit and I want to keep.*

Jackie gives a beautiful description of the concept of wholeness that becomes fragmented as traumatisation separates the self from the Self as people are reconstructed from the abuse they experience. Jackie does not have "borderline personality disorder", as she has been labelled. She is not a woman who "does not want to heal", as her psychologist told me. She is a woman trying to make sense of her painful experiences as she works to re-define her identity after so many others have tried to construct her out of their own pain and painful abuse on her.

As people talked with each other it was possible to observe how they began to reconstruct themselves from the fragmented parts of the person they had become as a result of the abuse and pain in their lives.

Transgenerational transmission of trauma

The transmission of trauma from one generation to another is complex and must be understood in the whole. The generational traumatic transmission or transference discussed here operates at two levels: intergenerational and transgenerational. Another aspect of transmission will also be discussed—incidences of transpersonal psychic transmission which cannot be explained in any rational manner, but which occurred during the fieldwork and were recorded in field notes.

Cameron (1998) discusses the differences between intergenerational and transgenerational transmission of trauma. Referring to the work of Apprey (1996), she suggests it would be more appropriate to refer to intergenerational trauma as "trauma passed down directly from one generation to the next, while transgenerational trauma would be trauma transmitted across a number of generations, for example from a grandparent, through to a grandchild" (Cameron 1998: 13–15). Root (1992) refers to secondary traumatisation—the experience of being traumatised by the trauma of another through witnessing another person experiencing trauma. All these are evident in experiences narrated by Lorna and Don and, to a lesser extent, by the others.

Lorna talks of witnessing the racist abuse by the reserve manager on her father, which is the secondary traumatisation to which Root refers. Lorna also articulates her father's traumatic transference of his own distress onto both herself and her siblings, by his behaviour once they have left the reserve. (It is important here to acknowledge that we do not know the story of Lorna's father.)

It would be assumed that the father's removal to and incarceration on the reserve as a child would have had a traumatic impact on his parents; similarly for Lorna's mother, who was brought to the reserve at an early age.

This is the intergenerational aspect of trauma transmission. Lorna also expresses the feeling of distress of her mother when white people came into her house to inspect it. (Lorna herself keeps a clean and ordered residence— anybody could walk in at any time of the day or night and inspect it and she would judged an exceptional housewife; her home and workplace is a beautifully welcoming place to visit, both for the way she keeps it and more importantly for the welcome she provides.) She also describes passing on to her son the rage or *madness* within her as she held the knife at his throat. These impacts are now affecting her grandchildren in a transmission of trauma across four generations. Lorna knows this. Fortunately, in her healing, she does not blame herself—although *there are times when I didn't think they would forgive me. I guess there is still stuff in them that comes up for them at times, but all I want to be today is the best person I can be [and] I have a good, very close relationship with [my children] today.*

In all instances there is also the traumatic reinforcement of trauma as people in their relationships re-traumatise themselves and each other. Lorna again demonstrates this, firstly in her childhood sexual abuse, later when she refers to *the sexual thing* that occurred when she was drinking. The issue of sexuality is so painful for people who have been abused that, down the generations, people experience a silencing, and are forced to live in denial and potential re-victimisation.

Mary refers to this in talking about her mother's reaction after her rape as a child: *Mum was pretty upset. ... She never talked to me about it after I came back from the doctor ... One thing I know now I am an adult woman ... it really shook Mum up. **It kind of froze her** too. She couldn't talk about it ... there were **things she said that made me feel a lot of shame** at the time ... I know she wasn't blaming me... but there were things that she said—**how she behaved—what she did** at the time and afterwards even though we never talked about it again, that **I knew had brought up shame for her** too. I think that's why I felt so much shame because it was a big shame job for her.* "You never got to understand what something like this meant for her?" *Oh no! It's a closed book. Even now she is an old woman and I try to talk to her adult woman to adult woman she just closes off. When we had that fight she even cried. I've never seen my mother cry before so I don't push it. I don't try.*

Mary here is referring to a traumatic reinforcement of her original trauma by her mother who, for whatever reason, could not talk to her about the incident, and transferred some of her own feelings of shame onto the child. All of the women described similar reactions within their families to their sexual abuse, and in the workshops overall this was a recurring theme.

At the time of the interviews the men were only just beginning to disclose and explore issues of sexual abuse, yet all three men name this as a factor of their childhood; a high proportion of the men in the workshops (80 per cent) disclosed similar experiences. Society's denial of sexual violence on boys and young men is a transference of its own pathology, its own unhealthy denial, onto others.

A number of situations of traumatic reinforcement are also evident in the narratives. The inappropriate treatment of

Lorna in the mental institution is one example. Her experience is similar to another who wrote at one time:

> They said I was paranoid schizophrenic. I was put in a ward up at the hospital. One time I went off, I was yelling and screaming. It took six of them to hold me down and inject me. It is only now that I can see what had happened to me in there was what happened to me as a child—being held down and abused. And I was fighting them nurses off in the same way I'd fought [my other abusers] off (Atkinson 1998: 5).

Len names the link between his grandfather, his father's behaviour and his own experiences and behaviours. *My father was a very strong powered person ... it comes from my grandfather ... we had a lot of rules and if the rules weren't kept he got obsessed ... once I hit a man chewing an apple with his mouth open. Crazy, eh. In our house, you couldn't leave the table until everything on your plate was gone ... eating ... force-feeding until I vomited.* Coupled with his other experiences of excessive discipline—*leather belt or cane—scary—a big man—waiting in my room sometimes it taking hours for him to come—that was the most scary—never a chance to explain—* the links are clear between his own traumatisation and behaviours impacting on him across generations.

Don provided a number of instances when what could be called "psychotic" episodes appeared to have links to the traumatic experiences of previous family members, which he said at the time he had not previously known about. At times he appeared to be acting out other people's trauma, or other people's trauma enmeshed with his own. Aboriginal traditional healers who were present at one episode said he was living "too much in the past ... he's back with the old people and he's got to come back here". Much more work has to be done on this for it to be discussed in any depth. It is necessary, as this book clearly demonstrates, to voice a caution before diagnosing any Aboriginal person from a Western medical psychiatric paradigm. Certainly there is an important point to be made: at no time did any of the informants in the We Al-li program as a whole provide any evidence that they had received help in psychiatric or other mainstream mental health treatment except as a short-term bandaid to hold the crisis in check. Many of them detailed experiences which could only be described as further abuse on them, and which reinforced and compounded their trauma.

When Lorna makes the link between her own feelings as a child—that she could *never be good enough*—to the *feeling of the place*, she names the significance of *place* to many people. *Place* has its own energy, its own memory, its own pain transference and healing capacities which are held across many generations. *Places* hold trauma just as people do. Many Aboriginal people talk about the energy and memory of traumatic events, such as a massacre, being retained in a place, a site or a location until ceremonies of healing—a smoking or similar cleansing action—can occur. Lorna's childhood sexual abuse is held in that particular place and made more complex in relation to the milieu of the *place*. It is unsafe to talk about it in *this place. This* is where the abuse occurred, and to break the silence of denial (there) would result in punishment. The child would be blamed, and further abused, for speaking the truth. This is significant for Aboriginal people generally as they struggle with the need to name the abuses which are now within their families and communities as part of the cyclic patterns of transmission of violence and its resulting trauma across generations.

Figure 1 is a six-generational genogram, a composite of genograms owned by two members of the group. It links the historical events of frontier intrusion into Aboriginal lands with the resultant epidemics, massacres, starvations and removals of people to reserves, to the next period of protracted traumatisation, which was the removal of children and intense government surveillance of Aboriginal lives; and on to the third level, which acknowledges the intensity of present-day government attempts to rectify past wrongs

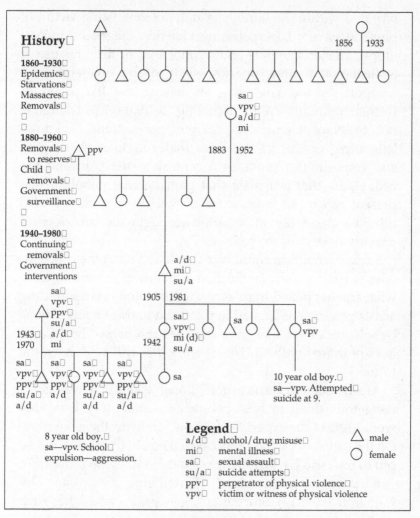

Figure 1
A six-generation genogram

while making no allowance for the levels of traumatisation in the lived reality. The fourth, fifth and sixth levels demonstrate the increase in intra-family violence in its multiple complexity and compounding effects.

The genogram traces one line of a family down the generations, listing the known traumas documented or narrated within the family: sexual violence, being victim of physical violence, perpetrating violence, diagnosed mental illness, suicide attempts and alcohol and/or drug misuse. It is clear that trauma, unacknowledged and unattended to, compounds and compacts, increasing the likelihood of further traumatic events occurring. To name this trauma is not to place blame on previous generations. Acknowledgement of the trauma-lines that run through families and communities provides a context to the pain and the behaviours that articulate that pain, so that people in the present can make more sense of their lived reality. It also provides necessary information to begin the processes of providing services for healing.

Such a genogram could be extended to chart the descendants of each person in the first generation shown, to trace what has happened in relationship to trauma compounding across generations located in *place*, and to trace interventions by self and others that have changed and helped heal in the lives of those involved. This is work that will be done in the future.

At one stage a health professional asked if it was not a dangerous thing to help people construct story lines that would reflect the experiences of the family in the genogram. On the contrary, "what cannot be talked about can also not be put to rest: and if it is not, the wounds continue to fester from generation to generation" (Bettelheim 1984, cited by Cameron 1998: 13). Story maps, genograms and other such methods help make links that explain the present. They also provide the means by which people can feel safe to begin to talk together, to come to grips with the past, which is the beginning of healing, to find resilience in their actions on which a new future is dependent.

Summary
In this chapter I have analysed people's narratives in relationship to the trauma experience. The narratives demonstrate that child-harm can result in considerable child

trauma which has ongoing consequences for the developing adult. Childhood experiences in parenting or institutional situations have been traumatic for many Aboriginal people. However, each of the people in the participant group demonstrated child-coping skills that allowed them to get on with their lives consequent to the trauma. They developed competencies that enabled them to function reasonably until a crisis occurred which triggered a return to the unresolved trauma. At the same time, in some aspects of their lives they demonstrated incompetencies in behaviours that were clearly based in previous trauma, and for which they did not receive adequate help.

Although people named violence in their lives, they did not provide detail. Rather, they focused on the feelings and behaviours which resulted from their own experiences of violence. Although there are links between victim and perpetrator behaviours, it is not always possible to define which is which. Lorna in particular showed the ill-defined line between perpetrator and victim. Ben, Don and Len all clearly showed the links between their childhood experiences of violence and their transference into adult behaviours that continue the cycle. It is more likely that people will feel safe to look at their perpetrator behaviours if they are also safe to explore their victimising experiences. Alcohol and other drug use was symptomatic of trauma and was used as a coping mechanism, but this in turn created more distress for the people concerned.

All the participants had multiple episodes of wanting to harm the self, and five had attempted suicide. By the ability of people to describe their experiences, the fragmentation of identity in trauma was made clear. What was not made as clear as it could have been by the Aboriginal members of the group, was the level of racism that is a normal functioning aspect of this society, and how this racism, both overt and covert, creates and compounds traumatisation. Lorna, Ben and, to a lesser extent, Mary show this, while Don was more particularly focused on the pain within his family. Transgenerational aspects of trauma were demonstrated both in societal situations and in families, both by overt transmission and by numerous acts of omission.

To understand in more detail the competencies which are integral to people's ability to cope and transform their lives as they work to address their experiences of violence and trauma, Chapter Five analyses the healing processes as concepts and practices of healing emerged from the narratives.

Chapter Five

The Way of the Human Being II: The healing story

> I am inspired by the knowledge that we can take this pain, work
> with it, transform it, so it becomes the source of our power.
>
> bell hooks and Cornel West 1992

The previous chapter examined the layered contexts of people's lives in order to develop a deeper understanding of the experiences and effect of violence. It was seen that trauma may be compounded down the generations as people act on each other from their own places of pain.

Naming and examining the problem is only a small part of what needs to occur, however. It is also important to consider and document processes of recovery or "healing". Participants also talked of their experiences of healing, of a need to heal, of a search for healing, of a deep desire for healing: *can Halo House be my healing place then?—I was looking for healing.*

Not all people had the same understanding of healing, or ascribed the same meaning to the term. It is important to discuss what healing means and how it occurs. This chapter explores the themes that emerged as people talked about their healing experiences.

Healing as an awakening

Healing as awakening refers to the phenomenon of people becoming increasingly conscious of their own needs in multiple domains of their individual and collective existence, and of an acknowledgement that these needs were unmet.

During the workshops people talked about healing a lot, but when they were asked to define what they meant, they were forced to unravel meanings to what had previously been an esoteric concept. Even in the process of defining healing they were awakening, at deeper and deeper levels, to their own healing needs. When asked about the meaning of healing, Mary and Jackie discussed their own experiences and understanding prior to coming into the workshops and after experiencing the workshops. *I don't think most **Murri** people have any idea about healing. A lot of people I know think healing is just going to the doctor and getting fixed up—getting some pills or something like that. **Getting somebody else to do something for them. Faith healers—religion**, stuff like that. That's what I thought too.*

Jackie had a similar concept to Mary, but in her discussion placed the healing process into an awakening to her own needs. ... *Healing is a really confusing word. When I first thought of it I thought I would go along to a workshop and all this pain was going to be healed. All my life **I thought that you went to a doctor or a psychologist or a psychiatrist** when you felt unwell and **he** would fix you—make you better. You would get healed. I can see now that is an unreasonable expectation. But it's the expectation of most people.* She began to tease out the aspects of healing that reflect the trauma of people's lives when they have been torn apart by painful experiences, and her own experiences of trying to receive help or "healing" for her pain. When Jackie says, *we might have to find a new word beside healing. Healing doesn't really fit,* she is awakening to her own healing needs and the fact they have not been met by the traditional medical approaches. *When I was looking for healing, I was in the deepest black hole depression and I couldn't see any way out. I had just come out of over twenty years of a really violent marriage. I thought I could just get on with my life but there came a time when I had to talk about it.* Here Jackie describes the crisis that often occurs after people have seemingly got on with their lives consequent to traumatic experiences, and also in the awakening, just before the movement into healing.

Trauma does not just go away. It has to be worked

through. *It was hard to find someone I could trust.* Once trust has been broken it is hard for trauma victims to trust again. Being able to trust sufficiently to explore the story of the pain, in its depth, is an essential part of the healing process. *A friend came to stay and once I started to talk, I couldn't shut the door when that person went away. I had no control over all the feelings that were just flooding from me. Everything was over-whelming me.* Jackie names the flood-gate of emotions that often open when healing begins and won't close once the story starts to come.[1] *I went to the doctor and he put me on antidepressants but they made me worse. I became suicidal. I had never thought of it before but now I was feeling suicidal all the time.* Jackie here names her experience, and the experience of Lorna, Mary, Don, Ben and Len, that sometimes traditional Western medical and psychological responses to people who are traumatised have not been adequate, and did not help them in the healing process. It is vital to understand that traumatised people are not sick. They are not mentally ill. They do, however, have specific needs that deserve to be met.

Jackie continues in her understanding that she did not get her needs met: *I went to a psychologist. He was a very quiet gentle type of person and so it was easy to talk to him. But he talked way above my head about things I couldn't grasp and couldn't understand. I had no concept what he was talking about. It didn't seem to relate to any of my problems or the things I needed to talk about. He wasn't really into the story of what was behind why I was feeling like I was. He said the story didn't matter. He was into, if you believed in spirit, he believed you should just relax and follow your inner thoughts and "spirit would heal". I was really trying to understand what he was talking about because **I had gone to him for help.***

---

1 Many Aboriginal people across Australia are at present suffering similar crises—because the reality of their pain at their removal as children has been unleashed by the Stolen Generations inquiry, or because they have begun to acknowledge themselves as living in abusive environments as a result of increased public attention to domestic violence/sexual assault issues—yet can find no help for their needs.

There is a vital part of Jackie's story here that needs to be fleshed out. The counsellor she went to told her to *believe in spirit* and *spirit would heal*. This is an incomplete concept of the inner healing process. It denies the pain the person is in, which precludes being able to access the inner healing process and the deeper knowledge of the Self, how it has been hurt and how it can heal. In her own wisdom Jackie names that: *I wasn't in a place where I could put into practice what he was trying to say even if I could understand it. You have to be at a* **certain stage through the pain before you can hear things like that***. The other voices I had—that I was stupid, that I was bad, were louder. I was really mixed up and I didn't know really, who I was.*

When Jackie was asked to describe what she meant when she said, "I was really mixed up—I didn't know really, who I was", she described the jigsaw concept of identity fragmentation defined towards the end of the previous chapter as the search for identity—fragmentation and separation. As she says: *I'd been controlled and manipulated for so long that I didn't know who I was.* She continued to give a powerful concept of her definition of healing: *I was really desperate when I applied to go to the workshops and I thought I would go along and all this pain would be healed and at the finish I would just walk away—healed, but now I know differently.* **Healing to me now means learning. It's an educational process of learning about myself at a deep level, what has made me who I am. That's healing.** Jackie has gone on to apply this concept in undergraduate studies, where she is now receiving high distinctions for her work.

Lorna has also described an inappropriate response to her healing needs: *I was locked away many times for my drinking.* "Did they help you in there?" *No. Most of the times I was sedated. I remember waiting on the veranda for my husband. He says he came through the door and he said, "Hello Sweet. How are you going?" And I said, "Oh hello. I don't trust too many men, but you look like a nice man so I'll talk to you. I'm just waiting for my husband and babies." He was very upset because I was so pumped up with drugs.* "Did they sit and talk to you about the kind of things we are talking about now?" [Note: Lorna's trauma story is already emerging when she says "I don't trust too many men."] *It didn't help. They just gave me tablets and wanted me to have shock treatment.* Lorna's husband awakened to the fact that the treatment Lorna was receiving for what others labelled a mental illness was not helping her, and he worked to get her into an Aboriginal Alcohol Rehabilitation program, which did help. He knew enough of her story to know that first she needed to stop drinking, and then she had to deal with the underlying trauma stories that were contributing to her need to drink. The awakening to what is healing, the potential to help healing happen, and the means of accessing it in the lives of people—these are vital considerations in the development of healing programs for Aboriginal people.

Healing as an experience of safety

The healing of trauma requires the establishment of an environment of safety, without judgement or prejudice.

In trauma healing there is always a significant or triggering event that intervenes or intrudes into a person's situation, which can be experienced as a crisis or emergency. Under such circumstances people need to feel safe and be safe. This can only occur in situations of cultural safety. Cultural safety is the identification a person makes with factors that are derived from the culture, belief systems or worldviews that allow them to feel safe while being with those to whom they have gone for help.

The world is often experienced as unsafe. Sometimes people may not even know they are in pain; a government program, such as the National Domestic Violence Awareness Program or the Inquiry into the Removal of Aboriginal Children from their Parents, may trigger awareness of their actual reality, of the source and extent of the pain that has been denied or buried. It may be young women innocently talking about sex, as in Jackie's case. A television program may bring up denied knowledge, as in Len's reaction to the sexual abuse in boys' homes, which forced him to face the part of himself he had disowned because it was too painful. The trigger may be a research project such as this one, where people are asked questions and have to face things that have previously been blocked out of their consciousness; or it may be a natural occurrence that takes on supernatural dimensions, such as a death of a close loved one. Often people are functioning in pain, with behaviours that don't make sense to themselves or others until context is explored as the stories unfold.

A significant event may be a crisis which triggers a further crisis; or the event may be a seed planted by another person, which is not fully heard at the time, but which becomes relevant at a later time of crisis. For example, Don's grandfather planted a seed at a time when Don was busy drinking: *Grandfather was getting old. He would be awake when I came home from the nightclubs 4 or 5 o'clock in the morning. Just before he died he said to me: "If you ever want to get yourself well again … you do whatever you need to do."* This instruction from his Elder, the senior member of his family—*"do whatever you have to do to get yourself well again"*—became pertinent when his grandfather became terminally ill, a crisis because his grandfather had been his only stable anchor since the death of his grandmother. Don's world was again unsafe. *Grandfather took sick. During the time that he was in the hospital—my body was doing crazy things. I thought I was going off my head. They said I was schizophrenic.* Don needed to find a place of safety within a cultural context that could provide support to his crisis needs, and he did, at Halo House, the residential alcohol and drug awareness centre in Rockhampton.

Ben also found safety at Halo House: *I **feel safe** here. I know it's a safe place for me. When I came to the workshops I had feelings—for the **first time ever**—feelings of **security** and **safety**.*

The reason it is important to deliberately create this safe environment, with rules established by the group, is that in so many instances participants have been living in situations where they were unsafe, where lore has broken down and law is inadequate, where family and community structures are disintegrating and there are no rules. They may also have had laws imposed on them which are discriminatory, of which they feel no part and to which they have no commitment. Each person (including all facilitators) must be involved in the process of making rules to live by as people begin the process of relating to each other at a deep level. The workshops were run on a set of rules that were non-negotiable: no harm to the self; no harm to another; no harm to property; no alcohol or drugs on site; and no sexual harassment or activity during the times of the (residential) workshops.

Len, who had such a flooding of feelings for most of his life that were often expressed in inappropriate ways on himself or others, found that in the safety of a supportive group *you just felt safe—to do things, to express yourself, to get out what was inside. It felt comfortable. You didn't feel like you were a fool if you cried or if you got angry. Being allowed to express anger in the workshops was brilliant, just brilliant. You were safe.* Here Len acknowledges that feelings can be expressed without the aid of drugs.

Don links the expression of feelings to spirituality, which is interesting in consideration of Thomas Moore's observation that the "soul is the place of deepest feeling". He also turns the negative label somebody else has given him into a positive, when he feels safe to explore himself in depth: *I learnt that it is good for me to cry and let out my anger in a way that doesn't hurt myself or other people ... that it's good to be mad, silly, womba. I found out a lot about my spirituality when I did this.*

Lorna emphasises that she had many reasons why she needed to have a safe place to begin to heal. *I **needed** to have a **safe place** where I could talk about my pain, all the pain that I have had in my life, my drinking, in my marriage, my childhood, to be able to sit and feel free enough to talk about it and get it out of me. I had it in me for so long, for too long.* The process of establishing safety is also part of the processes of reconstruction of community.

Healing as community support

The narratives demonstrate that trauma healing requires a supportive environment with people who care. Supportive families are vital in healthy healing, and, if not a supportive family, at least people who have been through or who understand what the person is going through.

In Don's case the seed had been planted; the trigger was the crisis of his grandfather's illness and death. When a crisis comes, however, the person may be forced to make decisions, to do something to meet their needs. In some cases their action goes beyond tackling the immediate crisis, taking them into other unresolved traumas that happened many years ago. There may be a build-up of crisis after crisis, until the situation becomes almost unmanageable; indeed, for some people, outside enforced intervention occurs.

It is crucial for people at this time to be able to make choices about what kinds of services are suitable for them and to access a variety of services. Some people need one-to-one contacts; others function better in a group. All of them need a safe, controlled environment where they can work through the "trauma" emergency with skilled people, so they emerge strengthened, knowing they have had the courage to do their own painful healing work. Some may need the quiet revitalising of their country and Elders who do no more than listen.

Both Don and Ben show separately what worked for them: in both cases they received an invitation from an aunty—*My cousin, and my aunty, tribal way, gave me a choice*—who saw her nephew in the street and knew he was in crisis, and invited him to either enter Halo House or attend the We Al-li workshops. In Don's case: *I was wanting to get off the grog so I came down to Halo House to talk to somebody. Aunty was there doing some painting. She said sit down and have a bit of a talk. I had to make a decision whether I would go into hospital and be pumped up with drugs and have the psychiatric doctors try to make me well again, or come down to Halo House. I was wanting to get off the grog so I came down to Halo House.*

At this time a person needs help and support to deal with the initial crisis and to uncover suppressed and denied stories and feelings, if this is appropriate, as they relate to the present crisis. This was so in the case of these two men. Ben was invited by his aunty to come to a We Al-li workshop because she knew he was in crisis: his father had suicided; his marriage had broken up; he had just unsuccessfully attempted suicide; he was drinking to excess (but it would not have helped if anybody had told him that). She did not lecture him, but invited him to a weekend workshop being run jointly by Halo House and the We Al-li program. Ben recalled: *You know what I was like at the first workshop—suicidal and depressed and it was the workshop that helped me feel I could do something for myself and so I moved to Halo House. [The workshops] helped me to make up my mind that I had a drinking problem.* He came back to the next one. From there he made the decision to enter Halo House and undertake a period of rehabilitation for his alcohol misuse.

In Don's case, his aunty saw him in the street and invited him to attend a meeting at Halo House. She knew his grand-father was ill and that his family were concerned for him. At Halo House he met people he knew and people who had been in similar situations to him. *I knew people here. Some of the people here had been in the same kind of experiences I was going through.* In his crisis he found what he needed—a safe place for him to be at this critical time—and community support: *What helped me most was being in a safe place ... the best thing about Halo House is I know it's a safe place for me.* When he said *people are here with my medicine*, it was originally assumed he meant pills, until he continued. ***My medicine** is people who are willing to **listen** to me when I want to talk about what is happening inside me ... with **my spirituality**.*

Don's concept of what medicine he knew he needed is powerful and compelling in its articulation of what is wrong with society generally. People do not listen to each other, and they are more likely to label a person as *womba*—crazy, criminal—than to consider that the behaviour of the person may have context—they may be articulating distress or they may be in a spiritual emergency. A spiritual emergency is where the deep structural layers of cultural and spiritual knowledge and knowing can begin to emerge to heal the trauma of the past if the emergence is responded to appropriately.

In the reciprocity of relating, Don also names the learning that comes from listening to others. *My medicine is listening to other people too. The first time I was listening to others talking, I thought they were talking about my life. Their experiences were like my experiences. Their feelings were like my feelings. I wanted to know how did they know my story and what it felt like to be me?* Don names here the power of the group process for Indigenous peoples, the learning from each other and the relating that allows the sharing of knowledge essential to healing. *I am not alone* is powerful medicine for people who have felt completely isolated, unheard, unacknowledged in their pain, even within large extended families and dynamic communities.

Don was also supported by his mother and he learns from her previous experience. *Mum was very good. She is very understanding because she has gone through the same things I've gone through. When she was going through it I thought she was mad [laughs] because—she had all these sicknesses, she was scared to go outside—she was scared to be locked up—she didn't want to sleep in her own room—she didn't know where she was, and I didn't know where she was either.*[2] *But she got through it and she is a lot happier in herself. When I realised what I went through I went back to her and said Mum, I had a spiritual awakening.*[3] *I wasn't going off my head, I wasn't having a nervous breakdown.*

---

2 Often when people act from their pain in crisis, family and workers experience fear because they do not understand what is happening and the pain triggers their pain. They therefore try to block off the expression of the pain, either (in the family) by hospitalising the person, or (in the institution) by medicating the person.

3 This term of Don's, and his description of his mother in crisis, are similar to the terminology Stanislov Grof uses to describe a "spiritual emergency": see for example *Stormy Search for Self* (Grof and Grof 1990) and *The Adventure in Self Discovery* (Grof 1988).

*I was having a **spiritual awakening**. Why didn't somebody tell me?* In this regard healing is also giving a positive name to what seems to be a negative experience. In fact many such "spiritual emergencies" can be an opportunity for change and healing, if responded to in an appropriate manner.

Rebuilding a sense of family and community in healing

It has previously been argued that the single most important restorative need for people who have been victimised is a supportive and caring family and community. When Jackie was *looking for healing* she felt alone in the world. She did not have a family who could support her. *I have no family in the true sense of the word, but I have made friends with people.* Part of her healing process was to begin to rebuild a sense of family, of community, with people around her. These people became her family, and yet there were still fears in her that something might go wrong. *I'm building a family—it's still hard for although I consider some people family, because the blood tie is not there, you don't know whether it can survive the turmoil of a relationship.* Nonetheless, the process of rebuilding is healing in itself as boundaries are explored and relationships worked through.

Ben names the experience of healing as rebuilding, or the development of community: *I enjoy all the closeness, the sharing with the other people. That was my problem. All my life I sort of felt nobody ever really cared but since I've been in the workshops I've met other people who also have problems and they **share** the same **pain,** the same anger and we all **care** for **each other**. It makes me feel good because I know I am wanted. I feel a **part** of **something**. It's given me **new life**.*

Healing as ever-deepening self-knowledge

The narratives demonstrate that healing at its most fundamental level is an ever-deepening knowledge, of the deep structure of the self and the layered and multiple parts of who the person is, at both biographical and transpersonal levels, culturally and spiritually.

Jackie explains: *The first workshop ... it was the safest workshop ... that's when I started to understand about myself and how you have to look at your story about how you became who you are.* Jackie confirms the importance of feeling safe. *We bonded into a family and I felt a really good feeling at the end of the workshop.* Communal processes of working together are also important, as she demonstrates. She goes on to name the beginning stages of finding the self as an early stage of healing. Before that time she could have been called a survivor (of child rape, of domestic violence); now she was taking the first steps to begin her own healing work. *I knew that **talking would help me find out a bit more about myself**. It would help me find out **the bits of me that were really me** and **the bits of me that were not really me.***

There are conscious choices people may need to make in healing. Lorna's change process occurred because she made a choice. *I made my own choice ... simply because I needed to be with my husband and family. **They were important to me. That decision** when I put down the drink ... **it's changed my life—** with my children ... when I was drinking I didn't have a relationship with them. We were like strangers. I used to hurt them and chase them and tell them I didn't want them around and after going through rehabilitation I came home and needed to build bridges with my children. I didn't think they would forgive me. I have a different relationship with them now ... a very close relationship with them.* It was only after Lorna "put down the drink" that the deeper work of healing the early abuses of her childhood could be undertaken. Lorna also names the ongoing legacy, the need to be aware that healing must occur across generations. *I guess there is still stuff in [my children] that comes up for them, as a result of their childhood, that they will have to deal with in the future.* But for Lorna, *I realise today I am only in control of me, I can't control them, and I am not responsible for them, only for myself.* This does not mean that Lorna does not grieve for the years when, for many reasons, she was unable to be the kind of parent she wanted to be, but rather that she has taken the responsibility to work on herself in an ongoing process of healing. That way she can be a better mother and grandmother today.

As people begin to feel safe and share with each other the deeper parts of their pain and demonstrate their courage, which results as people are with each other in the deep listening process, shifts in perspective occur. Hence Jackie and Mary name healing as a transforming process that creates a shifting perspective: *Today **I think and see myself differently** than I did two years ago—things that I had always thought about myself, **understanding them and understanding how I came to think things about myself that were not true**.* Mary saw the power of being able to make choices. *Healing is facing up to the fact that **you've got choices**. There is no need to live all your life in your pain. You can always get out of it. Knowing that you have choices is a healing thing itself and it shifts you from that place you never thought you could get out of, you just accepted and you know you can't change. **Healing is knowing you can change things in your life**.* Healing therefore must not be considered an outcome, but rather a process of engagement and understanding, of change and growth.

The story of healing can emerge in many different ways in a person. Dreams, for example, can provide context to the story and help a person face painful truths, as Mary demonstrates: *In the dream ... I was running around frightened and alone trying to rescue the babies. I was frantically rescuing the children from the river. [At the same time] I was angry at the women for not rescuing their children. [When I woke] I realised how exhausted I felt and asked myself why I was always trying to rescue people all the time. And I began to **understand how angry I feel because people are not doing what I thought they should be doing**.*

Lorna also names the critical need not to blame or find fault with others in the story, which diminishes the self, but to focus on self-awareness. *Healing began when I realised I had to **look at myself**. I had spent half my bloody life **looking at my** *husband and trying to get **him to change**, his family and my family. The only time the changes began to come was when I put down the drink and started to have a really good look at **me** to find my own story.*

This does not mean that there are not serious social implications in abuse stories—on the contrary, "the environment, family systems, school system, and city are all involved in every abuse situation, even those that occur within the secrecy of the home" (Mindel 1995: 111–13). Racism and sexism will continue to exist and govern the behaviour of many people in society. While it is acknowledged that many government programs actually increase the trauma instead of responding to the human distress, the focus in this work has been on having people involved in their own self-determination and self-healing.

The critical factor for each of the people in the narratives was the empowerment that came when they realised that the power for the change process was contained within them, and did not have to be abdicated to others. In taking this power to themselves, they became more able to work towards change within the systems that have previously functioned abusively on them.

The use of ceremony in healing

The purpose of ceremonies is healing through action and meaning-making. Ceremony is the observance or practice of a ritual which gives meaning to aspects of the life story. Telling and listening to stories can be ceremonial and therefore healing. In ceremonies we celebrate the awareness of our lives as sacred. *Dadirri* was used as a ceremonial process of aiding deeper listening. *Dadirri* "renews us and brings us peace. It makes us feel whole again. One of our ceremonies that brings about this wholeness is the Smoking Ceremony" (Ungunmerr 1993a: 34). The workshop activities and the narratives demonstrate that ceremony is healing.

Two important ceremonies were used within the workshops. There was the daily ritual of *Dadirri* (capitalised here to denote the ceremony), which was performed each morning so that the work of the day could begin, and a Smoking Ceremony which followed. The Smoking Ceremony was always carried out under the direction of people on whose country the workshop was being held. All work was conducted within a circle. *Dadirri* and the Smoking Ceremony comprised the experience of the contemplative time in the circle each morning before the other work commenced.

Mary described her experience of the circle as valuable learning: *Sitting in the circle and talking to each other—you call it reflective discussion—was the most valuable learning.* **We learnt from each other***. Just being able to hear other people's fears and things was powerful.*

Once the morning *Dadirri* ritual had been conducted, people were able to listen to each other more deeply. The ceremony created an atmosphere of care for one another and a consciousness of the honouring in the listening to each person's stories.

In the multiple losses that are part of traumatisation, grief is an important but often unresolved issue. People can become disconnected, not only from themselves but from others in their families and communities.

The practice of *Dadirri,* as it was observed within We Al-li, and more particularly the Smoking Ceremony, restored connection and provided a cleansing reconnection that enabled a renewal of relationships. When *Dadirri* is used within a circle, the circle holds the vulnerability of the person who has suffered the loss in sacred trust; it provides the space for them to be open and revealing of the depth of their pain. This provides the means by which the loss can begin to heal as others support them in their grieving.

Len first came to the workshops when invited by one of the Aboriginal participants after a suicide attempt. He says that he was **looking for a spiritual thing***, like the church, something really* **spiritual***, and* **cultural***.* He found, however, *it was far different than what I had expected. I thought we would be* *talking about what was spiritual. What we talked about was* *ourselves.* **Ourselves***!! Yeah! It really opened my eyes. It was a big* *turn-around for me when I began to understand that we are sacred* *beings.* **It was spiritual but not in a church way, and it was** **cultural but it taught us about ourselves***. Yeah. That was good.* The ceremonies of the circle, of *Dadirri* and the Smoking Ceremony brought a cultural spirituality to the group that provided its own healing atmosphere.

Cultural and spiritual identity in healing

It is important to acknowledge that many people were already searching for meaning and life purpose, and this search was connected to cultural and spiritual identity. In seeking a cultural and spiritual identity they were looking outside themselves as this society teaches us to do. They had not come to understand that the essence of "who they are" is an articulation of both their cultural and spiritual being. The story is present but its value has rarely been acknowledged. It is this aspect of healing from trauma that needs to be built on as the narratives indicate its relevancy in healing action.

Culture is the set of beliefs, values and rules for living that are distinctive to a particular human group. It is passed from generation to generation in a complexity of relationships, knowledges, languages, social organisations and life experiences that bind diverse individuals and groups together. In such interactions people develop an individual and collective sense of who they are and where they belong. Culture provides meaning and purpose to life, and is usually anchored in a particular place—a past or present homeland (Royal Commission on Aboriginal Peoples 1995: 25). Culture is a living process, and when there is strong cultural continuity people become imbued with a sense of identity, well-being and life purpose. Culture, spirit and identity are linked across time and place to country and kin. Healing occurs when these re-connections begin to be made.

Don's identity was located in the past, while his reality was the painful present. *All my life I been dreaming—dreaming about being like my ancestors, not fifty years ago or two hundred years ago. I don't want to be like them ancestors. I wanted to be like the thousands of fifty years ago when my ancestors used to heal themselves, go out bush—let all their energies out in the bush, and heal themselves. I want to be like them ancestors.* While his process of remembering was painful, and while there were difficulties in recognising and naming much of the actuality of his lived experiences, he also had help. *I feel I've always been a spiritual person. I always had a great belief in my ancestors and the old ways. I believe my spirit [another word for spirit as used here could be consciousness or soul] can contact his [grandfather's] spirit or any other spirit that I want to contact. When he was dying I started sending healing power to him so he could see the light and I asked my Creator—Moonda Nghadda— my Rainbow Serpent, to guide him towards the light because Nan was on the other side waiting for him. The Real Old People [The Ancestors] and Grandfather and Nan, they think it great what I am doing.*

Don names the depth of cultural and spiritual ways of being which are in the deepest tissues of Being and which can be called on to aid healing. *It seems like a dream now. Mother Earth and everything about her seemed to be within me from when I can first remember. Aboriginality, culture, corroboree, paintings, music, singing, dance. I know now they were in me.* This reflects the work of Deborah Bird Rose in *Nourishing Terrains of Aboriginal Australia* (1996: 35–6); Aboriginality, culture, spirit, land are implicit in identities who have created a country through thousands of years of human activities, which continue in the human psyche and the land in the present.

Don also began to re-make himself, to find for himself a new identity: *because being black isn't the colour of my skin— being Aboriginal isn't the colour of my skin. Not what-so-ever. I feel about myself being multi-cultural—being Aboriginal is being all kinds of races and creeds within me;* and he also began to find a new life purpose: *after I heal myself, I am willing and needing and wanting to heal all multi-cultural peoples right around the universe.* In saying this, Don demonstrates that as people heal they begin to express meaning and find purpose beyond their own self-limitations. In this sense, healing is a transformative and transcendental process.

Healing as transformation and transcendence

Participants demonstrated through their testimonies that healing is a process of transformation and transcendence. It is the ever-unfolding expression of knowledge of the Self. In the processes of transformation the Self is viewed with acceptance and compassion and a curiosity towards the change process. With the knowledge that change is possible must come the knowledge of choices and an access to services relevant to the transformation process. The desire for change can then be met.

The process of healing is to be able to look at the Self through a different lens. Bronwyn Fredericks writes about her experience of the workshops and gives a powerful description of using her courage to find deeper layers and make meaning out of her story in the complexities of a whole life of relating.

> The workshops enabled me to look at my life, my family, my friendship circles and my work environment. I saw how they all interface with each other, how they are sometimes supportive and sometimes abusive. I examined my own behaviour patterns in my personal and working lives. I was able to explore my experiences of being abused and how I have been, and can be abusive. One way I like to explain is: from the time I was born my life has been recorded on a tape. Sometimes when I hear, see, touch, smell and sense something, my tape rewinds. When this happens I remember and think about what happened in the past, the hurt, the pain, the upsets. Other times, I'd block the rewind because I didn't want to remember, think of, or deal with the issues. We Al-li for me has been a process of daring to take my tape, to load it in the tape recorder and rewind, play, rewind and play, dealing with the past, digging down deep into the crevices of where I buried my deepest hurts, re-experiencing some of the feelings, the tears I did, and I didn't cry, the screams I never let out and all the emotion, secret and shame that for a

long time I have attempted to hide and bury. One day I know if I keep going along my healing journey when I hear, smell, touch, see and sense something, I'll think back and I'll be able to say "yes that did happen and yes I'm OK" (Fredericks 1995: 23).

Jackie names the transforming process that occurred for her when she began to cast aside her old patterns of thinking and relating. While previously she had felt a victim of other people's behaviour on her, she is now taking responsibility for herself and is becoming truly empowered. She says: *Healing for me is learning how to look at things in a different way. Understanding how these things came to be in my life. Owning my own things, and not taking on board other people's things. Being responsible for what I am responsible for, and not taking on what other people are responsible for. Also learning how to deal with different situations — how to interact with other people — how to lessen conflict — how to work through things with people in a good way — how to see things from another person's point of view. [It is] also learning how to express myself without blaming other people. All of that's healing and that's what I learnt in the workshops.*

Mary names a factor that applies particularly to Aboriginal peoples who have been subjected to cultural and spiritual genocide and that often eludes people who have been made powerless, or who have placed all their power in others, and look to others for help. This applies particularly to Aboriginal peoples who have been subject to cultural genocide. *Saddest thing is [Murri people] don't even realise that they've got all the coping mechanisms and they've been healing themselves all these years. And if this was pointed out to them, things would really start to happen. They would build on it, because they know things are wrong, but they just don't know what to do about it.*

Mary names important factors here. As Aboriginal people demand that society generally look at its own abusive behaviour, they are forcing a healing process to occur for Australian society generally (that is, if Australia as a nation can take the courage to involve itself in an educational process of learning about itself at a deep level and if

Australians are willing to look at what has made us what/ who we are). What is needed now is for this process to be taken to the individual, family and community level, for only a small section of the process of healing has so far been entered into. Just as society has to look at itself, so do individuals, families and communities. As Mary says, Murri (Aboriginal) people need to come to accept that they do have the *coping mechanisms*, skills and knowledge, *and they've been healing themselves all these years* in their struggle to rise above the multiple traumatisations of a past era. These are vital skills, knowledge and coping mechanisms to recognise and on which to build. Non-Aboriginal peoples must concede to this.

As Mary also points out, *one of the things I've learnt in the workshops — the **pain isn't a bad thing** even though it might seem like a really bad thing. Going into the pain was **some of the best learning experiences** I've ever had. You go back into the most shittiest experience, and afterwards you realise that if it hadn't happened you wouldn't be **who you are**, you wouldn't have grown.*

At the same time, Lorna talks about the multiple layers she had to be prepared to address when she entered rehabilitation to get off the grog. *Putting down the drink helped. Then I was able to **have a good look at myself. Change happened. My attitude** toward my marriage, my husband, me. There were things in the rehab that I **started to like about myself** ... being black being black. ... Healing takes place when I feel well enough in myself to talk honestly about ... what happened to me, **what it was like** for me. This is what I found. **Healing is action.** I can sit and talk and talk about healing, but I had to **do the work** and it is **hard work** because it meant for me to go to workshops like We Al-li where I can **clean out that pain.** I realised today that I am **only in control of me.** I am not in control of my husband or my children or other people. I can't control them and **I am not responsible for them**, only for myself.* Lorna acknowledges that the work of healing is hard, and she demonstrates the blameless courage and a willingness to do what must be done, ingredients that come with deepening self-acceptance, and the self-confidence of discovering for herself who she is and what made her who she is.

Integration in healing

In situations of human atrocity with its resulting traumatisation, a person or group may lose their sense of direction. Life becomes meaningless. If life is meaningless, a person has no reason for living. The fabric and soul of relations and beliefs in and about people fragments and fractures. The intricate web of relations that binds people together no longer holds. People lose the knowledge of who they are, and they no longer know life as meaningful. The loss of purpose can create multiple greater losses. There may come a time when it seems proper to commit suicide, at both individual and group levels. The loss of purpose is passed down across generations as people, disconnected from life meaning, feel powerless and may inflict purposelessness onto the place and people where they live.

Without purpose, the past-present-future becomes weighed down with question marks: Who am I? Where do I come from? Why am I here? Where am I going? When the questions cannot be answered, life becomes more meaningless, more purposeless; and eventually the questions cannot even be asked. This is the condition of extreme apathy and anomie.

This explains the situation of so many young Aboriginal people who came into the workshops at different times and who felt no sense of either a valued present or a possible future in this country. So often they were engaged in senseless acts of violence on themselves and others. If there was any interest, it was generally focused on the past or the future. The past was the stories and milieu of pain, anger, humiliation, dispossession, alienation, marginalisation, rage —supported, often, by behaviours that maintained and increased that rage. The future was focused as a culture taken from videos, television, American movies, often those movies that depicted the future as "a bombed out planet, no trees, no communities, smashed bodies, blood and gore",[4] with no connection to their lived reality. Their felt powerlessness to change their situation created a cyclic situation where conditions could not get better, only worse. It was therefore important to help those who came to the workshops during the fieldwork to find meaning in situations that seemed hopeless, and in which they felt powerless. Frankl has said: "what counts and matters is to bear witness to the uniquely human potential to transform a tragedy into a triumph, to turn one's predicament into a human achievement" (1978: 43).

All the participants indicate that healing is not a simple journey nor an easy road to take. It is always bumpy and there are many ups and downs. It is hard work. Not everybody wants to heal, for as Don points out, *people are afraid of what they will find.* Often the process of healing appears to others to be some sort of mental crisis, as Len describes (and Don has previously described about his mother and himself): *After I came out of rehab I used to cry every day. I cried for months and months when I first came out, but now it's getting less.* And each day brings something different: *Sometimes I go back to it, when it's a really hairy day, but I know now I can't give up because things are starting to change.*

Facilitators of healing (counsellors or therapists) must therefore *know themselves,* as Mary discovered. *My expectations were to just get some tools to help our mob. I wasn't counting on all that stuff coming up for me and having to work through it. I don't think it really occurred to me that I would have to work on myself first before I could help my mob.* Len adds another dimension to this concept of the work of helping the healing/educational processes to occur for another. *There is a difference between allowing something to come out, and forcing it out. I've seen that a lot in rehabs and when you talk to psychiatrists. You have to think it out. But in the workshops, it **just***

---

4 I asked a group of young men from one of the prisons to draw me the future and generally that was the vision of the future they drew.

*flowed out, it came from the **heart and it was a heart healing**. It didn't come from the head*. He describes a natural non-intrusive process where the educator, working in a good way with a person, could be described as a midwife, an attendant at the birth of new knowledge, new understanding of the Self.

As Jackie explains: *Healing occurs with people sitting together in healing circles, maturing through their stories, realising change only comes if they make it come. Change is hard work and painful. My changes started with We Al-li in sharing stories, feeling strong because of the support of others, bonding into a family, coming to know I was lovable, **learning we are all unique and important**.* People can only heal when they know themselves to be of value and have a sense of their own worth.

During the workshops Mary discovered things about herself she had not previously valued. *I never realised I had so many skills and resources, you know, coping skills. I pretty much thought my life was a mess, but yeah, after being in the workshops I could see that I had **in-built skills** that were always there, were always there but I hadn't recognised they were a skill in the first place.*

From the beginning, a number of issues became clear, not the least of which was the realisation that in many cases people had lost their knowledge of the whole self and their sense of life purpose. Initially, people felt life had no meaning; often they were in a crisis of cultural and spiritual identity. This changed during the time they worked together.

What was apparent in those who came to the workshops was their desire to make meaning out of their lives and the activities in which they were engaged. It is appropriate to include here a poem written by William Gulf of Woorabinda during a We Al-li workshop at the Haven, Emu Park, in 1995.

> "Why are we here?"
> "We are here for learning."
> "What have we learnt?"
> "We have learnt
> to respect ourselves

and others
through sexuality,
religious beliefs, environments,
families, cultures, traditions, arts."

"All these things
are part of me, part of us all."
"By learning, by knowing,
by trying to understand
what I hold in my hand."

"To reach out
to those who need help."
"To grasp
the learning one has to offer,
and to work for a better,
healthier lifestyle,
but always keeping in touch
with one's own
spirituality and culture."

"This is my Dreaming."
"How I live and learn
from day to day
with my thoughts and deeds
I hold in my hand."

©William Gulf, Woorabinda, 1995

William expresses a deep learning and wisdom. This was his own meaning-making of the workshop activity, which in the broader sense could also be a statement about the activities and purpose of life. In his poem he also makes a statement about the valuable knowledge that comes from within the Self as people explore together, who they are individually and collectively.

Summary

This chapter has explained the experiences of healing that emerged from the narrative of Chapter Three, and the activities of the workshops of We Al-li. The workshops involved an awakening to the deep inner, often unmet, needs for healing. Healing required experiencing feelings of safety in what had previously been experienced as an unsafe world. When people work together to create safety for each other they rebuild community, and what emerges is a deepening self-knowledge not just of the individual but of the group—community is made in this activity. The ability to begin to rebuild the essence and experience of family and community, therefore, is an essence of healing processes. The group who were involved with We Al-li used principles of ceremony to add the healing processes, which strengthened aspects of the cultural and spiritual identity. Because the groups were mixed, often a sharing of cultures occurred as well. The transformational processes of healing were integrated as people settled into the knowledge that healing never ends, that the journey is long and hard, but that in transcendence the changes that occur strengthen and empower the person and the group for ongoing change and growth.

The chapter demonstrates that a healing relationship is potentially present whenever one person comes to another to share pain. One of the participants wished to change the word *healing* to *education*—educating the self about the Self. In the narratives the group demonstrated a powerful process of soul-searching, and significant insight and understanding of their own lives. This was observed during the taping of each person's story, and it also occurred as people worked together, shared together and listened to each other in the We Al-li workshops and the *dadirri* circles. Healing is a group interaction.

A healing relationship between people who are working to listen to each other in *dadirri* is important because it holds the potential for reacquainting people with their own self-healing abilities. For people who have been colonised this is doubly important, so that they begin to feel and reclaim the power within themselves to change who they have been made by the colonising processes and who they have tried to be to counter this colonisation. The "real self" only emerges once people have been able to name and know the "constructed self" (how we have been constructed by others) and the "ideal self" (behaving in the way we think people want us to behave).

The work of We Al-li was experiential. It was developed so that people could explore in safety their own lived experiences, and learn from them. It was also developed so that we who worked together in the participatory action work of the study could ask and answer the questions: How do people heal? What works, and why does it work?

The processes of healing within the workshops of We Al-li and the dialogues of the group who shared their stories affirm the knowledges and skills of Indigenous healing practice and their value within the whole world context in the need to acknowledge human traumatisation if violence is to be dealt with world-wide. The processes of We Al-li involved a special form of communication—of remaking community, communicating the care and concern of others for the individual and collective pain. In the shared process of being together in *dadirri*, people received, individually and collectively, the reason and the strength to begin to heal.

The next chapter makes links between the theory and practice of violence/trauma stories, and healing stories. Research in this field is analysed in relation to what has been explained so far, in the attempt to understand the phenomenology of acts of violence and experiences of trauma, and healing from trauma.

Chapter Six

To Unite Hearts and Establish Order

We need to talk the language of healing,
the language of courage and hope,
and in so doing name that each disaster or crisis
(in our lives)
is also an opportunity.
For with crisis or tragedy,
comes the invitation to move into the heart place,
which reconnects us to our soul
and brings spirituality to our lives.

Adapted from Robert Theobold

The chapter presents an Indigenous community healing model using four educational activity circles for re-creating lives and constructing life meaning from disorder and distress.

Cultural tools which assist healing: a model for community action

Chapter Two explored Aboriginal worldviews, which are relationship-centred. "Who I am" as an Aboriginal person could be described as the multiple inter-subjective experiences of being-in-a-world-of-relationships. These are the relationships that have been made by, and in turn have characterised, Aboriginal peoples throughout time: enduring connections held across generations with ancestors who have made us what we are, with the country which has formed us and has been formed by us in ceremony and ritual; the interconnections and interdependencies between people in kinship and other affiliations, and with the corporeal and non-corporeal world. These are fundamental considerations in constructing any healing process.

The core business of "Being Aboriginal", according to Stanner (1979: 143) and substantiated by Ungunmerr (1993a: 34), was the ceremonial activities used to unite people and establish order from within the normal human interactions of relating, and the chaos of natural disaster and human discord. An example of such ceremonial action was provided in the *prun* (Roth 1984: 1902, 15). Such ceremonies of healing conflict are important to reconsider today.

The structured work in the We Al-li process was an attempt to re-create ceremonies of healing in the contemporary situation. The study demonstrated that it is possible to build cultural safety through the use of cultural tools that would allow Aboriginal people to address the violence and heal the trauma that has become part of our day-to-day lives. In the course of the study, participants sat together over many long hours of *dadirri*. *Dadirri* provided not just the cultural protocols and practices of the research, but also became a way of life that participants entered when they became involved with We Al-li. For most participants this way of life continues. *Dadirri* is the processes of listening, observing, and reflecting, learning and re-learning, and acting with integrity on what has been learnt. In *dadirri*—the reciprocity of working together, sharing stories and learning from shared life experiences—participants worked to support each other in their pain and, in the hope that there is a way through the pain, they engaged in mutual healing.

The six participants who share their narratives here reflect, to various degrees, the life stories of many of the larger group of participants who came to the We Al-li workshops during the time of the study.

The study showed that violence as trauma fragments people's sense of self, identity, family and community, and fractures the loving and enduring connections of family and community that provide structure to human lives. The key finding was that healing, while hard work, is possible.

Healing is an awakening to the unmet inner needs of the Self, acknowledging the layered unexpressed pain of being unheard. Healing is the activity of working to have that pain recognised and heard, in reciprocal actions with others. These are fundamental cultural tools that have been part of Aboriginal ways of relating or being-in-the-world for millennia.

This study demonstrated that, within an Aboriginal cultural context, people do not heal alone. Because all people have the need to be part of supportive and caring families and communities, the study found that individual healing helps to rebuild families and communities, which in cyclic action, helps again in individual healing processes. Healing also strengthens the cultural and spiritual group identity which allows people to be contributing members of the society in which they live. Healing transforms pain and provides meaning and purpose to life. People whose narratives comprise the basis of this book are examples: they now have life purposes to help others who have been in similar situations to their own. They all desire to reconnect to, and work to repair, the country and community relationships that have been damaged.

Figure 2, based upon these findings, reconceptualises the crisis that Aboriginal peoples face today, in light of the critical need to address issues of violence in all its forms, as outlined in this book and in other works such as the report of the Aboriginal and Torres Strait Islander Women's Task Force on Violence (1999). There is a need to name this critical time as both a challenge and an opportunity. The challenge to Aboriginal people is to take the courage to begin to acknowledge the fracture in family and community relationships, and the opportunity is to show Australians generally that such reconciliation can be done. The diagram is built on the assumption that healing involves education at its most fundamental and deepest level.

The diagram is made up of four circles. Circles one and two are the worlds that were and are. Circles three and four

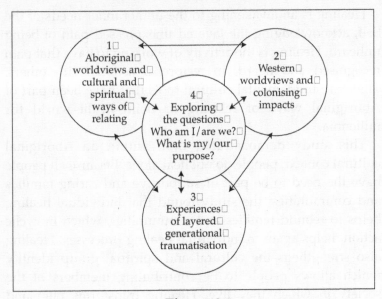

Figure 2
The circle of healing: Who am I? Who are we?

are the work that is being done and that has to be done for healing to happen. The first circle represents the Aboriginal world-of-relating before colonisation. There is a need to name the cultural strengths and weaknesses of those times, and bring those valuable cultural strengths into the present and let go of the weaknesses.

The second circle represents the Western worldviews and colonising impacts. The colonisers brought both good and bad. Aboriginal peoples, indeed all Australians, need to know what to keep and what to discard from what has been introduced by the invaders and immigrants.

Circle three represents the layered transmission of trauma down the generations and the experiences of this traumatisation that have largely formed who we are today. This is described in the narratives of Chapter Three, representative of the larger group, and is analysed in Chapter Four. There is a need to give value to these experiences, renaming the knowledge and the skills derived from such experiences as profound learning. These are the knowledge and skills we need to acquire to begin to deal with the levels of violence escalating throughout the world.

Unfortunately many people are caught in this circle, in cycles of painful abuse and self-abuse; in conflicts of identity, and the devaluing of the Aboriginal cultural and spiritual heritage. People should no longer remain victims of their past. The time has come to move to circle four and begin the work of healing.

Circle four is the work of the present and the future, demonstrating the educational work that has to be done, and the integrity, knowledges and skills that are available to facilitate people moving from victim/perpetrator/survivor, to be creators of a future free of violence. The educational work of circle four, which must be done by all Australians, is to achieve optimal health or well-being. This exists

> when a person experiences Self as an integrated whole that encompasses the body, the emotions (soul), the mind and the spirit. This state of health experienced as a pervasive sense of well-being can only occur through connection with other Selves —"without you there can be no me". To become whole the Self needs to be experienced and expressed from the inside and recognised from the outside. Hence the critical context for both health and healing is the interpersonal (Self–Other) relationship (Fewster 2000: 1–2).

Circle four, then, is the place where the life-long questions are asked and answered: Who am I? Who are we? What do I/we desire to be? What is my/our potential and purpose? What is the meaning of this life?

This circle represents the culturally safe places that must be created for the trauma stories to be told, the safe environments where people can give context to their lives through the narration of their experiences, making sense of their own realities, and, in the demanding process of healing, find a shared and new way forward. Circle four represents the healing places where people can sit in ceremonies of mutual care, in *dadirri*, and return to the work to which

Stanner (1979) refers, the important business of "uniting hearts and establishing order". While this is the vital work that faces all humankind, it is the foundation of Aboriginal cultural responsibilities as demonstrated in the current studies. Rose alludes to these responsibilities as she explores the worldviews of the Yarralin:

> Our lives are part of an oscillation which has preceeded and will succeed us. This sense of cosmic vastness can lead to a sense of our own insignificance. Yarralin people rarely understand human life in this way. The end point of sequential time is now. All that preceeded us and all that comes after depend on us. What we do matters so powerfully that to evade our responsibilities is to call down chaos (2000: 217).

An appropriate process now, is that Indigenous peoples demonstrate the way forward from the chaos that has evolved from colonial conquest, on this continent and elsewhere.

The rest of this chapter will focus on what is likely to be found in the work conceptualised and undertaken in circle four, derived from the understandings and knowledge that came from the findings of this study, and in the circle work that occurred in We Al-li.

Acts of violence and experiences of trauma

When participants were first recruited into the study, they were preoccupied by their pain. They revealed stories of violence that were "crying out to be told". These were accounts of acts of violence that they had witnessed, or experienced, or perpetrated. In many instances, during the activities of the We Al-li workshops and in the taping of the narratives, a participant would say, "I've never told anybody this before." After sharing an experience of great tragedy and sometimes indescribable violence, participants would say, "Oh, I feel better now." The relationship between the actions of violence and the experiences of trauma became clearer. In fact as participants went deeper into the pain of their experiences, their stories altered in emphasis. As they put context to their stories, as they made sense of what they had experienced, they began to move beyond being "victim" or "perpetrator" of abuse, to see the strength in their survival and their ability to change. While disempowerment and disconnection are core experiences of psychological trauma, reconnection and empowerment occur when people choose to reclaim and make sense of their stories (Herman 1992: 133). Obviously "telling the story" is only the beginning of healing. Nonetheless it is a vital first step. The experience of violence must be understood for its essential contribution to feelings and behaviours that influence situations of trauma across generations.

Violence, trauma, and child development

The study provides evidence to support the work of the Aboriginal and Torres Strait Islander Women's Task Force on Violence (1999: 32–4): that childhood experiences of violence are, in many cases, traumatising experiences that may have serious impacts on child development that can continue to transmit trauma across generations. Such experiences are often associated with feelings and thoughts that result in coping behaviours, which in themselves may compound the traumatisation as the child moves into adolescence and adulthood (Tedeschi and Calhoun 1995: 18–19). The experience therefore is both "feeling and thinking", from which action (or inaction) results in a circular process which is often re-traumatising and compounding. What is clear is that the impact of particular events at different times in the life cycle will have different consequences.

A child's personal identity is believed to be established by late adolescence. When the trauma occurs in childhood, the experiences are more likely to affect identity formation, and the consequences may therefore be carried into adult life. Consequently, the thinking, perceiving and reacting that result from traumatic childhood experiences may form the basis of many adult thoughts, feelings and behaviours (Tedeschi and Calhoun 1995: 18, 19). Each of the participants demonstrates this, and their narratives support the findings of Raphael, Swan and Martinek (1998) at different levels. Ben, for example, makes the connection between his violent behaviour on the streets as a young man to the child who has to hold in the anger because it was unsafe to feel and act on the feelings. He is *full of anger* towards his mother's violators, and he expresses *anger/shame* at his own feelings towards his father after the suicide, as well as feelings towards his father for his father's inability to fulfil his need to be parented. He acts out these feelings on the streets of his home town on friends and strangers.

Lorna names the link between her childhood experiences, the feeling and thinking which resulted, and her adult drinking and violent behaviours towards her self and others, such as her husband and children. In this she supports the findings of the Aboriginal and Torres Strait Islander Women's Task Force on Violence (1999: 28–32), which sees the traumatic transference of trauma as a vital consideration in the development of service delivery to Aboriginal victims and perpetrators of violence.

Each of the participants demonstrates Herman's point: traumatic memories resemble the memories of young children, in that victims are unable to give a verbal description of the trauma experiences, but the feelings in relationship to the trauma are indelibly encoded in their memory; and that often their adult behaviour resembles an enactment of the suppressed feelings of the original trauma (1992: 38).

Violence, trauma, and family and community fragmentation

The findings of this study show that actions of violence, and therefore experiences of trauma, can have a complicated and disabling effect that can fragment relationships in families and communities across generations.

Violence is more likely to occur between people who are closely linked emotionally and therefore vulnerable to each other (Duran *et al.* 1998: 345–7). In many cases the violence is the acting out of previous trauma on those people who are in close association, because in day-to-day associations a relative may unknowingly trigger unhealed and dissociated memories or needs. Traumatised people often find themselves re-enacting some aspect of the trauma scene in a disguised form without realising what they are doing (Herman 1992: 40). Herman says people in pain are often self-focused and are unable to listen to or understand the needs of others, even their own children, as Lorna has demonstrated.

Relationships are precious to people who have reason to fear abandonment and separation, who have come from unstable family backgrounds, or who have feelings of low self-worth. The study supports previous research that demonstrates that disrupted childhood attachment is an important factor in understanding people's adult behaviour (Raphael, Swan and Martinek 1998). Furthermore, children may feel abandoned; if their cry of pain is unheard, this appears more critical than the actual abuse itself (Herman 1992: 101) and has profound effects on adult relationships. When people do not have a secure sense of their own self-worth, obsessive jealousy or excessive control may become a factor in how they relate to others. As previously stated, the three male participants in the narratives presented here all had destructive jealousy which governed their relationship behaviours. Many other male and female participants in the study displayed similar behaviours. When people feel jealous they may be looking for validation of their self-worth outside themselves. Such people may also unconsciously be involved in power struggles within their relationships, they may try to manipulate and control the other person and the situation (Herman 1992: 80–1). Such people may have a fixation on the romantic aspects of male–female associations. During the time of the study people began to report that they now understood that what they expected from an adult relationship was often based upon unmet needs from childhood and that these needs could never be met in adult life.

In trauma the self feels fragmented, with a resultant sense of loss of identity. The fragmented self is unable to establish and maintain stable relationships, as all of the men in the study group demonstrated. For many Aboriginal people the fragmentation of self has been compounded by the enforced physical separation of people from their families and communities (Raphael, Swan and Martinek 1998).

An important finding of the study was the awareness of the ramifications across generations of the impacts of government policies on people removed in the actual implementation of the policies. Don, for example, felt the chaos in his family situation contributed to his own chaotic functioning. Yet a source of continuing pain for him was that when his behaviour became too chaotic he was placed in government care. He was unable to understand the impacts of previous removals in his family and could not "make sense" of the family dysfunction. The current findings demonstrate that in many instances, the Aboriginal sense of belonging to families and to community and cultural group has been shattered and often feels irretrievable, and this creates deep grief and anger in the individual and in groups as a whole.

The study group related experiences of violence both within the broader community and within the (extended) family. Greater feelings of betrayal and alienation accompanied the violence that occurred within the family than the violence committed by strangers, particularly authority figures. As Rose has pointed out, with young people (such as Don and Ben), there is much "hostility and despair ... directed primarily toward their own kin. They know that in turning against their family they violate one of the first and most basic tenets: that country and people take care of their own." They turn against their families because they feel that some older people are engaging in a form of self devouring predation ... [that their] lives, bodies and wills have been controlled by others for other's purposes and they have not been protected, defended and nurtured in return. Through violence, young people turn outwards, testing, in a manner that is guaranteed to fail, whether others really do care about them (Rose 2000: 182–3).

The young have not been given a context or construct to understand the traumatic experiences of the old, which continue to govern the behaviour of many older generations. The violence therefore moves down the generations, changed yet formed by previous government and societal acts of violence. These are experienced as trauma, which continues into the present in further actions of violence within families and communities.

At different levels all the participants in the study felt betrayed by their families. When a person experienced violence from outside the family and the family was unable, for whatever reason, to meet the person's needs, the betrayal and alienation were more deeply felt. In fact anger or rage was often directed at members of the family who it was perceived did not protect the person, or who did not respond appropriately to the person's needs after abuse had occurred from outside the family. In the participant group, rarely was anger felt or expressed towards the actual abuser(s). More often anger was expressed towards those who, for whatever reason, did not listen to and acknowledge the truth of the felt violation. In support of Rose's work (2000), when participants felt unheard in their pain they were often angry without knowing why, and would sometimes turn that anger on themselves, or on others within their families, or on society generally. Herman says that feelings of rage and fantasies of murderous revenge are normal responses to abusive treatment. In adulthood, abused children are often "rageful and sometime aggressive ... lack[ing] verbal and social skills for resolving conflict, and approach[ing] problems with the expectation of hostile attack" (1992: 104). This has major implications for the healthy functioning of families and communities. The study also revealed that the violence of self-harm/suicide and harming of others is closely related. The violence of harming the self as opposed to harming another is sometimes a preferred option by some people, but more often the behaviours are complex and circular.

Much healing work has to be done in families and communities fragmented by past government policy and by the rage turned inward, or in Baker's terminology, "the psycho-social domination—the cultural genocide" (1983: 39) that is also called "internalised oppression". In some Aboriginal families and communities, psychic prisons have been built, and people "have become simultaneously prisoner and warden and even executioner" (Baker 1983: 40). A powerful tool for healing includes family and community story maps which help people make sense of situations across generations which have long seemed senseless, and are becoming increasingly harmful and dysfunctional (functioning in pain and with difficulty).

Violence, trauma, and alcohol and other drug abuse

This study provides evidence to support the suppositions of Homel, Lincoln and Herd (1999) and Gagné (1998). While Aboriginal people themselves say alcohol is a huge problem, alcohol and other drug consumption "cannot be understood or given meaning except in relation to the dependent situation of Aboriginal people within the Australian state" (Homel *et al.* 1999: 3) and the transgenerational trauma in Indigenous lives. The study also lends support to the hypothesis by Gagné that "colonialism is the seed of trauma because it leads to dependency, then to cultural genocide, racism, and alcoholism" (1998: 358). Each of the narrators used alcohol or other (illegal and legal) drugs to alleviate a number of needs stemming from unhealed trauma.

The assertion has been repeatedly made that alcohol does not cause violence (Adams 1988: 176–99). Nor should alcohol and other drugs ever be used as a mitigating factor to excuse any act of violence. It is vital, however, to recognise the twin roles that alcohol and other drugs have played. Both historically and today, they have brought about many deaths and injuries through violence in Aboriginal family and community breakdown, and general ill-health; and they have also been used as a self-medicating tool in dealing with the effects of trauma.

Alcohol in particular has been at the core of family and community dysfunction, as Don demonstrates in regard to his family. The generation now using multiple drugs grew up seeing their fathers and uncles drinking and fighting. As the previous generations provided negative role models (resulting from their own trauma experiences and behaviours), subsequent generations have witnessed drinking and the resulting fights. Consequently they copy this behaviour. Some young people do not require alcohol or other drugs to be violent, but the drug use compounds and intensifies violent actions. The power of violence as trauma is already in their bodies and souls and must be expressed in some way. Again, alcohol and other drugs are now used in "coping with feelings" by peoples in chronic communal traumatic distress (Herman 1992: 44), and the resulting intense release of the rage spreads, complicates, and compounds the traumatisation into epidemic proportions.

Aboriginal people's use of alcohol and other drugs is, in many instances, connected to the traumatisation in violence that has occurred over generations, and the multiple losses within families and communities through removals and through early death from ill-health or risk-taking, suicides and homicides. Those who are flooding with emotions may use alcohol to try to numb the intensity of their feelings; conversely, when they are numb and unable to feel (as Len explained), alcohol can allow them to feel more intensely. The drugs may therefore function to release feelings (Herman 1992: 34–44).

May has said that drug addiction is another aspect of powerlessness (1976: 284). Different drugs have different effects. Some drugs anaesthetise the feelings, while others intensify or release them. The three male participants describe how, at various times, they acted differently while under the influence of different drugs. Drugs can provide relief from the profound and continuous feelings of pain from the original trauma; yet, as Len has described, they may also intensify feelings and allow uninhibited acting out, with the result that un-boundaried acts of violence may occur.

Traumatised people often use alcohol and other drugs as forms of self-medication and as a means of coping with feelings (Robin *et al.* 1996). The use of alcohol and other drugs enables the expression of pent-up feelings of rage or despair without the person or group having to take responsibility for the consequences that may result—that is, the rage that may be expressed as violence (Reser 1990). All the men in the study group demonstrated this. Ben's and Len's rage was expressed both against family members and in street violence, in every instance, while they were drunk or under the influence of other drugs.

In a group environment, alcohol may also provide a sense of community. Lorna described the role that alcohol played in meeting her need to be in *community*, and *to have a feeling of belonging*, which she experienced while drinking in the group. Studies done on cumulative trauma and post-traumatic stress disorder in American Indian populations and with American Indian Vietnam veterans (Manson *et al.* 1996; Robin *et al.* 1996) show how alcohol may be used in groups or families to cope with feelings of fear, guilt, sorrow, agony, horror from previous experiences, and as self-medication of unresolved grieving needs. Being "blanked out", the veterans cried together and related the stories of Vietnam, without having to remember in the morning how they cried or fought (Manson *et al.* 1996: Robin *et al.* 1996). Such behaviour is the "coping with feelings" to which Reser (1990) refers and is described by Len, Lorna and Don in particular.

Violence, trauma, and race and gender injustice

While racism was not a big factor in the overall discussions, it was fundamental in the experiences of the Aboriginal people involved in the study; in fact, it was normalised in the day-to-day experiences of the Aboriginal participants in the group. The study demonstrates that issues and experiences of racism are a cumulative compounding trauma (Baker 1983; Duran *et al.* 1998; Gagné 1998; Raphael, Swan and Martinek 1998), often obtuse and covert. Until it was drawn out in the interviews and workshops, racism was often unacknowledged by the study group as a relevant factor. The experience of racism was such an everyday occurrence that it was unacknowledged and unrecognised. At the same time, discussions promoted feelings of anxiety, diminishment, fear and rage, which were based in half-remembered memories of other forms of abuse, thus triggering behaviours that seemed senseless if viewed in isolation.

The experiences of the Aboriginal women in the study support the work of Huggins (1994) and Moreton-Robinson (2000) demonstrating that race and gender cannot be separated. In the study, the Aboriginal women named many levels of being silenced as women, and as "black" women, illustrated by both Lorna and Mary in their narratives and many other women in the study. Mary felt, at a number of levels, she was silenced about her experiences of being a woman, and her experiences of being a black woman and an abused woman. This silence was imposed, she believed, by society generally, by early religious indoctrination, and by her own mother and male members of her extended family and community.

For Aboriginal men, the struggle to affirm and assert black male masculinity was always present. For this reason, it was a profound struggle to acknowledge childhood sexual violence in the group. Intense shame was always present in such disclosures, as opposed to the anger or grief at physical violence or neglect. Many times during the field studies male participants expressed the real fear that, if other men found out that they had been sexually abused as children, they would be considered "less than men". There was also a feeling (generally unspoken unless specifically questioned) that they would more likely be further victimised in already abusive environments. The study therefore highlights the vital need to create environments where painful truths can be disclosed in safety and where the potential of further abuse has been reduced as much as possible.

As Solomon suggests, because men in particular are often unable to talk about their feelings, many issues remain unresolved (1997: 6). Men may therefore articulate their pain in destructive acting out in their relationships or on the streets. While most victims of violence do not become perpetrators, some do, and trauma seems to amplify the common gender stereotypes. "Men with histories of childhood abuse are more likely to take out their aggression on others, while women are more likely to be victimised by others" (Herman 1992: 113). Over the time of the study it became clear that those men who had witnessed violence in childhood against the female members of their families were more likely to perpetrate domestic violence as adults. In contrast to much of the present feminist writings on domestic violence (Yllo and Bograd: 1988), men who witnessed male-on-male violence were more likely to follow this pattern of social behaviour. The violence of Aboriginal men against Aboriginal men is as high as, if not higher than, their violence against Aboriginal women. This pressures us to find explanations for the violence that is presently a part of Aboriginal life experiences, beyond those extrapolated by feminist theories. Furthermore the study shows that women, often victims of violence, may also be perpetrators. To ignore this denies them the right to healing action which can help change their behaviour.

The study's findings substantiate the research which shows that children who experience sexual abuse are more likely to be re-victimised or to harm themselves than to victimise other people (Herman 1992), although in some cases a child who has been sexually assaulted may re-enact the abuse on other children. Because the study found high levels of child sexual violence against young Aboriginal men, as well as young women, there is a critical need to address sexual health issues with strategies that are gender-specific and culturally safe.

The women in the study behaved differently to the men in the way they expressed their feelings. They also had completely different experiences to the men in the way society dealt with their needs or pain. Firstly, it was legitimate for women to seek and receive help, even though the help was often inadequate, whereas it was not considered proper for men to even talk about or give context to their pain. Men were more likely to have negative interactions with law enforcement agencies, whereas Lorna described how the police behaved positively towards her. Don and Ben were considered to be behaving normally in their fighting and drinking, both by their families and by the community generally. However, there came a time when their behaviour was labelled criminal; their experiences with the criminal justice system did not help them change, but rather increased their trauma.

For the non-Aboriginal participants the primary issues were gender socialisation (that is, the social structures and cultural norms which make boys into men and girls into women), and inadequate or inappropriate parenting. In many participants, sexuality was formed by the destruction of safe boundaries in childhood. Two common forms of behaviour resulted: general promiscuity with a clear lack of sexual boundaries, which resulted in unstable relationships with high levels of jealousy (Herman 1992: 109); and the reconstruction of rigid boundaries with puritanical attitudes towards sexual matters that would substantially restrict sustaining relationships.

The most important and dominating factor for both Aboriginal and non-Aboriginal participants in the study, however, was the community and family denial and suppression of childhood experiences of violence, which became complex and compounded as people used drugs, drank, and acted out their distress towards others and themselves. The study clearly showed, and is supported by other research (Raphael, Swan and Martinek 1998; Duran *et al.* 1998; Gagné 1998; Mala 2000), that many life scripts were established by unhealed child trauma, compounded and made more complex by issues of race and gender in social situations, and the inability of families or communities in crisis to meet critical needs.

Violence, trauma, and criminal behaviour
The study provides clear evidence to support Wilson's (1988a, b) work with Vietnam veterans, that violence as trauma is often linked to what society then labels as criminal behaviour.

Violence (as trauma) deconstructs the self, and, in reciprocal action, reconstructs the self. Such action may be called criminal behaviour. In the experience of violence a person feels powerless. In the expression of violence a person feels powerful. When acted out, violence (as trauma) unites the different parts of the story that have made the person feel powerless or powerful. The action is often expressed without rationality and in chaos, as evidenced by the six people whose narratives appear here and the broader group involved in the study. A person expressing their anger and hate in violence must become unfeeling and detached. Yet the acting out is a reconnection (often unrecognised) to the original feelings of anger and hate, and is a release for the body and the psyche. Traumatised people are often involved in risk-taking and reckless exposure to danger (Herman 1992: 22). Violence may therefore be a symptom of trauma and a symptom of recovery from trauma (Wilson 1988a). Such an understanding is an important consideration in the development of treatment programs for both victims and perpetrators of violence and in alcohol and drug programs.

Violence, trauma, and poverty cycles

The study found there is a cyclic relationship between trauma and poverty. While Ochberg (1988) says being victimised by violence creates poverty cycles, this study also suggests that poverty contributes to violence and trauma.

Don's family was chronically poor. The condition of chronic poverty can be traumatising, and conversely trauma can create poverty across generations. Children who live in situations where they experience violence are often unable to settle at school, which was Don's situation. Don did not receive any validation at school. Don illustrates that children who do not have experiences of self-worth at home or at school are more likely to use alcohol and other drugs early in life as a strategy to cope and to escape. Because Don was unable to settle at school, he (and other young people like him) is less likely to have access to the knowledge and skills that come through the education system and which will enable them to compete in the employment market. The education system in fact may be a further point of trauma for Don and others, as it teaches them to devalue who they are. The Australian education system provides examples of this until recent times, and Duran *et al.* give examples in other colonised countries such as America (1998: 344).

It is well-documented that women as victims of violence enter a socio-economic spiral that can lock them into poverty which is difficult to escape (Ochberg 1988: 11–13). Men who have been victimised as children are more likely to enter offending patterns which prevent them from contributing to their own social and economic well-being. As one person in the study, who had spent considerable time in prison, said: "Blackfellas go into jail alcoholics and come out junkies." Prison programs generally do not provide life skills, nor allow them to deal with original trauma which is a fundamental part of their offending cycles.

Not only does violence as trauma sentence people to poverty, which is illustrated by all the participants. As the study demonstrates, it is also difficult to break out of the poverty cycles unless healing is helped to happen. Social structures, all too often, reinforce both the poverty cycle and the traumatic action.

Across generations: conflicting memories, feelings, and behaviours

The study found that participants often demonstrated conflicting memories, feelings and behaviours down the generations which compounded the traumatisation. In fact most participants in the study, at the beginning of the exploration of their experiences, were unable to describe the details of the actual experiences except to use "feeling" words. Herman has written of the difficulty traumatised people have to describe their experiences (1992: 67). In the experience of a violent act, participants said as children they felt *scared, fearful, frightened, shamed, insecure, powerless*. The participants described believing they were *dirty, bad, weak, a failure*. These descriptions were childhood labels they took into themselves from their early experiences. They felt like non-persons, with no, or little, identity of their own, powerless over who they had become, and how they were continuing to be victimised, even by their own actions. This supports Baker's findings of the psycho-social dominance which is a fundamental aspect of colonising processes (1983: 40).

Generally the participants suppressed their feelings of anger or rage. These angry emotions emerged in adolescence and early adulthood, often in violent actions against others, and in physical ill-health and emotional distress in later life (Tedeschi and Calhoun 1995: 21–4). Angry emotions were secondary to the profound grief at the loss of the Self as inviolate (Herman 1992: 69–71). As participants felt safe to explore their feelings in more depth, the stories of their violations began to emerge in more detail. All of the study group provided evidence that supports the work of Raphael, Swan and Martinek that Aboriginal people often have multiple layers of trauma stories across generations, of loss of the Self, of childhood, of identity, and a profound grief for the powerlessness, torment and pain they continue to feel (1998: 327–37). The extent of the feelings had often previously been unacknowledged or pushed down, but the stories elicited as part of the current research exposed the variety of the losses and traumatisation. Feelings became deeper as the stories emerged in more detail and people began to link feelings to thoughts, and hence to the acted-out scripts of their own lives and within their families and communities. While this was a painful process, it also proved to be liberating in the long term.

Another important consideration to emerge from the study is that different people may have conflicting and different memories of the same event. Survivors of trauma often tell their stories in highly emotional, contradictory and fragmented ways which undermine their credibility (Herman 1992: 1). Furthermore, children may have clear, sometimes frozen, memories of traumatic events that diverge from the recollections of adults who were present (Tedeschi and Calhoun 1995: 18). During the time of the study, the children of some of the participants also talked with me about their memories and feelings of growing up under the circumstances described by their parents. At other times the parents of the participants talked about their memories. Thus three generations were confiding in me. The study supports the complexity and compounding nature of traumatic experiences and memories, but it also provides a greater understanding of the danger of placing a memory into the context of a fact or truth, whatever "fact or truth" is.

The essential lesson is that each person has their own memories, which do not always completely correspond to the memories of others. Each is right. None is wrong. These are memories. People can have different experiences of the same event. Age differences may also account for the differing experiences. For example, Mary had a memory of a violent event that had occurred when her daughter was less than three years old. Mary had not even realised her daughter had been present at the event, but the daughter, twenty years later, was able to relate with great clarity some of the extremity of the situation: the blood on the wounded person, the kind of weapon the assailant had, the smell of alcohol on the assailant, and the loudness of the voices during the time of the crisis. Mary had no recollection of these details. Nor could she understand her daughter's continuing distress at the experience (indeed, anger at her for *allowing it to happen*), until she listened to her daughter relate the experience many years later. Mary developed a different understanding of her own experience through being helped to see it through her daughter's eyes; and her daughter began to see that the event was not as horrific, for the other participants, as her three-year-old mind had experienced and therefore categorised it. In Don's case, his memories are strong and clear and have been substantiated by other members of his family, who have been shocked to realise that events that happened over twenty years ago are still held as traumatic memories in Don's life today, experiences they had not understood could have significant traumatic memories for him. In another instance, two sisters who were part of the overall study had conflicting memories of the behaviour of their father—one eulogises him, while the other has clear and distressful memories of him being both drunk and violent towards her mother and herself (substantiated by the mother and other brothers and sisters). The other sister disagreed with her memories of their father and there was hostility between the two over the differences.

Participants also demonstrated that they may hold conflicting feelings of love/hate towards family members, which remained unresolved at the time of the study. Herman explores this confusion in depth in relationship to people who have been held in captivity (1992: 75–95).

Aboriginal people are told that their families and communities are places of caring and sharing, yet today many young people are growing up in places of pain and disorder. The previous generations underwent the experiences of the first two periods of colonisation as defined by Baker—frontier physical violence, and structural violence in enforced welfare dependency, restrictive legislation and child removals (1983: 44). These older generations have acted out their own rage and terror within their families and communities.

The generations of the present, therefore, have a totally different experience than their parents and elders. They have grown up in situations where pent-up rage, aided by alcohol consumption, has been released into the chaos of family and communal dysfunction.

Violence is both life-destroying and life-giving. Feelings of anger and rage, if worked through to resolution, can be life-giving. When people are made powerless, one option they have is to believe and accept they are helpless to help themselves. Feeling powerless, people may feel a numbness of spirit, anxiety and depression, a sense of hopelessness. They become apathetic, accepting what has happened as "their lot in life" (Erikson 1976). Chronic depression and anxiety were present in all the participants to various degrees.

The other option is to feel angry. Anger is a normal human response to a boundary violation. Each of the participants who felt anger or rage at their childhood violations was also expressing their "right to life"—their right to be heard and seen in their pain, their right to not be violated. Often the anger or rage was undirected and confused, however, which only made things more complex. Ben's undirected rage was aimed at anybody. So was Len's. Participants in the study spoke of the feelings they had of powerlessness and helplessness at the violations to themselves, and the flooding and uncontrollable anger they experienced. In many instances they expressed this anger on others in violent action. Yet what they demonstrated was that under the anger is always grief at the loss experienced in the violation. As each person accessed and shared the deep grief (as the primary emotion resulting from loss in the violation), they began to connect more deeply and enduringly with others in healing activity.

In summary, acts of violence and experiences of trauma are like the "pebbles in the pond" to which Figley (1986) refers. The experiences contain many layers of pain that are inexplicable to the outside observer and often cannot be described by the traumatised person. The body may speak what the tongue cannot (Wong and McKeen 1992). The study showed clearly that a human response to trauma is an increase in alcohol and drug misuse, self-harming and suicidal behaviour, and violent acting out towards others and self. There is a corresponding decrease in stable relationships and parenting skills as traumatised children become adults, acting in pain and with difficulty in their responsibilities towards the next generation. Although each participant demonstrated the diversity of the human response to the trauma experience, they also demonstrated that, at its deepest level, the experience of trauma that results from actions of violence is similar for all people. It is a profound blow to the psyche and identity which must be repaired in healing action.

Herman has set out a staged process for healing from trauma:

1. Establish safety for the trauma stories to be told.
2. Reconstruct the trauma story.
3. Restore the connections between survivors and their communities (paraphrased from Herman 1992: 3).

The situation is a little more complex for Aboriginal Australians, where some communities themselves are all too often in crisis; where violence has now been called epidemic; and where professional skills for working with traumatised populations are limited and unsustainable through inadequate resourcing for the work that has to be done. A trauma recovery program should emphasise identification of trauma symptoms among children and adults, and use methods of expression such as storytelling, drawing, writing, dancing and drama, based on Aboriginal cultural tools, for healing. Health workers and other professionals who work directly with traumatised children and adults must strengthen their knowledge about child development in relationship to adult functioning, trauma and grief theory, and develop their listening skills so that healing action can occur. They also must be supported in their work so that they do not burn out. Although the work will be difficult, it must be done.

Change and healing: making connections

A significant part of this study was the insights that emerged as participants found and began to narrate their stories, and in so doing came to know themselves at deeper levels, and to make sense of their life experiences. The study asked the questions: What personal and social experiences assist change? What is healing and how do people heal? What cultural tools promote healing and change?

Within the study group, such insight or wisdom came only after revisiting old, unresolved pain, and much hard work. This is the work of circle four as described earlier in this chapter. The narration of the violence, the trauma stories have to be told. This is fundamental to the beginning of healing. The activity reaches underneath constructed racism and other forms of abuse, and begins to deal with its consequences, its outcomes.

In the early stages of the study, the decision was made to use a non-hierarchical learning/teaching style called Circle-Work. The decision to allow feelings and experiences to be revisited, to test the textbook knowledge of others by our own experiences as researchers and researched in relationship, was a legitimate method of research supported by Herman's trauma recovery work (1992: 29). Non-hierarchical, participatory research was also reflective of the integrity of *dadirri*. Some may see the circle as people sitting together discussing their troubles, not unlike group therapy, or a focus group discussion, as in social science research. Such descriptions are inadequate, however.

It is important to list several reasons for the decision to use the symbol of the circle in the educational processes of We Al-li, and the research method of the project. For instance, the symbol of the circle was used deliberately to break down hierarchical structures between teacher and student, counsellor and client, researcher and researched. The use of the circle was based on the fundamental belief that, while all humans have different experiences and different skills to contribute, all are of equal value, have equal worth, and have something of importance to share in the whole-of-life learning of the community. Each individual story is relevant to the whole, making the whole story complete, allowing the community to make more sense out of the fragmentation and perceived senselessness that is their present experience.

Mary, for example, talks of how the sharing in the circle helped her to perceive people in a different way. *The workshops changed my whole attitude on how to relate to people. I also learnt about not judging why people have certain ways without fully knowing what their story was. I think my biggest learning was that everybody has their own stories—you just never know what they have been through.*

Participants come to share, understand and assist other participants. Hard work was undertaken by all in the circle to try to achieve common goals and harmonious balance. The circle can build positive feelings of self-worth, of belonging, of a shared sense of community. Mary explains how the circle became a place where people were able to confront and move beyond issues of race and gender. *For instance one of the other women in the group who was a white woman, just hearing her experiences as a young person. They almost mirrored mine. That was an incredible thing for me to hear. I've never matched up with a white woman before like that, who had just had the same experiences as me—I could see how we coped with it, almost pretty much in the same way. It was good to know that somebody else had had the same experiences like me, and had moved on, like me. It was good having a white woman in the group. It was a good thing to have the two mobs together in the group. Just as a group of blackfellas, we pretty much had similar experiences and depending on where people are at, that could be a dangerous thing. We could be feeding each other's anger and bitterness. It was valuable to understand that white people go through negative experiences in their life too.*

The circle was also a place where people could confront issues of race and gender in safety, enabling them to express deep pain, work through feelings and acquire new insights. In many cases bridges of understanding were built. There was often tension in the circle, but from this tension growth can occur if people choose to learn from their pain.

Apart from *Dadirri*—the ceremony which began each day—the strongest cultural tools for healing were story-telling, art, music, dance, theatre, and reflective discussion, which themselves are functions of *dadirri*. Such tools were used to bring to the front the painful stories of trauma and provide experiences of being listened to, of being acknow-ledged, of reconnecting with others for healing.

As participants conceptualised how painful experiences had shaped their lives, they also began to reshape and redefine the experiences, so that the reality of the actual phenomena to which they had been held captive for so long began to take on a different meaning. Making connections such as these was a fundamental change process of immense significance. The research process was therefore an essential component and "trigger for change" as participants became actively involved in investigating and making sense of their own realities.

Personal and social experiences which assist change and promote healing

The study revealed that there is rarely just one trigger for change that sets a person on a journey of transformation. More often a series of small incidents nudge the person into situations, at both personal and social levels, where they are forced to make a decision, or a series of decisions, on which they have to act. If they do not act, often the power to do so is taken from them by a society that tries to control the painful expressions of their crisis or distress. The study also highlighted that, as people try to change their circumstances, institutional intervention may act as a re-traumatising agent.

For some people who came into the We Al-li workshops, the change triggers had been occurring for a number of years. For example, Lorna faced a series of crises before she was presented with the option to enter rehabilitation because, her family told her, they would no longer support her dysfunction. What worked for Lorna was not the psychiatric unit at the local hospital but the Aboriginal alcohol rehabilitation centre she attended.

In fact, not one of the participants in the study was able to name a positive outcome they had experienced with mental health professionals. Generally the professionals clearly lacked race and gender analysis in their approach to the needs of their clients as they were defined by the participants.

For others like Ben the trigger for change was a crisis "in the moment". He had been stumbling from small crisis to crisis until he "stumbled" into the workshops through the invitation of his aunty, who herself had already travelled a similar road. She knew what he needed. What worked for Ben was the support of this member of his (extended) family, and the communal support of people in the We Al-li workshops.

From the study, there would appear to be two critical times in the life-span when people are more likely to experience crisis because of previous unresolved trauma: in adolescent or early adult years, and in middle age when some particular stress triggers a return to an old unhealed trauma. In either case there seems to be truth in the statement that a "dark night of the soul" is necessary before people can move to a point where they are willing to contemplate the levels of change required. They realise it is necessary to shift their consciousness sufficiently to discover alternative ways of living to those that have maintained, and in many cases intensified, their trauma. One person had described this time as being in a desert where there was "no life, no hope of anything but endless pain and hopelessness". In the very naming of this stuck place, movement occurred for that person.

At such times of crisis, the awakening to the pain brings an opportunity to heal and grow. This became a critical time of change in the lives of many participants. The change process was always connected to healing—"making whole again". Healing can also be defined as "educating the self about the Self", and was always in relationship with others—the Self/ Other validation. This is a critical factor in understanding, if we are to begin the process of helping people heal from violence-related trauma.

What was clearly shown in the study is that, at times of crisis or change, it is vital for people to have access to educational opportunities, resources and programs of healing to meet their needs and support the desire for change. However, such personal and professional educational opportunities are not available to most Aboriginal people. In this study, the workshops of We Al-li fulfilled this criteria. If such personal (and professional) educational opportunities are available, as illustrated by the participant group, people can then begin to make their own choices to access the other educational services to continue their change, growth and healing.

What is healing and how do people heal?

Apart from the creation of educational opportunities, what are the needs of people who are in a crisis from trauma and who have entered a change or transformational process? What is healing, and how do people heal?

The findings of the study with reference to healing needs are clear, and they correspond with the work of others such as Herman (1992), Tedeschi and Calhoun (1995), Duran *et al.* (1998), but in some instances they diverge from them. They also highlight some of the critical factors that are needed for healing action to occur within Aboriginal situations, which are not present within Australian society generally.

Since psychological trauma involves a disconnection from others, it was assumed at the beginning of the research that healing or recovery could only occur within the context of relationships which could allow reconnection and re-formation of supporting relationships (Herman 1992: 134). Brave Heart-Jordan calls this a group treatment model, in which the restorative factors incorporate sharing experiences, the reclaiming of hope and courage, collective mourning, and social support (1995: 114). According to Brave Heart-Jordan, substantiated by the work outlined here, short-term treatment models work, providing enough empowerment for people to become the author and arbiter (Herman 1992: 133) of their own recovery, so long as they can continue to access what they need to support their change and growth.

Firstly, people in the study demonstrated the need to feel safe before they could look honestly and openly at who they are and the context and content of their lives, or examine their trauma stories. A safe place is an environment where people can begin to find the parts of themselves that have become lost, the fragmented bits of stories that have been too painful and shameful and so have been disowned, pushed down and denied. The five basic rules of the We Al-li workshops, as we have seen, were: no harm to the self; no harm to another person; no damage to property; no drugs or grog on site; and no sexual activity during the workshop. Each of the participants spoke of the importance of that feeling of safety in the group over and over again.

In the We Al-li workshops, rules established by the participants were broken at different times, and in each instance it damaged the safety of the group with, in some cases, serious implications. An important fact that was learnt was that rules need to be revisited and re-established from time to time.

Another learning from the study was about assumptions: a person who has professional qualifications, and therefore (presumably) professional ethical standards, does not necessarily abide by the rules that they help the (client) group establish. This is an important consideration for setting up the safe environment of circle four. It is a critical factor often missing from service delivery within Aboriginal organisations.

Secondly, the study showed that, once safety has been established, people must be allowed to find and explore their individual and collective stories, to become self-aware. Storytelling is both a strong cultural and educational tool and a healing ritual among Indigenous peoples. In this instance, the stories were the life experiences of those working together in the circle. A series of action-learning experiences was created to help the stories flow naturally from people: *Lifting the Blankets, Past–Present–Future, a story map, a loss history graph* were different experiential modules developed and used in the workshops. One of the participants describes her experience:

> With the first workshop, Lifting the Blankets, all the hurts came up. We saw them in the blankets, and we wrote them on the wall. Some, you wouldn't even have thought of naming yourself. I think sometimes we just look at ourselves, this is what happened to me. But now I could see the whole picture. The men there, and the other women, all of us, we all shared our experiences. I was sexually abused as a child and I thought that was a separate issue but now I could see that other people also had that happen to them. I could see that it was part of a bigger picture. The loss history graph was really powerful. When I put down all the different things in my own personal story, things that had happened to me, the people who had died, I didn't feel bad, just stronger that I had survived all this. And lighter because it was really like those blankets had been lifted. Also I could understand why sometimes I find it hard to cope. Now I understand why and I make decisions to take more care of myself. I can say No louder (Priscilla Iles in Atkinson, Fredericks and Iles 1996: 4).

Storytelling should be a healthy part of childhood learning. In the group narratives, as participants talked together in the workshops, they taught each other from their own experiences, and healing happened for them by the work they did together. Gaining an awareness of the stories or life experiences that make them who they are is a most important part of healing for people, for everybody needs to know *who they are* at deep structural levels of their being.

When adults are frightened of the truth of children's stories, however, they work to suppress them. Children's comments, queries and observations can inadvertently identify or point to the past painful experiences and trauma of adults, in families or communities where this trauma is being expressed in inappropriate behaviour towards children in the present. "Like canaries in coal-mines, our children are reacting to elements in their environment. What is happening to our children is an indicator for our society" (Tripcony 1999: 1). Each of the participants, as children, had the stories of their experiences suppressed. Lorna felt unable to tell her truth about her childhood sexual abuse for if she did she *would be flogged*. When Don played by himself and walked down to visit his grandparents he was labelled *womba* (mad) by his family. Mary and Jackie experienced the silencing of their child rape experiences. In a healthy society children are heeded, not repressed.

The third point that emerged in the study is that healing occurred as participants felt and expressed the depth of their feelings in safety to themselves and others. Emotional release was a critical factor in reclaiming themselves.

Recovering the story will often take a person into deep feelings. In one instance a young man just out of jail took part in a workshop. When the participants were asked to make a story map, he expressed the opinion that this was "bullshit child's play". He was invited to participate by watching and listening to the others, and as he watched and listened he started to cry. Asked if he wanted to speak, he placed an empty rum bottle with cigarette butts he had collected in the centre of the room. In tears, he then explained that, as he had listened to the other participants sharing their story maps, he had seen the empty rum bottle under the building where the workshop was taking place, and it struck him, *like a sledge hammer in my gut—that is my life—an empty rum bottle—that's all I have to show for it.*

Helping people find the depth of their pain in "the story" also provides the means by which they can move through the pain to create new stories. However, workers need to be aware that, when feelings begin to emerge, they and other participants may feel frightened that the emotions will explode into violent actions. In fact this never happened. The only violence that occurred in the workshops was when people chose to suppress, rather than deal with, their pain. They consequently misdirected their rage onto selected others in a cold, covert manipulative manner by gossip and back-biting.

The narratives helped lead the storyteller deeper into their story. Suppressed and generally turbulent feelings often rose during this time. In fact the stories explained the feelings. For many participants these feelings had long been a part of their life, but not clear or strong as they were during the time of the work in the circle. Participation in the circle allowed them to understand their feelings. This led to deeper self-knowledge and the ability to make choices for change. Understanding the feelings helped the participants to understand the "craziness" of their situations and actions. Stories and the feelings attached to them helped participants to make connections, gain awareness and understand how they had been formed and how they can re-form themselves. They now had choices on which they could act.

Anger, for example, was seen to be masking a deeper emotion—fear, sadness, sorrow, anguish, or grief—that would emerge after the anger had been expressed. This connection was made many times by participants in the study. Under these feelings, the deeper story of what had been lost would emanate. This was the material that could be worked with. It was evident that feelings could be fully felt and expressed within the safety of a group that had consciously and structurally built safety.

Often the feelings of anger or grief were overwhelming. During the term of the study, however, we saw that healing began when participants started to reconnect with their feelings, and hence the experiences that are the foundation of the rage/hate or loss/grief. Many participants had previously been extremely fearful of the depth of their anger or grief. *I can't feel. If I did I would get mad. I would go really mad and I would kill someone.* When participants had created safe boundaries, they could feel, and express what they felt, without worrying about what others would think of them, or their own personal safety. Thus they became better able to express their distress in less destructive ways. Because of the deep and often turbulent feelings which govern trauma behaviour, and which generally accompany healing, the challenge in the work of circle four is to find ways in which people can heal with the least fear and anger possible.

Witnessing other people's expression of deep feelings was also important. During the workshops many participants became distressed when somebody became angry. This was either because they had been taught that they should not be angry, or because they had witnessed anger expressed as violence. Participants began to distinguish the feelings of anger/rage, which are legitimate, from the behaviour of violence, which is not legitimate.

The study found that the fourth stage of healing was helping participants make sense of their own stories in relationship to the collective, communal story. The concept that people can make sense of their own lives seems un-realistic in societies where value is placed in the expert knowledge of others, and the authority, expertise and power of those "expert others" over them. Yet the importance of allowing people collectively to tell and to make sense of their own stories proved the single most important outcome of the study. This approach is reflected in Western therapies—in the writing and practice, for example, of Narrative Therapy. People became expert over their own lives. They began to link their own stories to the stories of older generations within their families and communities.

Brave Heart-Jordan demonstrates "the Lakota intervention model which includes catharsis, abreaction, group sharing, testimony, opportunities for expression of traditional culture and language, and ritual and communal mourning" (1995:

114). She says, for example, that Wounded Knee and the generational boarding-school trauma cannot be forgotten. She found that:

- education about the historical trauma leads to increased awareness about trauma, its impacts and the grief-related effects;
- the process of sharing these effects with others of similar background and within a traditional Lakota context leads to a cathartic sense of relief; and
- a healing and mourning process was initiated, resulting in a reduction of grief effects, and experiences of more positive identity, and an increased commitment to continue healing work both on an individual and community level (Duran *et al.* 1998: 351).

This was also the case within the work described here. An important added factor, however, was to help participants locate their own trauma within the network of global colonisations and histories—seeking answers to questions about why colonisers needed to leave their own countries, to colonise and subordinate other groups (Baker 1983: 33). In Australia, many Aboriginal people have ancestors who have come from countries where there have been traumatic upheavals and dispersals; an important connecting and healing factor was the linking of these human experiences into the whole.

The fifth stage of healing which emerged from the study is the acknowledgement of the multiple layers of loss and grief that must be worked through. There is no implicit healing. One layer uncovers another layer; this is the educational process of finding the story of *who I am* in all its multiple dimensions, complexities and depth. Such educational experiences can become an exciting (yet painful) journey of self-discovery. The narratives demonstrate that, while each person deep down knows themselves and what they should do for themselves, the work of healing takes courage and is long and hard. In the work of healing, a person's rage may deepen and seem uncontrollable for a while. Grief may feel so deep as to be bottomless and despairing. For this reason, the work of healing needs words of courage and of hope that there is a way through. This book reproduces the dialogue of the participants to demonstrate the strength and tenacity they displayed to grow from the experience of *sitting in the fire* of the pain of their experiences. Ceremonies of healing were essential to this process.

The final stage of the process occurs naturally. As people work through the layers, not necessarily in the linear stages expressed here, they intrinsically enter a process of transformation. They begin to express themselves in different and creative ways, to write, paint, dance, and make positive changes in their lives. All the participants started painting or writing poems during the workshop activities, some of which are included in here. Many of the artworks used to express and give context to painful experiences have since been shown in art exhibitions.

Healing was shown to be transformational as people entered an evolutionary process of reclaiming the natural creativity of childhood, or of a "primitive—original—primary" humanness. As participants worked to make meaning out of what had previously not made sense to them, they entered a process of transcendence that became a co-creative union with others, where a sense of meaning and life purpose emerged and was strengthened. Life took on a new direction. Of the six people whose stories are reproduced in Chapter Three, five are now undertaking university studies. None of them had previously studied at a university.

Indigenous values and practices in healing

This chapter began by outlining the educational processes in the four circles of awareness, essential to recreating lives and re-establishing order from the disorder of Aboriginal lives today. The study found that there are practices and values which promote a deeper understanding of the human condition. The most powerful cultural tool used was the reflective discussion that occurred in We Al-li as participants began to make sense of themselves and their realities. As participants went on to spend a considerable time in solitary reflection, to do family history work, to locate themselves (their family lines) in history (story mapping), to read or discuss psychology and sociology, they worked to make meaning for themselves of who and what they were. They also painted, wrote poems and songs, kept journals, all of which became a record of their journey of healing and which strengthened their cultural and spiritual identity. Such activities brought an integration to the healing processes.

Another unexpected outcome was that altruism and co-operation emerged. So much has been written about humanity's innate aggression and the selfishness and egotism that is supposed to govern human behaviour. Yet many research findings also show that in times of crisis humans have a tendency toward altruistic behaviour; in fact, humans are more likely to come together in support of each other when a crisis or disaster strikes. Wilson, in looking at over a hundred natural disasters, found strong patterns of altruism among disaster victims which seemed to be part of the recovery process (quoted in Dalai Lama and Cutler 1998). She found that working together to help each other tended to ward off later psychological problems that might have resulted from the trauma (Dalai Lama and Cutler 1998: 59). Yet in long-term trauma, altruism is not always possible, for people are generally functioning in permanent crisis mode. More often, the bureaucratic response to the trauma disrupts the natural human capacity for altruistic behaviour (Erikson 1976).

However, as participants worked together to make sense of their own stories, listening to each other and experiencing the pain of others, their altruistic, co-operative natures re-emerged. People became more able to listen to another person's story with empathy for the person's pain. They began to support each other in healing, and at many other levels of their lives, in ways they previously had not considered possible or been able to attempt. Often the participants would make a comment about a trauma story belonging to somebody else which demonstrated deep psychological insight, far beyond some of the professional workers who during the time of the study "looked in" from the outside without participating. Many of the participants have moved on to work with others who are in pain, and they demonstrate an altruistic and empathic response to the needs of other people, with therapeutic skills and sensitive insight for working with people for healing.

A question must be asked. "Who is a healer or who helps healing to happen?" Based upon the current findings, the answer must be that all healing is self-healing. The person walking with a participant acts as an educator to an emerging new knowledge, helping to strengthen the deepening understanding of the Self, and helping to build bridges of communication and understanding between the person and others.

In naming the essential role of counsellor/therapist/psychologist/psychiatrist as an educator, the root of the word "educate" should be considered: the Latin *educatus* means "to lead out from, to bring forth". Education draws out from the "student of life" new knowledge about themself and their world, and what is already there as potential. Thus the task of education—or healing—is to facilitate people's discovery of themselves, their own nature, and their place in the world and value to the world. As people come to know themselves better, they become increasingly able to be with another person in the same process, without judgement or prejudice.

As Grof (1976) has made clear, the healing processes are not the treatment of diseases or disabilities, but rather an "educational adventure in self-discovery". The person called "client" is the main protagonist with full responsibility. The "therapist" or "counsellor" functions as a facilitator or educator, creating a supportive setting for self-exploration, and occasionally offering an opinion or advice from acquired wisdom based on their past experiences. The essential attribute of this person is not the knowledge of specific techniques; although these may be a prerequisite, they are quite simple and can be learned in a relatively short time. The critical factors are the facilitator's own "stage of consciousness development, degree of self-knowledge, ability to participate without fear in the intense and extraordinary experiences of another person, and willingness to face new observations and situations that may not fit any conventional theoretical framework" (Grof 1976: 375).

Over the period of the workshops a questionnaire was used to find out from participants what they felt were the most valuable tools or activities of the workshops to help in their healing. Two of the most important responses received through the questionnaire, apart from *dadirri*, were the narrative processes and the reflective discussion which aided self-understanding. Other tools were also found to be relevant. Some people who are traumatised are unable to verbalise their feelings, so art became a powerful tool to allow the story to be told in a way that enabled another level of expression and self-exploration. Art is also used to integrate the healing. We did collaborative paintings which helped the group to start to work together as they blended their individual stories into a whole.

Similarly, we found some people are able to dance (or move) the story through their bodies. Dance was also used to help people feel what is inside them, and to express those feelings in creative movement. Drama has proved to be an excellent tool to allow safe learning to occur, to create further points for discussion and understanding about the trauma story. Often in role-playing people had flashes of insight essential to understanding their behaviour and to recovery. These multiple pathways provide holistic integration and are most effective within the group process, which appears to be stronger, for Indigenous people, than individual work. We found the pain was layered, and awareness and healing increased as the layers were worked through. Indigenous therapies emphasise both personal and professional development, for we found the professional skills were dependent on personal growth.

These were listed as the most important tools of healing by all who filled out the questionnaire. Participants stipulated the creation of a safe environment as essential in any healing process. They also experienced the sharing of individual stories with others in a group environment as a powerful way of making connection with others, of making relationships and remaking community.

A number of things happened in the sharing of life experiences and narratives. As each person listened, in *dadirri*, to the stories of the others in the group, they became able to listen more deeply to themselves. They found the same courage in themselves that they observed and named in others. As participants explored their own stories they began to change as they found words to describe feelings and experiences they had never previously given voice to, and had never told another person. Shared feelings expanded understanding and deepened relationships.

The use of *dadirri* in the research methodology and in the workshops was justified, for it verified the deep knowledge, wisdom and courage within the participants as they took opportunities for growth in their sharing. The deeper into their stories participants went, the more sense they made of their lives, at the individual, family and community level. They were able to name and map their own change processes, to find their own answers, to take the initiative and seek out other healing/educational experiences to support their growth. Participants felt safe to map the patterns of their lives that contributed to feelings, thinking and behaviour that had compounded their trauma stories. In so doing, they came to know at a deep level that they were capable of bringing changes to how they felt, thought and acted. From this, the change process accelerated.

The work of circle four is the work of deconstructing the violence/trauma experience and reconstructing a new story of healing and life-meaning. When participants were asked "Do you feel healed?", generally they replied that they felt better and more able to cope. At the same time all participants understood there is no state of "being healed", as if there could ever be a final outcome. There is no way to put an end to the pain, but it can be managed. Participants said, and demonstrated by their actions, that they were able to take more control of their lives, to make choices that mediate the cyclic pattern of destructive thoughts and actions.

The study found that there was always some triggering event, beyond the control of participants, that initiated the desire to do something about the "out of control" feeling of their lives. It is essential that government and non-government programs recognise these needs and desires and respond positively with programs that support the triggers that initiate change and promote healing.

The study found that the most essential step in healing is to establish a culturally safe environment to do the deeper work, which enables people to change their lives. The next step is to find and explore, both individually and collectively, the stories which make people who they are and which contribute to how they live their lives. The third step is to be able to enter the deep feelings that are often suppressed and unrecognised, or in other cases, extreme and uncontrollable. The fourth stage of healing is to individually and collectively make sense of stories (or histories and her-stories) that have previously seemed senseless. The fifth component of healing is to understand that there will be multiple layers of loss and grief and that healing is a process or a series of cyclic stages in which the memories and the pain appear to get worse before they get better, as the stories emerge in greater depth, and are re-formed and transformed. Finally, people have to be prepared for changes that will in many cases radically transform their lives.

Programs and practices which use the language and actions of courage and hope are essential for people in pain and who feel powerless and helpless. All too often the way through the pain seems incomprehensible and impossible. Leaders must lead by demonstrating their own commitment to healing, the process of finding "who they are" at the deepest level of their being. The state of "being healed" is the self-defined state of accepting our humanness, warts and all, as we go about the business of embracing our commonality and valuing our diversity in the work of making our environments and relationships meaningful, enduring and enriching.

Deconstructing violence and constructing life meaning and purpose

The way people behave is socially constructed as much as a result of the choices they make. O'Shane, in writing of the psychological impact of white colonisation on Aboriginal peoples, says:

> We are the most ancient people in the most ancient land on Earth. Yet, we question who we are, what we are doing here, where we belong. [The psychological impacts of colonial experiences] strike at the very core of our sense of being and identity. Many of our people assume any other identity than that of Aboriginal. [This is] the denial of self. Many say, as I have done for years, I shouldn't be here in this world. I don't belong (1995: 151).

However if people wait for society to repair the damage it has created over generations, they will wait a long time. We must be about the work of healing ourselves.

Chapter Two covers the layered constructions of violence towards Aboriginal peoples; the overt physical violence of frontier aggression; the covert structural violence of state interventions into Aboriginal lives; and the psycho-social domination or cultural genocide, our internal *questioning who we are, what we are doing here, where we belong*.

The Aboriginal and Torres Strait Islander Women's Task Force on Violence wrote of "lost fragmented people who do not know who they are, how they are hurting, or how they are hurting others", expressing concern for a "crisis in cultural and spiritual identity" (1999: 264). The report documented the excessive use of alcohol and other drugs which, the task force felt, contributed to and escalated that violence.

Langton gives validity to the creation of multiple, fragmented personalities and fractured identities with no clear sense of self, through the use of language in labelling. She points out that there are sixty-seven definitions of Aboriginality within the Anglo-Australian legal and administrative framework. Aboriginality, she says, is a construction of the colonisers, as is race. She argues that the fixation on classifying Aboriginal people "reflects the extraordinary intensification of colonial administration ... aimed until recently at exterminating one kind of Aboriginality and replacing it with a sanitised version acceptable to the Anglo invaders and immigrants" (1993: 28–9).

This aspect of colonisation, making, naming and labelling as *other*, enforces separation, fragmentation, devaluing, feeling excluded and being lost. Labels may also identify and stereotype people as the same—for example "all Aborigines are drunks", "all Aborigines are violent", as though there is no separate identity other than what is ascribed to them as a racial collective.

Similarly, society generally—mental health professionals and law enforcement bodies in particular—use labels to construct people as *other*, labels which categorise people as "mad" or "bad", boxing them into situations that may be inappropriate and which sometimes can damage or even destroy lives. Many people seem to need to categorise and diagnose others; labels are used as a kind of coping mechanism. While sometimes such labels may be helpful and appropriate, often they are not. People who are labelled as "violent" have trauma stories just as much as people who are labelled as "victim". The work of circle four aims to deconstruct such labels and allow those who have taken such labels unto themselves, and who in many cases continue to act in relationship to those labels, to reconstruct themselves, and to make new, positive stories from the old negative labels.

In the process of the workshops and in the documentation of narratives, participants in this study, many of whom had been labelled as "violent" or "victim" to various extents, as "bad" or "mad", connected with others who were also making meaning out of the pain of their experiences. Together they began to make connections in the relationships of who they were and what they had become.

It is true to say that present Aboriginal situations have been formed from the generational impacts of traumatic distress, and the forming and making has not always been to our advantage. Nonetheless, one important thing has not changed: Aboriginal peoples are still in the world of relationships. It is a world where cultural identities are not fixed, but are in movement between different positions, drawing on the multiplicity of cultural traditions now available to people. People feel fragmented because of the many factors that impact on them through the multiple intergenerational layers of colonisation. It is now important to bring these fragmented parts together, to give them meaning and value. Others have colonised us with their words and actions. We need now to decolonise ourselves. When we choose to decolonise—to deconstruct how we have been made, to take the time to explore the whole story—it can be a painful process.

> The process of re/membering some of my own, and some of my mother's people's experiences of racism has been painful. It has also been difficult to recognise and to name some of the ways in which many of us, as murris, have internalised the racism of the dominant australian culture and developed essentialist notions of aboriginality reinforcing racism (Holland 1996: 110).

It can also be a powerful journey of healing. "I am inspired by the knowledge that I can take this pain, work with it, recycle it so it becomes the source of my power" (hooks and West 1992: 78).

Such a journey must be shared. In the work of this study the observation was made over and over again that in talking and sharing together in the circle, as participants explored themselves to the depth they did, they entered a process of transformation *of their inner lives*, where the patterns and habits of thinking and feeling, as well as their sense of identity, purpose, direction and mortality, changed. Participants were engaged in a process of self-discovery as they remade themselves, "in an intersubjective process of dialogue, imagination, representation and interpretation" (Langton 1993: 33) of who they were and who they are.

Langton says, "both Aboriginal and non-Aboriginal people create 'Aboriginalities' ... in the infinite array of intercultural experiences, there might be said to be ... broad categories of cultural and textual constructions of [both individual and collective] 'Aboriginality'". Langton goes on to name the three broad categories of cultural and textual construction of Aboriginality, which also must be considerations in the process of healing from violence and trauma (1993: 33–4). These are:

- the experience of Aboriginal people interacting with other Aboriginal people in social situations located largely within Aboriginal culture
- the familiar stereotypes of Aboriginal people which have been produced by Anglo-Australians from within their own cultural constraints and pathology
- the constructions generated when Aboriginal and non-Aboriginal peoples engage in actual dialogue.

For healing to be allowed to happen within Aboriginal Australian societies, Aboriginal peoples must restructure their own dialogues—must begin to talk among themselves about the acts of violence and the experiences of trauma, and hence undertake the hard work to change, to name with courage and hope, the possibility of healing.

Similarly, non-Aboriginal people must begin to consider, to own their own pathologies and take the courage to talk together about who they are and what their contribution to the well-being or otherwise of the Indigenous peoples of this country has been over history and her-story.

Finally a collective dialogue must occur between us, from informed and courageous decisions to share pain and work for healing.

The greater truth that emerges from this study is that, although the work ahead will be hard, it can be done. The participants demonstrated this. The work that must be done is to tap the deeper collective consciousness and the deeper sense of self which allows a person to feel whole again, to help us all find meaning in what has been experienced and to share that meaning, that knowledge and wisdom, with others.

Frankl, in his book *The Unheard Cry for Meaning*, quotes a letter from a person in a United States prison:

> One of the greatest meanings we can be privileged to experience is suffering. I have just begun to live, and what a glorious feeling it is. I am constantly humbled by the tears of my brothers in our group when they can see that they are even now achieving meanings they never thought possible. The changes are truly miraculous. Lives which heretofore have been hopeless and helpless now have meaning (1978: 43).

Using different words and in another country, an Aboriginal woman—one of many who attended the We Al-li workshops over the years—spoke of having experienced great pain in the exploration of the truth of her abuse, and struggling to find meaning out of the pain of her experiences, and those of her family. She wrote the following poem:

> "As I sit and watch the sea
> I feel the waves deep inside of me,
> I feel the song of a bird,
> I feel from somewhere deep within
> I don't know why."
> "But I am all these things."
> "I am song
> I am wind
> I am sea
> I am light
> I am laughter

I am love
And to you my friends
These simple gifts I bring."

© Hazel Kaur 1995
We Al-li workshop, The Haven, Emu Park.

"These simple gifts" are similar to the gifts Miriam Rose Ungunmerr refers to in *"Dadirri:* Listening to One Another", when she says to non-Aboriginal people: "We know our white brothers and sisters carry their own particular burdens. If they let us come to them we may lighten their burdens" (1993a: 37).

As Herman has said: "Remembering and telling the truth about terrible events are prerequisites both for the restoration of the social order and for the healing of individual victims" (1992: 1). Healing must take place, particularly for Aboriginal people, the Indigenous peoples of Australia, so that we can go forward together, with the "invaders" and "immigrants", and truly have a collective Dreaming for "what is and what could be". Ungunmerr provides the invitation, and the participants in We Al-li demonstrated it can be done.

Summary

This study highlights the fact that violence is an everyday occurrence in the lives of many people, more particularly Aboriginal peoples suffering the continuing impacts of colonisation which has shaped human interaction in Australia (indeed internationally) across many generations. Actions of violence have clear traumatisating effects which reach down those generations in ways that have formed and re-formed people, their families, communities and societies generally. Traumatic loss has been experienced at many levels which has influenced the formation of the child into the adult. Individuals take such feelings and behaviours into their associations with each other to continue and compound the trauma process at personal and social levels of human interaction. Expressions of such traumatic loss can be seen in adults who feel inadequate in their day-to-day functioning;

in the victim/perpetrator behaviours common in many families; in the escalating worldwide dependency on alcohol and other drugs as coping mechanisms; in the self-harm and risk-taking that occur when people can find no meaning to their existence and have no sense of purpose for their day-to-day activities. Fragmented and fractured identities contribute to the continuing escalation of violence between people. The future therefore feels meaningless, and people articulate their felt sense of powerlessness and lack of life purpose in violent acts on themselves and others.

At the same time the findings in this study suggest that, while trauma has shaped the lives of many people in Australian society, especially Aboriginal peoples, healing is possible. Healing can be described as a journey of self-discovery as people engage together in educating themselves about themselves. The findings suggest that if Australian society were to engage in a process of healing, of *educating the self about the Self,* reconciliation at the very core of what "reconciliation" means would occur. The findings show that healing involves the processes of awakening to the pain of unmet needs and working to have those needs met in reciprocal relationships with others. Healing also involves understanding that community is not a unified whole. Rather, it is a dynamic set of processes or activities of diverse and autonomous parts all in vital relationships, which are interacting and interdependent, forming and re-forming within the whole, in movements of growth and change. The work of healing is about transformation and transcendence: people change as they work through conflictual and re-harmonising activities with each other. The study shows that for this activity to be supported and sustained, work must be done to bring to consciousness these natural human processes in a structured and safe way. Furthermore, support services must be provided to help integration to occur.

A model for healing has been proposed, using education as a foundation, the educational process of educating the self about the Self, answering the questions, *who am I/who are we,* in the relationships between the self and others. The model comprises the four circles of human activity linking past-present-future into one, where safe and healthy places are created for people to work together for healing. In these places people are helped to fully understand the past from the various cultures that form us collectively as a people, and understand their contribution to making us *who we are* in the present. The knowledges, skills and wisdom that are essential for human progression must be brought from the past through the present into the future.

In renaming the pain of circle three (the traumatic experiences of our colonisations) as a place of profound learning and acquisition of strength, skills and courage to survive, the work of circle four becomes the creative process of actively fashioning a new future.

Safe places need to be established with appropriate funding, as a matter of priority, where the layered loss and grief, and the expressions of distress that are so often labelled by society as "bad" and "mad", can be dealt with in a healing way. The pain associated with the work of healing is not bad and will not kill, but the choice not to heal has the possibility of destroying the planet, and its diverse human and non-human inhabitants.

In memoriam: 12 June 1994—21 June 1998

In this dream I am in a large house with lots of windows and no furniture. My two sons and daughter-in-law are with me in the house. A savage beast /destroyer (B/D) is raging around outside the house, trying to get in. This B/D wants something we have in the house and I am not sure—is it us or is it a little bird in a cage?

My daughter-in-law is really upset and frightened and just wants the savage beast to go away. "Give him what he wants," she says. I feel irritated with her yet calm in myself. "We will not give him anything—he'll only want more and more," I tell her but I am frustrated with her, for being hysterical, being "womanly".

My two sons are macho and want to go out and fight the B/D. But I am worried if they fight it, it will get even more aggressive and its rage will get out of control and it will break into the house, which it could with the incredible strength it has, and it will destroy us. They, too, are frightened, but are showing their fear in wanting to go out and fight it to make it go away. I tell them not to fight it. They say, "Okay, we'll give him the bird and he will go away." I say, "No—if all it wants is the bird, then let the bird fly free from the cage and out the window. The B/D will follow it. If we sacrifice the bird to the B/D because of our fear, it will kill the bird. If it sees the bird fly out the window it will forget about us and will chase the bird as it flies away, but it won't catch it—it'll just go away as it chases the bird."

My two sons won't listen. They are about to open the window of the cage to give the bird to the B/D, and although I disagree, I am conscious the decision is theirs, and accept with a touch of impatience that they must make their own decisions. I am not frightened of the menace or presence of the B/D, and am confident in myself that all would be well if we did what I suggest and just let the bird fly free. I am frustrated and irritated that my two sons and daughter-in-law can't understand what I feel and know.

I move into a half wake–half dream state, and in this "non-ordinary state of consciousness", the dream continued , but I am conscious of making choices in the dreaming state. I wanted to find out more about the B/D and so I become it. I am **Death**. As Death, for a moment, I feel rageful, beastly, overpowering, hateful, but suddenly I am distracted by the bird which is now free of its cage. As I follow the bird I suddenly am the bird, which becomes an eagle as it flies into the sky.

As the eagle I am hovering in the skies above the house and I can look down with detachment at the people in the house. I am no longer angry at them for their "stupid" [my judgement, I am now aware of the judgemental aspects of myself] behaviour, but I am aware that I am too detached, almost superior, so I make the choice to come back down to the earth where I land on a tree. Immediately I sense all the parts of the tree, the life cycles, leaves falling, insects, animals, the earth that is nurtured and nurtures the tree, the eagle—we are all one. I sense that death is nothing more than a stage in the ongoing cycle of life, death, rebirth.

I woke up in a contemplative state, and spent the rest of the night thinking and writing about my capacity for judgement, judging my daughter-in-law and sons (one for the "womanly weakness" of hysteria, and the others for their "manly machismo"); the rage in me (the Beast/Destroyer) and my need to be freely involved in life (the bird in the cage, the eagle, the tree). The feelings of being beastly and the rage were okay so long as I did not put them out on, or judge, others. I also spent a long time thinking about the life-death-rebirth cycle, and for the first time began to have a sense of peace in a growing awareness that it was okay, there is birth-life-death-rebirth and it is okay. I wrote in my journal for some time about the meaning of life and the meaning of death, and felt a deeper understanding and a sense of peace afterwards.

On 21 June 1998 my son was killed in a sporting activity in which he was flying with eagles—hang-gliding. At the time of his death and afterwards I was considered by some people to be "not coping with my grief" because I was calm and at peace within myself at the funeral and afterwards. Eighteen months later when I was re-reading my journal and came across this entry, I realised that it was this dream and the inner understanding and awareness that came from it that helped me cope in the way I did with my son's death.

In the few months before this dream I had been having a number of dreams of a Holocaust nature—people on conveyor belts being taken to "gas chambers", women all lying down in rooms with doctors performing conveyor-belt operations, corpses in train station death chambers. Over and over again I experienced the anger I felt at those people for "just lying down and dying". In reflection I think this was part of my response to what I was hearing in the field about the violence in the day-to-day lives of people. These dreams also reflected my impatience, intolerance and sense of urgency to have people "wake up" because so many of our young people were dying of injuries due to violence and I was hearing the stories each day in the field.

This dream has given me my present philosophy about the deaths in our communities as a result of the violence—I no longer feel the depth of despair that I previously felt. I do, however, feel passionately "involved in life", and I am more committed to, have more energy for, am now more focused on, working towards change without the judgemental attitude I had towards others who have a different road to journey. I accept death, no matter how tragic, as part of a larger story over which I have no power. The only power I have is to journey with those in the present, to take the opportunities we have now to make our country a safe and healing place to live, for our children and grandchildren.

Healing Dreaming

What began as a PhD study became for me a personal fast-track to change. Over the time of the study, as well as collecting field notes as I recorded people's narratives, I also kept a personal journal. The journal documents my own change processes. My concepts of the definition and construction of violence were challenged daily. My own preconceptions, bias and judgements of the behaviour of others were also challenged. At every level I was confronted with myself. One particular part of the change process for me was an increase in dreams. In retrospect I have been able to see the significance of these dreams, both in my personal life, and in relation to the study. I began this book with a dream. I would now like to close with a dream, to show how my conscious awareness was influenced by dreams (or the other way around), and to demonstrate the influences of my unconscious being brought to the conscious.

Dream: 2 June 1996

I am walking down a darkened road. On each side of the road is dense bush. In the bush someone is crying. The sound of the crying is an intense desolation, despair, sorrow and loneliness. I know that I can (and must) provide comfort to the person/animal by singing or humming or making a sound—any sound. I open my mouth but nothing comes out. I try and try to make a sound.

As I do so, I become aware of an old Aboriginal man, painted and feathered, with white hair and a white beard, ahead of me in an open, cleared part of the bush at the end of the road. I know that if I can reach him I will be totally protected from the pain of this terrible noise, that I could totally trust this old man to look after me. I strain to reach him, to make a noise. I am able to make a noise—a humming sound—and at that time I find I am carrying a young child, of two or three years old, in my arms. The child is lying face down across my arms and is limp and still. I do not know if she is alive or dead.

I look back up for the Aboriginal man in the deep gloom, but he is gone. Instead, I see in front of me a face of a woman, sad, disembodied—just the outline of her face, and two intense eyes straining to communicate with me. I wake up sobbing, my heart pounding, my grief intense and despairing.

After I woke up I cried, for some time in a deep despair, and then as I settled I began to feel—to know—that the child, and the woman, was me. I was aware that I needed to do some healing work for myself. I wondered how much of what was coming to me in the fieldwork, the stories people were sharing with me about their violence/trauma experiences, was being carried by me, remaining in me. I wondered how much this dream related to my own childhood and my situation as an adult woman. I continued to feel a very deep connection to the old man in the dream—his face remains clear within me even today.

Some years later, in fact in 1998 not long after my son's death, my mother told me she had obtained a photo of my great-grandmother and great-grandfather, both of whom had died before I was born, and neither of whom I had ever seen in a photo. My sister had been doing family history and had obtained details about great-grandfather and two photos. We had always known that my great-grandmother was an Aboriginal, Jiman, woman. In the early 1980s I had tried to trace my great-grandfather. His parents were listed as two convicts who were living in the Grafton region. I therefore assumed that he was "white". My father, who had lived with his grandparents, had only ever described him as a gentle old man who always had a garden full of water-melon, and who loved children. My father never described the colour of his grandfather's skin. When I went down to my mother's to look at the photo, I found that my great-grandfather was an Aboriginal man, born in the Grafton region of a convict man and an Aboriginal woman. The face of the man in the photo who is my great-grandfather was also the face of the old man in the dream. In fact the two people looking back at me from the photos were the "great-grannie" who beckoned me to go to her, as I describe in the dream at the beginning of this book, and the old man at the end of the road, as I describe in the dream above.

I do not have a desire to analyse or theorise about these experiences. They are experiences from which I have grown and learnt, and *that is enough*. I am, however, more and more aware that there are things that are provable, tangible and real; and there are things that are unprovable, intangible and just as real. I can only repeat the words of Stanislav Grof, a man who has studied human consciousness all his life: "We know nothing about the human psyche."

The work of my PhD was always more than a study program for me. I needed to find answers to the "problems" of violence within our communities. This violence continues to escalate. During the time of the study I helped write the report of the Aboriginal and Torres Strait Islander Women's Task Force on Violence in Queensland. At that time we heard of and documented acts of violence that for me are indescribable and incomprehensible except within the context I have tried to present here. I also developed the Indigenous Therapies Program out of the work of We Al-li. Each of the people who came into the studies, who participated in the workshops, who sat with me in deep conversation in a sharing of *dadirri*, gave me insight and answers, changed me in ways they will never know. I am a different person now to the woman who applied to undertake the PhD in late 1992.

Towards the end of the fieldwork in the workshops of We Al-li, there were times when I observed myself, both subjectively and objectively, in the process of relating to the critical and highly emotional issues of the moment, issues of human pain that came out of previous violence experiences.

I observed that I was no longer responding from my own emotional reactivity, but totally aware of each person's subjective interaction, including my own. At such times I felt a complete focusing of all my perceptual and experiential faculties on the collective stories of the group as a whole, yet I remained aware of each as a diverse, unique individual in the whole, a heightened awareness and feeling of oneness. At times such as these, as I *listen*, I believe I am allowed to witness, to feel, to perceive, *to know* the individual and collective experiences in their fullest and deepest possible way (Keller 1985: 118), the strength and courage in people, and the human capacity to heal, which is inspiring. This for me was the experience of *dadirri* at its deepest level. That has been the profound privilege of this study.

"My feet are planted firmly on and in this earth."
"I feel the footsteps of the old people rise up,
gladdening my heart, telling me I *do belong*."
"Seeds full of promise,
full of potential, abound in my life."
"Breeze, like a spirit, fills my lungs.
Like a bird in flight
my spirit takes wing and soars."
"Anger, like a fire in my belly, grows and burns,
cleansing my essential self
as I find new and appropriate ways to express it."
"The gentle candle-flame burns forever in my heart,
a symbol of the fluctuating ebb and flow—energies of life."
"Water, water, the salt sea of my sweat
and tears as I continue my inner journey—
processing anger, through grief to crystal clear
clarity of mind and soul."

"Water, water reminding me of my origins
in the sea in the womb."
"Grace descends like a gentle rain
Earth Wind Fire Water
Ceremonies of healing—We Al-li."

© Nicki Apps 1995
Written at the final We Al-li workshop for 1994,
The Haven, Emu Park

Bibliography

Aboriginal and Torres Strait Islander Women's Task Force on Violence (1999) *Aboriginal and Torres Strait Islander Women's Task Force on Violence Report.* Brisbane: Queensland Government.

Aboriginal Coordinating Council (1988) *Community Justice in Northern Queensland: Problems of Implementation and Development.* Cairns, Qld: ACC.

—— (1990) *Submission to the Royal Commission into Aboriginal Deaths in Custody,* Cairns, Qld: ACC.

Adams, D. (1988) "Treatment Models of Men Who Batter" in *Feminist Perspectives on Wife Abuse,* pp. 176–99. Ed. K. Yllo and M. Bograd. Newbury Park, Calif.: Sage.

—— (1989) "Feminist-Based Interventions for Battering Men" in *Treating Men Who Batter,* pp. 3–23. Ed. P. Lynn Caesar and L. K. Hamberger. New York: Springer.

Akbar, D. (1994) *Let the Healing Begin: State Workshop Report,* Adelaide: Aboriginal Family Training, Education and Awareness Resource Centre.

—— (1995) *No Shame—No Violence: The Report on the South Australian Aboriginal Men's Gathering,* Adelaide: Aboriginal Family Training, Education and Awareness Resource Centre.

Allen, J. (1982) "The Invention of the Pathological Family: A historical study of family violence in New South Wales" in *Family Violence in Australia,* pp. 1–27. Ed. C. O'Donnell and J. Craney. Melbourne: Longman Cheshire.

American Psychiatric Association (1994) *American Psychiatric Association: Diagnostic and Statistical Manual of Mental*

Disorders, Fourth Edition, Washington, DC: American Psychiatric Association.

Anderson, I. (1996) "Aboriginal Well-Being" in *Health in Australia: Sociological Concepts and Issues*, pp. 57–78. Ed. C. Grbich. Sydney: Prentice Hall.

Apprey, M. (1996) "Phenomenological Psychology and Literature: Subjects in apposition, subjects on urgent, voluntary errands", unpublished paper, Virginia: University of Virginia.

Armstrong, K. (1998) "Children Living with Domestic Violence", *Aboriginal and Islander Health Worker Journal* (Brisbane), vol. 22, no. 2, pp. 4–8.

—— (1999) "The Impact of Traumatic Childhood Experiences in Children's Lives with Particular Reference to Traumatised Children raised in Institutional Settings", *Aboriginal and Islander Health Worker Journal*, vol. 23, no. 2.

Atkinson, C., Atkinson, J., Lester, J., and Hartley, J. (1998) "Submission in Response to the Model Domestic Violence Laws Discussion Paper", unpublished, Canberra: Office of the Attorney-General.

Atkinson, J. (1989) "Violence in Aboriginal Australia", unpublished paper, Dept of Aboriginal Affairs, Brisbane.

—— (1990a) "Violence in Aboriginal Australia: Colonisation and Gender", *Aboriginal and Islander Health Worker Journal*, vol. 14, no. 1 (Part 1) and no. 3 (Part 2).

—— (1990b) "Working with Families", paper presented to the Indigenous Education Workers Seminar, University of Queensland.

—— (1990c) *Beyond Violence: Finding the Dream* (video and booklet). Ed. National Domestic Violence Education Program. Canberra: Office of the Status of Women.

—— (1990d) "Violence Against Aboriginal Women: Reconstitution of Community Law—The Way Forward", *Aboriginal Law Bulletin* (Sydney), vol. 2, no. 46.

—— (1991a) "Stinkin' Thinkin': Alcohol, Violence and Government Responses", *Aboriginal Law Bulletin* (Sydney), vol. 2, no. 51.

—— (1991b) "Report From Queensland on the New Directions Workshop", *Aboriginal and Islander Health Worker Journal* (Brisbane), vol. 15, no. 6, November–December.

—— (1992) "Flat Tires and Medicine Wheels: A report from the Women and Wellness Conference in Canada", *Aboriginal and Islander Health Worker Journal* (Brisbane), vol. 16, no. 1, January–February, pp. 12–19.

—— (1994) *Violence against Young Women*, published conference paper, Queensland Youth Forum Making a Difference, Brisbane: Queensland Government.

—— (1995) "Aboriginal People, Domestic Violence and the Law: Indigenous Alternative Justice Strategies" in *Future Directions: Proceedings of the Queensland Domestic Violence Conference*, Brisbane: Queensland Government.

—— (1996) "A Nation is Not Conquered", *Aboriginal Law Bulletin* (Sydney), vol. 3, no. 80, pp. 4–9.

—— (1997) "Indigenous Therapies: An Indigenous Approach to Transgenerational Trauma", paper presented at conference, Trauma, Grief and Growth: Finding a Pathway to Healing, University of Sydney, May.

—— (1998) "Making Sense of the Senseless: Feeling Bad, Being Mad, Getting Charged Up" in Conference Proceedings *Having it Both Ways: Dual Diagnosis, Alcohol, Drugs and Mental Illness*, University of Melbourne.

Atkinson, J., Fredericks, B., Iles, P. (1996) "Indigenous Therapies", paper presented at the Rural and Remote Mental Health Conference, Broken Hill.

Atkinson, J., Kaur, H., and Doyle, D. (1996) "We Al-li Past Present Future: the Changing Cultural Face of Indigenous Healing Processes", paper presented at the Mapping Regional Cultures Conference, Central Queensland University, Rockhampton, July.

Atkinson, J., and Moreton-Robinson, A. (1990) "Violence as Contagion: Gender Relations in Aboriginal Communities in Queensland", paper presented at the Women and Anthropology Conference, Adelaide.

Atkinson, J., and Ober, C. (1995) "We Al-li—Fire and Water:

A Process of Healing" in *Popular Justice and Community Regeneration: Pathways of Indigenous Reform*, pp. 201–18. Ed. K. Hazlehurst. Westport: Praeger Press.

Auerbach, A. B. (1968) *Parents Learn Through Discussion*, New York: Wiley and Sons.

Australian Aboriginal Affairs Council (1990) "Australian Aboriginal Affairs Council Briefing Document", unpublished. Darwin.

Australian Bureau of Statistics (1996). *Census*. Canberra: Australian Government Publishing Service.

Australian Institute of Criminology (1989) *Violence in Australia*, Canberra: Australian Institute of Criminology.

Bacon, W., and Lansdowne, R. (1982) "Women who Kill Husbands: The battered wife on trial" in *Family Violence in Australia*, pp. 67–94. Ed. C. O'Donnell and J. Craney. Melbourne: Longman Cheshire.

Badgley Report (1984) *Report of the Committee on Sexual Offences Against Children and Youth*, 2 vols, Ottawa.

Baker, D. G. (1983) *Race, Ethnicity and Power*, London: Routledge and Kegan Paul.

Baker, S. A. (1991) *Family Violence and the Chemical Connection*, Deerfield Beach: Health Communications Inc.

Bandura, A. (1973) *Social Learning Theory*, New York: General Learning Press.

Banks, J. (1987) "A Developmental Perspective on Black Family Violence" in *Violence in the Black Family*, pp. 247–59. Ed. R. L. Hampton. Lexington, Mass.: Lexington Books.

Bass, E., and Davis L. (1988) *The Courage to Heal*, New York: Harper and Row.

Beckett, J. (ed.) (1988) *Past and Present: The Construction of Aboriginality*, Canberra: Aboriginal Studies Press.

Bell, D. (1983) *Daughters of the Dreaming*, Melbourne: McPhee Gribble/George Allen and Unwin.

Bell, D., and Ditton, P. (1980) *Law: The Old and the New: Aboriginal Women in Central Australia Speak Out*, Canberra: Aboriginal History for the Central Australian Aboriginal Legal Aid Service.

Bell, D., and Nelson, T. (1989) "Speaking about Rape is Everybody's Business", *Women's Studies International Forum*, vol. 12, no. 4, pp. 403–16.

Bell, R. (1994) "Prominence of Women in Navajo Healing Beliefs and Values", *Nursing and Health Care*, vol. 15, no. 5, pp. 232–40.

Berg, B. (1995) *Qualitive Research Methods for the Social Sciences*, Boston: Allen and Bacon.

Berger, P. L., and Luckman, T. (1966) *The Social Construction of Reality*, Maryland: Penguin.

Berlin, I. (1986) "Psychopathology and its Antecedents among American Indian Adolescents", *Advances in Clinical Child Psychology*, vol. 9, pp. 125–52.

Berndt, C. H. (1989) "Retrospect and Prospect: Looking back over 50 years" in *Women, Rites and Sites*, pp. 1–20. Ed. Peggy Brock. Sydney: Allen and Unwin.

Berndt, R. M., and Berndt, C. H. (1988) *The World of the First Australians*, Canberra: Aboriginal Studies Press.

Black, C. (1981) *It Will Never Happen to Me: Children of Alcoholics*, Denver: MAC Publishing.

Bolger, A. (1991) *Aboriginal Women and Violence*, Darwin: Australian National University North Australia Research Unit.

Bourke, C., Bourke, E., and Edwards, B. (1994) *Aboriginal Australia*, St Lucia: Queensland University Press.

Bopp, M., and Bopp, J. (1997) *Responding to Sexual Abuse: Developing a Community-based Response Team in Aboriginal Communities*, Ottawa: Solicitor-General Canada, Aboriginal Corrections Policy Unit.

Bowker, L. H., Arbitell, M., and McFerron, J. R. (1988) "On the Relationship Between Wife Beating and Child Abuse" in *Feminist Perspectives on Wife Abuse*, pp. 158–74. Ed. K Yllo and M. Bograd. Newbury Park, Calif.: Sage.

Bradshaw, J. (1988) *Bradshaw on the Family: A Revolutionary Way of Self-Discovery*, Florida: Health Communications.

—— (1990) *Homecoming*, USA: Bantam.

Braun, B. G. (1993) "Multiple Personality Disorder and Post-traumatic Stress Disorder: Similarities and Differences" in *International Handbook of Traumatic Stress Syndrome*. Ed. J. P. Wilson and B. Raphael, New York: Plenum Press.

Brave Heart-Jordan, Maria Yellow Horse (1995) "The Return to the Sacred Path: Healing from Historical Trauma and Historical Unresolved Grief among the Lakota", PhD Dissertation: Smith College School for Social Work, Northampton, Mass.

British Columbia Task Force on Family Violence (1992) *Is Anyone Listening?* Victoria, BC: Minister for Women's Equality.

Broome, R. (1982) *Aboriginal Australians*, Sydney: Allen and Unwin.

Brown, D. (1971) *Bury My Heart at Wounded Knee*, London: Vintage.

Brownmiller, S. (1975) *Against Our Will: Men, Women and Rape*, New York: Bantam.

Burbank, V. (1994) *Fighting Women: Anger and Aggression in Aboriginal Australia*, Berkeley: University of California Press.

Burgmann, M. (1982) "Black Sisterhood: The situation of urban Aboriginal women and their relationship to the white women's movement", *Politics*, vol. 17, no. 2, pp. 23–37.

Butler, S. (1978) *Conspiracy of Silence: The Trauma of Incest*, California: Volcano Press.

Butlin, N. (1982) *Our Original Aggression: Aboriginal populations of southeastern Australia, 1788–1850*, Sydney: Allen and Unwin.

Cameron, S. (1998) "Aboriginal Experiences of Psychological Trauma: Personal, Intergenerational and Transgenerational", Master's Thesis, Victoria University.

Cantor, C., Neulinger, K., Roth, J., and Spinks, D. (1998) *The Epidemiology of Suicide and Attempted Suicide Among Young Australians: A Report to the National Health and Medical Research Council*, Brisbane: Griffith University.

Carlson, R., and Shield, B. (eds) (1988) *Healers on Healing*, USA: Rider Press.

Carr, W., and Kemmis, S. (1986) *Becoming Critical: Education, Knowledge and Action Research*, London: Flamer Press.

Carrillo, R. (1992) *Battered Dreams: Violence against Women as an Obstacle to Development*, New York: United Nations Development Fund for Women.

Carter, E. (1987) *Aboriginal Women Speak Out*, Adelaide: Adelaide Rape Crisis Centre.

Cato, N. (1976) *Mr Maloga*, St Lucia: University of Queensland Press.

Chorover, S. L. (1980) *From Genesis to Genocide*, Cambridge, Mass.: Massachusetts Institute of Technology.

Choo, C. (1990) *Aboriginal Child Poverty*, Melbourne: Brotherhood of St Laurence.

Clarke, C., and Fewquandie, D. (1998) "Indigenous Therapies: Old Ways of Healing, New Ways of Being", paper presented at Rural Mental Health Conference, Ballina, NSW.

Clarke, C., Harnett, P., Atkinson, J., and Shochet, P. (1999) "Enhancing Resilience in Indigenous People: The Integration of Individual, Family and Community Interventions", *Aboriginal and Islander Health Worker Journal* (Brisbane), vol. 23, no. 4, July–August, pp. 6–10.

Clunies-Ross, M., Wild, S. A. (1982) *Djambidj: An Aboriginal Song Series from Northern Australia*, Canberra: Australian Institute of Aboriginal Studies.

Commission of Inquiry into Abuse of Children in Queensland Institutions (1999), *Report*, Queensland Government.

Commission for the Prevention of Violence against Women (1990) *Report to the Mayor and City Council of the City of Santa Cruz*, California.

Commonwealth Department of Health (1998) "Review of the Commonwealth Aboriginal and Torres Strait Islander Substance Misuse Programs", unpublished draft.

Connolly, S. J. (1998) *The Oxford Companion to Irish History*, Oxford: Oxford University Press.

Consedine, J. (1995) *Restorative Justice: Healing the Effects of Crime*, New Zealand: Ploughshares.

Cook, James (1893) *Captain Cook's Journal* (ed. Wharton), quoted in M. Dodson (1994) "The End in the Beginning: Re(def)ining Aboriginality", *Australian Aboriginal Studies*, vol. 1, pp. 2-13.

Corbin, J. (1986) "Insurrection in Spain: Casa Viejas 1933 and Madrid 1981" in *The Anthropology of Violence*, pp. 28–49. Ed. D. Riches. Oxford: Basil Blackwell.

Council for Aboriginal Reconciliation (1994) *Walking Together: The First Steps*, Report to Federal Parliament, Canberra: Australian Government Publishing Service.

Cowlishaw, G. (1988) *Black, White and Brindle*, Cambridge: Cambridge University Press.

—— (1990) "Feminism and Anthropology", *Australian Feminist Studies*, vol. 11, Autumn, pp. 121–2.

Crawford, E. M. (1996) *Famine: The Irish Experience*, Belfast: Queen's University.

Crolty, M. (1996) *Phenomenology and Nursing*, South Melbourne: Churchill Revirptir.

Crow Dog, M., and Erdoes, R. (1990) *Lakota Woman*, New York: Grove Weldenfeld.

Cummings, E. (1993) "Customs and Culture: The Current Situation in Relation to Violence against Aboriginal Women", *Aboriginal and Islander Health Worker Journal* (Brisbane), vol. 17, no. 6, November–December, pp. 15–17.

Currie, D. W. (1988) *The Abusive Husband: An Approach to Intervention*, Toronto.

D'Abbs, P., Hunter, E., Reser, J., Martin, D. (1993) *Alcohol Misuse and Violence: Alcohol-Related Violence in Aboriginal and Torres Strait Islander Communities: A Literature Review*, Canberra: Australian Government Publishing Service.

Dalai Lama, His Holiness, and Cutler, H. (1998) *The Art of Happiness: A Handbook for Living*, Sydney: Hodder.

Danieli, Y. (1980) "Families of Survivors of the Nazi Holocaust: Some long- and short-term effects" in N. Milgram, *Psychological Stress and Adjustment in the Time of War and Peace*, Washington, DC: Hemisphere Publications.

—— (1982) "Families of Survivors of the Nazi Holocaust", *Stress and Anxiety*, vol. 8, pp. 405–21.

—— (1988a) "The Heterogeneity of Postwar Adaption in Families of Holocaust Survivors" in *The Psychological Perspectives of the Holocaust and its Aftermath*, pp. 109–27. Ed. R. L. Braham. New York: Columbia University Press.

—— (1988b) "Confronting the Unimaginable: Psychotherapists' reactions to victims of the Nazi Holocaust" in *Human Adaption to Extreme Stress: From Holocaust to Vietnam*, pp. 219–38. Ed. J. P. Wilson, Z. Harel and B. Kahana. New York: Plenum Press.

—— (1988c) "Treating Survivors and Children of Survivors of the Nazi Holocaust" in *Post Traumatic Therapy and Victims of Violence*, pp. 278–94. Ed. F. Ochberg. New York: Brunner/Mazel.

—— (1989) "Mourning in Survivors and Children of Survivors of the Nazi Holocaust: The Role of Group and Community Modalities" in *The Problems of Loss and Mourning: Psychoanalytic Perspectives*, pp. 427–57. Ed. D. R. Dietrich and P. C. Shabad, Madison: International Universities Press.

—— (ed.) (1998) *International Handbook of Multigenerational Legacies of Trauma*, New York: Plenum Press.

Davison, T. (1995) "Some Preliminary Resources for Competence-Based Approaches to Facilitating Learning", unpublished.

Dawson, S. E. (n.d.) "Navajo Uranium Workers and the Effects of Occupational Illnesses", unpublished, Department of Sociology, Social Work and Anthropology, Utah State University.

Daylight, P., and Johnstone., M. (1986) *Women's Business: Report of the Aboriginal Women's Task Force*, Canberra: Australian Government Publishing Service.

DeBruyn L. M., *et al.* (1988) "Helping Communities address Suicide and Violence: The Special initiatives Team of the Indian Health Service", *American Indian and Alaska Native Mental Health Research*, vol. 1, no. 3, March, pp. 56–65.

Deloria, V., and Lytle, C. (1984) *The Nations Within: The Past and Future of American Indian Sovereignty*, New York: Pantheon.

Dobash, R. E., and Dobash, R. (1979) *Violence against Wives*, New York: Free Press.

—— and —— (1988) "Research as Social Action: The Struggle for Battered Women" in *Feminist Perspectives on Wife Abuse*, pp. 51–74. Ed. K. Yllo and M. Bograd. Newbury Park, Calif.: Sage.

Dodson, M. (1993) *Aboriginal and Torres Strait Islander Social Justice Commissioner's First Report*, Canberra: Australian Government Publishing Service.

—— (1994) "The end in the beginning—re-(de)fining Aboriginality", *Australian Aboriginal Studies*, vol. 1, pp. 2–13. Canberra: Australian Institute of Aboriginal and Torres Strait Islander Studies.

—— (1995) *Aboriginal and Torres Strait Islander Social Justice Commissioner's Third Report*, Canberra: Australian Government Publishing Service.

—— (1998) *Home: Social Justice: Speeches: The End in the Beginning*, Canberra: Human Rights and Equal Opportunity Commission.

Draper, M. (1991) "The Family in Context" in *Family Violence: Everybody's Business: Somebody's Life*, pp. 30–56. Ed. Family Violence Professional Education Taskforce. Melbourne: Federation Press.

Duran, E., and Duran, B., (1995) *Native American Post-Colonial Psychology*, Albany: State University of New York Press.

Duran, E., Duran, B., Yellow Horse Brave Heart, M., Yellow Horse-Davis, S. (1998) "Healing the American Indian Soul Wound" in *International Handbook of Multigenerational Legacies of Trauma*, pp. 341–54. Ed. Yael Danieli. Plenum Press: New York.

Edwards, C., and Read, P. (1989) *The Lost Children*, Sydney: Doubleday.

Edwards, W. H. (ed.) (1987) *Traditional Aboriginal Society*, Adelaide: Macmillan Press.

—— (1993) *An Introduction to Aboriginal Societies*, Wentworth, NSW: Social Science Press.

—— (1994) "Living the Dreaming" in *Aboriginal Australia*, pp. 65–84. Ed. Colin Bourke, Eleanor Bourke and Bill Edwards. St Lucia: University of Queensland Press.

Elder, B. (1988) *Blood on the Wattle: Massacres and Maltreatment of Aboriginal Australians since 1788*, Sydney: New Holland Publishers.

Elkin, A. P. (1954) *The Australian Aborigines: How to understand them*, Sydney: Angus and Robertson.

Ellis C. J. (1985) *Aboriginal Music: Education for Life*, St Lucia: University of Queensland Press.

Epstein, B. (1979) *Children of the Holocaust: Conversations with sons and daughters of survivors*. New York: G. P. Putnam.

Erikson, K. (1976) *Everything in its Path*, New York: Simon and Schuster.

—— (1994) *A New Species of Trouble: The Human Experience of Modern Disaster*, New York: Norton and Company.

Evans, R. (1982) "Don't you remember Black Alice, Sam Holt: Aboriginal women in Queensland history", *Hecate*, vol. 8, no. 2, pp. 7–21.

—— (1991) *"A Permanent Precedent": Dispossession, Social Control and the Fraser Island Reserve and Mission, 1987–1904*, Ngulaig Monograph no. 5, Aborigines and Torres Strait Islanders Unit, University of Queensland.

—— (1992) "A Gun in the Oven: Masculinism and Gendered Violence" in *Gender Relations in Australia: Domination and Negotiation*, pp. 197–218. Ed. Kay Saunders and Raymond Evans. Sydney: Harcourt Brace Jovanovich.

Evans, R., Saunders, K., and Cronin, K. (1975) *Exclusion, Exploitation and Extermination: Race Relations in Colonial Queensland*, Sydney: Australia and New Zealand Book Company.

Fahy, E. T. (1994) "Transculturalism: Still Winking and Speaking in Code", *Nursing Health Care*, vol. 15, no. 5.

Fanon, F. (1963) *The Wretched of the Earth*, New York: Grove.

Farrell, W. (1993) *The Myth of Male Power*, Sydney: Random.

Fawcett Hill, W. M. (1977) *Learning thru Discussion*, Beverly Hills: Sage.

Fee, E. (1981) "Is Feminism a Threat to Scientific Objectivity?" *International Journal of Women's Studies*, vol. 4, pp. 378–92.

—— (1988) *Critiques of Modern Science: The Relationship of Feminism to Other Radical Epistemologies*, Australia: Pergamon.

Ferguson, M. (1980) *The Aquarian Conspiracy*, Los Angeles: J. P. Tarcher Inc.

Ferrante, A., Morgan, F., Indermaur, D., and Harding, R. (1996) *Measuring the Extent of Domestic Violence*, Sydney: Hawkins Press.

Fewster, G. (2000) "To Health with You", *Shen*, vol. 25, Spring, pp. 1–2.

Figley, C. (1985a) "From Victim to Survivor: Social Responsibility in the Wake of Catastrophe" in *Trauma and Its Wake: The Study and Treatment of Post Traumatic Stress Disorder*. Ed. C. Figley. New York: Brunner/Mazel.

—— (ed.) (1985b) *Trauma and Its Wake: The Study and Treatment of Post Traumatic Stress Disorder*, vol. 1, New York: Brunner/Mazel.

—— (1986) *Trauma and Its Wake: Theory and Research of Post Traumatic Stress Disorder*, vol. 2, New York: Brunner/Mazel.

Finkelor, D. (1983) *Common Features of Family Abuse: The Dark Side of Families*, London: Sage.

—— (1984) *Child Sexual Abuse*, New York: Free Press.

Finkelor, D., Hotaling, G. T., and Yllo, K. (1988) *Stopping Family Violence*, Newbury Park, Calif.: Sage.

Frankl, V. E. (1962) *Man's Search for Meaning*, New York: Simon and Schuster.

—— (1978) *The Unheard Cry for Meaning*, New York: Washington Press.

Fredericks, B. (1995) "A Participant's Response to Recreating the Circle with We Al-li: A Program for Sharing and Regeneration", *Aboriginal and Islander Health Worker Journal*, vol. 19, no. 2, March–April, pp. 22–3.

—— (1996) "Fitzroy Indigenous and South Sea Islander Women's Workshop, 30–31st March, 1996", unpublished, Rockhampton: Aboriginal and Islander Community Resource Agency.

Fredericks, B., and Atkinson, J. (1997) "We Al-li: The Creation of a Healing Program—Healing the pain and trauma associated with colonisation", *Community Quarterly—Community Development in Action*, no. 43, June.

Freire, P. (1972) *Pedagogy of the Oppressed*, Harmondsworth, Mddx: Penguin.

Fried, H. (1990) *The Road to Auschwitz*, London: University of Nebraska Press.

Fox, N. (n.d.) *The Promise of Postmodernism for the Sociology of Health and Medicine*.

Gagné, M. (1998) "The Role of Dependency and Colonialism in Generating Trauma in First Nations Citizens—The James Bay Cree" in *International Handbook of Multigenerational Legacies of Trauma*, pp. 355–72. Ed. Yael Danieli. New York: Plenum Press.

Garbarino, J., and Ebata, A. (1987) "The Significance of Ethnic and Cultural Differences in Child Maltreatment" in *Violence in the Black Family*, pp. 21–38. Ed. R. Hampton. Lexington, Mass.

Geffner, R. *et al.* (1989) "A Psycho-educational, Conjoint Therapy Approach to Reducing Family Violence" in *Treating Men Who Batter*, pp. 103–33. Ed. P. L. Caesar and L. K. Hamberger. New York: Springer.

Gelles, R. A., and Straus, M. A. (1977) "Determinants of Violence in the Family: Toward a Theoretical Integration" in *Contemporary Theories About the Family*, vol. 2. Ed. W. R. Burr *et al.* New York: Free Press.

Gibbs, M., and Memon, A. (1999) "Indigenous Resource Management: Towards a Strategy for Understanding Collaborative Research", paper presented to the International Symposium on Society and Resource Management: Application of Social Science to Resource Management in the Asia-Pacific Region, Brisbane, 7–10 July.

Gibson, M. (1987) "Anthropology and Tradition: A Contemporary Aboriginal Viewpoint", paper presented to ANZAAS Conference, Townsville, Qld.

Giddens, A. (1989) *Sociology*, London: Polity Press.

Giorgi, A., Fischer, W., and von Eckartsberg, R. (1971) *Duquesne Studies in Phenomenological Psychology*, 4 vols, Pittsburgh: Duquesne University Press.

Gilligan, C. (1982) *In a Different Voice: Psychological Theory and Women's Development*, Cambridge, Mass.: Harvard University Press.

Girdler, M. (1982) "Domestic Violence: Social Solutions" in *Family Violence in Australia*, pp. 138–54. Ed. C. O'Donnel and J. Craney. Melbourne: Longman Cheshire.

Glaser, B., and Straus, A. (1967) *Grounded Theory Strategies for Qualitative Research*, Newbury Park, Calif.: Sage.

Goodall, H., and Huggins, J. (1992) "Aboriginal Women are Everywhere: Contemporary Struggles" in *Gender Relations in Australia*, pp. 398–424. Ed. K. Saunders and R. Evans. Sydney: Harcourt Brace Jovanovich.

Gondolf, E. W. (1988) *Men Who Batter*, Florida: Human Services Institute.

Gonzalez, M., and Gilmore, K. (1992) *Desperately Seeking Justice: A Resource and Training Manual on Violence against Women in a Culturally Diverse Community*, Melbourne: CASA House.

Gordon, R., and Wraith, R. (1993) "Responses of Children and Adolescents to Disaster" in *International Handbook of Traumatic Stress Syndrome*, pp. 561–75. Ed. J. P. Wilson and B. Raphael. New York: Plenum Press.

Graham, D. R., Rawlings, E., and Rimini, N. (1988) "Survivors of Terror: Battered Women, Hostages, and the Stockholm Syndrome" in *Feminist Perspectives on Wife Abuse*, pp. 217–33. Ed. K. Yllo and M. Bograd. Newbury Park, Calif.: Sage.

Graham, I. (1995) "Reflective Practice: Using the action learning group mechanism", *Nurse Education Today*, vol. 15, no. 1, pp. 28–32.

Graham, M. (1995) in *Search for Meaning*. Ed. Carolyn Jones. Sydney: Australian Broadcasting Commission.

Green, A. (1993) "Childhood Sexual and Physical Abuse" in *International Handbook of Traumatic Stress Syndromes*. Ed. J. P. Wilson and B. Raphael. New York: Plenum Press.

Griffith, J. (1991) *Beyond the Human Condition*, Sydney: Foundation for Humanity's Adulthood.

Grof, C., and Grof S. (1990) *The Stormy Search for Self*, Los Angeles: Tarcher.

Grof, S. (1976) *Realms of the Human Unconscious: Observations of LSD Research*, New York: Viking Penguin.

—— (1984) *Beyond the Brain: Birth Death and Transcendence in Psychotherapy*, Albany: State University of New York Press.

—— (1988) *The Adventure in Self-Discovery*, Albany: State University of New York Press.

—— (1991) *The Holotropic Mind: The Three Levels of Human Consciousness and How They Shape Our Lives*, New York: HarperCollins.

Grossman, R. (1984) *Phenomenology and Existentialism*, London: Routledge and Kegan Paul.

Gun-Allen, P. (1986) *The Sacred Hoop: Recovering the Feminine in American Indian Traditions*, Boston: Beacon Press.

Gusman, R. D., *et al.* (1996) "A Multicultutal Developmental Approach for Treating Trauma" in *Ethnocultural Aspects of Postraumatic Stress Disorder: Issues, Research and Clinical Applications*, pp. 439–58. Ed. A. J. Marsella *et al.* Washington, DC: American Psychological Association.

Hamberger, L. K., and Lohr, J. M. (1989) "Proximal Causes of Spouse Abuse: A Theoretical Analysis for Cognitive-Behavioral Interventions" in *Treating Men Who Batter*, pp. 53–76. Ed. P. L. Caesar and L. K. Hamberger. New York: Springer.

Hamilton, A. (1981) *Nature and Nurture: Aboriginal Child-rearing in North Central Arnhem Land*, Canberra: Australian Institute of Aboriginal Studies.

Hampton, R. L. (ed.) (1987a) *Violence in the Black Family*. Lexington, Mass.: Lexington Books.

—— (1987b) "Violence against Black Children: Current Knowledge and Future Research Needs" in *Violence in the Black Family*, pp. 3–20. Ed. R. L. Hampton. Lexington, Mass.: Lexington Books.

—— (1987c) "Family Violence and Homicides in the Black Community: Are they Linked?" in *Violence in the Black Family*, pp. 135–56. Ed. R. L. Hampton. Lexington, Mass.: Lexington Books.

Harré, R. (1993) *Social Being*, Oxford: Blackwell.

Harris, J. (1990) *One Blood*, Sydney: Albatross.

Hart, B. (1988) "Beyond the 'Duty to Warn'. A Therapist's 'Duty to Protect' Battered Women and Children" in *Feminist Perspectives on Wife Abuse*, pp. 234–48. Ed. K Yllo and M. Bograd. Newbury Park, Calif.: Sage.

Hartman. C. R., and Burgess, A. W. (1988) "Rape Trauma and Treatment of the Victim" in *Post Traumatic Therapy and Victims of Violence*, pp. 152–74. Ed. F. Ochberg. New York: Brunner/Mazel.

Hassan, R. (1995) *Suicide Explained: The Australian experience*, Melbourne: Melbourne University Press.

Hawkins, D. F. (1987) "Devalued Lives and Racial Stereotypes: Idealogical Barriers to the Prevention of Family Violence among Blacks" in *Violence in the Black Family*, pp. 189–205. Ed. R. L. Hampton. Lexington, Mass.: Lexington Books.

Hawks, S. R., *et al.* (1995) "Review of Spiritual Health: Definition, Role and Intervention Strategies in Health Promotion", *Science of Health Promotion*, vol. 9, no. 5, pp. 371–8.

Hayes, L. (1998) "Children of the Grog: Alcohol, Lifestyles and the Relationship to Foetal Alcohol Syndrome and Foetal Alcohol Effects", submitted in partial fulfilment of a B.App.Hc. (IPHC) Honours, University of Queensland.

Hazlehurst, K. (ed.) (1995a) *Legal Pluralism and the Colonial Legacy*, Aldershot: Avebury.

—— (ed.) (1995b) *Perceptions of Justice*, Aldershot: Avebury.

—— (ed.) (1995c) *Popular Justice and Community Regeneration: Pathways of Indigenous Reform*, Westport: Praeger.

—— (1996) *A Healing Place: Indigenous Visions for Personal Empowerment and Community Recovery*, 2nd edn, Rockhampton: Central Queensland University Press.

Herman, J. (1992) *Trauma and Recovery*, London: Harper-Collins.

Herman. J. L. (1988) "Father–Daughter Incest" in *Post Traumatic Therapy and Victims of Violence*, pp. 175–96. Ed. F. Ochberg. New York: Brunner/Mazel.

Herth, K. A. (1994) "The Root of it All: Genograms as a Nursing Assessment Tool", *Journal of Gerontological Nursing*, vol. 15, no. 12, pp. 32–7.

Hiatt, L. R. (1965) *Kinship and Conflict*, Canberra: Australian National University.

Hobson, I. (1990) Address to the Communities Futures Conference, James Cook University.

Hoff, L. A. (1988) "Collaborative Feminist Research and the Myth of Objectivity" in *Feminist Perspectives on Wife Abuse*, pp. 269–81. Ed. K. Yllo and M. Bograd. Newbury Park, Calif.: Sage.

—— (1989) *People in Crisis*. California: Addison-Wesley.

Holland, W. (1996) "Mis/taken Identity" in *The Teeth are Smiling: The Persistence of Racism in Multicultural Australia*, pp. 97–110. Ed. Ellie Vasta and Stephen Castels. St Leonards, NSW: Allen and Unwin.

hooks, b., and West, C. (1992) *Breaking Bread*, Boston: South End.

Homel, R., *et al.* (1998) *Pathways to Prevention: Developmental and Early Intervention Approaches to Crime in Australia*, Canberra: National Crime Prevention, Attorney-General's Department.

Homel, R., Lincoln, R., and Herd, B. (1999) "Risk and Resilience: Crime and Violence Prevention in Aboriginal Communities" (work in progress).

Horton, D. (ed.) (1994) *The Encyclopaedia of Aboriginal Australia*, 2 vols, Canberra: Aboriginal Studies Press.

Horton, M., and Freire, Paulo (1990) *We Made the Road by Walking: Conversations on Education and Social Change*, Philadelphia; Temple University Press.

House of Representatives Standing Committee on Aboriginal Affairs (1987) *Return to Country: The Aboriginal Homelands Movement in Australia*, Canberra: Australian Government Publishing Service

Huggins, J. (1994) "A Contemporary View of Aboriginal Women's Relationship to the White Women's Movement" in *Australian Women: Contemporary Feminist Thought*. Ed. N. Grieves and A. Burns. Melbourne: Oxford University Press.

Huggins, J., and Blake, T. (1992) "Protection or Persecution: Gender Relations in the Era of Racial Segregation" in *Gender Relations in Australia*, pp. 42–57. Ed. K. Saunders and R. Evans. Sydney: Harcourt Brace Jovanovich.

Hughes, J. (1980) *The Philosophy of Social Research*, New York: Longman.

Human Rights and Equal Opportunity Commission (1991) *Racist Violence: Report of National Inquiry into Racist Violence in Australia*, Canberra: Australian Government Publishing Service.

Hunter, E. (1990a) "Images of Violence in Aboriginal Australia", *Aboriginal Law Bulletin*, vol. 2, no. 46, Aboriginal Law Centre, Sydney: University of New South Wales.

—— (1990b) "The Inter-Cultural and Socio-historical Context of Aboriginal Personal Violence in Remote Australia", draft.

—— (1990c) "Using a Socio-historical Frame to Analyse Aboriginal Self-Destructive Behaviour", *Australian and New Zealand Journal of Psychiatry*, vol. 24, pp. 191–8.

—— (1993) *Aboriginal Health and History*, Melbourne: Cambridge University Press.

International Society for Traumatic Stress Studies (1998) *Childhood Trauma Remembered: A Report on the Current Scientific Knowledge Base and its Application*, Northbrook, Ill.: ISTSS.

Janov, A. (1975) *The Primal Revolution*, London: Abacus.

Jebb, M. A., and Haebich, A. (1992) "Across the Great Divide: Gender Relations on Australian Frontiers" in *Gender Rela-*

tions in Australia, pp. 20–41. Ed. K. Saunders and R. Evans. Sydney: Harcourt Brace Jovanovich.

Johnson, V., Ross, K., and Vinson, T. (1982) "Domestic Violence: Cases before Chamber Magistrates", in *Family Violence in Australia,* pp. 28–51. Ed. C. O'Donnell and J. Craney. Melbourne: Longman Cheshire.

Johnson, V. E. (1986) *Intervention: How to Help Someone Who Doesn't Want Help,* Minneapolis: Johnson Institute Books.

Jones, C. (1995) *The Search for Meaning,* Sydney: Dove.

Joseph, M. (1987) "The Religious and Spiritual Aspects of Clinical Practice: A neglected dimension of social work", *Social Thought,* vol. 13, no. 1, pp. 12–23.

Jung, C. G. (1964) *Man and His Symbols,* New York: Dell Publishing.

Kashani, J., Daniel, A., Dandoy, A., Holcomb, W. (1991) "Family Violence: Impact on Children", *Child Adolescence and Psychiatry,* no. 312, March.

Kawagley, A. O., and Barnhardt, R. (1997) "Education Indigenous to Place" in *Ecological Education in Action,* Fairbanks: Suny Press.

Keller, E. F. (1985) *Reflections on Gender and Science,* New Haven and London: Yale University Press.

Kelly, L. (1988) "How Women Define Their Experiences of Violence" in *Feminist Perspectives on Wife Abuse,* pp. 114–32. Ed. K. Yllo and M. Bograd. Newbury Park, Calif.: Sage.

Kidd, R. (1997) *The Way We Civilise,* St Lucia: University of Queensland Press.

Kirby, D. (1991) "Violence in the Family" in *Family Violence: Everybody's Business: Somebody's Life,* pp. 60–90. Ed. Family Violence Professional Education Taskforce. Melbourne: Federation Press.

Kirk, J., and Miller, M. L. (1986) *Reliability and Validity in Qualitative Research,* Newbury Park, Calif.: Sage.

Kirz, Demie (1988) "Not-So Benign Neglect. The Medical Response to Battering" in *Feminist Perspectives on Wife Abuse,* pp. 249–66. Ed. K. Yllo and M. Bograd. Newbury Park, Calif.: Sage.

Knight, D. (1986) "Fighting in an Australian Aboriginal Supercamp" in *The Anthropology of Violence*. Ed. David Riches. Oxford: Basil Blackwell.

Labonte, R., and J. Feather. (1996) *Handbook on Using Stories in Health Promotion Practice*, Ottawa: Health Promotion and Programs Branch, Health Canada (Cat. No. H39–378/ 1996E).

Lambert, J. (ed.) (1993) *Wise Women of the Dreamtime*, Vermont: Inner Traditions International.

Lane, G., and Russell, T. (1989) "Second-Order Systemic Work with Violent Couples" in *Treating Men Who Batter*, pp. 134–62. Ed. P. L. Caeser and L. K. Hamberger. New York: Springer.

Lane, P. jnr, Bopp, Michael, and Bopp, Judie (1998) *Community Healing and Aboriginal Social Security Reform: A Study prepared for the Assembly of First Nations Aboriginal Social Security Reform Strategic Initiative*, Lethbridge: The Four Worlds International Institute for Human and Community Development.

Langton, M. (1983) "'Medicine Square': For the Recognition of Aboriginal Swearing and Fighting as Customary Law", BA Hons Thesis, Department of Prehistory and Anthropology, Australian National University, Canberra.

—— (1988) "Medicine Square" in *Being Black: Aboriginal Cultures in Settled Australia*, pp. 201–25. Ed. Ian Keen. Canberra: Aboriginal Studies Press.

—— (1993) *Well I Heard it on the Radio and I Saw it on the Television*, Sydney: Australian Film Commission.

Langton, M., *et al.* (1991) "Too Much Sorry Business: The Report of the Aboriginal Issues Unit of the Northern Territory" in *Royal Commission into Aboriginal Deaths In Custody National Report*, vol. 5, pp. 275–511. Canberra: Australian Government Publishing Service.

Lassiter, R. F. (1987) "Child Rearing in Black Families: Child Abusing Discipline?" in *Violence in the Black Family*, pp. 39–53. Ed. R. Hampton. Lexington, Mass.

Ledray, L. (1986) *Recovering from Rape*, New York: Henry Holt.

Lifton, R. J. (1967) *Life in Death*, New York: Simon and Schuster.

—— (1993) "From Hiroshima to the Nazi Doctors: The Evolution of Psychoformative Approaches to Understanding Traumatic Stress Syndromes" in *International Handbook of Traumatic Stress Syndrome*. Ed. J. P. Wilson and B. Raphael. New York: Plenum Press.

Lifton, R. J., and Olson, E. (1976) "The Human Meaning of Total Disaster", *Psychiatry*, vol. 39, pp. 1–18.

Loos, N. (1982) *Invasion and Resistance*, Canberra: Australian National University Press.

Lorenz, K. (1988) *The Waning of Humaneness*, London: Unwin.

Lucashenko, M. (1996) "Violence Against Indigenous Women: Public and Private Dimensions" in *Women's Encounters with Violence: Australian Experiences*, pp. 378–90. Ed. S. Cook and J. Bessant. Newbury Park, Calif.: Sage.

Lucashenko, M., and Best, O. (1995) "Women Bashing: An Urban Aboriginal Perspective", *Social Alternatives*, vol. 14, no. 1, pp. 19–22.

Macksoud, M. S., Dyregrow, A., and Raundalen, M. (1993) "Traumatic War Experiences and Their Effects in Children" in *International Handbook of Traumatic Stress Syndrome*. Ed. J. P. Wilson and B. Raphael. New York: Plenum Press.

Madanes, C., with Keim, J. P., and Smelser, D. (1995) *The Violence of Men*, San Franciso: Jossey-Bass.

Malone, T. P., and Malone, P. T. (n.d.) "Selficide", unpublished.

Mann, C. R. (1987) "Black Women Who Kill" in *Violence in the Black Family*, pp. 157–86. Ed. R. Hampton. Lexington, Mass.

Mann, C. R., and Lapoint, V. (1987) "Research Issues Relating to the Causes of Social Deviance and Violence among Black Populations" in *Violence in the Black Family*, pp. 207–35. Ed. R. Hampton. Lexington, Mass.

Manson, S., *et al.* (1996) "Wounded Spirits, Ailing Hearts: PTSD and Related Disorders among American Indians" in *Ethnocultural Aspects of Post-traumatic Stress Disorder:*

Issues, Research and Clinical Applications. Ed. T. Mersella *et al.* Washington, DC: American Psychological Association.

Marcus, P., and Rosenberg, A. (1989) *Healing their Wounds: Psychotherapy with Holocaust Survivors and Their Families,* Pzraeger: New York.

Marsella, A. J., Friedman, M. J., Gerrity, E. T., and Scurfield, R. M. (1996) *Ethnocultural Aspects of Post-traumatic Stress Disorder: Issues, Research and Clinical Applications,* Washington, DC: American Psychological Association.

Martens, T., *et al.* (1988) *The Spirit Weeps: Characteristics and Dynamics of Incest and Child Abuse with Native Perspectives by Brenda Daily and Maggie Hodgson,* Edmonton Canada: Nechi Institute.

Martin, D. (1976) *Battered Wives,* California: Volcano.

Martin, K. (2001) "Aboriginal People, Aboriginal Lands and Indigenist Research: A discussion of re-search pasts and neo-colonial research futures", Master of Indigneous Studies thesis, James Cook University.

Marx, E. (1976) *The Social Context of Violent Behaviour,* London: Routledge and Kegan Paul.

Maslow, A. (1968) *Towards a Psychology of Being,* New York: Van Nostrand Reinhold Company.

—— (1971) *The Farther Reaches of Human Nature,* New York: Viking Press.

Mathiasen, S. S., and Lutzer, S. (1992) *The Survivors: Violations of Human Rights in Tibet—Healing in the Tibetan Exile Community.* Esbjerg, Denmark: Sydjysk Universitescentre of Fortatterne.

Matthieson, P. (1983) *In the Spirit of Crazy Horse.* United States: Harvill/HarperCollins.

May, R. (1976) *Power and Innocence: A Search for the Sources of Violence,* New York: Norton.

May, T. (1997) *Social Research: Issues, Methods and Process,* Buckingham: Open University Press.

McEvoy, M. (1990) *Let the Healing Begin: Breaking the Cycle of Child Sexual Abuse in our Communities,* Merritt, BC: Nicola Valley Institute of Technology.

McGrath, A. (1987) *Born in the Cattle: Aborigines in Cattle Country* Sydney: Allen and Unwin.

—— (1995) *Contested Ground*, Sydney: Allen and Unwin.

McGregor, H., and Hopkins, A. (1991) *Working for Change*, Sydney: Allen and Unwin.

McKendrick, J. H., and Thorpe, M. (1994) *The Mental Health of Aboriginal Communities*, Melbourne: Department of Psychiatry, University of Melbourne, Victorian Aboriginal Health Service.

Meggitt, M. J. (1962) *Desert People: A Study of the Walbiri People of Central Australia.* Sydney: Angus and Robertson.

—— (1966) "Indigenous Forms of Government Among the Australian Aborigines", in *Readings in Australian and Pacific Anthropology.* Ed. Ian Hogbin and L. R. Hiatt. Melbourne: Melbourne University Press.

Memmott, P. (1990) "Aboriginal Cultural, Social Problems and DIC Victims: A report to the Royal Commission into Aboriginal Deaths in Custody", unpublished, University of Queensland.

Merlin, F. (1988) "Gender in Aboriginal Life: A Review" in *Social Anthropology and Australian Aboriginal Studies.* Ed. R. M. Berndt and R. Tonkinson. Canberra: Aboriginal Studies Press.

Merwin, M. R., and Smith-Kurtz, B. (1988) "Healing the Whole Person" in *Post Traumatic Therapy and Victims of Violence*, pp. 57–82. Ed. F. Ochberg. New York: Brunner/Mazel.

Miller, A. (1983) *For Your Own Good: Hidden Cruelty in Child-rearing and the Roots of Violence*, New York: Noonday.

—— (1991) *Breaking Down the Wall of Silence: The Liberating Experience of Facing Painful Truth*, New York: Dutton.

Mindell, A. (1989) *The Year 1: Global Process Work—Community Creation from Global Problems, Tensions and Myths*, London: Arkana-Penguin.

—— (1993) *The Leader as Martial Artist: Techniques and Strategies for Resolving Conflict and Creating Community*, San Francisco: HarperCollins.

—— (1995) *Sitting in the Fire: Large Group Transformation Using Conflict and Diversity*, Portland, Oreg.: Lao Tse Press.

—— (1998) *Dreambody: The Body's Role in Revealing the Self*, Portland, Oreg.: Lao Tse Press.

Mobbs, R. (1991) "In Sickness and Health: The sociocultural context for Aboriginal wellbeing , illness and healing" in *The Health of Aboriginal Australians*. Ed. J. Reid and P. Trompf. Harcourt Brace Jovanovic.

Mollica, R. (1988) "The Trauma Story: The Psychiatric Care of Refugee Survivors of Violence and Torture" in *Post Traumatic Therapy and Victims of Violence*, pp. 295–314. Ed. F. Ochberg. New York: Brunner/Mazel.

Moore, T. (1992) *Care of the Soul*, New York: HarperCollins.

Moreton-Robinson, A. (2000) *Talkin' up to the White Women: Indigenous Women and Feminism*, St Lucia: University of Queensland Press.

Morgan, G. (1983) *Beyond Method: Strategies for Social Research*, Newbury Park, Calif.: Sage.

Morphy, H. (1984) *Journey to the Crocodile's Nest*, Canberra: Australian Institute of Aboriginal Studies.

Mow, K. E. (1992) *Tjunpari: Family Violence in Indigenous Australia*, Canberra: Aboriginal and Torres Strait Islander Commission.

Mowbray, C. T. (1988) "Post-Traumatic Therapy for Children Who are Victims of Violence" in *Post Traumatic Therapy and Victims of Violence*, pp. 196–212. Ed. F. Ochberg. New York: Brunner/Mazel.

Mugford, J. (1989) *Domestic Violence: No. 2 in Violence Today Series*, Canberra: Australian Institute of Criminology.

Myers, L. W. (1987) "Stress Resolution among Middle-Aged Black Americans" in *Violence in the Black Family*, pp. 237–45. Ed. R. L. Hampton. Lexington, Mass.: Lexington Books.

Nakata, M. (1998) "Anthropological Texts and Indigenous Standpoints" in *Australian Aboriginal Studies*, Australian Institute of Aboriginal and Torres Strait Islander Studies, pp. 3–12.

Napolean, H. (1991) *Yuuyaraq: The Way of the Human Being*, Fairbanks: Center for Cross-Cultural Studies.

National Aboriginal Health Strategy Working Party (1989) *A National Aboriginal Health Strategy*, Canberra.

National Health and Medical Research Council (1991) *Guidelines on Ethical Matters in Aboriginal and Torres Strait Islander Health Research*, Canberra: Commonwealth of Australia.

NiCarthy, G., Merriam, K., and Coffman, S. (1984) *Talking it Out: A Guide to Groups for Abused Women*, USA: Seal.

Nolan, C. (1991) "Family Violence: A Child Protection Issue" in *Family Violence: Everybody's Business: Somebody's Life*, pp. 203–28. Ed. Family Violence Professional Education Taskforce. Melbourne: Federation Press.

Nordstrom, C. (1993a) "Treating the Wounds of War", *Cultural Survival Quarterly*, pp. 28–30.

—— (1993b) "Global Disorder and Beyond: Overcoming Cultures of Violence", paper presented at Sydney University on conference on New World Disorder.

Nordstrom, C. and Robben, A. (eds) (1995) in *Fieldwork under Fire: Contemporary Studies of Violence and Survival*. Berkeley: University of California Press.

Novak, J., and Robinson, G. (1998) "'You Tell Us': Indigenous Students Talk to a Tertiary Library", Australian Academic and Research Libraries Journal, vol. 29, no. 1, pp. 13–22.

Nurcombe, B. (1976) *Children of the Dispossessed: A Consideration of the Nature of Intelligence, Cultural Disadvantage, Educational Programs for Culturally Different People, and the Development and Expression of a Profile of Competencies*, Honolulu: University Press of Hawaii.

Ochberg, F. M. (ed.) (1988) *Post Traumatic Therapy and Victims of Violence*, New York: Brunner/Mazel.

O'Donnell, C., and Craney, J. (1982a) "Incest and the Reproduction of the Patriarchal Family" in *Family Violence in Australia*. Ed. C. O'Donnell and J. Craney. Melbourne: Longman Cheshire.

—— and —— (eds) (1982b) *Family Violence in Australia*, Melbourne: Longman Cheshire.

O'Donnell, C., and Saville, H. (1982) "The Social Construction of Child Abuse" in *Family Violence in Australia*, pp. 155–75. Ed. C. O'Donnell and J. Craney. Melbourne: Longman Cheshire.

O'Leary, E. (1998) *Gestalt Therapy: Theory, practice and research*, Great Britain: Stanley Thormes.

Ong, N. O. (1985) "Understanding Child Abuse: Ideologies of Motherhood", *Women's Studies International Forum*, vol. 8, no. 5, pp. 411–19.

Ontario Native Women's Association (1989) *Breaking Free: A Proposal for Change to Aboriginal Family Violence*, Ontario.

Orr, L. (1991) "Explanations of Family Violence" in *Family Violence: Everybody's Business: Somebody's Life*, pp. 94–126. Ed. Family Violence Professional Education Taskforce. Melbourne: Federation Press.

O'Shane, P. (1995) "The Psychological Impact of White Colonialism on Aboriginal People", *Australasian Psychiatry*, vol. 3, no. 3, pp. 149–53.

Payne, S. (1990) "Aboriginal Women and the Criminal Justice System", *Aboriginal Law Bulletin*, vol. 2, no. 46, October.

—— (1992) "Aboriginal Women and the Law" in *Aboriginal Perspectives on Criminal Justice*. Ed. C. Cunneen. Sydney: Sydney University Institute of Criminology.

Pearson, M. (1991) *From Healing to Awakening: An Introduction to Transpersonal Breathwork*, Valley Heights: Inner Work Partnerships.

Pence, E. (1989) "Batterer Programs: Shifting from Community Collusion to Community Confrontation" in *Treating Men Who Batter*, pp. 24–50. Ed. P. Lynn Caesar and L. K. Hamberger. New York: Springer.

Pence, E., and Shepard, M. (1988) "Integrating Feminist Theory and Practice: The Challenge of the Battered Women's Movement" in *Feminist Perspectives on Wife Abuse*, pp. 282–98. Ed. K. Yllo and M. Bograd. Newbury Park, Calif.: Sage.

Perls, F. (1973) *The Gestalt Approach and Eye Witness to Therapy*, USA: Bantam.

Peterson, N. (1970) "Buluwandi: A Central Australian Ceremony for the Resolution of Conflict" in *Australian Aboriginal Anthropology*, pp. 200–25. Ed. R. M. Berndt. University of Western Australian Press for the Australian Institute of Aboriginal Studies.

Petrie, T. (ed. C. C. Petrie) (1904) *Reminiscences of Early Queensland*, Brisbane: Watson and Ferguson.

Pierce, R. L., and Pierce, L. H. (1987) "Child Sexual Abuse: A Black Perspective" in *Violence in the Black Family*, pp. 67–85. Ed. R. L. Hampton. Lexington, Mass.: Lexington Books.

Pilisuk, M., and Parks, S. H. (1986) *The Healing Web: Social Networks and Human Survival*, Hanover: University Press of New England.

Pittaway, E. (1992) *Refugee Women—Still at Risk in Australia*, Canberra: Refugee Council of Australia, Australian Government Publishing Service.

Poole, M. (1991) "The Status of Women in Australia" in *Family Violence: Everybody's Business: Somebody's Life*, pp. 1–26. Ed. Family Violence Professional Education Taskforce. Melbourne: Federation Press.

Price, G. A. (1963) *The Western Invasions of the Pacific and its Continents*, Oxford: Clarendon Press.

—— (1972) *White Settlers and Native Peoples*, Westport: Greenwood Press.

Ptacek, J. (1988) "Why Do Men Batter Their Wives?" in *Feminist Perspectives on Wife Abuse*, pp. 133–57. Ed. K. Yllo and M. Bograd. Newbury Park, Calif.: Sage.

Pynoos, R. S., and Nader, K. (1993) "Issues in the Treatment of Post-traumatic Stress in Children and Adolescents" in *International Handbook of Traumatic Stress Syndrome*. Ed. J. P. Wilson and B. Raphael. New York: Plenum Press.

Queensland Domestic Violence Task Force (1988) *Beyond These Walls*, Brisbane: Department of Family Services and Welfare Housing.

Quinn, J. F. (1988) "Healing: The Emergence of Right Relationship" in *Healers on Healers*. Ed. R. Carlson and B. Shield. London: Rider.

Raphael, B., Swan, P., and Martinek, N. (1998) "Intergenerational Aspects of Trauma for Australian Aboriginal People" in *International Handbook of Multigenerational Legacies of Trauma*, pp. 327–39. Ed. Yael Danieli. New York: Plenum Press.

Ratford, A. J., Harris, R. D., Brice, G. A., Van der Byl, M., Monten, H., Matters, D., Neeson, M., Bryan, L., and Hassan, R. (1990) *Taking Control: A Joint Study of Aboriginal Social Health in Adelaide with particular reference to stress and destructive behaviour, 1988–1989*, Monograph 7, Adelaide: Flinders University of South Australia.

Rees, S. (1991) *Achieving Power: Practice and Policy in Social Welfare*, Sydney: Allen and Unwin.

Reid, G. (1982) *A Nest of Hornets*, Melbourne: Oxford University Press.

—— (1985) "Queensland and the Aboriginal Problem, 1838–1901", PhD thesis, Australian National University.

Reid, J. C. (1979) "A Time to Live: A Time to Grieve: Patterns and Processes of Mourning among the Yolnger of Australia", *Culture Medicine and Psychiatry*, vol. 3, pp. 319–46.

Reser, J. P. (1990) "A Perspective on the Causes and Cultural Context of Violence in Aboriginal Communities in North Queensland: A Report to the Royal Commission into Aboriginal Deaths in Custody", unpublished.

Reynolds, H. (1981) *The Other Side of the Frontier*, Townsville, Qld: James Cook University Press.

—— (1987) *Frontier*, Sydney: Allen and Unwin.

Rhodes, D., and McNeal, S. (eds) (1985) *Women against Violence against Women*, London: Only Women Press.

Riches, D. (ed.) (1986) *The Anthropology of Violence*, Oxford: Basil Blackwell.

Rifkin, S. (1986) "Lessons from Community Participation in Health Programmes" in *Health Policy and Planning*. Ed. Barbara Power. Oxford: Oxford University Press.

Rigney, Lester-Irabinna (1997) "Internationalisation of an Indigenous Anti-Colonial Cultural Critique of Research Methodologies: A Guide to Indigenist Research Methodology and its Principles", paper presented at the Annual International Conference of the Higher Education Research and Development Society of Australia, July, Adelaide.

—— (1999) "The First Perspective: Culturally Safe Research Practices On or With Indigenous Peoples", paper presented at the 1999 Chacmool Conference, University of Calgary, Alberta, Canada.

Rinpoche, S. (1992) *The Tibetan Book of Living and Dying*, USA: HarperCollins.

Rintoul, S. (1993) *The Wailing: A National Black Oral History*, Melbourne: William Heinemann.

Robin, R. W., Chester, B., and Goldman, D. (1996) "Cumulative Trauma and PTSD in American Indian Communities" in *Ethnocultural Aspects of Post-traumatic Stress Disorder: Issues, Research and Clinical Applications*. Ed. A. J. Marsella *et al.* Washington, DC: American Psychologists Association.

Rogers, C. (1977) *Carl Rogers on Personal Power*, New York: Delacorte Press.

Romero, M. (1985) "A Comparison Between Strategies Used on Prisoners of War and Battered Wives", *Sex Roles*, vol. 13, nos. 9–10.

Root, M. (1992) "Reconstructing the Impact of Trauma on Personality" in *Personality and Psychopathology: Feminist Reappraisals*. Ed. L. Brown and M Ballou. New York: Guilford Press.

—— (1996) "Women of Colour and Traumatic Stress in 'Domestic Captivity': Gender and Race as Disempowering Statuses" in *Ethnocultural Aspects of Post-traumatic Stress Disorder: Issues, Research and Clinical Applications*. Ed. A. J. Marsella *et al.* Washington, DC: American Psychological Association.

Rosaldo, R. (1995) "Subjectivity in Social Analysis" in *The Post-modern Turn: New Perspectives on Social Theory*. Ed. S. Seidman. New York: University of Cambridge Press.

Rose, D. B. (1986) "Passive Violence", *Australian Aboriginal Studies*, vol. 1, pp. 24–30.

—— (1987) "Consciousness and Responsibility in an Australian Aboriginal Religion" in *Traditional Aboriginal Society*. Ed. W. H. Edwards. Adelaide: Macmillan Press.

—— (1996) *Nourishing Terrains: Australian Aboriginal Views of Landscape and Wilderness*, Canberra: Australian Heritage Commission.

—— (2000) *Dingo Makes Us Human: Life and Land in an Australian Aboriginal Culture*, Cambridge, UK: Cambridge University Press.

Rosenbaum, A., and Maiuro, R. D. (1989) "Eclectic Approaches in Working with Men Who Batter" in *Treating Men Who Batter*, pp. 165–95. Ed. P. L. Caesar and L. K. Hamberger. New York: Springer.

Rosewater, L. B. (1988) "Battered or Schizophrenic? Psychological Tests Can't Tell" in *Feminist Perspectives on Wife Abuse*, pp. 200–16. Ed. K Yllo and M. Bograd. Newbury Park, Calif.: Sage.

Roth, W. E. (1984) *The Queensland Aborigines*, vol. 11, Bulletins 1–8, *North Queensland Ethnology from the Home Secretary's Department—Brisbane 1901–1908*, Melbourne: Hesperian Press.

Rowe, D. (1987) *Beyond Fear*, London: Fontana.

Rowley, C. D. (1970) *The Destruction of Aboriginal Society*, Ringwood, Vic.: Penguin.

—— (1971) *Outcasts in White Australia*, Canberra: Australian National University Press.

Roxburg, T. (1991) "Support Services" in *Family Violence: Everybody's Business: Somebody's Life*, pp. 130–68. Ed. Family Violence Professional Education Taskforce. Melbourne: Federation Press.

Royal Commission into Aboriginal Deaths in Custody (1991) *National Reports*, 5 vols, Canberra: Australian Government Publishing Service.

Royal Commission on Aboriginal Peoples (1995) *Choosing Life: Special Report on Suicide Among Aboriginal Peoples*, Canada: Community Way.

—— (1996) *Report of the Royal Commission on Aboriginal Peoples*, Canada: Ministry for Supply and Services.

Sackett, L. (1978) "Clinging to the Law: Leadership at Wiluna" in *Whitefella Business*. Ed. M. C. Howard. Philadelphia: Institute for the Study of Human Issues.

Sanders, M. (ed.) (1995) *Healthy Families: Healthy Nation*, Brisbane: Australian Academic Press.

Sansom, B. (1980) *The Camp at Wallaby Cross: Aboriginal Fringe Dwellers in Darwin*, Canberra: Australian Institute of Aboriginal Studies.

Saunders, D. (1988) "Wife Abuse: Husband Abuse; or Mutual Combat" in *Feminist Perspectives on Wife Abuse*, pp. 90–113. Ed. K. Yllo and M. Bograd. Newbury Park, Calif.: Sage.

—— (1989) "Cognitive and Behavioural Interventions with Men Who Batter: Application and Outcome" in *Treating Men Who Batter*, pp. 77–100. Ed. P. L. Caesar and L. K. Hamberger. New York: Springer.

Saunders, H. (1975) "Women Hold up Half the Sky", *Identity*, no. 6, October.

Saunders, K., and Evans, R. (eds) (1992) *Gender Relations in Australia: Domination and Negotiation*, Marrickville, NSW: Harcourt Brace Jovanovich.

Saville, H. (1982) "Refuges: A New Beginning to the Struggle" in *Family Violence in Australia*, pp. 95–109. Ed. C. O'Donnell and J. Craney. Melbourne: Longman Cheshire.

Schaef, A. W. (1985) *Women's Reality: An Emerging Female System in a White Male Society*, New York: HarperCollins.

—— (1992) *Beyond Therapy: Beyond Science*, San Francisco: HarperCollins.

Schechter, S. (1982) *Women and Male Violence: Visions and Struggles of the Battered Women's Movement*, Boston: South End Press.

—— (1988) "Building Bridges Between Activists, Professionals, and Researchers" in *Feminist Perspectives on Wife Abuse*, pp. 299–312. Ed. K. Yllo and M. Bograd. Newbury Park, Calif.: Sage.

Schweitzer, R. (1996) "A Phenomenological Study of Dream Interpretation among the Xhosa-Speaking People in Rural South Africa", *Journal of Phenomenological Psychology*, vol. 27, no. 1, pp. 72–96.

—— (1997) "Phenomenology and Qualitative Research Method in Psychology", unpublished.

—— (1998) "The Application of a Phenomenological Methodology to the Study of Indigenous Healing in Australia", unpublished.

Scutt, J. (1982) "Domestic Violence: The Police Response" in *Family Violence in Australia*, pp. 110–20. Ed. C. O'Donnell and J. Craney. Melbourne: Longman Cheshire.

—— (1983) *Even in the Best of Homes*. Melbourne: Penguin.

Shalit, B. (1991) "The Law and Family Violence" in *Family Violence: Everybody's Business: Somebody's Life*, pp. 169–202. Ed. Family Violence Professional Education Taskforce. Melbourne: Federation Press.

Shkilnyk, A. (1985) *A Poison Greater than Love*, New Haven: Yale University Press.

Silko, Leslie Marmon. (1977) *Ceremony*. Middlesex, UK: Penguin Books.

Silver, S. M. (1986) "An Inpatient Program for Post-Traumatic Stress Disorder: Context as Treatment" in *Trauma and Its Wake, vol. 2: Theory and Research of Post Traumatic Stress Disorder*. Ed. C. Figley, New York: Brunner Mazel.

Simpson, M. A. (1993) "Bitter Waters: Effects on Children of the Stresses of Unrest and Oppression" in *International Handbook of Traumatic Stress Syndrome*. Ed. J. P. Wilson and B. Raphael. New York: Plenum Press.

Sinclair, J. M., *et al.* (2000) *Collins English Dictionary and Thesaurus 21st Century Edition*, England: HarperCollins.

Singe, J. (1988) *The Torres Strait People and History*, St Lucia: University of Queensland Press.

Small, J. (1990) *Becoming Naturally Therapeutic*, New York: Bantam.

Smallwood, G. (1996) "Aboriginality and Mental Health" in *Mental Health and Nursing Practice*, pp. 103–18. Ed. M. Clinton and S. Nelson. Sydney: Prentice Hall.

Smith, E. D. (1995) "Addressing the Psycho-spiritual Distress of Death as Reality: A Transpersonal Approach", *Social Work*, vol. 40, no. 3, pp. 402–13.

Smith, L. T. (1999) *Decolonizing Methodologies: Research and Indigenous Peoples*, Dunedin, NZ: University of Otago Press.

Smith, S., and Williams, S. (1992) "Remaking the Connections: An Aboriginal Response to Domestic Violence in Australian Aboriginal Communities", *Aboriginal and Islander Health Worker Journal* (Brisbane), vol. 16, no. 6, November–December, pp. 6–9.

Smith, S., and Williams, D. G. (eds) with Nancy Johnson (1997) *Nurtured by Knowledge: Learning to Do Participatory Action-Research*, New York: Apex Press.

Solomon, Z. (1997), untitled paper presented at the "Trauma Grief and Growth—Finding a Path to Healing" Conference, Sydney 1997.

Sparks, T., and Sparks, C. (1989) "Doing not Doing", unpublished.

Stanko, E. (1988) "Fear of Crime and the Myth of the Safe Home" in *Feminist Perspectives on Wife Abuse*, pp. 75–88. Ed. K Yllo and M. Bograd. Newbury Park, Calif.: Sage.

Stanner, W. E. H. (1963) "On Aboriginal Religion: VI Cosmos and Society Made Correlative", *Oceania*, vol. 33, no. 4, pp. 239–72.

—— (1968) *The Boyer Lecturers 1968: After the Dreaming*, Sydney: Australian Broadcasting Commission.

—— (1979) *White Man Got No Dreaming: Essays, 1938–1973*, Canberra: Australian National University Press.

—— (1987) "The Dreaming" in *Traditional Aboriginal Society*. Ed. W. H. Edwards. Adelaide: Macmillan Press.

Stark, E., and Flitcraft, A. (1988a) "Personal Power and Institutional Victimisation: Treating the Dual Trauma of Woman Battering" in *Post Traumatic Therapy and Victims of Violence*, pp. 111–14. Ed. F. Ochberg. New York: Brunner/Mazel.

—— and —— (1988b) "Women and Children at Risk: A Feminist Perspective on Child Abuse", *International Journal of Health Services*, vol. 18, no. 1, pp. 97–118.

Stavropoulos, P. (1995) "Representation and Resistance", *Social Alternatives*, vol. 14, no. 1.

Steavenson, A. (1991) *Un-happily Ever After*, Brisbane: Queensland University of Technology.

Steel, S. (1990) *The Content of Our Character: A New Vision of Race in America*, New York: St Martin's Press.

Stockton, E. (1995) *The Aboriginal Gift: Spirituality for a Nation*, Alexandria: Millennium Books.

Stone, H., and Winkelman, S. (1989) *Embracing Ourselves: The Voice Dialogue Manual*, California: New World Library.

Stone, H., and Stone, S. (1993) *Embracing Your Inner Critic*, San Francisco: HarperCollins.

Stratmann, P. (1982) "Domestic Violence: The Legal Responses" in *Family Violence in Australia*, pp. 121–37. Ed. C. O'Donnell and J. Craney. Melbourne: Longman Cheshire.

Strauss, A., and Corbin, J. (1990) *Basics of Qualitative Research*, Newbury Park, Calif.: Sage.

Subandi, Mr (1994) "A Psychological Study of Religious Transformation among Moslems who Practice *Dzikir Tawakkal*", MA thesis, Queensland University of Technology.

Summers, A. (1975) *Damned Whores and God's Police*. Ringwood, Vic.: Penguin.

Swan, P. (1988) "Two Hundred Years of Unfinished Business", paper presented to the Australian National Association for Mental Health Conference, in *Aboriginal Medical Service Newsletter*, September, pp. 12–17.

Swan, P., and Raphael, B. (1995) *Ways Forward: National Consultancy Report on Aboriginal and Torres Strait Islander Mental Health*, 2 vols, Canberra: Australian Government Publishing Service.

Swigonski, M. E. (1994) "The Logic of Feminist Standpoint Theory for Social Work Research", *Social Work*, vol. 39, no. 4, July.

Sydney Rape Crisis Centre. *Surviving Rape: A Handbook to Help Women become Aware of the Reality of Rape*, Sydney: Redfern Legal Centre Publishing.

Task Force on Violence, *see* Aboriginal and Torres Strait Islander Women's Task Force on Violence.

Taylor, M., and Hammond, P. (1987) "See How They Run: Battered Women in Shelters in the Old Dominion" in *Violence in the Black Family*, pp. 107–19. Ed. R. L. Hampton. Lexington, Mass.: Lexington Books.

Tedeschi, R. G., and Calhoun, L. G. (1995) *Trauma and Transformation: Growing in the Aftermath of Suffering*, Newbury Park, Calif.: Sage.

Tesch, R. (1990) *Qualitive Research Analysis Types of Software Tools*, New York: Falmer Press.

Tonkinson, M. (1985) "Domestic Violence among Aborigines", paper prepared for the Domestic Violence Taskforce.

Tonkinson, R. (1972) *"Nagawajil*: A Western Desert Aboriginal Rainmaking Ritual", Ph.D. thesis in Anthropology, Vancouver: University of British Columbia.

—— (1990) "The Changing Status of Aboriginal Women: 'Free Agents' at Jigalong" in *Going It Alone? Prospects for Aboriginal Autonomy: Essays in Honour of Ronald and Catherine Berndt*, pp. 125–47. Ed. R. Tonkinson and M. Howard. Canberra: Aboriginal Studies Press.

Trigger, D. (1986) "Blackfellas and Whitefellas: The concept of domain and social closure in the analysis of race relations", *Mankind*, vol. 16, no. 2, pp. 99–117.

Tripcony, P. (1999) "Indigenous Children's Issues and Underlying Factors", paper presented at the Children's Commission Research Forum, Brisbane, June.

Trudgen, R. (2000) *Why Warriors Lie Down and Die*, Darwin: Aboriginal Resource and Development Services Inc.

Tuhiwai Smith, L. (1999) *Decolonizing Methodologies: Research and Indigenous peoples*, Dunedin, NZ: University of Otago.

Unger, S. (1977) *Navajo Child Abuse and Neglect Study*, Baltimore, Md: Department of Maternal and Child Health, Johns Hopkins University.

Ungunmerr, M. R. (1993a) *"Dadirri*: Listening to One Another" in *A Spirituality of Catholic Aborigines and the Struggle for Justice*, pp. 34–7. Ed. J. Hendricks and G. Hefferan. Brisbane: Aboriginal and Torres Strait Islander Apostolate, Catholic Archdiocese of Brisbane.

—— (1993b) "The Spirit of the Bush" in *A Spirituality of Catholic Aborigines and the Struggle for Justice*, pp. 37–8. Ed. J. Hendricks and G. Hefferan. Brisbane: Aboriginal and Torres Strait Islander Apostolate, Catholic Archdiocese of Brisbane.

United Nations Office (1989) *Violence against Women in the Family*, New York: United Nations Office at Vienna Center for Social Development and Humanitarian Affairs.

Ursano, R., McCaughey, B., and Fullerton, C. (1995) *Individual and Community Response to Trauma and Disaster: The Structure of Human Chaos*, Cambridge: Cambridge University Press.

Valent, P. (1993) *Child Survivors: Adults Living with Childhood Trauma*, Melbourne: William Heinemann.

Van de Kolk, B. A. (1987) *Psychological Trauma*, Washington, DC: American Psychiatric Press.

Venbrux, E. (1995) *A Death in the Tiwi Islands*, Cambridge: Cambridge University Press.

Vogal, M. L. (1994) "Gender as a Factor in the Transgenerational Transmission of Trauma", *Women and Therapy*, vol. 15, no. 2.

Volkman, S. (1993) "Music Therapy and the Treatment of Trauma-Induced Dissociative Disorders", *Arts Psychotheraphy*, vol. 20, pp. 243–51.

Waldegrave, C. (1990) "Social Justice and Family Therapy— A Discussion of the Work of the Family Centre Lower Hutt New Zealand", *Dulwich Centre Newsletter*, no. 1, p. 1.

—— (1998) "The Challenges of Culture to Psychology Postmodern Thinking" in *Re-visioning Family Therapy: Race, Culture and Gender in Clinical Practice*. Ed. M. McGoldrick. New York: Guildford Press.

Walker, L. E. (1979) *The Battered Woman*, New York: Harper and Row.

—— (1984) *The Battered Woman Syndrome*, New York: Springer.

Walker, R. (1985) *Applied Qualitative Research*, Great Britain: Gower.

Wanganeen, R. (1994) "Self Healing and Spiritual Reconnection: How to Heal and Reconnect to Your Spirituality for Your Own Well-Being", *Aboriginal and Islander Health Worker Journal* (Brisbane), vol. 18, no. 2, March–April, pp. 9–15.

Watson, L. (1987) "Sister, Black is the Colour of my Soul" in *Different Lives: Reflections on the Women's Movement and Visions of Its Future*, pp. 45–52. Ed. J. Scutt. Melbourne: Penguin.

Weisinger, H. (1985) *Dr. Weisinger's Anger Work-out Book*, San Francisco: Volcano.

Whitfield, C. L. (1989) *Healing the Child Within: Discovery and Recovery for Adult Children of Dysfunction Families*, Florida: Health Communications Inc.

Widom, C. (1993) "The Cycle of Violence", paper presented at the Second National Conference on Violence, Australian Institute of Criminology.

Wignall, D. (1992) "Working with Anger: An anger-processing exercise", *The New Physicians' Newsletter: A Quarterly Journal of Whole Person Medicine*, vol. 1, p. 6.

Wijkman, A., and Timberlake, L. (1984) *Natural Disaster: Acts of God or Acts of Man*, London and Washington: International Institute for Environment and Development.

Wild, S. (1986) *Rom: An Aboriginal Ritual of Diplomacy*, Canberra: Australian Institute of Aboriginal Studies.

Williams, B., and Gardner, G. (1989) *Men, Power Sex and Survival*, Elwood, Vic.: Greenhouse Publications.

Williams, N. M. (1987) *Two Laws: Managing Disputes in a Contemporary Aboriginal Community*, Canberra: Australian Institute of Aboriginal Studies.

Williams, N., and Jolly, L. (1992) "Gender Relations in Aboriginal Societies Before White Contact" in *Gender Relations in Australia*, pp. 9–19. Ed. K. Saunders and R. Evans. Sydney: Harcourt Brace Jovanovich.

Williams, R., Swan, P., Reser, J., and Miller, B. (1992) "Changing Oppression Social Environments," in *Psychology and Social Change*, pp. 297–316. Ed. David Thomas and Arthur Veno. New Zealand: Dunmore Press.

Wilson, J. (1986) in *Trauma and its Wake*, vol 2: *Theory and Research of Post Traumatic Stress Disorder*. Ed. C. Figley. New York: Brunner/Mazel.

—— (1988a) "Understanding the Vietnam Veteran" in *Post Traumatic Therapy and Victims of Violence*, pp. 227–53. Ed. F. Ochberg. New York: Brunner/Mazel.

—— (1988b) "Treating the Vietnam Veteran" in *Post Traumatic Therapy and Victims of Violence*, pp. 254–77. Ed. F. Ochberg. New York: Brunner/Mazel.

Wilson, M. N., Cobb, D. D., and Dolan, R. T. (1987) "Raising Awareness of Wife Battering in Rural Black Areas of Central Virginia: A Community Outreach Approach" in *Violence in the Black Family*, pp. 122–31. Ed. R. L. Hampton. Lexington, Mass.: Lexington Books.

Wilson, P. (1982) *Black Death : White Hands*, Sydney: Allen and Unwin.

Women's Research Centre (1989) *Recollecting Our Lives*, Vancouver: Press Gang Publishing.

Wong, B., and McKeen, J. (1992) *A Manual for Life*, British Columbia: PD Seminars.

—— and —— (1998) *A Manual for Life* (2nd edn), British Columbia: PD Seminars.

Wright, A. (1997) *The Grog War*, Broome, WA: Magabala Books.

Wyatt, G., and Riederle, M. (1994) "Sexual Harassment and Prior Sexual Trauma Among African–American and White American Women", *Violence and Victims*, vol. 9, no. 3.

Yllo, K. (1988) "Political and Methodological Debates on Wife Abuse Research" in *Feminist Perspectives on Wife Abuse*, pp. 28–50. Ed. K. Yllo and M. Bograd. Newbury Park, Calif.: Sage.

Yllo, K., and Bograd, M. (eds) (1988) *Feminist Perspectives on Wife Abuse*. Newbury Park, Calif.: Sage.

Zuber, S. (1996) *New Directions in Action Research*, New York: Falmer Press.

Index

Kick the Tin
Doris Kartinyeri

When Doris Kartinyeri was a month old, her mother died, and Doris was removed from the hospital and placed in Colebrook Home. A moving testimony from one of the Stolen Generation.

With a Foreword by Lowitja O'Donoghue, Doris Kartinyeri's story allows the reader to understand how it felt to be separated from family and from the Ngarrindjeri culture into which she had been born.

ISBN: 1875559-95-7

Ngarrindjeri Wurruwarrin: A world that is, was, and will be
Diane Bell
Winner, Gleebooks Award for Cultural or Literary Critique, NSW Premier's Awards

A magisterial work .... every Ngarrindjeri person I have spoken to applauds this book. Ethnographies of this sort are usually avoided for any number of reasons, not the least of which is the sense that attempting such a study is too hard. That Bell attempts and succeeds in this without sacrificing scholarship or standards is a magnificent achievement.
 Christine Nicholls, *Times Higher Educational Supplement*

ISBN: 1875559-71-X

Daughters of the Dreaming
Diane Bell

[Daughters] represents a major contribution to our knowledge of past and present Aboriginal societies and demonstrates the significance of women in every aspect of community existence.

Isobel White, *Aboriginal History*.

Voices of the Survivors
Patricia Easteal

Powerful and moving stories from survivors of sexual assault.

ISBN: 1-875559-24-8

Beyond Psychoppression
Betty McLellan

A guide to therapy which explores the intersection between the personal and the political.

ISBN 1-875559-33-7

The Will to Violence: The Politics of Personal Behaviour
Susanne Kappeler

Sexual violence, racial violence, the hatred of foreigners: how should we understand these and other forms of violent human behaviour?

A brilliant and original analysis.

ISBN: 1-875559-46-9 (pb) 1-875559-45-0 (hb)
(Available from Spinifex in Australia and New Zealand only)

If you would like to know more about Spinifex Press
write for a free catalogue or visit our website

Spinifex Press
PO Box 105, Mission Beach,
Queensland, Australia 4852
women@spinifexpress.com.au
www.spinifexpress.com.au